PRAISE FOR
City of Ice

ICE LAKE

Also by John Farrow

CITY OF ICE

John Farrow

ICE
LAKE

HarperCollins*PublishersLtd*

For information address
HarperCollins Publishers Ltd.,
55 Avenue Road, Suite 2900,
Toronto, Ontario, Canada M5R 3L2

www.harpercanada.com

HarperCollins books may be purchased
for educational, business, or sales
promotional use.
For information please write:
Special Markets Department,
HarperCollins Canada,
55 Avenue Road, Suite 2900,
Toronto, Ontario, Canada M5R 3L2

First mass market edition

Canadian Cataloguing in Publication
Data

Farrow, John, 1947–
Ice lake

1st mass market ed.
ISBN 0-00-648538-3

I. Title.

PS8561.A785I23 2002   C813'.54
C2001-902537-8
PR9199.3.F455I25 2002

OPM 9 8 7 6 5 4 3 2 1

Printed and bound in the United States
Set in Monotype Baskerville

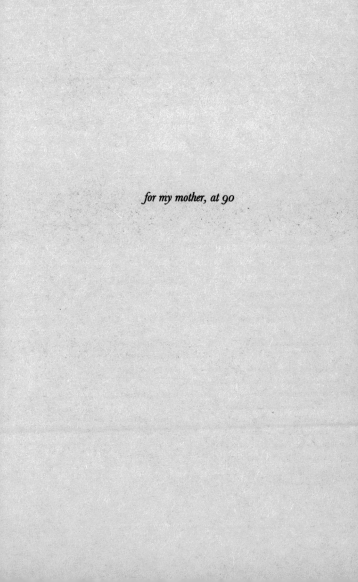

for my mother, at 90

———

Cocktails for the Dead / 1
The Influence of Dark Matter / 179
Bloodwork / 449

ICE LAKE

COCKTAILS
FOR THE DEAD

1

A BODY, AFLOAT

Sunday, February 13, 1999

Ensconced in an ice-fishing hut on the Lake of Two
Mountains, northwest of Montreal, Sergeant-Detective
Émile Cinq-Mars was gazing through a frosty pane of
glass as a red Ski-Doo, paced by a brisk wind, crossed
the snowbound lake from the east and veered toward a
broad bend in the shore. A child was clinging to the
driver's waist. The two appeared to be headed for the
same community of fishing shacks where he was holed
up waiting for a stranger to arrive.

Roaring, the machine doffed a squall of snow in its
tracks.

Along the perimeter to the ice-village, the Ski-Doo
throttled down and followed streets on the snow
marked by discarded Christmas pines. The driver was
a woman, her body shape now evident in a snug-fitting
snowmobile suit. A woman had called him down here.
Cinq-Mars kept an eye on this one, but she did not
approach his shack, stopping instead beside an orange
shanty where her daughter leapfrogged off the seat.
The child sprinted about ten steps before her mother
called her back. She skidded to a halt. Grasping her
helmet and pulling her head out from under it, the girl
shook her brown curls and fidgeted while her mother

braved the cold with bare fingers, yanking up the girl's hood and tying a bow under her bright-red chin. Free at last, the seven-year-old scampered loose to knock on a nearby door.

The woman shut the machine down. She flipped through a key-ring, then snapped open the padlock on her shack, and Émile Cinq-Mars returned to fishing.

Inside her hut, the woman dropped her own and her child's helmet onto a bunk, then pinned her mittens to a line. Unzipping to the waist, she extracted her arms from the sleeves of the snowmobile suit, the upper portion collapsing behind her like a second skin not wholly sloughed off. She removed her minnow bucket from the stovetop and put it on the floor, then set about striking a fire.

She ignited newspaper, kindling and logs in the cast-iron stove.

Then awaited warmth.

The woman gazed out the window upon winter, at the white, barren lake spotted with Ski-Doos and the colourful spinnakers of ice-sailors, shining under the sun. In her thirties, she was not one to wear makeup on a daytime outing. Her low, abruptly raked forehead, the chiselled cut of her cheekbones, and the thrust of her nose seemed to have been carved as much by life as by birth and genetics. The features suggested a strong constitution and a body accustomed to stressful labour apart from the demands of motherhood. She wore her light-brown hair in a buzzcut with longish tufts at the nape of her neck.

The shack was primitive and small. Plywood over two-by-fours, the windows and doors salvaged from a job site, the hut included the critical necessities—a pot to pee in, another for washing up, a stove for both cooking and warmth, a mattress that, when thawed, cushioned the tumult of bodies and comforted them for a short rest afterwards. Similar to other huts in the neighbourhood, hers had been coloured with leftover paint others had discarded. While many shacks were rented by the day or the weekend, hers was leased for the entire season, which allowed her to keep cutlery and pans, dry goods that could bear being frozen, extra clothes, blankets and children's toys on the premises, as well as her own fishing tackle.

To occupy the time she broke the surface ice in her minnow bucket and baited a hook in the cold. She opened the floorboards to reveal her fishing hole. She'd been up to the shack the night before, so the hole hadn't frozen much—with a heavy steel bar she put a crack in it. She tapped all around the circle to loosen new ice, breaking the block into pieces, a familiar routine. The dark patch at the surface was difficult to discern in the shade. Her eyes were not fully accustomed to the dimmer light of the cabin and the greater dark within the cavity. Only when she tried to push the chunks under the thick ice of the lake did she encounter a problem. Something she could barely see—a sort of floating debris. Finally, she got down on her knees and raised the chunks of ice up, placing them on the surface of the lake below the cabin floor.

In the circle of the fishing hole, pearls of ice clung to a knotted tangle of hair.

A head lay afloat, face down in the lake.

Later she would not be able to explain why she did this, why she had to touch it, as if to be assured that a body remained attached. Only when she was certain did she commence a rapid series of gasps followed by a spectacular array of upper-register screams.

Émile Cinq-Mars was lost in thought while observing miniature, diamond-like crystals wicking higher on his line. All morning long he had ignored his partner, Detective Bill Mathers, often fixing his gaze instead on a vertex where the ascending beads of ice on his line met the shack's smoky warmth, a point he could manipulate by bobbing his hand.

Both city cops, one significantly older than the other, had spent most of the morning slumped inside the ice-fishing hut over an opening sawed between their boots. A wood fire that should have kept them warm crackled in an iron stove. On one side was a bench sufficiently long for a man as tall as Cinq-Mars to stretch out on. The one opposite, on which Bill Mathers sat, had been cut short to accommodate the door. A thin line of smoke leaked through a joint in the stovepipe and every ten minutes or so one man or the other opened the door to circulate fresh air, inadvertently releasing the cabin's heat and keeping them both well chilled.

Mathers sat with his shoulders hunched as though he'd never been warm in his lifetime. He had no clue why he was there. Cinq-Mars had not told him, and he couldn't believe it was only to fish. In the finest of seasons he cared little for fishing, and to be baiting hooks in the dead of winter under the onslaught of a twenty-knot nor'wester rattling the rough-hewn, plywood hut, out on a frozen lake he believed might crack apart and immerse them, combined what he perceived as an exercise in futility—fishing—with a regimen of discomfort—fishing in February—that bordered on misery. He was waiting for his partner to reveal himself, but his patience was ebbing quickly.

Before he'd made up his mind to confront Cinq-Mars, he was distracted by a frantic shriek outside. Glad for the interruption, he was first to the door to investigate the racket.

"Émile," he said, not liking what he saw.

"What's that caterwaul?"

Out on the frozen lake, a woman was wailing and calling for the cops. She'd fallen to the ice on her hands and knees, having fled a shack in too big a hurry to pull up the top portion of her snowsuit. Helped by an equally frantic neighbour, she struggled to her feet again, shouting for the police.

Oddly, she was half crawling and sliding in their direction, as if she knew where cops might be found.

"Looks like we're on the job," Mathers commented dryly.

"Not exactly our jurisdiction," Cinq-Mars pointed out, but he was rising to have a look for himself and retrieving his line.

"Beats fishing," Mathers said.

Both men took the time to don their winter garb before venturing onto the ice. Others were running over to check on the fuss, and Cinq-Mars and Mathers walked across and showed their gold shields to bully their way through the gathering throng. At the sight of their badges, the stricken woman perked up considerably. In French, "This way! Come quickly, I'll show you! There's a dead guy in there! He's dead!" Whatever horror she had viewed was supplanted now by a need to impress upon the authorities the depth of her distress.

The cops walked quickly behind her.

Bill Mathers entered first. He crouched down on the cabin floor. "Émile."

Cinq-Mars peered over his partner's shoulder. The circular ice-hole was partially filled with water. A few inches below the surface floated the back of a human head, the long hair beaded with ice, the face plunged into the frigid lake. Mathers pulled the victim up by the hair, raising him a few inches. The condition of the neck was the only evidence Cinq-Mars required—shock-white, the skin bulging where ice had frozen and expanded within the corpse, causing lumps. "Make sure," he instructed.

On the floor, a hooked minnow flapped, obviously just baited by the woman. Cinq-Mars took a folding knife from his pocket and, over the ice, gave the little fish a quick deep cut across the throat.

Mathers pulled the head as far out of the water as he could. He had to reach down, as the surface was about two feet thick, and kneel way over to get a look at the face. Swollen, white, and bloated with ice. The eyes frozen. Ice bulged from the mouth and points glistened within his nostrils where they caught sunlight refracted through the smudge on a side window. A man's face, which Mathers returned to the water, the death confirmed.

"Secure it somehow."

Cinq-Mars needed to create a barrier around the shack. The curious were bumping in behind him. He was helping the woman pull on her snowsuit and instructing a neighbour to take her inside somewhere else when her daughter came running up and promptly stuck to her mother's leg. The bond seemed habitual, the woman scarcely noticing the bulky appendage. Cinq-Mars ordered others out of the shack and away from the door, which didn't stop them from gathering at the windows and peering inside.

Offered the use of three cellphones, he accepted one from a tall, plump man, then asked a second favour of him. "Would you mind keeping people away from the hut? It won't be easy."

The man checked out the gathering, considering whether the task was worth the hassle. He chuckled and shook his head. "I can try," he agreed.

"Thanks." Cinq-Mars returned inside, where Detective Mathers splashed his fingers in the water. "What've we got?"

Mathers had looped strands of high-test fishing line through buttonholes on the dead man's jacket and shirt and tied the free ends to the feet of the cast-iron stove. "He didn't fall through here. He's not coming out this hole either unless we open it up." The head pretty much blocked the entire cavity. His shoulders would never pull through.

"There can't be that many places to fall in. He could've drifted for miles, poor bugger. Probably he went through on a snowmobile, out where the current's fast and the ice is thinner. That's awfully surprising, though, in this weather."

"Would you care to consider the facts first, Émile?" Mathers vigorously rubbed his freezing wet hands.

"Such as?"

"Your theory doesn't explain the bullet hole."

He looked at him then, and the younger detective nodded that he was serious. He pointed to the back of his own neck. "In here, out the front. Low down. Here." Mathers indicated the soft spot at the base of his throat.

Cinq-Mars punched a number into the phone.

"SQ?" As Montreal Urban Community cops they were off their island, away from their professional turf. On major crimes in which a coroner became involved, *La Sûreté du Québec,* the police force for the province, would be granted jurisdiction over any small-town department.

Cinq-Mars shook his head no, and spoke into the phone, requesting the number for the local police for Vaudreuil-Dorion.

"Why them?" Mathers asked as soon as he'd signed off.

"Their fishing hole."

"Murder, Émile. They'll have to turn it over."

"They'll remain an informed party. A small-town police chief might appreciate being let in, enough to share the news back again. Give it to the SQ right off the bat and we'll be cut out, that's for certain."

"Do we want to be cut in?"

"Like you said," Cinq-Mars told him in a whispered murmur, and this came as a surprise, "it beats fishing."

Mathers waited for Cinq-Mars to finish his second call before asking, "Émile, why'd we come out here today? Were you tipped on this?"

"Don't you know? We're here for *doré*, Bill. What you English call walleye. If I happen to hook a whale instead, should I let it get away?"

Mathers guessed that his chain was being ceremoniously yanked, although with Cinq-Mars it was hard to be sure. "What now?"

"Smile. You're on Candid Camera."

At that, the handsome younger man looked up. A video camera perused the premises through the frosty rear window, zooming down for a close-up of the dark fishing hole where the ice-encased corpse gently bobbed, then pulling back to once again include the cops.

"Tonight, partner," Cinq-Mars warned him, "you'll be on the evening news."

"I'll spring for the popcorn if you buy the beer."

Cinq-Mars returned outside again. Although the big man he'd conscripted had managed to keep most of the curious back, the cameraman and a few others were incorrigible. He thanked the man for his phone and returned it to him, then stood off to one side. The detective had a little more breathing room now and he used the space to look around, take in the scene, get a feel. Gusts chased snow-hares onto shore. The huts of the fishing village, mostly decorated with wild colours, their chimneys gently smoking against the backdrop of snow and ice, made for a colourful view in one direction. In the other, above the steep bank at the waterside, mostly new homes and a small strip mall were a blight, crowding out the few old farmhouses that still remained. Behind a set of brick condos at the edge of the bay, an office tower dominated the skyline, a dozen floors of concrete and glass, the tallest building for seventy miles west. North, hedged by rolling hills, the frozen landscape could be any large lake where winter held court. To the east, the curvature of the earth and trees on the opposite shore concealed the island city of Montreal.

It was not just any lake, anywhere, Cinq-Mars acknowledged with a certain grim understanding. *Lac des Deux-Montagnes*, the Lake of Two Mountains, was close to home, marking this death, this corpse in the water, as being in his own backyard. Jurisdiction or not, a murder at his favourite fishing hole had captured the city cop's attention.

He was a famous detective, one of the old breed. At least, that was how the media liked to portray him. When he himself thought about the "old breed," he envisioned cops from the Night Patrol during Montreal's heyday as a centre of vice, during the 1930s, '40s, and '50s. Those guys would bulldoze a brick wall to bust into a prostitution warren, or careen through skylights into gambling dens. They'd engage in wild shootouts with equally notorious mobsters. He supposed that he was likened to those guys because he was independent, and did not fare well within a system which relied heavily on teamwork, computer analysis, statistics and science. He preferred to get into the heads of criminals, figure them out, trap them by anticipating their behaviour. He had made the style work for him, and he'd benefitted over the years as well from crackerjack informants. While he didn't smash and raid and jump down skylights if he could help it, he did have a reputation for the surprise thrust, the pivotal, deft exploit.

Fame was a tool, he'd learned. People who might be reluctant to inform on crooks because they were scared, or because the crooks were neighbours or family, or simply because they didn't like cops, opened up to Cinq-Mars because they enjoyed being in proximity to a legend. Speaking to a famous cop was different, it provided an incentive that some required. Many cops resented his ever-expanding reputation, and Cinq-Mars agreed that the situation wasn't fair. When you're dying for a break, you can't buy one, and when you've already received a hundred breaks, fate reaches into its grab-bag and tosses you a hundred more. His early career had been difficult, a slow plod. Now, information flowed, often without prompting.

Being a celebrity cop also had its downside. He had tried to explain to his fellow officers that his reputation drew nutcases to his side like cockroaches flushed from the woodwork, and he had tried to convince them that the kooks wasted a huge chunk of his time. His colleagues dismissed his difficulties as minor. They'd trade problems with him any day, and Cinq-Mars could guess their reaction to this latest episode. Today, the woman who had phoned and coaxed him down to the ice had been a no-show, and yet she had placed him in close proximity to a murder. A mysterious voice. She had sounded intelligent, youthful, concerned, intense. Somehow, she had known his home number. He'd been enticed. Now this. Johnny-on-the-spot. Pure luck. Reason for his fellow cops to hate him all over again.

Around the hut, fishermen huddled in the bitter cold. They pounded their feet on the ice and slapped their hands together to keep them warm. Breath chugged in the cold like the vapour of automobiles stalled in winter traffic. A talkative, spirited bunch, primed with alcohol despite the early hour, they did their best to draw the policeman into conversation. Distracted, Cinq-Mars declined. Along the shoreline, squad cars were racing, cherries flashing, coming his way.

So it begins, he was thinking. *Just like always.*

Oddly, he could not shake the sensation that this time was different. This time, he'd been on the scene—almost next door at the moment the body was being discovered—and, truth be told, he had been invited to the scene, something he had yet to admit to Mathers.

While it was not true, to his knowledge, that the murder had gone down under his nose, he could not alleviate the sensation that somehow, in some way, his nose was being rubbed in this death. The geography and the timing, not to mention his invitation to the rendezvous, had conspired to make this personal.

At a strip mall a half-mile away, Lucy Gabriel paced and fumed. She'd been back and forth between the donut shop, for coffee, and her car, a Honda Accord, six times, and still the person she had arranged to meet had not shown up. Inside the donut shop, a friend, a slim young man, was keeping the same vigil, only he was far more relaxed.

Lucy burst through the shop's door once more and stormed across to their table. "What do you think? Maybe Andy went straight there." She kept her voice low, hushed, urgent as she stood over him. "He could be talking to Cinq-Mars right now! Let's check it out."

"Andy knows he's meeting us here, Luce. If he's not here, I can promise you that he's not there." He sipped his hot chocolate.

"Then where is he?"

"That," he stressed, "I don't know. If he is on the lake, then I can guarantee you that he wants us here. No closer than here. Come on, Lucy. Sit down, warm yourself. Your teeth are chattering."

"This isn't working," she grumbled as she slid into the booth. "Cinq-Mars won't wait forever. If Andy doesn't show—"

"—we'll find another time. Andy's not the most reliable guy on the planet, plus he's working both ends against the middle. You know what that means."

"No, what does that mean?"

She was finally wearing down his outer reserve. "Luce, if Werner Honigwachs crooks his little finger, Andy has to run, and we're automatically postponed.

He wouldn't be able to let us know. I expected something like this to happen. Give it another half-hour,
after that we'll call it a day. And Lucy—"

"What?"

"No more coffee. You're wired, girl. You're way too
jumpy."

"I got a bad feeling."

"That's what comes from drinking coffee by the
barrel. Relax!"

She lasted about twenty seconds before wanting to
bolt. "I'll just go down to the shore. I won't step on the
ice. I'll take a look around, make sure Andy's car's not
there. How can that hurt?"

The young man sighed. "Tell you what. You stay
here. I'll go."

"Why you?"

"Because you can't be trusted. You'll charge onto
the ice and have your own powwow with the great
white cop. I'll check things out and be back in a flash. If
Andy shows, just drive him down to the lake and we'll
continue as planned. Okay?"

Reluctantly, she consented to the compromise. At
least they were doing something.

"Remember, Luce. About the coffee. Just say no."

A widening of the Ottawa River, the Lake of Two
Mountains is shaped somewhat like a dancing woman
with a flared skirt. At its western head the river passes
over and around a hydroelectric dam and gracefully
swims downstream through an elongated neck, then
fills at the bodice and narrows again at the waist. The
lake dramatically broadens as the skirt spreads outward
and then separates, about seven miles downstream
from the bonnet, into two legs. One becomes what is
known unofficially as the Back River, creating the
north shore around the island of Montreal. The waters

of the other plunge through rapids at its foot into the St. Lawrence River, forming the south shore.

Land around the lake is thinly populated. An Indian reserve, apple orchards, villages and two small towns, vast grounds for a monastery and an expansive provincial park occupy the north side. Homes poke out amid the canopy of trees along the southern embankment, until the trees yield to farmland at the eastern tip. On winter weekends, the lake is active with skiers, snowmobilers, and fisherfolk, and with those content to drive to a shack on the ice to drink and gab.

The Chief of Police for the Town of Vaudreuil-Dorion arrived in a squad car and descended the steep ramp from the road to the lake on foot. From a distance he struck Émile Cinq-Mars as being athletic, hale. Barrel-chested, he possessed good muscle tone for his age and took to the snow with a graceful lope. That he had chosen to leave his car on the road seemed worth evaluating. The Ford, a rear-wheel drive, likely would skid on the ice and the ramp's steep pitch. The man had exercised due care, meaning either that he had profited from experience—a good sign—or that he was remarkably cautious, a quality of indeterminate value.

Cinq-Mars returned to the shack where Mathers had remained with the dead man, partly for the warmth, as the stove-fire was blazing now, but principally to make himself difficult to dismiss when the chief went about his business. He produced his badge the moment the officer arrived, in case the fellow tried giving him the boot.

"Cinq-Mars," he stated, "MUCPD." Announcing that he was a member of the Montreal Urban Community Police Department would not earn him brownie points with a small-town chief, but there was no getting around that. "My partner, Detective Bill Mathers."

"You put in the call?" the chief asked.

"I did."

"How'd you get here?"

"We were fishing. Practically next door. Off duty."

"*Émile* Cinq-Mars?" the chief probed. Younger than him, about forty-five, he spoke with a gruffness born of self-doubt. Cinq-Mars worried that he'd made a mistake. He had hoped for a savvy small-town cop happy to have a significant crime to track down, but he ran the risk of landing a mayor's shoddy cousin, or some such.

"Yes, sir." At that moment, Cinq-Mars noticed the minnow bucket, where ice remained attached to the edges. The little fish hardly swam at all in the cold, but why was the water not frozen solid when the cabin was not yet fully warmed by the stove? A bucket of solid ice would take a while to thaw.

The chief shot him a glance and uttered a sound inside his chest, a cross between a harumph and a belch. "Chief Jean-Guy Brasseur. This is not your case."

"Did I say it was?"

"Have you disturbed anything?"

"When we first showed up, the body was on the cot. For safekeeping, we put him underwater."

"Your press clippings don't mean squat to me, smartass. All you city cops are crooked anyways."

Cinq-Mars could hear Mathers chuckling behind his back, enjoying his senior's predicament. "Country cops are bumpkins. Now then, we've insulted each other. What does that prove? Are you interested in this crime, or not?"

"The SQ will take it over."

"Give them a call. You might need them to blow your nose."

"Don't get smart with me, bud. What do we got here, anyways?"

"Thanks for taking an interest. There's a man under the ice, Chief. A bullet hole through his throat."

"A fishstick?"

Cinq-Mars was familiar with the reference to frozen corpses. "Pretty much."

The Chief did not kneel to have a closer look. He gazed down at the victim for a moment, then glanced about the shack. "How'd he get down there?" he asked.

"Floated in, I imagine," Cinq-Mars suggested.

"You were just fishing? That's a coincidence. You're carrying your shield, that's also a coincidence. Are you carrying an issue?"

"Habit," he acknowledged. At least this guy had half a brain. Cinq-Mars was beginning to appreciate a few of his meagre qualities.

"What about you?" the chief asked Mathers.

"Shield, yes. Always do. Issue, no. I prefer to catch fish with hooks, not shoot them." Mathers gave Cinq-Mars a scorching look. He could not believe his partner had carried a service revolver to go fishing on a week-end off.

"You're a famous detective," summarized Chief Brasseur. "A legend in your own time, they say. You're fishing, carrying a shield and pistol, when a body bobs to the surface near your hook. So I'm wondering, what did you use for bait?" A pair of constables arrived at the door and the chief ordered them to clear and secure the perimeter. He turned back to Cinq-Mars. "Did you say you called the SQ or not?"

"I thought you'd prefer to do that."

"Their case, bud. The coroner will assign it that way."

"You'll be privy."

"Don't count on it. Not with the SQ. What we know for sure is, you won't be."

"I happened to be on hand, Chief. I'm not fighting you on jurisdiction."

"What else do you know?" the younger man asked him.

"Excuse me?"

"About this case."

"I cleared civilians away and called the cops. That's the full extent of my involvement."

"You can't see any bullet hole from here," the chief reminded him.

"I discovered it, actually," Mathers put in.

"The body or the bullet hole?"

"The hole. The entry wound is in the back of the neck, under all that hair. The exit wound is out the front of the throat."

"Do you think I give a flying fuck? Tell it to the SQ, as if they need your input."

"We thought you might be interested in a homicide in your own backyard, Chief," Cinq-Mars interrupted. "Our mistake. Obviously, you'd rather hand out traffic tickets, investigate dog poop on lawns."

"Don't talk like that. Not to me. I warned you once."

"We've pulled you away from poop-'n'-scoop patrol, I can tell."

The chief responded with a snide laugh, then stepped up to Cinq-Mars, though he stood under the other man's nose. "I'm not interested in you, Cinq-Mars. I don't need you on my turf taking credit. You want publicity? You want to be a front-page cop? Go back to the city, don't sniff around here."

"I live out here. I'm a citizen."

"You're a TV cop, Cinq-Mars. I know your kind."

"You used to be on the force yourself, is that it? What happened? Did I get promoted while you got skunked?"

"You want to talk about promotions? I'm Chief of Police. You're a rat-shit Sergeant-Detective."

"How'd you get this job if you got trashed out? Who'd you marry?"

Chief Brasseur reached between his legs and gave his paraphernalia a hoist. "Up yours," he added.

"Call the SQ, Chief."

"You think I don't know why you called me? You expect I'll be your bum-boy from the little town. Sure, I'll call the SQ. They think even less of you than I do."

Cinq-Mars shook the tension from his shoulders as though he'd rather be throwing punches. "Listen. I was out here fishing. A woman screamed. We went over. We found a body in the water under the floorboards. I buzzed the cops. I'm a citizen. What's your problem with that?" If the local chief wanted to get under his skin, he was making good progress.

"You're right, I was on the force, so I know how assholes like you operate," the chief threw back at him, ignoring his question. "Every word you speak is two parts bullshit to one part jam. You're spreading it right now."

Cinq-Mars stared down the prodigious slope of his nose at this poor excuse for a civil servant. He'd seen much worse, but when men brought their pathetic grudges and grievances to the job, to any job, he felt no compassion. Ages ago he had given up trying to disguise that stance, and while he understood that cops were envious of him, he had ceased to care. "Sorry to interrupt your Sunday nap, Chief. I guess you can't function with the Super Bowl behind us. Why don't you just call the SQ before the body goes smelly."

"Wiseass. I'll make that call." Under his overcoat he wore a policeman's leather bomber jacket, and under that a microphone pinned to his shirt. He tapped it and called his station, his voice relayed through the transmitter in his cruiser. He informed his subordinate to forward the news to the SQ.

Finally, the chief bent to his knees and leaned over the hole. He pulled the deceased's head up by the hair and studied the face.

"He's thawing," Mathers noticed.

"What?"

"When I first looked at him, the face seemed more

frozen than that. Ice was poking out the nostrils. Not now. Maybe it's the warmth of the cabin."

"You got no jurisdiction here," the chief reminded them both. "Why don't you both buzz off?"

Cinq-Mars nodded. "I'm on my way."

"But not too far. Don't leave the lake until the SQ gets a crack at you."

Cinq-Mars left and marched briskly through the snow to his rental hut. He looked neither left nor right, and failed to acknowledge the questions of those on the ice awaiting news. Mathers raced to catch up, fearing that the door might slam in his face if he didn't duck inside soon enough.

"Do we stick around like he said?" Mathers asked in the cabin. A superior's command carried little weight with his partner. That the superior in this case came from another force made that order irrelevant.

Pacing the small quarters, Cinq-Mars considered what to do. He would have preferred to send Mathers home, except they had only one vehicle between them. "Bill, we stay. It'll be an education. Take notes on how the SQ botch things this time." He paused, and eyed his partner closely. When he spoke again he had lowered his voice. "There's something you should know, partner. Friday, I received a call. I was advised to rent a fishing shack on this lake this morning and wait for a visit. Someone with information to peddle. A woman's voice, that's all I know. Whoever called knows I fish here on occasion, and that was enough to arouse my curiosity. I didn't tell you for a couple of reasons. First off, it was liable to be a wild-gooser. I didn't want to get you excited for nothing—I wanted you to concentrate on fishing. Besides that, I gave my word not to tell. Point is, we have to hang out to see if my contact shows. If she does, after all this mess, that'll be good. If not, at least we can say it's been an eventful afternoon."

"Maybe you've received your information."

"Meaning?"

Bill Mathers motioned in the direction of the crime scene.

"That I don't know," Cinq-Mars admitted.

"I'll stay on one condition," Mathers negotiated.

"What's that?"

"No more bloody fishing. I've hooked my last minnow."

Lucy Gabriel was waiting outside in the freezing cold, her neck tucked deep into her collar, when her friend returned. He was no longer quite so calm and collected.

"What's up?" she asked him.

"Something's happened on the ice."

"What?"

"A death. You know how it goes, some old guy drinks himself into a stupor then freezes when his fire goes out. Or he gets excited reeling in a big fish and has a heart attack. It happens every few years. Anyway, there's too much activity out there, we're not meeting Cinq-Mars today."

Lucy was pounding one foot against the other to keep her toes warm. "We should find out what happened, don't you think? Camille's there—"

"Not both of us. I will. Go home, Lucy. I'll give you a ring later."

"Don't bother," she told him. "The day's shot. I'm going into the city."

"To do what?"

"Drink. Laugh. Be with people."

"I warned you, Luce. The coffee has you wired."

"The situation has me wired. You take it easy. We'll talk."

Pensive, Sergeant-Detective Émile Cinq-Mars ground his upper and lower molars together while Bill Mathers tended to the wood-burning stove. The junior officer discovered that if he played with the fire and arranged it to one side, less smoke leaked into the cabin, which made breathing more relaxed. Meanwhile the constant tinkering helped pass the time.

When the SQ arrived, Cinq-Mars didn't bother going onto the lake to greet them. "What kind of a uniform is that?" he mocked, watching through the frosty glass. "Whose idea was it to dress them up in brown shirts? Doesn't anybody understand the symbolism?"

"I think they're meant to be green," Mathers said, hoping to cool him down.

"*Green!* Who're they supposed to be, the Environment Police? Heaven help us if that's true. Cops should wear blue. True blue. These guys look like something scraped off a pasture."

Cinq-Mars sat back down awhile, wishing that he still smoked. Twelve years now since his last puff, time that had gone by in an eye-blink. He wasn't a reformed smoker who had learned to detest smoke. Half the time he wished he still indulged—not for the taste or to feed a craving or for the show, but just to help get him through those hours when he had nothing to do but wait, sit still and be bored, then wait some more.

Both men were startled by a fierce knock. The door sprang open without their invitation.

"*Sûreté,*" an officer informed them.

"As if we couldn't tell from the uniform," Cinq-Mars grumbled.

Mathers showed him a badge in return, and the young officer came in with an even younger, apparently pubescent partner in tow. They'd been told whom they'd find inside, and both men did their best not to appear impressed. They were intent on treating the city cops no differently than nuisance civilians.

"We're taking down everybody's name, then releasing them."

"Releasing?"

"Sending them home. Clearing the site. You're Cinq-Mars?"

"I'm pleased to meet you. My partner, Bill Mathers. Who's the Investigating Officer?"

"Sergeant Painchaud is the IO. He just arrived. You know him?"

Cinq-Mars shook his head and surrendered his phone numbers when asked. Mathers did the same.

"All right," the slightly older of the two said, "you can go now."

"I'll stay."

The officer was lean, arrow-straight, almost gaunt. His thin moustache stood out, a match for his heavy eyebrows. He was filling out his form with a pencil in his left hand, curling his wrist above the line he was inscribing. The remark seemed to fluster him.

"I don't know. You're not supposed to. Why would you stay?"

"I'm fishing."

"I'll ask about that."

"Go ahead. In the meantime, Officer, did you know that when addressing a superior from another force it's customary to use the appellation 'sir'? It's a courtesy. Is this news to you?"

"Yes, sir," the officer said, lowering his clipboard to his side and looking Cinq-Mars in the eye. "I didn't know that, sir. It's news to me, sir. I'll ask if you got to leave, sir, although it's possible Sergeant Painchaud will want to talk to you, sir, to see if you disturbed the crime scene, sir. Sir?"

Still seated on the cold wooden bench, Cinq-Mars had raised his hand, his palm aloft for silence. "Say 'sir' once more to me in that tone of voice and I'll shove you down this ice-hole and seal the hatch. Don't think I won't. Don't think I can't."

The officer chose to say nothing, then turned to leave.

"Wait!" Cinq-Mars advised him.

The aggrieved cop and his mute partner faced him again.

"Check the hole."

"Excuse me?" Quietly, the officer tacked on, "Sir?"

"Check the hole. This and every other one in the entire ice-village."

The officer wiped his leather-gloved hand down over his moustache, mulling the advice. "I'm sorry, sir, but I don't take orders from you."

"Fine." Cinq-Mars abruptly stood. "Be a useless fuck-up *Sûreté* cop. Screw up another investigation. Go ahead, make uselessness your life's work. Aspire to being an ignorant dolt, let it be your highest ambition, don't mind me."

The patrolman in khaki green was less inclined to leave at that moment. "What's down that hole?" he asked.

"That's the point. You don't know. You should want to find out."

The young officer considered his options. Leave in a huff. Depart quietly and seek advice elsewhere. Or look down the hole. He decided to beat a rapid retreat.

"What if another body's down there?" Cinq-Mars addressed the man's back. "What if bodies are down half a dozen holes in this village? What if you miss that? What if we've had a massacre here? How will that look? Doesn't it scare you that you might miss something so big?"

The man spun on his heel. He was ready to belt his tormentor, but instead sighed heavily, pushed past him and flung open the floorboards to the ice-hole.

Cinq-Mars leaned in behind him. "What do you see?" he asked quietly.

"Nothing!" the officer threw back at him.

"Nothing?"

"An ice-hole. Snow. Ice. Water. Nothing else."

"Good!" Cinq-Mars tapped him lightly on the shoulder in praise. "Now you know what's down there. Before, you didn't. I suggest you do the same thing in every cabin on this lake. If you come up with nothing, at least you'll have the satisfaction of knowing you've done your police work properly. Now get out. If anybody asks, tell them I'm staying put for now."

The uniformed officers departed, as if escaping Purgatory. Mathers was chuckling to himself and shaking his head.

"What's up with you?" Cinq-Mars barked.

"Sometimes I wonder how I survived being your rookie partner."

"Funny you should say that, Bill. Sometimes I wonder why I let you."

Mathers laughed louder, happy to be somewhat immune when Cinq-Mars rattled his cage. The flue had begun to smoke so he continued to tend the fire while Émile Cinq-Mars closed his eyes, ostensibly napping. They were interrupted by a knock on the door again. Both men waited, but this time the visitor did not barge straight in.

Cinq-Mars opened the door to another uniformed officer, one with rank equivalent to his own. The cop, however, was no older than Mathers, mid-thirties, with a loopy kind of grin, a side-angle smile. It was an infectious grin, which seemed genuine. "Sergeant-Detective Émile Cinq-Mars?" The man was holding out a gloved hand.

The older detective shook it.

"An honour, sir. I'm a big fan. My name is Painchaud—Sergeant Charles Painchaud. I'm the Investigating Officer on this case."

"Are you, now."

"So far. May I come in?"

An SQ cop with manners. This was novel. "Please."

Cinq-Mars introduced him to his partner. Mathers

mentally translated his name to mean *hot bread*, and
filed away the mnemonic reference.

"It's fortunate for us you were on the scene,"
Painchaud mentioned. "At least I know that nothing's
been disturbed. Do you fish here often, sir?"

"Several times a year," Cinq-Mars replied, sizing up
this new intruder. He was taken with his manner, and
especially with his ability to ask a pertinent question
while seemingly engaged in small talk. But the man's
size was disconcerting. He was unaccustomed to cops
so small.

"Any luck today?"

"Afraid not."

"That's not surprising," Painchaud offered.

Cinq-Mars was intrigued. "Should I be offended,
Sergeant?"

The *Sûreté* detective laughed heartily, and Cinq-Mars
could see that there was definitely something wonky
about his mouth. "I'm sorry, sir. I'm not suggesting
that you're a lousy fisherman. How would I know? Last
night was the full moon, a big night for fishing. The bay
was probably fished out. With Ski-Doos and four-
wheelers around for the weekend, you'd think fish
would know better than to get hooked this morning."

Cinq-Mars was willing to concede the point. "I
should have taken all that into consideration."

"But you never know, do you, when you're fishing,
what might show up?"

Cinq-Mars smiled and conceded that point as well.

"Sir, you asked my officer to check the holes. Did
you have a specific reason for that request?"

Sticking a hand down the back of his collar, Cinq-
Mars gave himself a good scratch between his shoulder
blades. His bulky clothing, the range of temperatures in
and out of the huts, and the smoke had made him itchy
all over. Feeling that he was being interrogated by
someone with skill also made him squirm. "I suppose I

should mind my own business. This is out of my jurisdiction, as you know. And even within my jurisdiction it would not be my case, because I'm not connected to Homicide. I suppose I should mind my own business and shut the hell up."

"No, sir," the detective replied, surprising him yet again, "you shouldn't. If you have something to contribute, I'm interested. Your reputation is immense, I'd be a fool not to consider your counsel, and I don't consider myself a fool, Sergeant-Detective, despite what you might think about the SQ."

Cinq-Mars met his eyes then. Clearly, his prejudices had shown, or had preceded him by reputation, and he had displayed them to the wrong person. "All right," he consented. "I'll tell you what I think."

"Thank you, Sergeant-Detective."

"Everything is conjecture. I have no facts."

"Understood."

Cinq-Mars sat with his feet wide apart and put his hands on his knees. "Sergeant Mathers identified an exit wound through the front of the throat."

"That's correct."

"The victim was shot through the back of the neck."

"Agreed."

"Who does that? Given the option, what killer shoots his victim through the throat? What I think happened is this. The victim was down on his knees. He was to be shot execution-style, through the back of the head. At the last second, either because he flinched or because he suddenly knew what was going on, he jerked up slightly. The gun that had been aimed at the back of his head fired, and he was shot through the neck."

The uniformed detective was nodding, but he had questions, objections. Cinq-Mars waited to see what they would be, to help him determine if this IO deserved more.

"How do we know that he was down on his knees?"

The right question to ask. "That's what the wound tells us. The killer's aim was suddenly deflected. That's the first clue. Had the victim been standing, and suddenly flinched, the bullet would still have travelled into his head, only the head would have been turned slightly. The entry line is downward, and the location of the exit wound says that the gun was pointed down at him."

"What's the second clue?" Painchaud asked. Cinq-Mars had dropped that remark to see if he was sharp enough to pick it up.

"The ice inside his face."

"It makes him look strange. Isn't it a case of water freezing inside him? It's cold down there."

Cinq-Mars opened the hatch to the ice-hole under the floor. Forming a pistol-shape with his fingers, he fired an imaginary bullet. "The victim is shot and immediately falls face down into the hole. He's still alive. He wasn't shot through the head or heart. He's still breathing and will be for a while longer. Why does his assailant not fire a second round? The first was no accident. Execution-style, remember. Has there been any sign of a second wound?"

"We won't know until we get him out of the hole. On first examination, no."

"For now, let's say there was one shot. Why only one? Because he needed noise to cover the sound, perhaps? Three or four snowmobiles are roaring towards his cabin—"

"Not the cabin where we found the body?" Painchaud wanted to verify.

"Some other one. I saw no sign that he was shot there. Now, snowmobiles are roaring up, and the killer entices or tricks the victim to check the ice-hole. Maybe to pull up a line, clear ice, something like that. The victim gets down on his knees and pulls up a fishing line. The killer takes out his pistol. The snowmobiles are roaring by, and when the sound is loudest the victim feels the pistol on his hair and jerks slightly. *Pop!* The killer fires. The head of the victim collapses into the water, but he's not dead. He's not able to save himself—he will drown there or bleed to death—but he's not dead. The killer cannot fire again—"

"—because the snowmobiles have moved on."

"Exactly. He's not sure what to do. His victim is thrashing around. Should he shoot him again? No. Let him drown? Either his head is underwater or it's just above the surface. Maybe he lifts him by the feet and pushes him down. Maybe he plants a boot on the back of the man's head. But he keeps him in the water. Only after he's been in the water awhile, and is quite dead, does he lift him up."

"Why?" Bill Mathers asked.

Cinq-Mars shakes a finger in the air. "The killer is not done with the corpse. We know this because the corpse freezes on land, not in the water. Water does not turn to ice when it enters a warm body. But water turns to ice when it freezes in a dead body left out in the cold. Perhaps the dead man remains in the hut with no heat, and overnight the water in his face, throat and lungs freezes and expands. Some drains off him and crystal-lizes in his long hair. Perhaps he's carried on a Ski-Doo sled across the lake and in the forty-below temperature freezes stiff. The thing is, before he is put back in the water, he freezes above ground. That's key. That's important."

Painchaud nodded thoughtfully. "So my men should be checking ice-holes for signs of blood and tissue."

"Not only here," Cinq-Mars admonished him, "but all around the lake. As soon as possible."

"Why do you think the victim was not shoved into the hole right away?"

"Good question, Painchaud. You must have your thinking cap on."

"Actually, Sergeant-Detective, some of us in the SQ have brains, contrary to the perception of our friends in the MUCPD."

Cinq-Mars chuckled. "*Touché*, my friend. Possibly, the victim did not fit into the hole, just as he does not fit the hole where he was found. The killer may have left him to go and find tools to open the ice. More likely, the killer might not have wanted him to be found where he was shot. I doubt that he would know to rely upon a current. He might not have expected him to be found until spring, and when he was, he wanted it to be as far away from the scene of the crime as possible. Or perhaps, and this is a long shot, the killer had specific reasons for having the victim found where he was. I'd want to make sure there was nothing keeping the victim in place, other than the fishing line tied to the stove, which Bill put on him. We must at least entertain the notion that he was deliberately left to be found where he was found."

"But how?"

"That's another good question," Cinq-Mars acknowledged, but he did not suggest an answer.

Painchaud jumped up from his seat. "I'll get on that right away. I hope it's not too late."

"Very good, Sergeant. Good luck with your case."

Painchaud held the door open a moment, admitting the frigid wind, before stepping outside. "Thank you, sir," he said, turning, "for everything." Then he was gone.

Mathers and Cinq-Mars waited in the cabin, listening to the howl of wind around the timbers and plywood surfaces, hearing the old wood creak. Mathers had a grin on his face.

"What?" Cinq-Mars finally bellowed when he had had enough. "What?"

"Émile Cinq-Mars," Mathers chortled, "confiding in an officer from the SQ. Will wonders never cease?"

"I didn't tell him any damned thing," Cinq-Mars huffed. But after a while he asked, gesturing broadly with his chin, "The guy seemed different from the others, though, didn't he? To you?"

Mathers nodded slightly. "Smaller," he conceded.

Sergeant Charles Painchaud strode across to the hut where the body had been found. The woman who had discovered it was inside trying to keep warm, and another woman was hovering around her, being helpful. Upon entering, he gave a slight nod to the friend, who understood that she was being asked to leave, and through a series of hand signals and facial expressions she understood also that she should gather up the woman's daughter and take her along. It took a while to get everyone dressed and out, and only when the door had closed did Painchaud give up the pretence of conducting an official police interview.

"Camille, I'm so sorry," he said, and pulled up a wooden chair to sit beside her.

"Charlie. My God. They've killed Andy. What're we going to do?"

"You didn't tell anyone you knew him?"

"I didn't know what to do," she confided. "I just started screaming. I figured Cinq-Mars was around somewhere. That he'd come."

"Okay, Camille, you did fine. Now, think, did you tell anyone you knew him?"

"No, I didn't. Was that wrong?"

"If it's found out that you knew him, you can always plead that you didn't look at his face."

"I told people I did. Look at his face, I mean. I don't know why I did it. I told people I lifted up his head to see if it was attached."

"Camille!"

"I was in shock! I *am* in shock! Damn it, Charlie."

"Okay, okay, take it easy." He held both her cold

hands between his, rubbing them. "It'll only be a problem if someone finds out that you knew Andy. I'm in
charge of the case, so the question probably won't
come up."

"What about Cinq-Mars?"

"He seems interested in what's going on. I'm going
to make that work for us. I'm going to keep him interested."

"Why don't we just tell him everything? We were
going to talk to him anyway."

"Andy's death complicates things. You knew him.
He's dead in your hut. Andy held so many keys that
could have helped you and Lucy. Now he's dead.
That's trouble. Lucy's in trouble. You are, too. I need
time to think this through."

She began to breathe heavily, and tears welled.
"Charlie, Charlie, they've killed Andy! Andy's dead!"

"Shhh, shhh," he whispered, both cautioning and
soothing her.

"How did he get under the ice in my hut?" The
mystery of it seemed to make her frantic. "Is that some
kind of warning? Do they know about me, too? Are
they going to kill me next?"

"Don't panic, Camille. It's a coincidence. They
would never warn you first." That seemed of slight
comfort, so Sergeant Painchaud moved across to the
bunk on which Camille was sitting and took her into his
arms. He rocked her and urged her not to worry, but
he knew that there was much to fear, and much that
was left unexplained. Eventually, the woman who had
crossed the ice on a Ski-Doo that morning only to find
a friend dead beneath her fishing hut calmed herself.

"Where's Lucy?" Camille Choquette inquired.

"She's gone into the city. To blow off steam, I
imagine."

Camille looked up at him, astonished.

"No!" he hastened to add. "She doesn't know about Andy."

"Oh my God. Charlie!"

"I know," he said. "I know. It's going to be rough on her."

They held one another in the stark, warm comfort of the shack.

That night, Sergeant-Detective Émile Cinq-Mars snoozed toward the end of the movie he was supposed to be watching with his wife, missing the romantic bits. He struggled to wakefulness when she got up to snap the tape out of the VCR and switch the television to the news. Groggy, he had a difficult time pushing himself farther out of the sofa's deep cushions. Clips from an earthquake in Colombia were depressing, and yet another uprising among Palestinians contributed to a sombre mood. They were watching a station out of Vermont, as his wife was American and preferred to catch the news from home.

"If we switch to the local channel you might see your husband in action," Cinq-Mars remembered.

"Why's that?" Sandra asked. She was much younger than him. She was sitting with her knees up, encircled by her arms.

"Some lout with a video camera was on the ice. He probably sold me off to the highest bidder."

"Then switch!" Sandra Lowndes enthused. "I never get to see you on the job."

A local French station was also finishing up the international news, but the lead story when they turned their attention to home was a murder on the Lake of Two Mountains.

"There you are!" Sandra cried out, seeing her husband peering down into the cavity where, the audience was told, floated a dead man's head. "Did you

touch him with your bare hands? Talk about a body
gone cold."

"Bill did the touching." The sad-sack Chief of Police
from Vaudreuil-Dorion received two seconds of
airtime. Much of the report was devoted to the amazing coincidence of star detective Émile Cinq-Mars
being, once again, in the right place at the right time.

Included in the report was information Cinq-Mars
did not know. The victim had been identified as
Andrew Stettler, an employee of a pharmaceutical
company known as BioLogika. When the company's
name was mentioned, the camera panned the tall
building at the head of the bay that overlooked the ice-
village.

Following her husband's thirty seconds of continued
fame Sandra switched back to the American channel,
while Cinq-Mars mulled the news that the dead man
had worked near the spot where his body had been
recovered.

Sandra punched off the tube with her remote
control, stretched and yawned. She fluffed her brown
hair back, then leaned way over and kissed her
husband. She was a handsome woman with lively eyes
and a quick smile. She had a soft, full mouth and gentle
lines across her forehead created by perpetually arch-
ing her eyebrows. She jumped up, grasped his hand
and pulled her man to his feet.

"You are not going to think about this all night,
Émile."

"That might not be possible."

"Wanna bet?"

Movie romance had her in the mood, and the detective was not about to pit himself against the bright twinkle in her eye. They departed the den in their country
home clasped in one another's arms, and Cinq-Mars
stretched out his free hand to turn out the lights.

2

ROLL CALL

Depending on the nature of the experiment, lab rats at Hillier-Largent Global Pharmaceuticals, Inc., were paid up to a thousand dollars for a weekend of their time and the indiscriminate use of their bodies. Applicants agreed to be inoculated, or scratched with a vaccine, or given drugs orally, or sprayed with decongestants, or plied with laxatives, and consented also to spending a weekend, Friday night to Monday morning, in the lab under observation. In a few experiments they were deprived of sleep, in others they were prohibited from leaving their beds except to urinate or defecate in pots, their urine and feces retained for study.

In any economy, stagnant or prosperous, a shortage of candidates rarely occurred. If the company advertised for healthy twenty-year-olds, non-smokers, with no record of prolonged alcohol abuse, the line of university students needing cash for spring break circled the block. If the company required octogenarians with a known history of heart disease, applicants were dropped off by relatives. They shuffled into line behind their walkers, checking pacemakers and pulse, sneaking a smoke to calm their nerves prior to the interview. If the company requested men with a previous history of heroin addiction, ex-convicts released from prison a few days earlier responded, as polite as choirboys, happy for three more days of detention, and they were joined by skid-row vets hoping to earn a dollar.

Inside the laboratory, where visitors' blood tests were conducted, a poster, out of the lab rats' sight, repeated a variation on an old adage: "Life is Shit, Then You Croak." The sign was meant to cheer up the technicians.

Lucy Gabriel, generally, did not require cheering up, although she had been responsible for erecting the sign. Affable and fun-loving, she was bright, eager and talkative, and took considerable pride in her work. She'd been chosen to interview the applicants who lined up for the Wednesday morning roll calls because of her natural affinity for the destitute. She treated them in a cordial and sympathetic manner. Being native didn't hurt. The poor suspected that she had known hard times herself, which eased their embarrassment at being there. Those who recognized her as an activist for Indian rights, someone who had spent time on the barricades during an explosive period in the history of her reserve, believed that they had placed themselves in good hands.

Men, of course, were delighted to discover themselves in the care of a beauty.

An aspect to conducting the interviews was keeping an eye peeled for special people. That Andrew Stettler caught her attention was no surprise. He had come on strong. She knew the type. Men of his ilk treated the program as a joke, a bump on the road, a story for the boys back at the bar.

As was the case with most lab rats, Andrew Stettler was down on his luck the day that he showed up. Lucy had no problem with that. She didn't judge people by their troubles. She still lived on the Kanesetake Reserve, where being down on your luck was commonplace, where hard times never ended. On occasion, she might grow impatient with men who chose to be boisterous about being broke, or who dismissed bad decisions as rotten luck, but she understood that people had a right to deal with misery in their own way.

Andrew Stettler's way was to be the life of any party going.

"Choose me," he demanded, wearing a wry smile upon entering her office. He had long black hair, curling where it rested on his shoulders, an engaging grin and a discernible brightness to his eyes. Sitting down in the chair in front of Lucy's desk, he splayed his big hands across the pale oak veneer. "Rich veins. You won't have to drill for my blood. I admit, the last time I bled, the colour was black. Alien ancestors, I'm guessing. Maybe the bullet poisoned me, who can explain it?" His chin was pointy, his neck longer than most, and his Adam's apple was particularly prominent. "For you, sugar, I'll bleed red. Looking at you makes me feel like a red-blooded American boy, which I'm not. I'm local talent. Canadian. A Montrealer, born and bred. Chances are decent I'll die here, too. I don't get around much anymore, but who can blame me? So many lovely beauties, how can I leave even one behind? Speaking about dating—"

"We weren't," Lucy interjected.

"Details," he said, waving a hand as though to dismiss her point. "We'll use the grand your company's paying me to take an enema—or whatever you got in mind—and we'll have ourselves a night on the town. Good food. Catch a movie. Drinks someplace. What do you say?"

"Name, please," Lucy asked. His smile had already snared her. The slight turn at the corners of his mouth expressed mischief, fun, buffoonery and an inclination, she supposed, for the erotic. She liked the darkness in his eyes.

"Call me Andy."

"What does your bank call you, Andy, in case we write a check?"

"Ah! That'll be Andrew Stettler. Since I don't see my name on a check too often, make it out to Andrew R. Stettler. A nice honky ring, don't you think?"

"If you say so."

"You're not white," he said.

"You're not blind," she murmured, and pretended to mark his form.

"Might've been. Half-blind anyway, until I saw you. Women in uniform never looked good to me before, but you've turned me right around on that one."

Her white lab coat did not constitute a uniform, but she wasn't going to argue the point. "Are you clean, Andy?"

He sniffed both armpits. "Lord God Almighty, I think I did take a shower this morning. Shaved, too. I smell like a cross between Irish Spring and Right Guard. So no, I don't stink, if that's what you're asking."

"I think you know what I'm asking." She typed his name into her computer.

He flashed that dark-eyed smile again. "What's your name, sugar?"

"Lucy Gabriel."

"Please to meet you, Lucy. I believe in a drug-free America, so I do my part by living in Canada. Seriously, though, I stay away from that shit. Bought me too much trouble in life. Lost me too many friends. Sample my blood, if you want."

"I'll do that, Andy. I positively will do that. But you can save us both time and trouble by answering honestly."

He brushed his big hands over the surface of the desk, smiled. "Clean for how long?" he asked.

"Six months would be nice."

"Next question. Clean of what, exactly?"

"Heroin. Crack. Cocaine. Amphetamines," she stipulated.

"Marijuana? Hash? Angel dust?"

"It'd be nice if you could give me six months from my list and six days from yours."

He stuck out his hand. "Agreed. Can I come back next week?"

"Ah …"

"Kidding!" He laughed. "I'm clean! I'm not saying it's been entirely voluntary, but I haven't toked up up since my last job. Your list never interested me. I'm one of the few guys alive who went to prison and actually came back a rehabilitated soul. I'm a walking, talking miracle, Lucy."

She had a backlog of applicants waiting in the corridor outside, but was in no hurry to finish with him. "Under occupation, what do I write? Miracle man? Religious nut? Jailbird?"

He laughed. "Funny you should ask. Let me talk to you about it. Any jobs with this company, Lucy? Real, permanent-type jobs, not this guinea pig stuff?"

She shrugged a shoulder. "You'd have to apply at Personnel."

"Drug company, right?" he went on. "I come here, I see video cameras in the lobby. I see employees showing photo I.D., punching in passwords. I'm thinking, they got security problems here. I can help with that."

"Try Pinkerton's."

He laughed again, as if she'd cracked a joke. "I can't be bonded, Lucy. But someone like me, I know things that would pin back the ears of a Pinkerton guard. If you have problems, I'm your man, the guy with solutions."

She decided on the spot to take him seriously. "All right, Andy. I'll give you a problem. Provide me with a solution."

For the first time, he sat back in his chair, cocky and cool. "Shoot."

"Let's say I wanted you to steal a truck. How would you go about it?"

Andy whistled. "Whoo-ee, aren't you the action figure! Are you serious?"

She smiled. "No, I'm not. It's a test. Are you all talk, or do you know things?"

He nodded vigorously, as if to indicate that the ground rules seemed fair enough and that he was only too eager to rise to the challenge. "All right. Let's see. The gangs, there's your problem. You don't hijack a truck anywhere close to the city without the approval of organized crime, not unless you want your clutch foot lopped off. Either you make a deal with a gang, or …" He seemed to suddenly lose himself in thought.

"Or what, Andy?"

"You're Indian, right?"

"So?"

"Heist a truck in the States. Then use your Indian friends—I'm just saying, maybe you have a connection—to let you drive the truck back across the border. Everybody knows Indians control the border. If what you want is the truck, pay your Indian friends with the contents. Cigarettes or booze."

His eyes had wandered to one side during his dissertation. Done, he looked back at Lucy Gabriel, and discovered that she was staring at him with a grave expression.

"What's the matter?" he asked.

She shook herself, as if emerging from a trance, and jumped up from her chair. "Would you mind waiting here a minute?"

"I got no pressing engagements."

Lucy quickly left the office.

She made her way down labyrinthine corridors, halting at a number of doorways to punch in a code, and entered an expansive laboratory. Lucy started work early, and the lab had yet to fill with its usual complement of technicians. Spotless, the walls and ceiling white, the tables a shiny stainless steel, the room was made eerie by silence. Lucy was pleased to find the man she was looking for there, which saved her an elevator ride three floors up to his office.

"Dr. Largent!" she called.

"Good morning, Miss Gabriel." A slight, mousy-looking man with distinctive blue eyes, Dr. Randall Largent brushed his tufts of hair into rampant bursts of white flame, as if performing an impression of Einstein. Under his laboratory smock he was dressed in his familiar pinstriped blue suit and tie. Sixty-two years old and a principal of the company, he was a creature of the executive suite, not the lab.

She strode up to him to whisper her information, and her employer placed a conspiratorial hand on her elbow, drawing her close as he lowered an ear.

"I've found the one for us! He's perfect! Perfection on a platter!"

"Calm down, Lucy."

"He's *exactly* what we're looking for. He's here as a lab rat. What should I do?"

Dr. Randall Largent sucked in his breath before announcing his decision. "Hire him," he suggested. He exhaled.

"Really? For the job?"

"No," he stipulated. "Hire him as a lab rat. Observe him over the weekend. See how he handles himself."

"Yes, but what if he doesn't show up for the weekend?" Lucy objected.

"Then he's not the man for us, is he?"

"I suppose not," she conceded. "But it's not a typical weekend, remember. It won't be easy."

"All the better. We'll see how he fares."

Hillier-Largent Global Pharmaceuticals, Inc., did

contract research, and Montreal was a major research centre. Whenever the exclusive license to a successful drug patent was expiring, competing companies developed their own versions for the marketplace. New variations required testing, if for no other reason than to adhere to government regulations. Drug companies had found it cost-effective and less messy to farm out this kind of work, and Hillier-Largent Global, a relatively small outfit, happily took on the contracts as a means to finance its own development of new drug therapies for serious illnesses. This weekend they were experimenting with a bowel cleanser, to be used when patients needed to prepare their intestines for examination. When Andrew Stettler had mentioned taking an enema, he'd been close to the truth.

Lucy nodded. "Okay, I'll do that."

"Good morning! What's up?" The question was posed by the other half of the company's letterhead, Dr. Harry Hillier, as he entered the lab. Harry was easily Lucy's favourite of the two, but he was not involved in all the company's enterprises. She knew things her boss did not. Bald across the top, with jet-black hair worn straight down on the sides, Harry had a horse-shaped face with large lips. He was no taller than Lucy. Everyone knew that Harry Hillier was the scientific brains behind the company, whereas Randall Largent managed the enterprise. Hillier was known as a bland stickler for the rules, while Largent had a reputation for fudging data, and nobody would put it past him to cook the books.

"Just working my way through roll call," Lucy cheerfully intoned. "It's under control now. Got to be going. Bye!"

She set off on the fly, sliding a little on the polished floors.

Andrew Stettler had left his seat and was examining a photograph perched on a filing cabinet as Lucy returned to her office. In the picture, Lucy was dressed in what she referred to as battle fatigues—an embroidered elk hide vest, denim shirt and tight-fitting, patched jeans. She was standing on an upside-down police cruiser, a fist clenched at her side, her other hand raised straight up clutching a rifle. Her face was painted with colourful streaks—war paint—and her mouth was wide open, apparently expelling a blood-curdling holler.

"Lucy, is this you?" Stettler asked, incredulous, as she took her seat.

"Yep."

"Jesus. I better not mess with you. That was during the Oka Crisis?"

At the beginning of the 1990s, an altercation between the police and her people had led to a conflict. A town near the reserve, called Oka, had blithely decided to expand the limits of its municipal golf course. The expansion absorbed land Mohawks considered to be their own, and they further believed that the land in dispute included sacred burial grounds. A classic confrontation. Whites pooh-poohed the notion of ancient burial grounds and faded treaties while deifying golf and every man's right to swing a club. Mohawks invoked centuries of grievances to marshal their defence of the piney woods and put up roadblocks. The SQ attacked. A cop was shot and killed, and the police contingent fled the woods like scared rabbits. The army was brought in next, and the stand-off between Indians armed to the teeth and soldiers with fixed bayonets absorbed the interest of the western world for weeks. Eventually, peace was restored. The Mohawks kept their burial grounds, while a few of their number did jail time.

"Oka Crisis … last weekend," Lucy deadpanned, "I

can't remember now. I'm always turning over cop cars,
it's hard to keep track."

"And I thought I was a bad boy."

She smiled. She liked him. "Listen. There's a chance
of a regular job."

"You're kidding me. Here?"

"Not here. But that's another story. Next week,
maybe, I'll set up a meeting with the president of
another company, a partner company of ours. He's
looking for someone like you."

"Why only maybe?" Stettler asked.

Lucy cocked her chin. "First, you have to get
through the weekend. I'm hiring you for the guinea pig
job. If you're not a troublemaker, if you behave, that
sort of thing, you'll get the interview."

"Lucy, that's great. Thanks."

"You won't be thanking me this weekend. You'll be
puking your guts out between attacks of diarrhea."

"Yeah?"

"Afraid so."

Andy gently nodded, accepting the conditions, and
flashed his seductive smile again. "How's that any
different from my usual weekend?"

Andrew Stettler walked away from Hillier-Largent
Global that morning, which was not unusual in itself, for
most lab rats arrived and departed by public transport or
on foot. Only a few drove, usually in old, rust-spotted
cars that dragged their mufflers. What made Stettler's
departure exceptional was that after he had walked a few
blocks and turned three corners he stopped and looked
around, then unlocked the door to a late-model Oldsmobile, tucking himself in behind the wheel.

Equally surprising, he drove to a house he owned.
Andrew Stettler lived on the upper floor of a duplex in
a congested, nondescript north-end neighbourhood,
and leased the lower portion of the house, connected

by an inside staircase, to his mother. He did not charge her more than the monthly allowance he provided for her, but for tax purposes they honoured the ritual of writing and cashing rent checks.

At home, Andy stripped out of the faded, rough clothes he had worn to the interview. He unlaced the worker's boots and tossed his old jeans into a heap. Then he dressed again, in a pressed shirt and creased trousers. A knock on the front door interrupted him.

Two raps, a pause, two more raps, a second pause, one final rap.

As always, secret code.

His one irritation about living in close proximity to his mother was her tiresome habit of visiting him soon after he arrived home. His complaints had caused her to delay her entry by a few minutes, but she could not resist coming up the stairs and sharing a word within the half-hour.

"Hi, Ma."

"Andy! You were up early this morning!"

"My prerogative, Ma."

"Where were you off to?"

"My business, Ma."

"I'm just making conversation." She was entering deeper into his apartment, scanning, sniffing slightly, curious as to whether or not he was alone.

"You taught me to be secretive, Ma. Don't complain about the results."

"Secretive about secrets, Andy. Not secretive for the sake of being secretive."

Never a tall woman, she seemed to be shrinking daily. Andy had wondered if the process would ever stop, or would she continue to shrivel until, one day, he'd be unable to find her amid her pillows and sheets unless she spoke up. Around the house, she tended to wear her bathrobe over her nightdress, and only when special guests were coming over did she bother to put on a proper outfit and don her cape. Mrs. Stettler was interested in the occult, and had belonged to a secret spiritual group while her son was growing up. Covert knocks and coded rings on the telephone, abrupt moves in the middle of the night and a strict prohibition against outsiders coming into the house had defined his childhood. The techniques came naturally to him now. He could lead a double or a triple life, deceive as easily as breathe. In her dotage, Mrs. Stettler restricted herself to reading tarot cards and hosting the occasional midnight seance. To her friends she was a harmless daffy duck, but her son had taken up the mantle of the secret life. Even she did not know what he did for a living, or how he managed in the world.

"Ma, I'm heading out soon. Is there something you wanted?"

"The *TV Guide*, dear. I've misplaced mine."

He smiled. She always had an answer, one that never sounded as though it had been divined on the spur of the moment. He had inherited the knack. Andy always had an answer, too.

After sending her on her way with the magazine and wolfing down a quick bite, he headed out for his squash club. This was a lengthy jaunt, for he preferred to live among a mix of French and immigrant populations while socializing in the more affluent English neighbourhoods farther away. He had to drive across the northern rim of the city into the western sector and get off the expressway in a community of shopping malls, bungalows, and split-level homes. Werner Honigwachs was waiting for him when he arrived, and the two shook hands.

"I got a call from Lucy," Honigwachs told him.

"Already?"

"She's hot to trot. She thinks I should hire you."

The two men chuckled.

Honigwachs carried himself with a presidential air.

He had a round face, with eyes set wide apart and the cheekbones unusually broad, flat plateaus. Although somewhat small, his nose was distinctive, the tip pushed slightly to one side. His black hair was trimmed to perfection, his fingernails equally well manicured. Trappings of his success were in evidence. Rolex watch. A substantial gold wedding band on one finger, on another a hefty topaz stone nestled in a bed of diamonds on a white-gold ring. The suit was a striped executive grey, a superb fit. Solidity exemplified his appearance, the large, square shoulders sloping to a heavyweight's chest. That he looked after himself was apparent to Andy, for his body type would noticeably sag if he let himself go. He was a six-footer, around two hundred pounds.

"She told me I had to get through the weekend first, prove myself."

"The weekend won't be easy," Honigwachs cautioned.

"I can handle it. The worse it is, the better for me. A little sympathy will help seal the bond between me and Lucy. You were right, Werner. She's a babe."

"Did you meet anyone else?"

"Nope. Wasn't introduced. She did leave to talk to someone—"

"Randall Largent," Honigwachs interjected.

"He's the guy onside, right?"

"Get that straight. Randall Largent, wild white hair, looks like a mad scientist. It's a studied look, incidentally. He's neither mad nor much of a scientist. Yes, he's the one onside. His partner is Harry Hillier, short, stooped, bald on top, baritone voice—he's not onside. Harry knows nothing about you."

"Largent knows."

"Largent knows and I know. Period. To everyone else you're a lab rat coming in from the cold."

"Except for Lucy. I'm the man of her dreams."

"So soon?"

"I got that feeling."

Werner Honigwachs whistled. "You work fast. Come on, let's grab a court."

Andrew Stettler trailed along beside his new client. He decided to forgo discussing his one slip that morning. He had mentioned to Lucy that she was going to give him an enema when he had had no way of knowing that information beforehand. He had passed it off as a fluke, a coincidental remark. For Andrew, as a professional industrial spy, the goof was worth noting. Mistakes could be dangerous. He was playing a part again. The time had come to step into the role. Play it smart, and play it for keeps.

Two and a half days later, early Saturday morning, December 11, 1998

The fluid that Andrew Stettler and the other lab rats were required to drink was a clear, sour-tasting concoction that caused horrific eruptions to assail the intestines. The ordeal was no fun for anyone. The lab rats were seated on pots for hours, evacuating their bowels without respite, while the technicians endured the moaning, the stench, the mess and the sadness that accompanies the humiliation of others.

A few volunteers were instructed to drink slowly, others more rapidly, the results observed and recorded. Among those who drank quickly, Andrew Stettler was one who also vomited frequently, sometimes simultaneously with diarrheal spasms.

Later, in the still of the night, Lucy visited him as he rested on a cot.

"Did I pass?" he wanted to know.

"How are you holding up?"

"My body is Jell-O, my mind mush, my insides feel like cold porridge. I'm fine, thanks. You?"

"If it makes you feel any better, the stench made me nauseous, too."

He smiled faintly. "Yeah, I feel a lot better. Tell me something. You've turned over police cars, had your picture taken carrying an assault weapon, for your job you get to torture men you should be dating. What makes you tick?"

She was impressed that he still had a sense of humour.

Lucy pulled up an aluminium folding chair and sat down by his cot. They were speaking quietly, respectful of the other lab rats sleeping around them. "If," she said, "you get the job, you know, the one in security, and if the job required stealing a truck—"

"I get the feeling sometimes you're not kidding me. Go on."

"And if—I'm being hypothetical here—if we need to steal a truck—I'm just saying *if,* I'm just giving you a puzzle—we'll need a driver."

"I'm your man. I can drive."

"No," she told him. "You're supposed to be the man with solutions, remember? Hypothetically, we'd need a driver who's not connected with either Hillier-Largent or the other company. You're already connected to us. You're drawing a paycheque for this weekend. We need someone totally unconnected—"

"No big deal."

"—who's HIV-pos," she added.

"Whoa, that's a complication."

"Possible?"

Andy tended to the rumblings in his stomach a moment, wincing as a constriction worked through him. "Not only is it possible," he said, "it's easy. I know exactly who to call."

"Really?" She was impressed again.

"No problem."

"You know an HIV-positive car thief?"

"Doesn't everyone? But seriously, his name is Luc Séguin, and he's not a car thief. He's a truck-jacker. Born to the trade. Third generation, he says."

"Get out of town! You know him?"

"That's my job. At least, I can make it my job."

She nodded, thinking about that. "Is he gay, this Luc?"

"Does it matter?"

"I was just wondering."

"He got AIDS in prison, from drug use, that's what he tells people. I know him well enough to say that he likes women, but things can happen inside. Who knows?"

The next growl through his gullet was a noisy one, and they both laughed a little. She touched his bare forearm where it emerged from the sheets.

"Why do you need someone with AIDS?" Andy asked. When she didn't answer right away, he added, "Hypothetically speaking, of course."

Lucy took a moment to consider whether or not she should answer. "The driver will see a few things. He'll meet people who are sick. It'll help if he's one of them. I can trust someone more if he's in the same situation as the people he's helping out."

"This is about helping people?"

"It is for me." She tapped his forearm. "I'm going to set up that meeting with you and Werner Honig-wachs," Lucy promised. "I think you'll get the job, Andy."

"That's great. I'm sorry it won't be for your company. It would be fun working together."

Lucy whispered, "Don't be so sure it won't happen."

"So many secrets," he whispered back. "You excite me, Lucy."

Smiling, she left him to his rest and his rowdy intestines.

3

EYE TO EYE

Lucy Gabriel stood by the side of the road near her home, her breath visible in the cold. The small bag she had packed rested at her feet. She was wearing cowboy boots, tight-fitting blue jeans that accentuated her long legs, and an old suede jacket. She kept her hands stuffed in the jacket pockets, her neck scrunched in the lambswool collar that once upon a time had been white but now was grey.

An old jalopy, hiccupping black smoke and looking shabby from a distance, as though its fenders had been banged into place that morning, puttered up, with Andrew Stettler slumped down in the front passenger seat, his raised knees pressed against the dash. Up close, the car reminded Lucy of the relics littered across her reserve. She looked at the sky, sighed, then tossed in her bag, piled into the back seat, and, leaning forward, received a peck on the lips from Andy. She held out her hand to shake the driver's.

"This is Luc Séguin, the guy I was telling you about," Andy said. To Luc he added, "Told you, man, she's a babe. Just don't treat her wrong. If you do, she'll overturn your car and stomp on it."

"I seen that picture in the paper," Luc said. He had

51

a scratchy voice. "That's why I brought a wreck."

"It's nice to meet you," Lucy said.

"Likewise, lady." He put the car in gear, which didn't seem so easy, and they drove on through the Kanesetake Reserve.

"Did you talk to your Warrior brothers?" asked Andy. He was sitting sideways and speaking to her through the gap in the front bucket seats.

"I wouldn't call them my brothers, exactly."

"You don't get along?"

"We don't see eye to eye—let me put it that way." She shrugged a shoulder.

Andy and Luc exchanged glances. Lucy guessed that Luc Séguin was around fifty-five. He could have been even older. His weathered skin was oddly pale, his blond hair trimmed right to the scalp. He was gaunt, and looked worn. Worn out, perhaps. She didn't know how ex-cons were supposed to behave, but he was measuring up to her vague preconceptions. His quiet felt more absent than solitary, as if he was accustomed to being in one place while mentally residing somewhere else.

"That surprises me. What do you mean?" Andy's tone had turned serious.

Lucy rotated her head, stretching her neck and easing an inner tension. The subject was no big deal to her, always more interesting to white people than her own. "If the mayor of some dinky town wants to take our land, if cops attack, if the army surrounds us and tries to cut us off from the world and starve us out, then you better believe we'll fight alongside each other, one Indian will die for another. But if the Warriors get an idea into their heads to turn the reserve into a gambling den, if they want to sell dope and weapons to the gangs, if they plan to educate our kids to be hewers of marijuana plants and drawers of cards from the bottom of the deck, that'll provoke a difference of opinion around here. Believe it. I'll fight alongside the Warriors if we're attacked. If they try to impose their will on the rest of us, I'm not afraid to kick Warrior ass."

They were driving through the reserve, where the homes were tidy and plain. A few showed the flag of the Mohawk Warriors, and a number of huts advertised cheap cigarettes and booze, smuggled in from the United States for sale to whites from the city. These were small enterprises, but big business was involved, and big business did not always play by the rules either. Tobacco companies manufactured Canadian brands in Puerto Rico and used Indians to smuggle them into the country through New York State, where their reserves crossed the Canadian border, undercutting high cigarette taxes intended to discourage the young from smoking. Tobacco companies believed in supplying their product at a reasonable cost, while the Warriors believed in doing good business.

Andy was shaking his head in admiration. "You never cease to amaze me, Lucy. I never pegged you as a politician."

"I believe in what's right."

The comment had Andy chuckling. "How about that, Luc? Ever worked on the side of truth and justice before?"

"Can't say so."

"Get used to it," Lucy told him. "You are now."

"The last time I checked, Lucy, hijacking trucks was not considered right."

"We're in this to save lives."

"How about that, Luc?" Andy pestered him. "You'll be a national hero."

"That's all right." He steered calmly through the swoops and curves of the country road. "Can maybe I ask you something about the Warriors, lady?"

"Ask me anything you want, Luc."

"Will they open the border to us? You're not seeing eye to eye with them, like you said, it makes me wonder about that there."

"That's a good question," Andy put in. "Will they?"

"No problem, guys. It's a business deal. We cross the border back and forth, they acquire a shipment of cigarettes. It's got nothing to do with being a Warrior or seeing things eye to eye. It's pure business."

Andy, for one, seemed satisfied. He twisted in his seat and faced forward. "That's good. I wouldn't want politics mixed up in any of this."

"Amen," Luc said. He downshifted as they entered a hamlet and a reduced speed zone.

"Everything's politics," Lucy murmured to herself.

"I heard that," Andy warned her, and reaching back between the seats he grabbed her knee.

They left the reserve and crossed over a bridge downstream at the busy rural town of Hawkesbury, then drove south cross-country into Ontario, keeping to the rural back roads. After an hour they passed into Indian land again, onto the Akwesasne Reserve. The name means "Land Where the Partridge Drums," referring to the birds' habit of drumming on rotted logs. As if in kinship, Warriors there had a reputation for warfare. The boundaries for the reserve crossed both the St. Lawrence River and the Canada–U.S. border, a quirk of geography that was proving to be a headache for the authorities and a boon to native enterprises, especially criminal ventures.

At a roadside shack that sold cigarettes, Lucy got out of the car and walked inside. She returned about five minutes later with a hand-drawn map. "Keep going this way for a bit. I'll tell you when to turn off."

After they turned off, the road narrowed and wound through trees. The forest became more dense and wild, and before long they glimpsed the frozen St. Lawrence River through the trees.

"Here!" Lucy called out. A small orange ribbon fluttered from a tree.

Luc had to stop and back up, then make a second turn, down toward the river.

At the bottom of the road they stopped at a command post. A Mohawk took one glance at the two white guys in the front seat and went back inside his hut, returning with a semi-automatic rifle in one hand, the barrel pointed at the ground.

Luc rolled his window down to talk to him, and the man leaned his weight on the doorframe. "Yeah?" he asked.

Lucy spoke to him in Iroquois from the back seat. When she was finished, the guard grunted, issued instructions, and waved them through.

"What'd he say?" Andy asked.

"Drive fast, follow the trees. When we get on the river, on the ice, stop for nobody, especially not Customs agents or Mounties, until we reach the other side. The river's frozen, but there could be holes. You need speed to cross the holes without sinking. Step on it, Luc."

Fast was a relative term, and Luc had no guidelines other than the issue of maintaining control over his junkheap on bare ice. For the sake of traction he accelerated slowly, despite Lucy's vocal whipping, and when he hit fifty miles an hour everyone believed he was doing fine. They followed a route marked by pines stuck in the ice. A pair of snowmobiles appeared to be in hot pursuit, and they were gaining, and from down the lake a four-wheel drive on a crossing lane also was overtaking them. Luc edged it up to sixty, bending his weight over the wheel to maintain control. His whole body shook wherever the ice was rippled. About halfway across, a vehicle approaching from the other side passed them at what had to be close to ninety, and that's when they knew that they were way too slow.

Luc pressed his foot to the floor. The relic fishtailed

on the ice. The doors and side windows rattled, and cold air rushed through a small gap in the floorboards with a flurry of snow, and the springs in the seats shook. Luc had the car up to seventy-five when he said, "Oh, shit." The embankment on the other side suddenly loomed ahead, a white mound on a white river, and he hadn't left himself room to stop, not on ice.

"We're dead," Andy stated simply.

"Shift down, Luc, shift down," Lucy called from the back seat, her voice urgent, but calm, insistent.

"Hang onto it yourself, lady." Luc spoke English without much of an accent, but he had a tendency to butcher phrases, especially when he was excited. He slowed the car by gearing down, which was a struggle, but the gearbox wouldn't allow him to go into first. He touched the snow on one side of the ploughed road with his tires. The snow sent the car swerving and the bodies in it rocked from side to side, but Luc wrestled with his steering wheel and recalcitrant clutch and unruly gearshift and kept touching the wheels on the right side into deeper snow. Near the edge of the river he announced, "Nope, we're not making it in this way," and made a move to put the car into a spin. The rear end fishtailed, then spun. Lucy howled and Andy let out a roar, hanging on, and the car twirled like a top. Luc said, "Maybe we do it this way," and the car catapulted off the opposite edge of the road and in that deeper snow finally stopped.

They were settled for no more than a second when Luc was gunning the car in reverse, then quick-shifting between first and reverse, the two passengers praying for the transmission to hold together. Then suddenly they were racing backwards, and Luc said, "Maybe this way," and they were on the ice-road again. He rammed the shift forward and the car leapfrogged a series of icy ruts and scaled the embankment.

They travelled thirty yards and stopped at the guard-house there.

Once again, Luc rolled down his window.

An Indian came over carrying an Uzi, put a hand on the roof over the driver's door and asked him, "Drive much?"

Luc looked shyly down. "I thought to myself I did all right."

"Oh yeah? Maybe we should have those scorecards, you know, the ones like they use for skaters, on the TV? Me, I'd put you down for five-point-two for technical skill, five-point-nine for artistic merit. How's that sound?"

"Pretty good. That's fair. Thanks."

"Anyhow," he said, "welcome to the United States of America." He stuck his head in the window. "Hey there, juicy Lucy, how're you doing?"

"Good, Brad, you?"

"Not so bad. I guess what I heard is true." He was a broad, square-faced man, about five-foot five, with a substantial belly. In the cold, his breath billowed as he spoke. He was wearing boots with unlaced flaps that overhung the toes. From time to time, the man moved his weapon from one hand to the other, then quickly changed it back.

"What do you hear, Brad?"

"I heard you only shack up with white men these days. That true?"

The challenge and animosity inherent in the statement chilled the men in the car. This was not going to be a friendly encounter, and at least two participants, Luc and the Indian, were armed. Any instinctive response Andy or Luc might have felt to defend the woman's honour was mitigated by being on foreign soil. This was the United States of America, but this was also hostile Indian land.

"You don't have that exactly right, Brad," Lucy told him, nonplussed.

Andrew Stettler was looking at her, hoping she had the sense to ease the tension here.

"How's that?" Brad asked.

"I only sleep with good-looking men. Now if that eliminates every Mohawk Warrior you know, including you, it can't be helped. I have my standards."

Brad had a mock smile on his face as he looked across at Stettler. "Ain't she a bitch?" he asked him.

Clearly, the man was waiting for an answer. Andy looked at him, then back at Lucy, then shook his head. "She has a way of sticking it to us guys."

The guard gave a little snort. "Lucy's a sad story. Isn't that right, girl? Folks died when she was young. She got adopted into the white man's world. We're glad to have her back, don't get me wrong, but the white man's world messed her up, there ain't no doubt about that."

"I know nothing about it," Andy said.

Lucy was shaking her head in the back seat. "Tell him the whole story, Brad," she lashed out. "Fill him in on the details."

Brad smirked. "You still got the bitterness in you, Lucy. It shows. The sun don't shine in your heart."

"Oh, sing me a lullaby!" Lucy stormed. "Where are the fucking violins? Or the tom-toms, or smoke, or whatever the fuck you want to use to make my eyes water?"

He was laughing now. "It ain't hard to get you going."

"Tell him, Brad. Tell him why my parents died young."

Abruptly, he stopped laughing. "White men don't need to hear that story. I don't need to hear it again."

"You brought it up! Tell them about the time the Warriors burned my parents' house down—"

"Nobody knew they were home, Lucy, that's what I heard."

"What are you saying? That it was okay to burn their house down, it's just too bad they were home? Good thing I slept in the garage or I'd be dead too."

"That's ancient history. Anyways, it was an accident."

"It was fucking murder, Brad. All over a goddamn difference of opinion about *zoning*. Now are you letting us through or what?"

Brad stood up straight and shook his head for a while in a deliberate and thoughtful matter. "You're coming back this way. That's what I was told."

"That's the deal."

"With a truckload of smokes."

"Which you get to keep."

"The truck stays with you. You move it to the other side, then move it back again. What's in the truck on the way back, Lucy?"

"You don't want to know, Brad."

"Maybe I do."

"No, Brad," she told him, enunciating each syllable, "you—don't—want—to know."

Brad chewed on the matter a moment. "All right," he decided. "Go on through. Do what you have to do. Understand one thing. I don't want nobody bleeding on Indian land. If you're bleeding, go someplace else. Don't bring trouble on us, we won't welcome your trouble. Is that clear enough?"

Dutifully, Luc and Andy nodded. In the back seat, Lucy scowled.

Brad thumped the top of the roof a couple of times and Luc Séguin drove on.

After they had driven off Indian land into upper New York State, Andy twisted around in his seat. "Never mind that eye-to-eye stuff," he said, "you don't get along with your Indian brothers *at all*. You're not even *friendly!*"

Lucy pursed her lips as if she wanted to spit. "Warriors burn down my parents' house, they kill my mom and dad and call it a mistake, I get adopted off the reserve, and when I grow up and come back they expect me to spread my legs for them? In their fucking dreams!"

"Easy, girl," Andy advised.

"Don't call me girl!"

"Then what should I call you?" he asked. "Miss Gabriel? Ma'am?"

"You," she parried, "you, you can call me—" Suddenly she caught herself and burst out laughing, her mood and the tension breaking. "You can call me 'sweetheart.'"

"Okay, sweetheart," Andy said, laughing too. "I'll do that."

Luc did not join in the fun, and after a while he asked, "What was he talking about, not bleeding on Indian land?"

"Look in a mirror," Lucy told him. "Look in a goddamned mirror!"

Andy glanced at Luc a number of times after that, finding him a hard man to read, then he looked back at Lucy. He explained, "Luc's sensitive about his blood. He also doesn't understand English perfectly."

The comment sank in, and Lucy reached forward and patted Luc gently on the shoulder. "He didn't mean anything by it, Luc. Just that you're white. That's what you'd see in a mirror. Nobody told him you have AIDS."

Luc nodded. He kept his eyes on the road. "Okay," he said after a while.

They drove on. Andy kept glancing back at Lucy, and finally he asked, "How come you slept in the garage when you were a kid?"

"Oh, piss off," she told him, and they drove on in silence after that.

Luc had planned the heist. The only aspect he could not handle himself was the border crossing, but the opportunity to cross freely, courtesy of the Mohawk Warriors, was one that he could not resist. Still, he wasn't clear on the parameters—specifically, what was in it for him. He had chewed it over with Andy.

"You're telling me that I jack a truck in the States and bring it back here."

"That's right."

"Full of cigarettes, but I'm going to *give away* those smokes to the Indians. I am doing this why?"

"You'll get paid."

"You know what it is a truck of smokes worth?"

"Nothing, unless you sell the smokes. You can't sell in the States, you have no contacts. You can't sell here, because how do you get the smokes across the border without the Indians? So the smokes are worth nothing to you or me."

"I'm dying, Andy, but I'm not dead. I'm doing charity why?"

"To help people out who are dying the same way you are."

"No," he said, shaking his head. "Nope. I need something out of this."

"It's a mission of mercy for which you get paid."

"For this I get to Heaven? Your guarantee is how much to me worth?"

His old pal from prison had a point. "Like I said, Luc, you're getting paid. It's sort of like being on salary."

"I'll get back to you on that," Luc told him.

He had then taken a few days to devise a counter-proposal. He agreed to hijack the truck and, after the Indians had emptied the contents, drive it back to Canada, where Lucy could transform it into a mobile lab. He'd be her driver, as she had requested, and return with her to the States. At the end of her operation, he'd use the truck for an enterprise of his own.

"What," Andy asked him, leery, "enterprise?"

"I got something going."

"What? I need to know."

"I do believe I can sell the truck. That's what I get out of it. The truck." A salary was not enough. He was a dying man. Death was expensive, he'd been finding out. He had expenses. If he was not entitled to a share of the cigarette action, he'd score on his own.

"Where?" Andy questioned him.

"I know a guy in Florida."

"Keep Lucy out of it."

"No problem."

Andrew Stettler accepted the deal, and Luc began to plan the truck-jacking.

Andy and Lucy dropped Luc off in town, then headed for the rendezvous point. They parked in a wooded drive, seldom used in winter but ploughed regularly, that led to a small electric transformer.

"I brought candles," Lucy said.

"I'll keep the motor running."

"We might asphyxiate ourselves. Or run out of gas. Who knows how long Luc will be? I'll light the candles. Keep the window open a crack. You'll be surprised how warm it stays."

After she had lit two candles, one on the dash and another between the front seats, Andy suggested that they get into the back.

"What for?"

"Guess."

"Now?"

"Did you have other plans? Appointments?"

She smiled. She got out to climb into the back but Andy, in his eagerness, crawled over the front seat and was there to greet her with a kiss.

"How do you like the candles?" She spoke between kisses. "Warm, huh?"

"What happens if we get carried away and knock them over?"

"We go up in flames. Together. Romantic. I can't tell you how many native boys and girls have gone out that way. You'd think we'd learn."

She kissed him, and settled into the warmth of his body and the easygoing excitement of his embrace.

"I can hardly ever tell when you're kidding me," he confessed. "Not when you talk about Indian things."

"If I were you, I'd assume I'm pulling your leg pretty much all the time."

His hand went to her breast then, surprising her, and he kissed her roughly.

"Here?" she asked. "It's not *that* warm."

"No?" He pulled away from her to pull off his own jacket, sweater and shirt, as if to challenge her, to dare her to do the same. "We'll make our own heat."

"Too corny for words."

"I'm showing no mercy today, Luce. This car. Two candles. I don't care how cold it is outside."

As she reached down and tugged her shirt out from her jeans, Lucy smiled. She loved this part. The moment when there was no turning back.

"Just so you know," she warned him as her shirt came off.

"Yeah?"

She moved over top of him, straddling him, kissing him from above, reaching behind to unfasten her bra.

"I'm not showing any mercy either."

Outside Massena, New York, a truck parked at the service entrance to a mall. Two axles. A separate cab. The rear box tall enough for a man to stand up in and just touch the ceiling on his toes, stretching. The vehicle had driven up from Ogdensburg, as usual, where it had been supplied with cigarettes for the northern communities of the state. At Massena, more than 90 percent of its cargo remained aboard.

A problem that Luc Séguin faced had to do with the education of the driver. In the region where he normally hijacked trucks, drivers were aware of the practice. If they transported cigarettes or liquor they were given hazard pay, and if they were intercepted, they knew enough to hand over the keys when asked to do so by a friendly highwaymen who shouldered an automatic weapon while his partner aimed a grenade-launcher at the cab door. Heavy weapons pacified the victims, and rarely was there any need for violence. Peaceful upper New York State, on the other hand, could be home to truckers who hadn't been educated. They might become emotional during the experience, or object to being robbed. They might resist. In Luc's plan, the operation had to be quick, startling, and decisive. The driver of the truck could not be allowed a moment to evaluate his choices.

The trucker stepped down from his vehicle just as Luc came around it from behind. They met at the midway point of the truck's length.

"Go back, please, to truck," Luc directed him, and he opened and closed his coat.

"Excuse me?" the man asked.

Already this was going badly. "Go back, please, to truck." He opened and closed his coat again.

"I don't follow you," the man said.

"No, don't follow me, go first!"

The clean-cut trucker wore a quizzical expression and scratched the side of his neck with one finger. "Sorry, Frenchie, I don't know what you're talking about."

Thinking fast, Luc decided that he had a problem. When he was nervous he did not speak English well.

Saying "please" was probably a mistake, it sent the wrong signal. And perhaps the deadly force of his pistol had not been apparent during the quick flashes he had given the man.

Luc opened his coat a third time, and held it open. A hand, thrust through the open pocket of his coat, gripped the pistol and pointed it at the other man's belly. "Get back in truck."

For the first time, comprehension registered on the driver's face. Looking down, he couldn't take his eyes off the gun. A weapon of that heft aimed straight at him had created instant terror.

"Easy, easy," he said, putting his hands up.

"Put down your hands! Get back in truck!"

The trucker was of medium build but still had fifty pounds on Luc. Around forty, he wore a wedding band on his ring finger. Luc could tell that he was already in shock and might not be able to hold himself together. He stayed right behind him as the trucker returned to the cab and climbed in, and Luc slammed the door on him. He moved quickly, and in a second was climbing up the passenger side. The door was locked. Luc nodded to the driver to lift the lock button.

The man thought it over, but only for two seconds, then leaned across and lifted it up.

"Good decision," Luc said.

"What do you want?" He was looking around for help but saw none. He kept raising his hands, wanting to hold them over his head, as if that was expected of him, but then he'd remember that he'd been warned not to do that.

"Drive," Luc commanded him. "Go where I tell you to go. Worry not so much. Don't think about dying. You won't die today if you do what I tell you to stay alive."

"You want the cigarettes," the driver said. He turned the key in the ignition and the engine started up.

"I want your smokes," Luc agreed. "I want your truck, too. You, I don't want. I don't want trouble. Understand?"

The driver didn't give him any trouble. They were already on the outskirts of town, and two quick turns put them on a lonely rural road. Luc didn't want to drop him off close to any farmhouse, but he had that planned. He urged him out of the truck in a wooded area where the man would have to walk at least four miles to the nearest phone, and that was only if he happened to choose the right direction, which was not the way he'd come. The man stood on the shoulder of the road, looking up, still worried that he might be shot.

"You got your coat?" Luc asked him.

"It's behind my seat."

Luc fished it out and passed it down. "You want these boots here?"

"Yeah, sure." Luc threw them down. "Thanks."

"Anything else you need from here?"

"My gloves are between the seats."

Luc dropped them into his outstretched hands.

"I wouldn't mind my house keys. They're on the same ring as the truck key."

Leaving the key in the ignition, Luc twisted them off the ring, tossing the collection down to the owner.

"Pictures of my kids, inside the driver's visor."

He handed those down carefully, not to soil them on the roadside snow.

"Thanks."

"No problem. We're finished now?" The man shrugged. "You're all right?" The man shrugged again, but fright or relief or tension or the snapshot of his children brought tears to his eyes. "Button your coat up," Luc directed. "Don't catch cold."

Luc drove off. About a mile down the road his own car pulled out from a driveway ahead of him with Andrew Stettler at the wheel and Lucy Gabriel in the back seat, turned to observe him. The vehicles continued down the country road in tandem, heading for a back entrance into the reserve.

Luc was pleased that nobody would be bleeding on Indian land, that everything had gone well. He didn't know how many crimes remained for him to commit in his lifetime. Time was becoming precious. He wanted to make the few jobs he had left to him count.

4

HEARTLAND

The same day, Monday, December 20, 1998

Sergeant-Detective Émile Cinq-Mars drove deep into the hinterland, through towns known to him as a child and across the hills, fields and woods of his youth. He was moving toward his family home, where his father continued to live, in the village where they had both been born, St.-Jacques-le-Majeur-de-Wolfestown. If the winter roads stayed clear, the trip would take less than two hours, driving west and north from Montreal. His heart was heavy, the journey a sad one, for he knew it might be his last trip home with anyone there to greet him. His father was dying.

The senior Cinq-Mars, Albert, had argued his way out of hospital, demanding the dignity of death in his own house, in his own bed. Imagining the scene did bring a rise to his son and caused the corners of his lips to curl upward. He sympathized with the doctors and administrators trying to reason with his father, only to be rebuffed in no uncertain terms. Albert Cinq-Mars held no illusions about his circumstances—in a short time he would die—but as a gesture of both courage and dignity, perhaps also as a tribute to his own life, he had insisted on choosing the environment for the great event. It was almost, his son was thinking as he drove—

and this part did not cause him to smile—as though his father wanted to turn his passing into an occasion.

Albert had called his son to let him know that if they were to talk again it was now or never. If they had anything more to say to one another, this would be the moment. "Émile, leave the thieves to count their loot in peace. Let the murderers sleep unmolested for a night, it'll give them time to reflect. Who's not worthy of a day's rest? Come on home, Detective, visit your old man."

"What's up, Papa? You know how it goes. I'm kind of busy right now."

"I'm busy too, Detective. My bags are packed. My passport's been stamped. I've accepted an invitation to knock on St. Peter's Gate, and apparently there is no time *but* the present. Christmas, you know, Christmas will be hectic. Even for those of us at death's door. Come before. I don't want to take chances."

"Papa—?" He immediately felt burdened, by the impending loss, by his silly excuse to delay a visit.

"One month. Next month. I'm betting on the one after that. If I lose, how does the winner expect to collect? In other words, I can't lose. For the time being, Émile, I'm home."

"You're *home?* The hospital discharged you?"

"I insisted. I have a nurse. I want to die in the house where I was born. You know me, I value symmetry."

Symmetry. Wasn't it just like his father to cling to modes and concepts even as his hold on life lapsed.

Driving into St.-Jacques-le-Majeur-de-Wolfestown, Émile Cinq-Mars braced himself. This was not yet the time for grief, he reasoned, that hour lay ahead of him. Obviously his father remained alert, as crafty and as philosophical as always. Tears later. Now, final words. Words from the heart.

Émile Cinq-Mars parked alongside the curb in front of his father's house. The driveway, which ran alongside the cottage to a tumbledown garage in the back, had not been shovelled recently, and likely would not be again for the season. Certainly the old man had nowhere to go. Presumably a neighbour was keeping the short walk and the stairs clear. Typical of Quebec architecture, the steps started almost at the curb, for in this climate no one wanted to shovel much. The detective climbed the stairs of his childhood home, invaded by a sense of that distant time, a poignant memory of his father as a young man meandering inside him, and a sense also of their love for one another—patient father, rambunctious child; proud father, world-weary adult son—resting upon his shoulders, his sensibilities, his heart.

The detective went inside without knocking.

His first surprise, although he should have expected it, was that his father had had his bed moved down to the living room, the sunny space just off the small foyer. He would negotiate the stairs to the second landing no more, and here he benefited from heightened stimulus. The broad window onto the street kept him entertained, as did the nearby television, while fragrant aromas emanating from the kitchen were a short drift away. Down here, Albert had no ready access to a toilet, but if a nurse was attending to him full time he had probably been reduced to using a bedpan anyway.

Émile went in quietly, not wanting to wake him.

The old head lay softly upon its pillow, hardly making an impression. The face was thin now, the hair as white as the snow outside. He seemed calmly asleep, despite the clutter of an intravenous bag overhead and the oxygen tanks attached with precious lifelines to his nostrils. A step caused a noisy creak, and Émile stood still. His father's head lolled to one side and the eyelids fluttered open. Before a word, before, it seemed, recognition, a smile appeared. No matter who had entered his vicinity, Albert would have a smile for the intruder.

If Death arrived this noisily, Émile Cinq-Mars speculated, his dad would greet him with a grin.

His eyes blinked rapidly, as though to dispel a haze, or decipher conflicting information. "That you, Detective?" his father asked. "You're about the right height."

"It's me, Papa. How are you?"

"Sleepy. Well. Come closer, Émile."

At first, Albert could not lift his arm for a handshake. Émile leaned down and kissed his father's cheek, then held his father's hand. After a few minutes he felt the old man's strength emerging from his sleep. The large, bony hand squeezed his, and they remained in that position for more than ten minutes until Émile stood and finally removed his winter coat.

He went through to the kitchen then and met the nurse, who was playing solitaire. She hadn't heard him come in. Cards had never been allowed in his father's house when Cinq-Mars was a boy, and he reflexively thought to object, catching himself in time. Not only would he sound silly voicing the prohibition, but his father would probably storm an objection, for not all the interdictions of his youth had withstood time's test. Few, in fact. Cinq-Mars poured tea for himself and his father and brought the cups through to the living room on a silver tray, an activity that awakened a sadness of a different order, for it evoked the routine of his mother bringing the tea in to her husband on the same tray. She'd been gone now for almost a decade.

"Papa. Tea."

"Splendid!"

Cinq-Mars worked the crank that raised the top of the bed, bringing his father up to a sitting position, and pulled up a chair for himself. He poured the tea and the two men drank quietly in the familiar, warm comfort of the house.

"Émile," Albert Cinq-Mars began. "I've been meaning to tell you something."

The French language had always been vital to
Albert. While he was familiar with the local dialect, he
had·been very particular about proper diction, exact
pronunciation, and the correct use of words. That life-
long discipline now stood him in good stead. Although
his voice was frail and dry, and he was obliged to pause
at length to catch a deeper breath, not once did he slur
a word. His lips and tongue found the precise elocution
for each sound. His diction alone, Cinq-Mars was
thinking to himself, could grease his way into Heaven.

"I've been meaning to tell you something myself," he
said to his father.

"I will go first," the old man announced. "I've been
thinking about this since your mother died. You were
so sad at the funeral, Émile. As devastated, I would say,
as I was. Rarely does one think of oneself in these
terms, but I realized then that some day my own passing would cause you grief. It is the way of the world,
but when you are a father, it is easy to forget what that
means to the son."

"I will grieve for you, Papa. I'm grieving now. I can't
help that. Nor will I resist it. But you understand grief,
you've grieved for others. I'll come out of it. I won't
forget you, but I'll emerge from my sorrow."

"Yes, yes," Albert recited impatiently, "but you are
jumping to conclusions, Detective, always one of your
faults."

Cinq-Mars smiled. The soul endures, he was thinking. This soul is no more near death than one yet to be
born. "Go ahead. I promise not to interrupt again."

"Thank you. I used to tell you, Émile, that I had
wanted to be a priest. I used to encourage you to be a
priest yourself. I wanted you to have the life that was
denied me."

Cinq-Mars knew the story well. War had interfered
with his father's vocation. He had decided to go to war,

that was his moral choice in response to the conflagra-
tion in Europe, although it was not the popular one in
Quebec. By the time he returned, which was before the
war's end due to an injury which had not occurred in
battle, his younger brother was enrolled in a seminary,
his own father was ailing, and he had to assume the
mantle of the family provider. Before he knew what
was happening to him, Albert had fallen in love and
married, and had a child on the way.

"I realized, at the time of your mother's passing, and
I don't know why I did not see this sooner, that all my
life I had been saying a cruel thing to you."

"Papa—"

"You promised," Albert shot back.

"Sorry. Go ahead."

"Saying that I would rather have been a priest—how
was that understood? Did my wife think that my
marriage to her was, for me, a poor substitute for the
Church? Did my son think that I would rather he had
not been born?"

Cinq-Mars gazed into the eyes of his father then,
until his father was the one who turned away.

"The life I lived," Albert Cinq-Mars stated once he
had again found the strength, "was the life I was meant
to live, one far richer than the one I had imagined for
myself. I have been blessed. My wife. My son. I was
never deserving of such riches."

With his hand on his father's cheek, Cinq-Mars
wiped a tear away with his thumb. He leaned forward
when he felt that he had attained sufficient emotional
control, for he knew that he wanted to tell him something, and not lose the force of his words to either grief
or sentiment. He whispered in his father's ear. "You
are the father of my being. I have lived a life very
different from yours, but you have always been my
pilot. I love you. Thank you."

Minutes later, after the nurse had taken away the cups, Albert beckoned for his son's attention once again. "I need a favour, Detective."

"What would you like, Papa?"

"I need you to be a detective for me."

Cinq-Mars was understandably puzzled. "Why? Is something missing? Have you been robbed?"

"Émile, I thank God that you did not become a priest. The Church finds itself in disrepair these days. I am glad, that you, like me, remain with the Mother Church, to keep her upright, but what a depressing place it can be for a priest! Around here, there are so few priests. Many parishes are vacant. Others are inhabited by nincompoops. Émile, my time is close at hand. When I receive extreme unction I want the words spoken by a man who believes them. I want them spoken by a priest who is a man of God, not some molester of infants. Émile, be my detective. Travel about the countryside. Find the nearest priest who will be adequate."

"Adequate?" the son asked.

"Who will not offend me. I do not wish to spend my last moments alive obliged to berate a priest. Or to bite my tongue to keep myself from doing so. I'd prefer to be comforted by a good man's sincerity than made furious by his ineptitude."

Cinq-Mars nodded. He understood. "I will find you a priest, Papa."

"Thank you, Detective. It won't be easy. If anyone can, it's you. You know, don't you, that I am proud of my detective son?"

Cinq-Mars held his father's hand in both of his. "When you first started calling me 'Detective,' Papa, I sensed a certain disdain in your voice. Don't worry. You haven't fooled me. As the years went by, I heard the change of tone. I know that you've been proud of me."

The old man shrugged, wanting, Cinq-Mars could

tell, one last jibe. "Who could not be proud? You were on television."

They both chuckled, but what saddened Cinq-Mars, what caused the tears in his eyes to flow freely, was the realization that they had said what they had intended to say, and their conversation was over. Their words had been spoken. At least his father, always his pilot, had given him work to do. His father had delivered him from the helplessness of idly waiting for a loved one to die and given him an important chore.

He grabbed a sandwich in the kitchen and questioned the nurse on his father's condition. She assured him that his pain and discomfort were being managed. Grateful for that, Émile Cinq-Mars left to track down a worthy priest. He brought to the assignment the same determination he'd have employed in chasing down a notorious criminal, and before the day was out, he had found his man.

5

A FIST AT THE SKY

Two and a half weeks later, Thursday, January 6, 1999

Preparing the truck's cab as a mobile laboratory, Lucy Gabriel was constrained not by cost but only by time and an overriding desire to simplify. Modest electrical current could be generated by a bank of batteries the engine charged. If more power was necessary, she could plug into an AC outlet. The electrician explained that he could supply her with a generator on the roof, but she was dissuaded by problems of maintenance and noise. Instead, she'd operate only a small refrigerator and make do with a bare-bones system.

To brighten things up, the interior of the truck was slathered with a coat of white paint. As she needed to protect the lab from prying eyes, in lieu of side windows she had two tinted skylights placed in the roof to both admit daylight and expel the heat of a southern sun. Cabinets were installed, with shelves and locking drawers, and file holders were screwed into the walls. Bunk beds were added against the forward bulkhead, each with small portholes and ventilation hatches, and the sleeping quarters were separated from the lab by a sliding curtain. Lucy expected to spend most nights in motels, but she was also prepared for roadside naps and occasional, nervy overnighters in city slums.

A third bunk was fitted down one side for the casual use of patients while Lucy drew their blood, or while they rested after consuming a large dose of drug cocktail, and an interior lock was added to the fold-down rear gate.

The exterior changed only slightly. The doors were repainted, and Crogan's Cartage became County Cartage. Ogdensburg was erased and became Champlain. Andrew Stettler had a fresh set of New York plates stamped. He was able to supply false registration and insurance papers as well, to match the legitimate plate number.

"How do you know how to do this?" Lucy asked him.

"Don't ask," he said.

"Why not?"

"Never ask that question."

"Why not?"

"Because, Lucy," he steamed, "you don't ask that."

He was a difficult man to pin down on just about everything.

"Pretty fancy," Camille Choquette commented, tongue-in-cheek, when she dropped by to inspect Lucy's progress. They'd been friends from the day that Lucy had started work at Hillier-Largent Global. They had shared an interest in science, one that had motivated them to overcome their backgrounds. Lucy's adoptive father had been a physician, one who had worked for a while on her reserve. His interests, particularly in science, had brushed off on her. Camille's roots were working-class. An education had not come easily.

"I added a few necessities, that's all," Lucy responded.

Camille coughed up a little laugh. "The first time you went to the States, you did it in your own car. Then you borrowed a beat-up van. Now you're travelling in a stolen truck with your own driver. What's next? A luxury bus?"

Lucy smiled. "I was thinking, maybe, private jet?"

"With a stretch limo on the ground."

"Stretch limo with a pool in the back."

"Air-conditioned motorhome with your own masseuse," Camille suggested.

"The masseuse I'll keep, but I won't drive a plush motorhome into Harlem."

"At least you're an Indian in Harlem. When I go, I'm strictly white trash."

"Ah, but *sexy* white trash, Camille," Lucy teased.

"Watch yourself, girlfriend."

The two worked in the lab together, and had been involved with this extracurricular project from the beginning. Camille had introduced Lucy to Werner Honigwachs, the president of a pharmaceutical firm where she used to work. The relationship between the two companies was vague to Lucy, although Camille seemed to be in the know. The two firms were competitors, and yet at the same time they would collaborate on certain projects. Lucy had reminded Camille on the way to meet the president of BioLogika that she already had a job. "Just talk to him," her friend had insisted. "Anyway, he's dying to meet the famous Indian rabble-rouser. I promised to introduce you."

Honigwachs, Lucy found out, was charismatic in a nasty-executive kind of way. He did nothing to present himself as charming, but he carried himself with authority, and his trim physique and good looks offered curb appeal. When he smiled, he looked like the man in the moon, his face round and bright. Lucy did not believe that she could be influenced by a man's position or wealth, but the way he moved attracted her, as did the understated cunning of that moon-like smile. She was also impressed that he knew a great deal about her and about the troubles across the river from his corner office.

"You're a passionate young woman," Honigwachs said, and Lucy was thinking, *Here we go, the seduction line.*

For this meeting she had worn a simple, full-length summer dress, a mauve pastel patterned with large hibiscus flowers. She knew that it showed off her copper colouring to advantage.

"Some people are passionate. Others have an office on the top floor."

"Passion can be an asset in our line of work, no matter what floor you're on."

"Really?" she responded dully, still sceptical.

"The world's confronted with a crisis, Lucy. In Africa alone, millions die every year. Here, thousands." He gestured while he spoke, stabbing at the air with his fingers, ardent. "We're the people—me, you, Camille, others—who've been charged with finding a cure, and finding it fast."

"Well," Lucy attested, taken aback, "you—maybe. Others—perhaps. But not me. All I do at Hillier-Largent is separate plasma from blood."

"You could play a more important role, if you wanted."

"You mean, if I left Hillier-Largent and worked at BioLogika?" She assumed that whatever job he had in mind included stepping out of her clothes.

He swatted the notion of changing jobs aside. "Here. Hillier-Largent. *Where* is not important. Just join the fight. Save people's lives, Lucy."

She was tempted to blurt out, "What do I have to take off to save these lives?" but instead she asked, "How?" The word was no sooner uttered than she realized that she had both created an opening for him and altered the direction of her life.

When Lucy departed BioLogika later that day with Camille, she nudged her new friend with an elbow. "Are you sleeping with him?"

"Well, *duh*, wouldn't you?" Camille hadn't dressed up. She was wearing a white blouse and blue business slacks.

"Not if he's sleeping with my best friend already."

"I got him first. At least, I'm first in line after his wife."

"That's okay. He's not my type."

"Yeah, right."

Some weeks later, Camille informed Lucy that her relationship with Honigwachs had ended. She offered no details. After that, Lucy wondered if she might be his next move, but it never materialized, although her work with the special project—which she considered to be *his* special project, although Honigwachs was careful never to attest to personal involvement in any direct way—intensified.

Camille was Lucy's immediate superior and her principal contact. Sometimes she talked to Randall Largent about general things, but when a project was underway her marching orders came through Camille. How, and via what source, Camille received her information was not known to Lucy, but she accepted the importance of a covert chain of command. All part of the fun. She accepted that she was not to know what even Camille seemed to know, ever, and she was not to ask questions. She had her job to do, an important one integral to their operation—administer advanced, untested drug therapies to the ill—but how they came into Camille's hands, and subsequently hers, had to remain a secret.

What lab prepared the drugs, which scientists were assigned to the project, who in the administration of BioLogika or Hillier-Largent Global was aware that drugs were to be tested on humans—for reasons of security, the information was privileged, and she was not in the loop. Similarly, she presumed that many of the people higher up the ladder were totally unaware that she was the one who undertook the distribution south of the border. The right hand was not to know the business of the left. So be it.

Naturally, she and Camille made assumptions about the chain of command, and they knew that Werner

Honigwachs and Randall Largent were involved. And yet, as far as Lucy knew, there was no direct communication or shared activity between the men and the women. Anyone tracing the activities of the women would be unable to follow any direct line to the men, and any investigation from the top down would similarly find a muddied trail.

Now the truck was just about finished. Lucy wanted plywood flooring installed, as walking on the corrugated aluminium had proven awkward. A proper floor would also benefit those who arrived on wheelchairs or on gurneys.

While Camille was inspecting the refurbished vehicle, a mischievous thought seemed to cross her mind, and she smiled in an insinuating manner.

"What?" Lucy demanded.

"Do you like this guy?" The truck was parked outside. They were shivering under their coats in the cold.

"Who?"

"Who. The King of England, who. Andy!"

"I like him," Lucy grudgingly admitted. "I'm not *crazy* about him. He's fun. He's—I don't know—"

"What?"

Lucy shrugged. "Private. You know? Secretive. We've made out at my place, but he's never taken me to his place. He won't even tell me where he lives. I asked if he was hiding a wife and kids at home. He tells me no, only a mother. Camille! He's been to jail, but he lives with his mother! Weird, you know?"

"Good in bed?" Camille pressed her.

Lucy blew out a gust of air.

"Really?"

"He's handled women before. He's rough. Use your imagination. Trust me, Andy will be done with me, sooner or later, he's that kind of guy. When the time comes, take him for a trial run. I won't mind."

"I'm off the market." Camille let her voice trail away.

Lucy gave her a long look. "You're getting serious with your cop buddy?"

Camille's smile confirmed the assessment. "I know what you're thinking. Charlie's the runt of the litter, but he's a sweet guy. That counts, right? He's good with my kid. Carole wants him to be her dad. Maybe I do, too."

Lucy kissed her cheek. "I hope it works out."

They both opted to jump down from the truck-bed rather than use the tailgate's hydraulic lift, and together they strolled away from the garage. Lucy had lent her car to Andy for the day and had phoned her friend for a lift. Of the two, Camille was older by about five years, and she was the stern one, taut and circumspect, with her short brown hair and chiselled bone structure. Lucy's loose gait and long, bouncy black hair announced her as the free spirit. Whatever their disparities, their zeal for this project united them.

"How's your end coming along?" Lucy asked, as she climbed into the car.

"Good! We've run up a solid booking. You'll be in New York, Philly, Baltimore for sure. We're still working on Newark and Atlanta."

"Newark I can do without."

"People get sick and die in crummy cities, too," Camille pointed out. "Anyway, I got the word today. You leave Monday night."

"What? Yikes! That soon?"

Camille started the ignition of her Mazda 626 and spoke in a hushed voice, as though to muffle her secret below the engine's rumble. "The cocktails will be ready tomorrow, Saturday at the latest. The code name for the project is *Darkling Star*. Put Sunday aside for orientation. I had a look. It's complicated this time."

"How come?"

"Different strokes for different folks. Dosages, combinations change. It all depends on the stage of the illness. You'll be playing doctor this time around."

Lucy nodded, determination firing her eyes. "I can do that."

Camille smiled. "We know you can," she assured her.

"We?" Lucy asked.

Oddly, her friend seemed flustered. "You know," she said. "Everybody."

"Who's everybody?" Lucy grilled her. The one thing about all the secrecy that irritated her was not understanding Camille's importance to the operation. Was she merely an intermediary, a dutiful soldier like her, or did she have a hand in the strategic planning? Usually, Camille came across as a peer, and certainly she presented herself that way, but at times it was obvious that her knowledge of the entire operation was at least somewhat more thorough and perhaps more intimate than Lucy's. Camille had initially recruited her, evidence that she was entrusted with sensitive responsibilities. She had been sexually involved with Honigwachs, and maybe still was, despite her announcement to the contrary. Lucy was not boundlessly curious about these issues, but they were ongoing irritants, and she was a tad jealous that after all this time, after all the risks she had taken for their project, she was not permitted to know things that Camille seemed to take for granted. She felt that Camille betrayed confidences sometimes, to her, and that if she were given a higher station she'd be better at keeping secrets than her pal.

"You know."

"No, I don't. Who's everybody?"

Camille looked directly into her friend's eyes.

"Werner knows I'm going? He's on top of this?"

"Lucy—"

"Who else? Who's everybody?"

"Randall Largent," Camille said in an agitated tone, trying to come up with names.

"Of course, but who else?" Lucy pressed. While, intellectually, she accepted the need for secrecy, she also believed that she should be trusted more.

"Andy."

"You talked to Andy? *He* thinks I'll be a good doctor?"

"Lucy—"

"What?"

"You know how it is."

"I don't, actually. Andy knows more than me now? Explain it to me, Camille."

Camille closed her eyes and gave them a gentle rub with the thumb and forefinger of her right hand. "Lucy, if there's something I can't tell you, then there's something I can't tell you. Just leave it at that."

Lucy thought about it. She nodded, reluctantly conceding ground. Truth be told, secrecy was one of the seductive attributes of the operation. She was a sucker for clandestine thrills. She was, after all, the point man, or point woman, the first one to put herself on the front lines. The only one, really, who stuck her neck all the way out. She'd have to continue to satisfy herself with that. "Okay. Let's go."

"Oh, now don't be pissed off."

"I'm not pissed off. Let's go, all right?"

"Lucy—"

"Drive!"

Five days later, Monday night into Tuesday, January 11, 1999

They had no choice but to drive by night. Once again, Luc picked Lucy up outside her place, as the route along the back roads successfully avoided weigh stations, truck stops, and any significant police presence that might compromise the anonymity of their vehicle.

The truck had a good solid feel on the road. Its prior use, transporting cigarettes, had put little strain on the suspension, which was sound, or the brakes, which were trustworthy. Yet it rattled.

Neither Luc nor Lucy talked very much on the way down to the border. Lucy was tired. As usual, she had worked through the weekend, testing decongestants on cold-sufferers this time. The lab rats had rested all day Sunday, though, which had given her the opportunity to study the regime for the drug cocktails she was taking south. That morning, after a breakfast of coffee and donuts, she'd discharged the sniffly, sinus-clogged lab rats, and during the day she'd catnapped amid bouts of worry and intervals of study.

Luc remembered the route through Indian land down to the waterside. The instructions were different for a night crossing by truck. Of all vehicles, a truck was the most likely to be intercepted on the ice by border patrols, so it had to move fast, lights extinguished, and aim for a pale-blue beacon on the opposite shore. No one except law enforcement had any business on the river at night, and therefore any presence had to be outrun or, in extreme circumstances, run over.

Lights out, Luc waited on the shore. He could just make out the pale blue beacon. "Don't run anybody down," Lucy whispered to him.

"I don't need for my life to end in prison."

"These Indians just talk tough. There's no need to run anybody down."

"I do my best not to. If they chase me, I will run. If they shoot me, I will die."

"Nobody's asking you to be a freaking martyr. Just get us across the ice."

"You are ready?" Luc put the floor-shifter in gear.

"As ready as I'll ever be."

"You can see the blue light?"

"Yeah. You? You're lined up."

"I see it for now. Let's go."

This time, he understood about speed. A crescent moon appeared and vanished amid scudding clouds, shining on the silver truck whenever it appeared. Luc drove hard, fast, his own vision hampered by the scant light, his eyes fixed on the opposite shore and the beacon.

"How fast?" he asked, not daring to take his eyes off the ice-road.

"Sixty. Sixty-five." As was the case with his old car, the American truck recorded speed in miles per hour.

The truck continued to accelerate. He could feel the drifts when he went off course, but at least the heavy vehicle was not thrown around by patches of snow. Soon he could feel the worn ruts on the ice and recognize a change of sound if he edged too close to the perimeter.

"Seventy-five, Luc. Oh, Luc. Eighty. God help us."

Luc hit ninety before it was time to begin slowing down, and he worked through the gears and was doing only about thirty as he charged up the ramp on the opposite shore. He kept the lights off through the dark woods, wending his way up the trail, and stopped at the guardhouse.

Brad came out and stepped onto the running board as Luc rolled down the window. "Hey, Lucy. How are you?"

"Good. You?"

"Super."

"You're working the night shift."

"Doing my part for my people, Lucy."

"Is that what they call crime these days?"

Brad cleared his throat. "I'd like to see what's in the back of your truck."

"We made an agreement. That's not part of it."

"Agreements change."

"No dice."

"Then turn back."

They couldn't see one another well, silhouettes in the dim light.

"Don't do this, Brad."

"Just so you know, it's not my idea. I got orders. I got to check you out."

In the overall scheme of things, it was not that big a deal. A matter of security and a matter of pride, for both Lucy and the Warriors. Lucy took her time, but she already knew she'd relent. "All right. Come see what you won't understand."

Beakers, burners, test tubes and test-tube racks, test-tube rack shakers, fluorescent lights, a fridge, cots, enough file folders to keep a small bank in order and row upon row of glass jars filled with what seemed to be colored beads.

"What are you planning to do, buy back Manhattan?"

"Very funny, Brad. You're hilarious."

"Explain it. Why hijack a truck and kidnap the driver—in case you didn't know, those are the charges— just so you can drive around with a stash of beads? You could be giving us Indians a bad name here."

Having come around to the rear of the truck with her, Luc was determined to let Lucy do the talking. He didn't understand anything anyway.

"They're not beads," Lucy told Brad. "They're pills. Drugs."

"You're into that shit? I'm surprised at you."

"Not those kinds of drugs. They're not recreational, Brad. They're medical."

"Yeah? If you say so. So what are you up to?"

"Saving lives. I'm on a mission of mercy. Other people suffer, too, you know."

"I don't get it."

"You're not supposed to," Lucy warned him.

Brad kept looking around the truck as though one

more clue might clarify everything. "I have to explain it to other people, Lucy. Right now, I can't." She saw that he was asking for help.

"These drugs aren't legal, Brad. Not yet, anyway. The government is holding up approval, pending tests. You're an Indian, you know about the government. I'm not waiting for the Minister of Health to wipe his bum while men and women die of AIDS. I'm going to help them right now. Can you explain that?"

Brad nodded. "I think so. Maybe."

"Try. There's nothing in it for the Warriors except what they already got, the smokes. Now can we go through?"

"Yeah," Brad said, suddenly subdued. "You're on your way."

Luc locked the tailgate again while Lucy hugged herself warm in the cab, then he climbed in beside her and Brad waved them through. The truck lumbered up the snowy incline that was cut through the trees, slipping a little on the icy patches, gaining traction wherever the rocks were bare.

Later that day, Tuesday, January 11, 1999

From a distance, smokestacks exhaling the dawn's grey haze, the spectre of New York City was an impressive, odd sight for travellers just down from the state's north woods, the buttress of skyscrapers an unreal illusion on the grainy horizon.

Lucy asked her driver to pull over. "Let's wait for the sun," she said.

Later, she asked, "Isn't it beautiful, Luc?" But Luc was taking advantage of the respite to sleep, and he stirred uncomfortably behind the wheel.

"Beautiful?" He stretched and yawned.

"I know. Beauty's hard to measure. We've come

through rolling hills, and they were beautiful, but this, too, is beautiful."

"Like the personality of an ugly girl is beautiful," Luc proposed.

Lucy was too baffled by what he said to bother figuring out what it meant. "It looks nice, Luc."

"A bunch of buildings?"

"With the sun coming up, and the ocean in the distance, and the lights of the city clicking on and off and the lines of traffic on the bridges. Luc! Look!"

"A bunch of buildings," he grumbled. "I thought you Indians liked nature."

"Got us figured out, huh?"

"Don't get mad. It's just what I thought."

She gazed at his profile then. He didn't see things as she did, and why should he? He had illness in his short-term future, possibly death. For him, the escarpment of buildings might evoke prison walls, not a new, unexplored world. She was young. He was middle-aged, without a future. She was out here to save lives. Luc didn't have a clue what he was doing with her. Naturally, he saw things differently.

"Sorry. Didn't mean to upset you, Luc. I've been catnapping while you've had a long drive."

"That's all right to me."

She returned her attention to the distant view. She thought she'd explain one reason why it was attractive to her eye. "My people built this city," she stated quietly.

"New York?" Luc challenged, doubtful. "Indians?"

She smiled. "People always laugh when they think of us selling Manhattan for beads. But it wasn't such a bad deal. Who do you think built the bridges and skyscrapers? Mohawks. Men from my reserve. My father was one of them. More people do the work now, but it used to be just us Indians who walked the high girders as if we were out for a stroll in the park. We lived pretty well off Manhattan."

Luc liked her story, she could tell by the subtle change in his expression. He was staring out at the city now, letting his imagination travel with her story.

"The Mohawk Warriors began as high riggers. Way up there, above Fifth Avenue, looking down on Central Park or Broadway, men from my reserve would discuss the ways of the world and the lives of Indian people. The men decided to change things. I'm not against the Warriors. God knows, I have a Warrior heart. What happens to a high rigger when buildings aren't going up, that's a tough question. The first Warriors asked tough questions like that. I don't think anybody shouted out, 'Let's call Bingo numbers!' But I bet somebody said, 'Look out for the red man first, and fuck the white man's ways.' Oh yeah, that was said."

They were quiet awhile, and even Luc appeared appreciative of the sun rising above the winter haze into a pale sky.

"Can I ask you something, Lucy?"

"Go ahead."

"What do you have in the back of this truck I drive?"

She reached across and touched his wrist. "You want to know what kind of trouble you're in?"

He shook his head. "Doesn't matter to me if I get five years or ten. The man can't take those years out of me because I don't got that many left to give him. But I would like to know the true nature of the wrong I'm doing."

Lucy stretched her muscles, stiff from the night's travel. "Luc, you're going to see some things you haven't seen before. Some sights won't be so pleasant, unlike the one in front of us now. Prepare yourself. Some things might disturb you. Even *you*, an ex-con. But we'll make a deal. If at any time you're not comfortable with what you're doing, let me know, all right? We'll talk about it then. For now, just drive."

"All right," Luc agreed. "I'll drive."

"Follow the signs to Paramus, New Jersey. We'll find a motel there."

The density of traffic increased on their drive down to the city and the sea. The buzz of the metropolis reverberated to the outskirts, where cars raced and trucks rumbled, and the tall, pear-shaped clerk at the motel desk looked up at them with disdain for interrupting his next bite of a morning omelette.

"May I help you?" he asked, and coughed. Lucy studied him, and felt quiet inside, because she knew he didn't mean or want to be offering help. And yet it was men like him, men of no particular distinction, who wore lesions on their foreheads like him, wore them as medals, yes, men like him that she had come to save, rescue from the dusty destitution of their lives brought on by the most menacing plague of all time.

"Yes," she said. "We'd like two rooms. One for me. One for my friend."

He shook his head. "Housekeeping won't have two rooms fixed up this early."

"That's not my problem," Lucy told him.

"You have to come back."

"Or—" she suggested.

"Or what?"

"Or there's another way."

"Lady—"

"Two rooms," she said. "Cleaned up, sheets changed. Twenty minutes. Where do I sign?"

Tourists, he was probably thinking, hating them all. "Sign here, lady." He indicated the visitor's card and offered a pen. "Your rooms will be ready soon. I'll fix them up myself."

"That's the spirit." After she had signed in, she

looked at him again. "I have something for those sores on your face."

He laughed her off. "No, lady, you don't."

"Yes. I do." She smiled and accepted the keys. "We'll talk."

The next day, early Wednesday morning, January 12, 1999

Camille Choquette lived with her daughter in a modest bungalow in a town that took its name from the adjoining lake, *Lac des Deux-Montagnes*. The location offered the advantages of a small town in the country, and yet, thanks to an expressway and a commuter train, she had ready access to her job at Hillier-Largent on the edge of the city. In winter, if she wanted to drop by the ice-fishing village or visit friends where she used to work at BioLogika, she'd speed across the lake on her Ski-Doo.

Awakening in the dark, Camille groped around for her nightgown, tossed off in a moment of passion. When the lost was found, she slipped the wisp of fabric, patterned with vines and dashes of colored flowers, over her head and down her torso. Then she tucked her feet into bedroom slippers, the ones with lambswool lining. She went through to the bathroom, where she took a long drink directly from the tap. Anytime she made these nocturnal strolls to fend off dehydration, she reminded herself to buy a humidifier, but somehow she never remembered when she was out shopping. Too many things on her mind, and the minutiae of daily living bored her silly. Drudgery wore her down. *Everything must change,* she thought to herself. *Everything will,* she vowed, as though a second voice had answered the first.

She flicked on the light and gave her short hair a hasty fluff. Camille had never been considered a beauty, but she made the best of her sharp features.

Given that she was already on her feet, she went

through to her daughter's tiny bedroom to confirm that the little girl was warm enough, and adjusted her covers slightly. According to the child's careful count, Carole was seven and three quarters years old. She had a habit of kicking the covers off while she slept, but tonight was resting calmly. Perhaps she had fallen asleep intent on sounds from the other room, which had kept her still.

Gently, Camille removed Carole's thumb from her mouth and gave her a gentle kiss on the forehead.

Back in her bedroom, her guest for the night had roused himself. "Leaving?" she asked.

"Pretty soon. If I can wake up."

"Just as well." She crawled under the covers and snuggled up against him. "I wouldn't want Charlie to pop in on us."

The caution took Werner Honigwachs by surprise. "Are you expecting him?"

She patted his shoulder. "He'd call first. But you never know, there's always a first time."

"You're living dangerously," Honigwachs teased.

Her right hand drifted south, finding his softened penis to tug. "What would you do if Charlie waltzed in here, wearing his gun?"

He chuckled. "My fast-talking skills would be put to the test."

"What would you say?"

"I'd tell him the truth."

That intrigued her. "What truth?"

"That I was doing him a favour, sparing him a life-time of misery with you."

"Wrong move, Wiener," she said, using her pet name for him and giving his testicles a rub. "He'd shoot you dead if you said that. Charlie believes in me."

The conversation and her attentions were helping Honigwachs wake up. "What would Charlie-boy do to you?"

"I'd promise to do that little thing he likes. He'd spare me."

"What thing?"

"I'm not telling."

"Have you done it to me?"

"Want me to? Turn over on your tummy and raise your butt."

"Forget it." He threw the covers off himself while Camille giggled at her own sauciness. Exposed to the chilly air, he moved quickly to dress. While he was tucking his shirt into his trousers, Honigwachs asked, "You're off soon, to the States?"

"In a few days. Lucy just got started. I like to check results after six days." Camille squatted on the bed, bunching the blankets around her. She was bobbing her chin and shoulders as if hearing a distant dance music.

"You're set? It won't be a picnic. I still think you should go with someone."

"Too risky. I can handle this myself."

"It'll be different this time."

"I'll manage."

Upon his arrival that night, Honigwachs had gone straight to her bedroom, so he found his overcoat there.

"See yourself out, okay, Wiener? It's too cold to get up."

He leaned across the bed to give her a kiss. "Take care, babe."

"Give your wife a hug for me, will you?" She laughed again.

"Say hello to Charlie. I'd still like to know what you're doing with a cop."

"What are you doing with a wife?" She hugged a pillow for warmth.

"She takes care of my home. My family. She's an asset in many ways. We have fun together."

"Ditto Charlie," Camille said. "He's an asset in so many ways. I'm probably going to have to break this off with you, Werner, sooner or later. Just so I can be more faithful to the boy. At least on the surface, if you know what I mean, until everything works out. When I'm super-rich, when I've outgrown him—I'll dump him then."

He leaned down once more and kissed her. "And Lucy? She no longer puts the two of us together?"

"I took care of that. She believes I'm utterly devoted to Charlie. Charlie thinks so too. Nobody can connect us."

"Be careful in New York, Camille."

"*Wiener!* Don't worry. I know what's ahead. I can handle it."

The same day, Wednesday, January 12, 1999

In the morning they drove onto Amsterdam Avenue in Upper Manhattan. Luc appeared to know his way around, although he was reluctant to give details of time previously spent in the city.

"I assume you weren't attending Columbia," Lucy said.

"What?"

"Never mind. I'm just being snobby. Hard-Knocky U probably gave you a well-rounded education. Did you get an athletic scholarship, at least?"

"What?" Either his morning coffee had been too weak or he really couldn't grasp the language when she teased him. Lucy was thinking that the trip could turn out to be an endurance test in one another's company.

"Sorry, Luc. Forget it."

When she reached the address on 126th Street Lucy was pleased to discover that not only were they expected, but a welcoming committee had prepared for their arrival. A skinny black man with a wide grin, a salmon shirt and grape-coloured pants was the first to greet them, and he did so with a sense of occasion.

"Saint Lucy herself, in the flesh, come from the clouds

in a big, bad truck. Virile trucker-man beside her. Girls are always trying to kid us that size is not important. Pocahontas-child, that's a big mother truck. What does a big truck say to me? Bigger is better and you're all for it."

"Hiya, Wendell. How's it hanging?"

"It's still attached, Saint Lucy, which I owe to you. Who's your darling friend?"

"Wendell, this is Luc."

"Luc! And Lucy! A tag team! I love it! Luc— *darling!*—I'm pleased to meet you. Come inside and meet the boys. You'll have to get used to us, sweetie, we'll be keeping your Pocahontas-child busy busy busy." He gathered up both visitors by the arm and strutted between them to the door. Wendell's head was elongated, narrowing at the top. The shape was accentuated by his haircut, which shaved the sides to a mere shadow while allowing the hair on top of his head to grow straight up, rising three inches above his scalp. He whispered to Lucy, loudly enough for Luc to hear, "Is he one of us? He seems so, I don't know, *severe*."

"Luc's HIV-pos," Lucy said. She hoped that it was all right with Luc to say so.

"Oh, darling, I'm so sorry. You poor thing!"

"But he's not gay."

"Sorrier still! Oh, sweetheart, the gay man's plague and you haven't enjoyed the fruits from the vine? That's heartbreaking!"

"Wendell."

"I'm devastated. Watch the step now, precious, the concrete is not as *concrete* as one might hope."

Inside the apartment, the full welcoming committee was equally pleased to see Lucy again, but considerably more sedate. Sadness prevailed for those lost since her last visit, as well as happiness for those whose lives had been preserved. Luc stood off to one side and observed the proceedings, quietly impressed by the number of people who treated Lucy as a saint. Men touched her arms, or her fingers, with a delicacy that struck him as unnatural, as though they were desperate for the touch but genuinely believed themselves unworthy to commit the simple act. Lucy, on the other hand, kissed the men's foreheads and gave them robust hugs. Tears flowed. The residents related how their lives had improved. Two were back at work, and three claimed to have been symptom-free for months. "You've given me back my life, my hope, my reason to live."

"You're a brave man, Jack. You didn't want to do it, at first."

"I was a 'fraidy-cat! But it's paid off." Jack had always carried weight, but now his skin hung on him sadly, the extra pounds gone. He wore a midriff girdle to keep himself looking trim.

"That's great. Still no guarantees. None last time, none now."

The man put up his hands and would not hear another word. "We're all at war, Lucy, like you told me. If I don't benefit, someone else will. The beauty, though, is that I *have* benefitted."

"Don't hog every last speck of her time!" Wendell butted in. "Who among us is not enthralled? Share, Jack, share!"

Down a dark corridor, in the back rooms, sick men awaited her. They smiled, and valiantly raised their heads to the sight and sound of her. Luc's stomach turned to see these ravaged bodies, the skin of one man a mere membrane over bones, the flesh gone. They smelled. The house smelled. Of disinfectant. Old vomit. Urine. A few had open lesions. These men also praised Lucy and what she had done for them, or for their friends. "My doctor told my lover a week. Here I am, Saint Lucy, *three months* since then. Not good months, but I'm here. I love beating the odds."

"Stick it out, Garrett. Maybe this time we can do better. Who knows?"

"Whatever it takes, Saint Lucy. If it's good for me, good. If it helps science, better. My doctor says, 'What are you doing, how are you staying alive?' He thinks he'll win the Nobel Prize if he can figure me out."

"But your lips are sealed, Garrett?"

"With bright pink paraffin! Not a peep escapes from me!"

After she had shared a word with everyone, and reminded each man again that she was offering no promises, Lucy addressed them as a group, offering the assurance that they were placing themselves at the leading edge of medical knowledge, dodging the ass-dragging government agencies, both American and Canadian. The men nodded, murmured a litany of complaint. Being on the edge, Lucy reminded them, meant hope. "As I've told you before, better to be a guinea pig for a new drug, with its risks, than taking the safe ones and dying. The day we have a cure will be months before it's generally available. What's the point of dying in that interval when you could get help? But it means taking a chance. You're the guys who take the risks. For that, you get to sample the latest drugs, and by letting us see them in action you help us move faster, so you're helping everybody who's sick. Our knowledge increases, and knowledge is what this race is all about."

She changed her tone after her speech, and became their physician. "I'll need a blood sample from each of you. We'll do that indoors. Later, *in an orderly fashion*— and that means no pushing and shoving in line, Wendell—come outside to the truck, one at a time. This will take a while, so your patience is appreciated."

"Patience? Time?" Wendell questioned. "Who has time? We're dying here, Pocahontas-child! You jabber jabber, we die die die. Will you get a move on? Or do I have to wait another *lifetime* to see any *results* around here?"

"Wendell, I have an especially long needle for you."

That had everyone laughing.

"There you go with that *size* fixation again. Bigger badder better, that's all you girls think about."

"Is that why you became one of us?"

The comment elicited a series of groans from the motley collection of lab rats. Expecting Wendell to give her one right back, to catch her on the hook of his wit, they waited, their breathing hushed. He seemed flummoxed, standing with his hands on his hips in a posture of irate indignation, chin high.

"Well," he gushed finally, "I suppose."

Which won the day, and the dying men whom Lucy had come to save enjoyed a laugh.

Luc's job, which he did faithfully, was to keep the vials of blood intact and together with the paperwork for each patient, without error. "Handle with care," Lucy warned him.

"I know why I am here now. A healthy man might infect his own blood."

"There's that. A cut could be dangerous," Lucy agreed. "Also, Luc, I need someone who won't freak out with these people. Who won't be scared to touch them, or be afraid to be in the same room, afraid to breathe the same air."

"You be careful yourself," Luc warned her.

"Yeah, yeah," she intoned, and waved off the danger.

"No," Luc said. "With the blood, be careful yourself."

She was touched by his obvious concern. "Thanks, Luc. I will. Don't look at me like that! I'll be careful. Go! Bring me the black bag from the truck, please." She crinkled her nose for him. "I get to be Doctor Lucy today."

Wendell was the first to offer his arm, and Lucy Gabriel drew his blood with care. Not trained as a nurse, she had nevertheless learned how to do this and to administer drugs intravenously. "What's your schedule like, Lucy? Got time to socialize?"

"I'm around, but this is strictly a working trip. Tomorrow and Thursday I'm in the Village. Friday's Newark."

"Newark! You *are* a saint. Thank God for the body-guard."

"I can take care of myself."

"Famous last words. Knock on wood, *immediately!*"

"We're done." She lifted up the tube with his blood. "Fine colour, Wendell."

"I wouldn't wish it on a vampire. So, no carousing?"

She shook her head lightly. "Do me a favour?" Lucy told him about the motel clerk in Paramus, whose name was Evan, and Wendell promised to give him a call.

In the truck, dressed in her grey wool coat against the chill, warmed also by an electric heater she had connected to the house power by running a line across the sidewalk, Lucy assessed each patient in turn. She administered an intravenous dosage and, after the consultation, selected the new cocktail. Pills were divided by size, shape and colour. Those whose illness was full-blown, who had not been brought back to good health by her previous visit, just kept alive, were placed on one sort of regimen. The healthiest went onto another, and those who were having manageable problems were given a variety of supplements. The work was tedious, as she had to be careful what she prescribed, and equally careful to note the dosage accurately. Each man checked and rechecked the prescription, the number of reds and blues, to be taken with what frequency and at what time of day. Each schedule was clearly written out, and although no patient was likely to be negligent, she stressed the importance of discipline. For some, the number of pills exceeded forty, while Wendell, relatively healthy, got off lightly with seventeen.

"Two less than last time," he noted. "A couple are big mothers, though."

"Wash them down with a shot of vodka, that's my advice."

"Will Camille be coming?"

"Tracing my steps, as usual. Expect her in a week. Maybe less. She'll call."

"Someday, Saint Lucy, when all this is over and we can go public, you'll be enshrined."

"I wish I could do more."

"You've saved so many!"

"You're saving lives, too, by agreeing to this."

"That's true." He put his hand on his chest. "*I* should be enshrined. Someday, I want my head on a quarter. I want monuments and universities named after me—streets, hospitals! Is it asking too much to have my own day?"

"You want to be a national holiday?"

"What do you think? Be honest. Is it too much?"

Lucy laughed, and kissed him, smack between the eyes.

On the drive home to Paramus, Luc and Lucy were quiet. She was weary, while he was preoccupied with all that he had witnessed. They agreed to hook up in an hour, which gave them time to freshen and change and catch a nap. Dinner was found down the road, a noisy walk along the edge of the highway. Luc opted for steak, Lucy, a shrimp pasta. Talked out from her day, she was just as happy to adopt Luc's quiet, grumpy demeanour.

After dinner, Luc walked Lucy back to the motel, then left again to return to a bar they'd passed. Lucy watched a little television until she couldn't keep her eyes open and switched it off. She snuggled in under the covers.

The rage of traffic would not make it a quiet night. She was still awake, listening to the trucks, a distant siren, the endless rush of cars, when someone knocked on her door. She looked through her peephole first, then admitted the motel clerk into her room.

He paced the floor after she had closed the door behind him. "I don't know," he said. "This is nuts."

She recognized the fear, the conditioned and rational aspect of any patient worried about treatment outside the usual medical boundaries. Her patients, however, were desperate men, grasping for hope, and all she ever had to do was to allow that desperation to supersede the old and useless logic.

"I'm not here to force you."

"I feel like I'm at a medicine show, buying snake oil."

"No snake oil, Evan. More importantly, I'm not here to sell you a damn thing. Was that not made clear?"

He was a bitter man, she could tell, angry and prepared to die while shaking a fist at the sky. To have hope and life and health sprung upon him upset his way of being. He now didn't know how to behave, or how to believe.

He looked at her finally, standing still, the shabby pear-shape of him exhausted, resentful and yet, ultimately, still longing for the miracle. Had the miracle come? His eyes appeared to wobble in their sockets. "I can't believe this," he said.

"You're here. In my room. Give me the word, Evan, and everything will change."

"You're not some nutcase with a lab in your kitchen? That's not what this is all about?"

"I represent a multinational, multi-billion-dollar pharmaceutical corporation. What we will do here, in this room, is illegal and would land me in jail, not to mention the corporate executives. But we have advanced immune-system therapies. You can wait a year and a half for further testing and government approval, although you might die by then, or you can start to be relieved of your pain right now. Tonight.

I'm tired, Evan. I've been saving lives all day. What do you say?"

His shoulders slumped, his lower lip trembling, Evan said, "I'm willing."

"Good. I need to take your blood. Then I'll plan the best scheme for you. After that, I'll give you a shot, which will knock you off your pins. Everybody today found the shot hard to handle. I'll give you your dosage, which you'll have to follow without any variance, to the letter."

"And that's it? No strings?"

"When it comes onto the market, it'll cost a fortune. For doing this now, it's free for you forever. It's also your best chance to live."

Reduced to working at a seedy hotel to keep going, perhaps a professional career ruined, and expecting only to eke out a brief existence until he died, the man was having to deal with the possibility of salvation. She had seen it so often before.

He sat down beside her. "If I didn't work here, in this shit-hole, I never would have met you."

Lucy put a hand on his forearm. "No guarantees," she said. "But everyone I've treated has improved or beaten the odds. All you have to do is agree to let my people follow up, and to keep your mouth shut."

"All right."

"What are you taking now?"

He shook his head. "Nothing. I can no longer afford anything. Anyway, what's the point?" He was not the tough receptionist he had been yesterday. He was on the verge of weeping.

She held his forearm on her lap and gently applied the cool rubbing alcohol to his arm with cotton batting. "It's okay," she whispered. "You'll get used to the idea of being well again."

"Oh, Lord," he nearly wailed, and the tears flowed. "Oh, Lord."

"Shhh, don't wake the other guests. Remember, you're going to feel weak and sick for a while. That's only natural."

"I've felt weak and sick for a year, but only on my good days."

He tried to laugh amid his tears. His body was shaking as she drew blood.

"How about that?" he asked. "I didn't think I had any of that shit left."

The next day, Thursday, January 13th, 1999

"Explain them to me," Luc Séguin asked.

The pharmaceutical array was impressive for its variety and colour.

Lucy smiled. "At the border, Brad thought I was smuggling beads, giving Indians a bad name. What he didn't know, those beads could probably buy back Manhattan."

"You think so?"

"Health is big money."

"Each one does something different?"

"Some of the pills are blockers, they simulate how the immune system protects cells. Others are fiercely strong anti-virals. Others protect the body from the pills, especially the stomach. Others cheat the body into attacking foreign organisms even when they're not there, again, taking the place of the immune system. Others treat the blood, feed the red cells to make them vigorous. Others—"

"Okay," he interrupted her, "I got you."

She wasn't ready to stop. "The large purple oblong pill? It works with the intravenous dosage I give. It's anti-viral, though it's still in development. Stops a host of illnesses. In its physical form, a virus is three-dimensional, with sharp angles. The pill works by seeking out a virus, then sliding into its grooves, gumming it up so that it can no longer feed. Isn't that amazing?"

Luc was duly impressed.

They were having breakfast in a small café attached to their motel busy with tradesmen and contractors. Lucy was having cereal and fruit, while Luc had opted for the eggs-and-sausage special. Dressed for another busy day, she wore a rose sweater over a checked shirt, beige pants, and cowboy boots. Never before, though, had she seen Luc wear such a fine shirt. Olive, it needed pressing but still looked smart. As usual, he had stuck to wearing jeans.

"When we move that one along," Lucy explained, "we'll not only be treating AIDS, we'll be curing everything from meningitis to the common cold. Like I said, there's big bucks if we can win the race. But for you, the news is you'll be okay if you develop full-blown AIDS."

"If?" he asked.

"When," Lucy acknowledged. "One of the problems we're facing is that the drugs lose their edge over time. The AIDS virus adapts. What we're going after now is called integrase. It's an enzyme with a bad job. It knits together the HIV genetic material with the victim's DNA, right inside the cells. You hijack trucks, Luc, integrase hijacks cells. Only after it does that can HIV begin to reproduce as fast as it does." She stopped to take a bite and give Luc a moment to process this information. "We already have protease-inhibitors, which block another HIV enzyme called protease and work at the later stages of replication, and we have AZT and ddI, which block an enzyme called reverse transcriptase and work at the early stages of infection. We've been trying like mad to devise a integrase-inhibitor to help people through the long and developing middle stages. What we're looking for is to find the spot, the exact spot, where we have to nail integrase, where we have to stop it, in order to shut it down. We're on it, Luc. Nobody knows this. But we're on it."

"That's good. I'll show you why that's good." Luc raised his shirt slightly to display a lesion on his stomach.

Lucy put down her spoon. "I didn't know."

"I used to be fifty pounds more weight. In prison, English guys they called me Fat Face. They won't call me that name no more."

"Luc," she said, leaning forward, "let me treat you. Let me get you early."

He sliced his sausage. When he had finished chewing, and thinking, he said, "You are a beautiful woman. It is for me to protect you."

"Luc—"

"It's not early for me. I am just doing pretty well right now."

"Let me stop it in its tracks."

He gazed at her awhile. "Yes. I will let you."

As if he was doing her a favour, indulging her fancy.

"All right," Lucy agreed, returning to her own breakfast, "I'll cure you, Luc. If you don't believe me, just watch."

"I know this you have done before. In my life, I never had a luck like that. I don't know what that is, luck. If I am wrong now, I hope you are right."

"Well, Luc, you'll be out of luck if you ever show me anything like that again while I'm eating."

He was puzzled, but after thinking through what she had said, Luc cracked a smile, and for the first time in her company, chuckled.

6

CLOSE WATCH

Five days later, Tuesday, January 18, 1999

Under special circumstances, drug companies were allowed to treat the terminally ill with experimental therapies, a rule that had been instituted since the onslaught of AIDS, given that the devastation of the plague demanded a more aggressive approach. It was not permitted, however, to treat the merely sick with drugs that had not come through government channels and had scarcely been tested on live rats, let alone humans.

For those in the executive suite, letting kittens out of the bag by administering new therapies to the public was perceived as dangerous. Competitors could embark on similar designs, and the advantage of a head start might slip away if a rival happened to get lucky. Any spectacular result hoisted a red flag and brought attention where it was not desired. Competitors had been known to buy drug cocktails from test patients to jump-start their own research. Secrecy was preferred in treating those who were not yet terminal, and secrecy was desired at all times to keep the competitive wolves at bay.

For Werner Honigwachs, President and CEO of the BioLogika Corporation, covert testing provided a unique opportunity outside the realm of science.

BioLogika was a publicly traded company. Stockholders needed to be kept happy. And yet Honigwachs was not inclined to share the full bounty of his company's potential with them. He was also a secret, silent partner and the majority owner of Hillier-Largent Global Pharmaceuticals, Inc. He had devised a plan whereby he would permit one company to flourish, driving up the market price of BioLogika, with the intention that ultimately, handed the right product or product-set, he'd allow Hillier-Largent to trump BioLogika. In this way he would be immunized from sharing the immense benefits, projected to be in the billions of dollars, with the riffraff—his word for stockholders.

The manoeuvres demanded finesse.

Compounding his troubles, the nature of the investors in his company was unusual. Honigwachs had begun his career as a scientist but had soon understood that nothing significant could happen in the lab without proper financing. He devoted his attention to attracting and, if necessary, extracting government research grants, which helped him to establish BioLogika in partnership with both Randall Largent and Harry Hillier. His next mission was to mine private funding. Biochemical research was difficult for banks to assess. They considered his projects wildly speculative, his results too far downstream. Confident that his people were moving into cutting-edge work, Honigwachs pioneered the field of contract research, doing the messy tests on human lab rats for his competitors in order to finance his own programs. Contract research was quick money, and so the banks were willing to finance his need for start-up capital in buildings and equipment, but he still needed bundles of cash for his more ambitious projects. He was engaged in a race in which winners ascended to enormous wealth while losers became blips on a computer screen, soon to be forgotten.

In his search for investors, Honigwachs fell upon an

untapped and bottomless pool of funds. He developed methods whereby his company would assist certain illicit flows of hard currency, which drew him into a circle that included the criminal elite and their financial advisers. Laundering money advanced his company's research. The next step, both in terms of keeping his financiers happy and moving his company forward, was an Initial Public Offering. Revenues from the stock sale benefitted both his secret partners and his company's research, and put him in a position to be able to participate in laundering ever larger sums.

On the positive side of the transaction, he had created cash flow. As a negative aspect, he now had to share his future profits in BioLogika with millions of shareholders, and these included mobsters. A ruthless biker gang that operated in Quebec, a chapter of the Hell's Angels, which did its business in cocaine, marijuana, prostitution and extortion—Honigwachs could only guess what else—generated millions, and the gang's greatest problem was sanitizing truckloads of cash.

Honigwachs obliged them.

His relationship with the gang meant being subject to their supervision. Vice-presidents came and went, and no one understood why, or what they did while they were around. In fact, they were envoys from the mob. As his plans progressed toward fruition, he was assigned someone who, unlike the others, had particular expertise and also status in the mob. Honigwachs had controlled how Andrew Stettler came into his company, first as a lab rat, then soon after as a security guard and an internal spy. The full range of his talents was at his disposal. That Stettler had appeared at all, however, had not been his doing. The young man had been imposed upon him as the price to be paid for the value of his connections. Werner Honigwachs needed to make BioLogika a success, not only to participate in the immense profit potential of biotechnology, but also to stay healthy, free from the hazards of chainsaws and car bombs. Others with a vested interest were keeping a close watch.

He called Stettler in to see him. The young man lounged in one of the guest chairs, slouching down, putting his feet up on the desk. Honigwachs didn't reprimand him. "What've you heard?" the company president asked.

"Lucy's moving south, finally, but she needs more product." A glitch had slowed her progress. In Greenwich Village, more patients had turned up than they'd planned for, probably due to a breach in security. The unexpected numbers required that she see people over a three-day interval, and that extra day had inflicted changes on her timetable. Lucy had then contacted Camille Choquette back in Montreal to alert everyone down the line, but when she was finally through in the Village, Newark messed up the alternate date, setting her back further.

"How about delivering it yourself?" Honigwachs said.

"Me?" This was a surprise, given the risks.

Honigwachs sat in his own chair and leaned back with his hands behind his head. He hated feeling intimidated by this callow youth. "What better excuse to go down there and check things out? Delays bother me. I don't want Lucy hanging around any one place too long."

"I could catch her in Baltimore."

"Excellent."

"Anything else?"

"Why not go through New York? Check on things there first."

"Isn't—?" Andy stopped, and waited.

"Camille? Yes. But Camille … Well, I'd like to hear your perspective, as well as Camille's." Honigwachs put his hands down and swivelled around in his chair, looking out at the ice-covered lake beyond his window.

"Keep your eyes and ears open, Andy. You don't understand the science, so I'd run everything by me when you get back. This is an important move, the last link in the puzzle. I don't want anybody to know more than they should, and that includes Lucy and Camille."

Andy nodded. He understood now why the mission was worthy of his talents. That Honigwachs might also appreciate having him out of his hair for a few days didn't bother him. It was understandable. "I'll pack a bag."

"Do that. I'll ready Lucy's supplies."

"How do I take that stuff across the border?"

Honigwachs waved a hand in the air, not interested. "You're the one with the heavy connections. You figure it out."

Andy nodded. He wasn't thrilled about the plan—he'd rather have avoided criminal exposure—but the prospect of seeing Lucy Gabriel again was incentive enough to go along with it.

The next day, Wednesday, January 19, 1999

Camille Choquette moved down the dim corridor in search of Room 44. Behind the doors, televisions recited the news, conversations were interrupted by bawling kids, walls thumped with music. When a door opened up ahead, she increased her pace, and waiting for her there was the black man she knew as Wendell.

"Thank God," he said.

"How are you?" she inquired as she came inside.

"I'll need help to get back to bed, Camille, that's how I am."

Sores on his feet made walking difficult. His breath was short, and he was feeling dizzy. "I only answered because I hoped, I prayed it might be you."

"That's sweet. Take it easy now, Wendell. Take it slow."

He groaned as she helped him into bed and immediately launched into a sustained coughing fit. "Am I going to die?" he asked when she was done.

"Why would I let you die?"

Camille took his temperature, checked his pulse and blood pressure, and examined the lesions that had erupted in a symmetrical design across his chest. She placed a stethoscope over his lungs and listened to the rumbling mucous there.

"I don't think the new cocktails are working," he surmised, his voice scarcely audible, as she was putting away her instruments.

"That's hard to say. Obviously, you're not doing very well."

"I'd offer you a drink, but frankly, sweetheart, it's too much effort."

"Don't worry about it, Wendell. But do you mind if I sit down awhile? That would be a huge favour. I've been run off my feet."

She sat in the big, soft armchair and watched the man close his eyes. The room was a hodgepodge, with wigs on the furniture, makeup on the bookshelves, photographs scattered about on the floor, as though the man had been rampaging through his past, or his memories. Camille shut her own eyes to enjoy a brief catnap, and when she opened them again, Wendell was snoring lightly. Camille observed him. When eventually he stirred, she offered, "I can help you. For today. Would you like that?"

He nodded gently, coughed, and sat up. Not one to remain quiet for long, he asked, "Camille, how did you get into this business? Are you a nurse or a scientist?"

"I'm in it for the money."

"Oh good. There are just too many damned saints in the world. I adore Lucy, though, she's one of the best. Camille. Save me, before you go, will you, please? I'm feeling so rotten."

Camille pulled up the sleeve on his pyjamas and dabbed the back of his biceps with rubbing alcohol. She returned across the room to her bag and loaded a needle, holding it up to the light of a floor lamp.

"Actually, I came upon my profession honestly," she told Wendell. "I had a brother. Paul. Loved him dearly. When I was fourteen I asked him to buy me drugs, I didn't really care what. We were both on the wild side back then." She moved back to the bed. "This'll prick a little, Wendell, nothing serious." She gave his arm a jab, to which he hardly reacted. "I don't know what happened, but that night my brother was killed. First he was shot through the face, right in the eye, and then his neck was cut half off."

"My God, Camille, I'm sorry. You poor thing."

She put away her implements. "I thought it was my fault. Maybe he was trying to steal drugs for me and that cost him his life. Who knows? I remember the funeral as if it was last week. The bones on his face, they'd been smashed in by the bullet, he didn't look like himself at all. He was painted in heavy, dreary makeup. The smell of the makeup made me sick. My father told me to kiss him, on the lips, that's what I was supposed to do, so I did." Camille dismissed her bad memory of the moment with a brief, sad smile. "I loved my brother, but I didn't like doing that. It was too creepy."

"No, that's a very sad thing for a child."

"Yes. Well. Life."

"So ... sad."

"Are you feeling drowsy, Wendell?"

"Yes, I ... suppose, I ..."

The sedative was taking effect. Camille fluffed the pillows and adjusted the blanket around him. Tenderly, she kissed his cheek. His eyelids flickered.

"Sleep awhile, Wendell. You need your rest. It'll help. It's okay, I can find my own way out."

So much devastation. So many sick men. She envied

Wendell his afternoon nap, drug-induced or not. She herself hadn't had many hours of sleep since her arrival in New York.

Nor did she enjoy many that night. Awakened by a telephone call, she was told the news of Wendell's passing.

"Oh no. No. Oh no, that lovely man."

Her caller was from their network, a patient himself. "There's more bad news."

"What? Tell me."

"It wasn't natural causes."

"What do you mean? It was AIDS."

"He was smothered. Suffocated. With his own pillow, the police say."

"Oh my God, no. No."

"Whoever did it sutured his lips closed."

"What? What are you saying? What?"

"His lips were sewn shut with thread. He was wearing make up, rouge spread messily on his cheeks. Lipstick. Silver eye shadow. With his lips sewn together. Who would do a thing like that?"

Camille remained awake in her hotel room, her stomach in a knot. At dawn, having given up trying to sleep, she ordered coffee. She had another day ahead of her, another round of visits. Everyone would be talking about Wendell. Probably they'd all be equally terrified and upset. She was not looking forward to her day.

The next day, Thursday, January 20, 1999

Luc changed, after Philadelphia. In Newark he'd had a fever, which had caused him to be drowsy and severely cranky, although the symptoms were appropriate for a body being introduced to a major chemical bombardment. He refused his breakfast on the cold, sunny morning of their departure from Philadelphia, and Lucy had to keep close tabs on him, making sure that he didn't fall asleep at the wheel.

When he declined lunch she got mad. He showed her the lesions on his right leg then, and the two fresh marks that had appeared on his back. "I don't feel right," he told her. He complained about the drugs she was giving him. They just weren't suited for him.

"Stick with the program, Luc. Without the cocktail, you'd be worse off."

"That's hard for my body to believe. My brain understands it. But my brain's never been a smart cookie."

After lunch, such as it was, at a roadside truck stop, Lucy drove. For a while, her companion felt ashamed about that, but he soon fell asleep. When she pulled over for diesel fuel, Lucy suggested that he move to the back of the truck, where he'd have air and light as well as a bed.

"I don't know," Luc told her.

"What don't you know?"

"I can't make it that far."

"I'll help you."

He hung his weight on her shoulder and slowly they made their way around to the rear. Lucy used the hydraulic lift to hoist them up, and she supported him again across to the bunk that ran fore and aft. After making sure that the vents were open, Lucy loosely strapped him onto the bunk with electrical cord. He was already nodding off. She threaded the cord through the belt loops on his trousers and tied him down more snugly. Then she locked him in, climbed back into the cab, and drove on.

Outside Baltimore, in the parking lot of their motel, she pulled the detritus of Luc Séguin back up to his feet. Their rooms were on the second floor, which was unfortunate, but Luc seemed to be getting a measure of his strength back and he struggled up the stairs with her. She settled him into bed and propped him up. He was keen on watching television, and it didn't matter what was on. With coaxing, he agreed to hot soup, which she made by pouring boiling water into a cup of instant mix, and Luc sipped it slowly. He seemed to be improving.

After she'd grabbed a bite for herself, she brought Luc his nightly dosage. He visibly recoiled, his body edging back into the pillows. His feet made slight, involuntary kicking motions under the blankets. "Now, Luc," she said.

"For other people it's good. For me, maybe not so much."

"You've caught a fever. That's all. The drugs came along after the fact. So let's be a big boy."

He was obedient, he did consume his medication, but in the middle of the night he pounded on the wall to wake her in the adjoining room. Lucy had kept his key, so she barged right in. Luc wasn't weak this time, he was energized and animated, but Luc was in agony, his muscles convulsing. He raved, spouting nonsense in French. Lucy soothed the tantrum of his body with cool compresses and comforting words. He'd had trouble breathing, which had brought him to the brink of panic. With a soft light on, and her easing touch and the tender lilt of her words, he relaxed, and the ordeal became manageable. Luc apologized for being a pest.

"Don't worry about it."

"I don't know what is wrong with me. I don't feel right."

"But you're feeling better now?"

Not wanting to be a greater nuisance, he agreed. "Yeah. I'm okay."

"Okay. I'll see you in the morning."

"Lucy? Can I ask you something? I keep thinking about it."

She suspected that this might be a ploy, that he was scrounging for questions to delay her departure. "Go ahead."

"Why is it that you were in the garage?"

"Excuse me?"

"When your father's house got burned down, you were in the garage. Why? You wouldn't tell Andy, but I keep wondering that to myself."

She could tell him, the story wasn't as complicated as he might imagine, but she was curious about his interest. "Why do you want to know?"

"It seems so sad to me." He shrugged with the weight of his gloominess. "I'm glad you didn't burn, that's not sad, but why did a little girl not go to sleep in her own house?"

Lucy sat down again on the edge of his bed. She smiled. "My father built the apartment above the garage for his father, but my granddad lived in it for only a few months before he died. A natural death, peaceful. Old age. I missed him, he was a great old guy, and he always had time for me, so I played in his apartment a lot. It was a bit like being with him. Then shots were fired at my house. Warning shots. They weren't intended to hurt anyone. Just to make a point. My dad was on the Grand Council and a few hotheads didn't like what he was doing. After that, he put me in my granddad's place to sleep. He was scared about stray bullets. As it turned out, being in the garage did save my life, only it wasn't a bullet that missed me."

She didn't tell him that she had watched the house burn. That she had seen her father through a window, arms raised, walking, on fire. She had never told anyone that and she never would.

"You were meant to live," Luc put in.

"I think that's true, Luc. But I don't think my parents were meant to die."

Luc watched her with a steady gaze. "You've been mixed up in things all your life."

"That's true too. You also. My intuition tells me that."

Luc responded with a slight shrug of his bony shoulders. "Nothing in my life was easy."

"*Is* easy," she corrected him.

"You are changing my English now?"

"Not your English, Luc, your attitude. You're a long way from dead. You're in the hands of Saint Lucy, didn't you know? Your luck has changed!"

"Tell that to my insides. After all this luck I'm having, my insides want back their old misery."

Lucy laughed with him and planted a kiss on his forehead. She sat on his bed with her legs curled under her and rested her chin in her palm. "Now, Luc," she directed, "you tell me something. How come you know your way around New York?"

Luc was shy about telling the story. In his late teens he had worked with an older friend who would journey to the Big Apple to buy electric guitars and other instruments. The quality instruments were rarely available second-hand in Canada, and when they were the prices were exorbitant. The two would respond to ads in the papers and run around from Queens to Harlem, Manhattan to Brooklyn, the Bronx to Staten Island. Returning to Canada, they'd pay the duty at the border, then sell the guitars and organs at a terrific mark-up in Montreal.

Lucy was puzzled by the story. Why was Luc embarrassed by his past?

Unaccustomed as he was to intimacy, he was reluctant to confess the true burden of his tale. He had been involved in the wheeling and dealing because it had helped make ends meet while he pursued his real interest. He had wanted to be a musician. "Me," he said, "in a band. Pretty dumb, huh?" An ambition that had died hard, and Luc was ashamed to admit that he had once had a dream, one that, today, seemed hopelessly farfetched. "One time, we stopped at this roadside restaurant, and when we came out the truck was gone, stolen. All the instruments, gone. I was so mad. My friend, he was bent out of shape, because all the money he had left in this world was in those guitars. We never had no insurance. Know what I did? I stole ourselves another truck, a small van, to get us home. My dad was a car thief and a truck-jacker himself, and his dad was that, too, before him, so it seemed like the right thing to do. Trouble was, we never made it across the border. I did time for that heist, and after that I was just another criminal, you know? When I got out I hadn't touched a guitar in five months, so I just started up stealing trucks with my dad."

One mistake had caused a slide. From a youthful dream of playing in a band, to dying of AIDS. Lucy felt the sorrow, the regret, of the man's life. She climbed off his bed and kissed him gently between the eyes, letting her lips linger there, consoling the very depth of him. After that, she fluffed his pillows, turned out the lights, and returned to her own room.

Just as she was closing her door, a foot was thrust in the jamb. Lucy gasped and jumped six inches. Instantly, she flung herself against the door and caught the intruder's knee in the gap. She propelled her weight against the door repeatedly, ramming the knee. The intruder cried out, "Lucy!"

She stopped a moment, keeping the knee pinned with her weight. "Andy?"

"Lucy, you're hurting me. *Jesus!*" She opened the door for him. He was holding his injured leg, while nodding to the room where she'd just been. "Are you sleeping with Luc now?"

"What're you doing here?"

"Are you cheating on me?" He looked like a wolf with his long wild hair and his dark eyes and the shadows of the night around him. He was wearing his usual bomber jacket but also a baseball cap she hadn't seen on him before, with the famous NY symbol of the New York Yankees.

"Ah, cheating? Like you don't cheat on me? Luc's sick. I was helping him out, that's all."

He closed the door behind him, as though he had needed that explanation first. Andy took her in his arms and kissed her.

Lucy had to reach up and move the peak of the baseball cap out of her way. Suddenly, the misery and sadness of the past days welled up inside her. Her work was exciting, but the endless kindnesses and the stream of suffering men took a lot out of her, more than she had thought she had to give. And now a man, whole and healthy, rocked her in his arms and his kiss plundered her senses and she hung onto him with all her might. The instant Andy broke away Lucy peeled off her dressing gown, and he was reaching under her top and she kissed him wildly, then yelped, as he lifted her off the floor and they tumbled onto the bed.

"Heaven help me," Lucy pleaded.

"What for?" He bounced right down on top of her. The bedsprings made a racket and Lucy laughed. He still hadn't taken that silly cap off and she did it for him, tossing it across the room. His hair, as black as her own, nearly as long, fell across both sides of her face as he peered down upon her. "What for?" he asked again, quietly.

"I always fall for bad boys."

"Am I a bad boy, Luce?" He worked himself up to a crouch, his mouth moving down to her thighs and legs quickly until he'd kissed her ankles, then grazing up her body, nibbling her like a beast on all fours, kissing her shins, knees, thighs, hip.

"You're so bad. The worst." Inner thighs. Her waist. He pulled her panties off.

"Yeah? You going to save me, Lucy? You going to reform me?"

"That depends." Her body twisted, and she cried out under the fury of his kisses.

"On what?" He gave her pubis a quick, teasing lick.

She was breathing harshly now. She didn't want to talk any more.

"On what?" he asked her again, and he licked her again, just as quickly.

"On how bad you are."

He laughed. He came up on his knees and turned her around on the bed. "You already said I'm the worst. You going to reform me, Lucy? Me, I got that to look forward to?"

"No," she whimpered.

"No?" He held her wrists behind her back in one hand, and leaned over to kiss her neck. She bucked under his grip, and thrashed her head around.

"No."

"You want me bad as I am." He turned her over again. "Huh?"

"Unhunh."

"Was that a yes? You want me as bad as I get?"

"Stop teasing me!"

"Answer me."

"Yes!"

He pushed her little top up and roughened her breasts with kisses, his whiskers scratching her, and then he returned to her mouth as he pressed his weight down upon her. She interrupted him by punching his back.

"What? Lucy?"

"Get out of those damn clothes!"

While he was doing that she peeled her top off, and kissed his flesh wherever it suddenly appeared, his chest, back, neck, stomach. Then thighs. And finally she devoured his penis and hugged him. All the while he infuriated her with his little laughs and salacious chatter, and then they were kissing again, body to body, and she wanted him as much as she had ever wanted a man.

"Condom!" she instructed breathlessly. "Condom!"

"Oooo, maybe yes, maybe no."

He took his penis and rubbed the head against her sex, and she fought him and squirmed underneath him. "Andy, no!"

He laughed that maddening laugh again and rubbed her pubis and that felt so good, but no, she couldn't. "Andy! No! Andy!" His laughter so infuriated her that she could just kill him, and then he was reaching into his cast-off trousers and retrieving his wallet. She watched as he pulled the condom over his penis and asked him again, "What are you doing here?" Then suddenly there was no time for talk and he entered her and held her arms pinned, and she moved with him. She let him do the work for a while, until he squatted above her and said, "Your turn," and now she was responsible for the movement, twisting and bending and humping her body against him, against his penis, until suddenly he slipped out and in the same move-ment he flipped her over, clutching her legs at the right moment and entering her from behind. She loved this attention and realized how much she had missed him, or this, or anyone, health, life, any respite from sickness and death, and her orgasm was upon her, and she reached back with one hand behind his muscled thigh and pulled him deeper, harder into herself, and when she came she knew that she was waking up the motel guests but she didn't care, she wanted to be loud and she could not help herself anyway.

She flat out yelled.

Andy wasn't done with her. He teased her to desire again, and made love to her again, more violently the second time, with her head pounding up against the wall, and this time when her release overwhelmed her he immediately followed. They lay in one another's arms, warm and spent and delighted.

"Andy," she asked after they had both napped awhile.

"Mmm?"

"What are you doing here?" She could hardly tell where her body ended and his began.

"What do you think? We got the word. You needed more product. So I'm here. Your delivery man."

She found this curious. "Who sent you?"

"I'm probably not supposed to say."

"You're moving up the ladder pretty quickly."

"I've got a nose for what's going on. To tell the truth, I begged for the job."

She liked the sound of that.

"So how's it going?" Andy asked.

Snuggling into him, she made a few noises he couldn't interpret.

"What does that mean?"

"Luc, for one thing. He's sick. I'm treating him, and he thinks the fever he caught was caused by the cocktail I made for him—"

"You're treating Luc?"

"He's full-blown, Andy. He's not just pos, he's full-blown."

"Shit," Andy said.

"What's wrong?"

"Nothing. Just, it must be crummy for you with Luc not feeling well."

"It's a drag, yeah. I'm sure he'll be better soon. How long are you staying?"

"I'm allowed to make the delivery, that's it."

She lightly traced his arm with her fingers. "I'm glad you came," she said.

"Is that some kind of pun?"

Lucy giggled. "No. Maybe. Yes! Why not? I meant, I'm glad you're here."

They kissed awhile before turning themselves to sleep.

In the morning, Lucy was disappointed but not surprised to find herself alone in the room.

After washing and dressing, she went in to see Luc. He related astonishing news. "Andy told me. Something's wrong with the drugs. I'm not supposed to take them no more."

She stood there, stunned, shaking. "What?" Lucy asked. "What?"

"They're killing people," Luc said. "The same as me, they're dying."

"Who? What are you talking about?"

"Your drugs, they're killing people. They've been killing me. Andy, he said he just came in from New York. Everybody's dying there, Lucy, from this, everybody you treated. It's a terrible thing that's happening."

She felt herself go light, woozy, faint. She could only dimly make out Luc's face, only vaguely discern his voice. Seeing him, she tried to tell herself, she tried to convince herself, that she could not possibly have been killing him all along. Luc. Dying. Not just sick, but dying. Because of her. Then she thought of the others, so many others, and Lucy Gabriel slumped to the floor and folded her knees up against her chest, and she rocked herself, and no matter what Luc did or said, she would not stop rocking. She sat on the floor of the motel room in Baltimore and continued to rock.

Where? she wondered. *Where's Andy? Why did he go?*

7

HOMECOMING

Ten days later, Sunday, January 30, 1999

Overcome with rage, and with a rumbling panic inside her, Lucy Gabriel had first cared for Luc Séguin before returning home. Erratic, distraught, she didn't know if she should run or hide or confront someone, understood only that the world was not as she had imagined. Her instinct to forge passionate bonds, so long nurtured within her culture and her political experience, warred against a renewed conviction that no one could be trusted.

The assault weapon that she had defiantly deployed during the Oka crisis had been stripped from her the day the army had negotiated its advance onto the reserve, but she still owned a shotgun for hunting mallards in season. She had arrived home on a Friday, and when Andy Stettler called on Sunday and insisted on paying her a visit, she waited for him in her apartment above the garage, the shotgun across her lap, a finger crooked around one of the twin triggers.

When he knocked, she didn't respond.

When he entered, she aimed both barrels at his belly.

"Easy, girl," he said gently, raising his hands chest-high.

"Fast-talking man," she warned him, "you better have something to say."

"Don't go off half-cocked. Aim the gun down, Lucy."

"At your balls?"

"Where's Luc?"

"None of your business."

"He's my friend," Andy pointed out.

"Good thing you didn't forget that. If you hadn't told him he was dying I would've killed more people. Nice of you to let me know, Andy." She crossed an ankle over a knee, and balanced the weapon across her calf, aiming now at the vicinity of his crotch, as promised.

"I let you know as soon as I found out."

"How do you figure that? You said diddly-squat to me!"

"Can I sit down, at least?"

"Suit yourself."

"Will you put the gun away?"

"No."

Andrew Stettler pulled up a wooden chair that long ago had lost its finish. Facing Lucy, he positioned himself the wrong way around on it, resting an elbow on the back and feeling more secure, perhaps, to have bits of wood between himself and the shotgun. Even now, she loved the way he moved his body, folding his long limbs with the easy confidence of a snake coiling itself on a rock. They confronted one another under the steeply sloped roof of the garage. At either end, the windowpanes were blotted with frost and windblown snow. Wind squealed around the walls.

"I'd been to New York. Luce, the news there was pretty grim. That morning with you, I called Camille for the latest report—the morning after we made love. I had to catch her early, before she went on her rounds. She gave it to me straight, and it was then, it was only then we decided to face facts. Camille and me. We couldn't call certain things coincidences, or accidents, any more. We couldn't kid ourselves that some people were having a run of bad luck. The evidence was mounting. We had to face facts. I didn't wake you. All right, maybe I should've. I went straight to Luc and gave him the word instead. Luc could tell you everything. I had a plane to catch. All hell was breaking loose." Andy grimaced at the bad memory. "To be perfectly honest with you, Lucy, I chickened out. All right? I didn't want to be the one to tell you. It was hard enough telling Luc. I was a wreck after that. Anyway, I had to shake a leg. I had to get home, find out what was going on."

"What was?"

"Lucy—"

"Don't Lucy me! I got *you* hired, not the other way around. The next thing I hear, you're telling Camille I'd make a good doctor. Well, thanks! Like you're giving me a pat on the back. How come is that? Since when are you directing things? You came in on this as a fucking lab rat, Andy, a lab rat. Suddenly, you're in tight with Honigwachs? He sends *you* to New York? To *Baltimore?* For *what?* When did this happen, anyway? Who the hell are you? How come, all of a sudden, you know more about everything than I do? Explain it to me. I really want to know."

Snow was melting off his boots, creating a puddle on the floor. He held one forearm across the chair back and another along a thigh, a rattler sliding over rock, his gaze cool and animal-like and sexual, even with a shotgun aimed at his vital organs. She loved his hands, those long, curled fingers.

"Lucy, listen to me," Andy started, and now his tone was grave. "I'm your best chance right now, so you have to figure this out in a hurry."

"*You're* my best chance?" she sneered. "Now I know I'm really fucked."

"I'm in tight with Honigwachs because I'm his security director right now. I got promoted. When he found out what I could do for him, he boosted me up the ladder."

"What *can* you do for him?"

He put both hands on the back of his chair now, as though to slither around it, to cover it with his full length, his legs coiled around the base. His long, black hair fell down one side of his face, casting a shadow across the other. "Bad boys don't grow on trees, contrary to public opinion. We're a breed apart. I know the criminal stuff, except I'm not interested in being a criminal no more. That's old, it's not for me. You know what they say, if you can't do the time, don't do the crime. I can't do the time, Lucy. I won't do the time. I'm sick of being inside. I want to live for a change. I want to be around girls, you know? But for somebody like me—I don't fit in this world, there's no place for me. As it turns out, I'm somebody Honigwachs can use, and that's been all right, until now."

"Now what, a crisis of conscience?" She jerked her shotgun up and down in rhythm with her words. "I'm supposed to feel sorry for you?"

He pushed a hand through his hair, tucking the longer strands behind an ear. She could see his face much better now, and it seemed that he had wanted that, that he had wanted to indicate that he should be trusted in this circumstance. "Lucy, you're in trouble here. You're in deep. Do you know that much? You brought drug cocktails down to seventy, eighty guys. Half of them are dead now."

She did not respond to his question right away, her gaze travelling off, and when she did speak she inquired, in a quiet voice, "Half?" Fear cascaded through her.

"About half, yeah."

"So we had guys who were going to die and a control group, placebo boys?"

"Could be," Andy acknowledged. "Something like that."

"That was never our thing. We promised no placebos. We told our people we would give them the best shot available, no control groups, no dummy drugs."

"Yeah, well," Andy noted, "maybe this time it was lucky."

That might be true, fewer men were dead, but she wondered where the larger betrayal began and where it ended.

"I know how much trouble I'm in," Lucy confessed. "I always knew that something could go wrong, that a drug might not work. But never, never in my wildest imagination could I picture this. I never signed on for this horror story."

"You weren't part of it," Andy said, "you couldn't have known what was going to happen."

"Of course I wasn't!" she threw back, offended by the suggestion. "I mean, I was part of it, but I didn't know what was really happening. Oh God. I know a judge and jury won't care about the difference."

"Where's Luc?" he asked her abruptly.

Lucy looked down, at her shotgun, then up. "He's dead, Andy."

They were quiet awhile, letting that news resonate between them.

"Tell me about it," Andy asked.

"There's not much to tell." Lucy looked away as she spoke. "I brought him to a hospital in Baltimore. He made a call down to Florida and the next day this hairy guy knocked on my motel room door—*big* hairy guy— and paid me cash for the truck. I took my stuff out and paid Luc the money. I knew about the deal. He was to get the truck. Luc put up the truck money for his hospital bills but he went down fast. I stayed for the five days he was alive. He could see the ocean from his room. That gave him an idea about his funeral. I took his ashes down to the harbour and floated them on a falling tide."

Andy had expected the news, but he had to adjust to the image. A friend—someone he had not known well, but they had been in the can together, and that counted for something—had been reduced to ash. He'd floated out to sea. Andy had drawn him into this escapade, and to this end.

"Lucy," he started up momentarily, then stopped. He put his hands on his widespread knees, thinking. "Lie low for a bit, okay? Say nothing to no one. Do nothing. No one should know that you treated Luc. If the wrong people find out, they'll guess that you know too much. Tell them only that Luc got sick and died. No details. He had AIDS, it happens. It upset you and that's what brought you home."

Lucy aimed her shotgun at the ceiling, the butt-end tucked into the base of her hip. Then she stood, paced, and put the gun down on her kitchen counter. She had her back to Andy and looked at him over her shoulder. "I can't just do nothing."

He stood as well, pulling the chair out from under him and setting it aside. "What's there to do?"

Lucy was gazing out her back window. The blackness outside reflected back her own image, but she wasn't seeing it. She saw only space, the dark, a void. "We can lie low, like you said, but we can also gather information. Figure out what happened, why, who was responsible." She turned around to face him. "We have to gather evidence, Andy. It's the only way."

"Dangerous, Lucy. If you just lie low—"

"Lie low, with the deaths of those poor men on my mind? Who knows how many? A few were my friends. I can't live with it. Besides, I don't want to go to prison for this, Andy, it wasn't my fault." Her body shook as she breathed deeply, a mix of rage and sorrow overtaking her. "I told them, I told my boys, leading-edge medicine is dangerous. Nothing's been tested. You take your chances. But, the worst I ever counted on was failure. Failure means my boys would die, but they would have died anyway. This wasn't mere failure, Andy. God. The drugs made them sicker. The drugs killed them a whole lot quicker than just having AIDS would've!" She breathed heavily, willing herself to calm down, without letting go of her anger. "I'm not a frigging martyr, Andy, but I sure don't want whoever's guilty—Honigwachs, presumably, but *whoever*—I don't want anybody getting away with this. I'll lie low, but I want justice for those dead men, for each and every one of them."

"Lucy, it's so risky right now—"

She turned to face him, putting her hands back on the rim of the counter behind her. "Choose, Andy. Whose side are you on?"

"Lucy, come on, I'm with you."

"Are you? Don't forget, it's risky and dangerous, quote, unquote."

"Come here," he invited.

That was difficult for her, to cross that expanse of floor, although she wanted to go there. She hesitated at first, crossing her arms under her breasts. Eventually, she put her arms down, and her feet stepped on the area rug, and she moved cautiously across the floor, circling him somewhat, not going straight to him. When they met, she pressed herself against him, and they held onto to one another, and she was grateful for the contact, for the pressure of his arms and the warmth of his body. She did not know whom to trust, she did not know whom to love, but she had to have this also, she craved affection right now. She had killed people, inadvertently she had destroyed many lives, and she needed to affirm that she was not the evil one, not the criminal here. Lucy sought justice for the dead. She wanted to uncover and expose the hard truths, she would see to it that the truly responsible were identified. But clasped in the arms of Andrew Stettler she also required absolution, and needed, desperately, to be touched, now, here, to be comforted.

Émile Cinq-Mars drove up to the rectory and parked along one side. Modest shelter from the wind was available there as he walked to the back door, his head bent forward and turned away from the stiffer gusts. One of the things he had liked about this priest from the outset had been his generous, friendly invitation to drop by anytime, and to use the kitchen door in the rear.

A light was on, and Father Réjean quickly responded to his visitor's knock. A night owl, he had been up with a book and a coffee.

"Come in, come in, Émile. Out of that weather. My goodness."

Cinq-Mars dusted the snow off his chest, then slapped his wool cap against his thigh to knock it from both the cap and his coat. "I hope I'm not intruding, Father Réjean. I know it's late."

"Nonsense. I'm delighted to see you, Émile. I'm pleased to have the company. I hope that you can assure me, though, that you haven't arrived with dire news."

"No. It's not that, Father." Cinq-Mars pulled his coat off, and the priest helped him with it and hung it on a hook. The detective unwound his scarf, stuffed it into the coatsleeve, and plunked his wool cap on the hook to dry. "My dad had a difficult time yesterday, so I came up. But he was much better by this evening."

"That's good to hear. It's a trial, I know. You're heading home?"

"Yes, Father." Cinq-Mars nodded with resignation. "No rest for the wicked. I have to work tomorrow."

"That's a long drive at night. You will be careful, Émile. Coffee?"

"Thanks."

"Now you won't consider me a 'whiskey priest,' will you, if I offer you a glass of Glenfiddich?"

"Are you a whiskey priest, Father?"

The priest shook his finger at him as Cinq-Mars took a chair at the long and narrow antique pine table. "I should remember that I'm talking to a detective."

"I'm happy to join you for a small one."

"Fine. Fine. I'd press a large one on you, but I know you have that drive."

"I'd accept a large one, or two, Father, if not for that."

The priest busied himself with glasses. He was a man of average height and build, although now that he was sixty his body had slumped. His hair was white and quite full, and he combed it straight back. He had a liverspotted forehead, soft, intelligent brown eyes, and a small, charming pug nose. He was wearing black, but not clerical garb—slacks and a heavy wool sweater. Over the door, as in most of Quebec Catholic households, hung a crucifix. Inside the kitchen, nothing distinguished the room from farmhouse kitchens for miles around. Old, a dark, sombre patina graced the woodwork, and the floor sloped gently in different directions, quietly buckling with age. Cinq-Mars felt comfortable here, not because he was in a priest's residence, but because he was in a home similar to those he had visited during his childhood.

The refrigerator door had pictures of children pressed to its surface with magnets, unusual in a rectory. In his investigation of priests, Cinq-Mars had learned that Father Réjean had had a previous existence as a part-time lecturer in economics. He had also been a husband, a parent, and a failed entrepreneur. Some years after the death of his wife, he had opted for the priesthood, and had actually made his way through the seminary while still an active single parent. His children were now grown, educated, off on their own in distant big cities, while Father Réjean had been assigned to the countryside, an entirely new environment for him.

"How's everything, Father?"

"Oh, you know." He brought the tiny glasses back full. "There are days when I think that my real job is to be a glorified social director. At other times I know I'm needed. And with you?"

Cinq-Mars put his elbows on the table and folded his hands thoughtfully. "There are days when I know I'm useful. Other days when I believe the criminals are fortunate to have such a bungling idiot as an adversary."

Father Réjean laughed. The two clinked glasses, and cried, *"Santé!"*

Both men enjoyed a sip.

"You can't believe that, Émile. You're no bungler."

"Some days you're right. I'm not. Then again, I've long believed that one of the most important aspects of my profession is learning to deal with failure. You have to be willing to make mistakes, and to suffer the consequences. Otherwise, in a job like mine, it's easy to become paralysed. I'll thank you to not to let the criminals know that. I wouldn't want to give them comfort."

"Ah, yes," Father Réjean noted, "comfort to the criminals. Now that would be my profession, wouldn't it?" He sat with a contented grin on his face, the wee glass held between the chubby fingers of both hands.

"Somebody has to do the dirty work, Father."

"Someone must!" he burst out. "But is that my job or yours, that's the question! Is it a dirtier job to comfort criminals, or to catch them?"

"I'll concede the high ground."

"You say that, Detective, but do you mean it? Or is it a ploy, culled from a policeman's bag of tricks, to lead me down a road of no return? You do that sort of thing, don't you, Émile?"

"What sort of thing?"

"Snare people in the maze of their character flaws."

Cinq-Mars laughed lightly, and took another sip of the single malt. "Let's just say, Father, that when those in your profession fail, I'm left to pick up the pieces."

The remark started the priest off on a deep-throated chuckle. At its conclusion, he proposed, "Let's just say, Detective, that when your work *succeeds*, my work begins. Then it's my job to go in and pick up the pieces."

Cinq-Mars wasn't going to allow him the final word. "It's a matter of faith, Father. I have faith that the bad guys will not enjoy incarceration. You believe you can redeem the irredeemable. Misfits can reform, that's true. Boys with wild hearts can straighten out. Men with troubles, or who took a wrong turn, sometimes choose to live properly for a change. But the bad guys, Father, the truly bad, once we turn the key on them, there's nothing for you to do but provide them with a diversion in an otherwise dull week."

"Our Lord might suggest otherwise."

"*Our Lord* said to the thief on the cross next to his, 'I'll see you in Heaven, buddy, there's nothing I can do for you down here.'"

The priest erupted into full-blown laughter. "Émile, who're you trying to kid? You're not a cynic. I haven't known you for long but I know *that*."

On the counter, the coffeemaker was starting to gurgle with a fresh pot, and the aroma filled the room.

"I'm not a cynic. I won't even pretend to call myself a realist. I'm probably a romantic, as sinful as that may be. *Ludicrous* as it may be, in this world. But there are bad guys, Father, who are not redeemable, not by you, and not by me."

"Your point being?" Father Réjean stood to pour the coffee.

"My point is ..." Cinq-Mars required a few moments to think about it. The priest had time to pour the coffee and stir in cream and sugar for himself. He remembered that the detective took his black. "My point is, my father is dying, and there is nothing that I can do about it except to ask … except to hope and pray that the latest drugs he's taking give him some comfort. In essence, Father, I pray to drug companies now, to doctors, and I thank God for nurses."

Placing the cups on the table, the priest sat down again. He spoke softly to Cinq-Mars. "Ask," he said.

The detective looked up. "Pardon me?"

"You started to say, that there was nothing you could do except ask. Ask what, Émile?"

"Ask that you go and see him."

"Of course. I will go tomorrow."

"I know it's not good enough."

"Émile."

"I'm a man of faith, Father. So I've thought. But I'm a man of faith who doesn't want his father to die. I'm aware of the inherent contradiction in that."

"You don't want him to suffer. But you know he will die, Émile." The priest looked at him with his small and deep-set eyes. "What's more, you know he's ready to die. You know that he's waiting to die. You know that there's nothing you can do about it. You're also quite right. Whatever I can do for him won't be enough. Priests, like cops, must learn to live with failure too."

The conversation had already helped. Émile Cinq-Mars wearily exhaled. He tried the coffee, which was hot and strong and a jolt to his system, and he laughed.

"What?" Father Réjean asked him.

"My father. He wanted me to find him a half-decent priest."

"Thanks for that, Émile. From what I hear, you're a half-decent cop yourself."

"You know what I mean."

"I think I do." The priest wore a wry grin. "And yet, I do not feel overwhelmed with praise."

"The point is, Father—" Cinq-Mars stared off into space a moment.

"Yes?"

"Now I'm wondering if the sly old codger didn't mean to find a priest for me. Not for himself so much. For me."

"Émile," the priest said, as the wind outside shook the doors and shutters, "I cannot betray a confidence. But your father is facing death with some anxiety, regret, fear, and, frankly, with a measure of rage. He is also prepared to get on with it and see it through. He's calm. He's ready. His conscience, much to your surprise, perhaps, might have been blemished in the past, but more importantly it is clear now. I think, Émile, that you should phone your wife and tell her that you won't be home tonight. The roads are too snowy, the north wind too strong. You'll travel when it's light out. In the meantime, you'll stay holed up with a renegade priest drinking whiskey."

"Renegade? You?"

The priest raised his glass and winked.

Cinq-Mars nodded. "Then what?" he asked quietly.

Father Réjean smiled. "Then comes the really scary part, Émile. I'll either hear your confession, or, better still—*scarier* still—we'll sit around in my kitchen, drink whiskey and chat. You can tell me about the bad guys. You can tell me about the boundless depths of evil in the world."

"That's the problem. I keep discovering new depths."

"The phone's on the wall, Émile."

Cinq-Mars was surprised by his own weariness as he pushed himself to his feet and crossed the room to make that call. Sandra was understanding, even glad, that he wasn't going to be out on the roads. Earlier she had counselled him to stay at his father's for the night.

When he returned to his chair, the whiskey bottle stood between him and Father Réjean on the table. Cinq-Mars helped himself. He took a long sip, then poured again, this time filling his host's glass as well.

"The murderers, the traffickers, the gangs, Father, they've been getting to me. They're impairing my judgment."

"How, Émile?"

"They've undermined my faith in the just. People in all walks of life have lacked courage. And the gangs have been teaching me how to hate."

"That's their job, Émile. The question is, what's yours?"

Both men took a long sip, and this time the priest in his winter kitchen poured.

The question was a more difficult one than Father Réjean might have supposed. At different times in his life, Cinq-Mars might have rejoined with a cavalier remark, "My job is to defeat them," or one that was merely pragmatic, "Put them in jail." Time had eroded easy conclusions.

"Bearing in mind, of course," Father Réjean encouraged him, "that you are a romantic."

"I suppose," Cinq-Mars sighed, "that my job is a prosaic one. It sounds uninspired to me. But if I combine my experience, my success, my failures, my observations, and my ideals—mix them all up in a blender—then here's the best that I can muster. It'll all sound a little boy-scouty. It already sounds foolish to me."

"Yes?"

"My job is to be ready."

The two men nodded. In time, each smiled, enjoying the company, the late hour, the drink.

"Émile," the priest said, "I have snifters in the living room. The chairs are more comfortable in there, as well. Shall we go through?"

"You *are* a whiskey priest," Émile Cinq-Mars remarked.

"For tonight, anyway." Father Réjean laughed.

Two days later, Tuesday, February 1, 1999

Camille Choquette kept the engine running in her Mazda 626 in order to operate the heater, and she gave her seven-year-old strict instructions to remain in the back seat. A tape that repeated the little girl's favourite children's songs played, and Carole had two dolls to dress and undress and a teddy bear to keep her company. Camille entered the restaurant where Werner Honigwachs was waiting.

Drinking coffee in a corner booth, he put on a show of being disgusted with his environment, to the point of scowling whenever he looked at a patron. He'd shudder, as if mortified. Camille guessed that he was merely disgruntled about being overdressed in a greasy spoon. When she arrived at his table, he grumbled, "Why this place?"

"Do you know anybody here?"

"If I did I wouldn't admit to it. But I don't. Who would want to know anybody who comes here?"

"Well, that's why we're here, Wiener."

"Don't use that name in public. As a matter of fact, don't use it at all."

"Nobody can hear me. That's another reason, *Wiener,* why we're here." The restaurant didn't pump out recorded music, but kept a golden-oldies radio station turned on with the volume high. Camille unwound her purple scarf and unbuttoned her overcoat before sliding into the seat across from him. She made eye contact with a waitress, who popped over with a coffeepot. "Tell you what, just make me a grilled cheese sandwich, all right? Two, actually. One to go."

"BLT," Honigwachs requested.

Accepting that the room was warm and that Honigwachs was refusing to remove his overcoat only out of disdain for the premises, Camille shrugged hers off where she sat, pulling her arms free from the sleeves. She brushed bits of wool fluff from her pale-blue cardigan and tugged the collar on her white blouse. She liked to keep men waiting. All set, she said, "So."

Leaning toward her, Honigwachs kept his voice down. "Have you spoken to Lucy?"

"I'm not sure that Lucy wants to talk to me."

"I don't like this," he conceded. "She's talked to Andy already—on Sunday. On Monday, she didn't show up at Hillier-Largent. How did she find out? She was supposed to administer the doses, provide the cocktails, then move on. She was supposed to be in another city before anybody got sick, and be home before she was any the wiser. The plan was, she'd never know. That way, she'd never ask questions. We weren't going to send her back down. Lucy wasn't *ever* supposed to find out."

"Andy Stettler spilled the beans."

"This you know for a fact?"

Camille shrugged. That she was calmer than he was pleased her. "It's how I'm betting."

Honigwachs shook his head. "Not possible. Not Andy."

She also leaned forward to whisper her opinion. "He called me, Andy did, from Baltimore, when I was still in New York. He wanted the latest news. What could I tell him? I knew that *he* knew the truth, he just didn't know that *I* knew. So I had to tell him. I had to tell him that we had lab rats who were dead and dying."

Werner Honigwachs raised his chin and moved his body back in his seat, as though to guard against her parry. "I don't get it. Why'd you have to tell him that?"

"Wiener, get wise in a hurry, will you? If I had lied to Andy, it would have been like telling him that I was in on it. Why else would I be covering up? So I was frantic, I was worried, I was concerned and I gave him the bad news in my frantic, worried, concerned voice. I told him what he already knew. What choice did I have?"

"So you think he told Lucy?"

"How else did she find out? *If* she's found out. Lucy never visited another lab rat after Andy's phone call to me. And now she's home. She never finished the job and she's come home. She's already talked to Andy, but she hasn't called me yet. What does she know and who does she trust? I'm betting that she knows everything and that Andy's not only her man, he's her conduit."

As the waitress passed by with food for other customers they stopped talking. When she was gone, Honigwachs stated the obvious. "I don't like this."

"*You* don't like it, *you!* I'm the one with the exposure here, Wiener, *me!* I'm the one who cleaned their sores. I did the body count."

"No, no," Honigwachs insisted. "It wasn't Andy. He couldn't have been the leak. You don't know his background like I do. He'd be the last one to talk."

She shook her head and gave a little laugh, as if both amazed and annoyed by his intransigence. "He asked me, I gave him an answer. We know he was with Lucy. After that, Lucy stopped treating rats. She disappeared for a while and then came home. That's all I've got to go on, but it adds up to something."

He breathed deeply, taking in the full dimension of their predicament. "I'll talk to Andy," Honigwachs decided. "But you have to contact Lucy."

Camille nodded aggressively, eager to make the call. "I can do that. I've got lots to say. I can vent about the disaster. I was just hoping she'd get in touch first."

"What's the difference?"

"I need a sign that she trusts me. That's going to be important."

Honigwachs's tone was intense, commanding. "I'm

counting on you, Camille. If she's suspicious of you, you've got to turn her around in a hurry."

"I've thought about it. I've got an idea."

She had to keep it to herself for another minute, as their food was arriving. Both ate rapidly, and Camille, in particular, wolfed her sandwich down. The second grilled cheese was neatly wrapped in wax paper.

"So what's the idea?" Honigwachs asked once the coast was clear.

"Okay. Andy told you that Lucy wants to gather evidence, right? So far it's the two of them, her and Andy. I'll convince Lucy that she'll need help. I'm going to squeeze my way in, and I'm going to do it by suggesting that my boyfriend joins us. And no, I don't mean you."

Honigwachs was appalled. Both his hands fell to the tabletop with a thump. "He's a cop!"

"Exactly. But he's my cop."

"No way, Camille, are you mad?"

She again leaned forward to drive her point home. "Wiener, if Lucy knows what I think she knows, sooner or later she'll bring information to the cops. Better we do it in a situation I control. I go to Charlie. I tell him that Lucy can't go down for the crime, because if she goes down, I go down. I work it so Charlie's protecting me. You're already protected. You're so well insulated you have nothing to worry about. No one can link any aspect of this to you."

"Andy can," Honigwachs put in.

"How come?"

"I sent him down with new stock for Lucy. I arranged that with him."

"You twit! You bonehead!"

"All right, a mistake, but Andy is on our side."

"That doesn't matter! You don't give anybody a job to do that can be traced directly back to you! That's *basic!* It's your own damn rule!"

"I made a mistake. Now drop it." He put his hands up as though to physically repel any countervailing argument.

Camille crossed her legs under the table, folded her hands on top of it, and straightened her posture. She seemed quite prim. She wanted to be the calm one. "Something happened in New York that you don't know about. At first, I didn't think it mattered. Just some strange New York thing."

"What do you mean? What happened?"

She cleared her throat. "One of our patients was murdered. Smothered with a pillow."

Honigwachs offered back a quizzical expression. He seemed unimpressed. "He had a friend, I'm guessing. It was a mercy killing."

"Well, whoever the *friend* was who snuffed him, also took the trouble to sew his lips together with a needle and thread."

"What?"

"I've been going over it in my head. Andy was in New York then."

"What are you saying? Come on, Camille. You're getting out there."

She lowered her voice so that he had to lean in to hear her. "How much do you really know about him? That's all I'm asking. If you think about it, you don't know Andy from Adam. He's a hooligan, with the charm of an angel. But what do you know? So think about it, Werner. At the very least, be careful around him."

He slumped back in the booth, and exhaled. "Oh God," he murmured.

Placing her elbows on the table, Camille crossed her arms. "This is what I'm thinking. We'll have our little playgroup to get to the bottom of all this. Me, Lucy, Charlie, Andy. By bringing in Charlie, I get Lucy to trust me. Because I'm bringing in a cop, it's a sign of my commitment, it proves that I want to know the truth just as much as she does, that I've got nothing to hide. Charlie will be anxious to defend me, but clueless. He'll let me know everything that comes through from the cop side of things. Me and Andy, we'll be on your side in all this, only Andy won't know where I'm coming from, so I get to keep an honest eye on him. Meanwhile, Lucy will be fighting her little fight, not knowing what's really happening. It's the only way, Wiener. I know Lucy. She's a demon! We can't let her take things out of our hands. Don't forget, I've got exposure here. I can be identified. I'm looking out for myself, not just you."

Werner Honigwachs studied her awhile. "You've been thinking about this."

"Somebody has to." She sipped her coffee.

"We need to know what they know." He spoke as though the course of action being suggested was his own.

"That's right. And if they learn more, we need to know that, too."

Honigwachs nodded. "There's a point—" he began to say.

"I know," Camille said softly. "I just can't bear to think about it. I won't think about it."

"If Andy is working for them against us—"

"No, please, don't think that way. Andy would cause such trouble! You know what I'm talking about."

Honigwachs engaged her eyes. "There's no immunity here. None. If someone needs to be removed from the scene, I won't hesitate."

"Please, don't talk that way. Would you even have the guts to do it?"

Honigwachs narrowed his gaze, continuing to nod, a rhythmic, menacing bob of his chin. "We're not there yet. But Andy would have to be finessed, if it came down to that."

"Oh, God. You would, wouldn't you? You'd have the guts?"

Honigwachs put his two fists together, side by side, facing forward. He then made a snapping motion, as though breaking a twig in half. "I think first," he told her. "When I act, I act. This is my time. I can feel it. I can feel how everything has been ordained. Nobody will step in my way. There's no point being stupid, but if I have to take out Lucy, I will take out Lucy. I'd do it right now, but I need to know what she knows. I need to know who she's talked to. Andy? Him too. Don't doubt me on that one."

Camille remained quiet, observing him for a while, then averting her gaze.

"It's a rough business," Honigwachs chided her. "You have to be in it for the whole game. Don't go squeamish on me, we don't have time for that."

"Don't speak of these things," she whispered. "Never again. Not aloud. Not in public."

He gazed at her coldly. "Stay on top of things, Camille. I want detailed, perfect reports of your meetings with the others. We won't go down that road unless it's absolutely necessary. But I need information."

"I'm on top of it. Now, tell me, Wiener, what about the science? Have we done it? Did we find what we're after? Have we marked the integrase enzyme yet?"

For the first time, he allowed a smidgen of a smile to sunny his sombre disposition. "I've talked to Largent. He thinks we've found the marker. He'll write up the tests as if they were performed on rats. That requires a certain amount of translation, and after that we'll pass the data through to Harry Hillier. It won't be long after that. Harry's brilliant, he'll locate the marker and figure out how to exploit it, at least in theory. He'll think he's won the Nobel Prize."

"Maybe he will."

Honigwachs laughed. "Whatever makes him happy. As long as I come away with about eight billion or more, they can elect him Pope for all I care."

"You'll get the check here, rich man? I have to scoot. Carole's in the car."

He nodded.

Camille covered one of his hands in hers and leaned very close. "You're the brains behind all this, Wiener. You set up the science, you set up the money end. Just remember, when the time came to get the job done properly and quickly you needed me. Hang tough. That's your only job right now. Don't think such dire thoughts! Everything will work as long as we do what has to be done. One little crisis with Lucy won't wreck anything."

She popped up from the booth then, excited by the next challenge. She wrapped herself up warmly and headed out.

She found Carole behind the wheel, pretending to drive, the keys in the ignition, the engine still running. A couple who had emerged from a Dodge Caravan were dismayed, but Camille Choquette murmured, "Lighten up," under her breath, and rewarded her daughter with a bright, happy smile. Then she discovered that her child had locked the doors.

"Open up, Carole. Open up for Mommy."

The little girl shook her head and stuck out her tongue.

Camille showed her the grilled cheese sandwich. "Do you want Mommy to throw it in the snow?"

Carole thought about that, and decided in the end that she'd rather unlock the front door. Her mother crawled in and commanded her to jump into the back seat. "Just for that little charade," Camille told her tersely, "I'm eating your sandwich myself. You'll just have to starve today."

That brought on protests and tears, and through it all Camille Choquette, driving away from the restaurant, made exaggerated sounds of pleasure as she consumed the grilled cheese. "Yummy," she said.

"Yummy, yummy in the tummy." The little girl pounded her fists against the back of the front passenger seat and wailed and her mother thought that that also was funny. She held up the final bite. Carole ceased her tantrum, hoping that it might be for her. Camille gave her a big smile in the rear-view mirror. *"Pop!"* She laughed, just before the bite vanished into her own mouth, and she chewed extravagantly while the child, astonished, stared at her with teary eyes, too shocked to bawl.

That week, Thursday, February 3, and Sunday, February 6, 1999

The three conspirators decided to meet at Lucy's house.

For reasons both apparent and unknown, each was wildly suspicious of the others. Andrew and Camille both believed that Lucy would be difficult to manage. She'd be obstinate in the face of any pragmatic proposal if it did not appeal to her intensely passionate nature. For her part, Lucy couldn't understand how Camille had been able to stick to the format of her job. Yes, she was supposed to examine the lab rats in the field and report her findings, but they were talking about human beings! Found dead and dying! How had she gone about her analytical work, calm and detached, as if detailing the march of a minor flu?

In the past, they had always managed to help people. The sick had been revived. The dying had had their days prolonged and the quality of their life improved. Suddenly, their patients had failed rapidly, succumbing overnight to a catalogue of plagues that relentlessly stalked them, now successfully. Yes, there had always been risks associated with administering untried drugs, but they had always had a beneficial, or at least a benign, result. That Camille had been witness to the carnage and had simply gone on about her work, just like always, as in the good old days of their successes, disturbed Lucy a great deal.

And Andy, why hadn't he returned to her room in Baltimore and warned her to stop? How could he have assumed that Luc would do that job? His explanation didn't wash.

Andy and Camille were leery of one another also. To Andy, Lucy's passionate conviction to help people made sense, it was true to her nature, but Camille seemed a cold fish to him, aloof. He did not know her well enough to say what motivated her, nor could he evaluate how she'd hold up under pressure. From the beginning, he had accepted her because Lucy did so, he'd gone along with her judgment. That Lucy was now distrustful raised a warning flag.

In turn, Camille distrusted him. She had heard through Honigwachs that he was vaguely linked to organized crime, whatever that might mean, but she also held to a private conviction that the poor boy was in love, and love could be a dangerous tonic to antisocial, criminal behaviour. People had been known to change, go straight, mend their ways to serve the tyranny of love. Even if he was trustworthy, lust or infatuation could distract him, cause him to slip. Camille would watch for any sign of weakness in him.

As Lucy answered Camille's knock, Andy was coming up the driveway in a rusty blue Chevy. He always seemed to be in a different vehicle. Camille was wearing a cockeyed smile and there were tears in her eyes, and at that signal Lucy did capitulate. The two friends hugged.

"Oh, baby," Camille whimpered, "this is so terrifying! It's so awful!" Both women wore jeans, as if their choice of clothes set the tone for the job ahead. It was time to work, to get things done, and to be practical. Nodding, the faces of dead friends they had both known vivid in her head, Lucy gave her pal another fierce hug.

Andrew Stettler was chugging up the stairs to her apartment above the garage. "Good," he said upon entering, "we're all here. Let's get down to it."

They thrashed things through. Being together proved their desire to tackle their problems as a group, but the discussion unearthed the doubts each had, and those had to be resolved.

"What Lucy's saying, Andy," Camille explained, "is that she doesn't buy it. You left her alone in Baltimore without telling her that she was killing people."

"Luc would tell her!" Andy protested, not for the first time.

"She doesn't buy into that theory."

"Well," Andy reiterated, appearing contrite, "it's not a theory. It's the truth."

Believing that Andy had been compromised by love, Camille encouraged Lucy to badger him, to see how he might respond. Stettler stood his ground. He had gone down to Baltimore with a job to do.

"I called Camille," he explained for the fifth time. "Together we decided that things had gotten out of hand. I told Luc, then got on a plane."

The explanation confirmed for Camille that Andrew Stettler was indeed the source of the leak—he had told Lucy, through Luc, about the deaths. But Camille now had to take into account the part that Luc had played in events, facts she hadn't been in possession of before. Luc had been treated by Lucy and had quickly failed. Sooner or later, Lucy would have understood the truth for herself, whether or not Andy told her. Sooner, obviously, was proving to be a problem, but telling her had not been fatal, given that she'd had evidence travelling alongside her, in the company of poor Luc. So his indiscretion, under the circumstances, was explainable. As well, Andy had been placed in a tough position, as his own friend was being treated and so was in mortal danger.

"How did that make you feel?" Camille asked him. Only after she had posed the question did she realize that it was inappropriate, given her position here. She was supposed to be one of them, not an agent for Honigwachs. She had wanted to know how he felt about the situation as a conspirator, but she was not supposed to have that information.

"What?"

She had to push on. "Luc being sick. How did that make you feel?"

"Listen," he said, and he placed a hand over his heart in an overt gesture of sincerity, "I've been a lab rat myself. You don't think that every time you inject somebody he doesn't have a twinge of fear, a worry? In New York you told me that things were bad. Then I find out that a buddy of mine is really sick, and it makes me wonder. I called for your latest report. I was hoping you'd tell me that things were getting better. That it was a freak situation. But that wasn't the answer you gave me. So I told Luc the bad news, then headed home, because this was a major security issue, and my job at BioLogika happens to be security."

The response, as Camille analysed it, suited the discussion alive in the room. She knew that Andy had already known that men were dying. He had been in on it from the beginning. He was privy to whatever Honigwachs knew. But what had possessed him to contact her? If he had already anticipated the problems he was facing now, then he was just plain brilliant, a genius in matters of deception. She admired him, but at the same time her antennae warned her to be careful. His explanation, she noted, did serve to placate Lucy.

"What about you?" Andy asked Camille. "Weren't you freaking out when you found people dead or dying? Didn't you report back with that?"

"Who to, bozo? The people behind this don't want to hear from us. Let's say it's Honigwachs. We can assume it's Honigwachs. But you know, he doesn't ever come out and say so. Nobody ever comes out and says they're doing it, or what we're doing is for them. I get my marching orders on the sly, secretly, coded. When things go wrong, like they did this time, I don't exactly have anybody to complain to, or to ask for advice. In this organization, you got to understand, the buck stops nowhere."

"I don't know, Camille," Lucy interjected, "we're talking about people dying."

"No, no, listen to me, I did call Honigwachs. I did call Randall Largent. They didn't want to hear from me. I kept trying to code it for them, to let them know that somehow they had to reach me and talk to me. When Andy showed up in New York, and then called from Baltimore, I figured that that was it. That was their way of getting in touch. Andy, I believed you were acting for the higher-ups, that that was my chance to let people know what was happening. Otherwise, I wouldn't have told you everything I did."

She thought that she was pretty brilliant, too—up there in the same league with Andrew Stettler—but Lucy did not seem to share the same impression.

"You set up the schedule, Camille, you could've found some way to track me down to stop me."

A difficult point to counter. Camille knew right away that she was in trouble here. "The schedule had gone kaflooey, remember? Not to mention, do you have any idea what it was like for me? Lucy, how did you feel when you found out about it? And you only heard about it word of mouth, a rumour maybe, nothing confirmed. Me, everyday I had to go into the houses of people who had lost their loved ones. I had to ask them really personal questions about the progress of the disease. I had to find out what this was all about. I had to visit the dying. Do you know, can you imagine, the torment they were in? I was upset, I was scared, I was trying to get in touch with Montreal and have them do something. I didn't *believe* what was right in front of my eyes. I thought about trying to get in touch with you, but how easy was that? I was in a daze, Lucy."

The speech was the best that she could do, but it didn't really clear up all the issues regarding her behaviour.

Camille added, "I'm sorry. I guess I screwed up." She kept her eyes downcast.

"It's understandable," Andy offered, "under the circumstances. It's not like anybody was prepared for this. The question is, what are we going to do? The two of you are in trouble, no matter how you look at it, but laying the blame on each other—I don't see how that works for anybody."

Lucy was tense, taut. She was sitting with her legs apart and her elbows on her knees. She covered her face with her hands, as though to conceal or perhaps contain her fury. She felt confused, apologetic and accusatory, and certainly she did not know what to do and had no solutions to propose.

Across from her, in the deep cushions of a sofa, Camille opted to play her magic card. In a weak position here, she had not been able to properly explain an aspect of her behaviour. She needed to elevate her position, and she needed to be trusted. "I think," she proposed, "that you guys should let me tell Charlie."

The suggestion altered the current in the room.

"What the hell for?" Andy asked.

"What are you thinking, Camille? Go straight to jail? Do not pass Go?"

She raised her hands in an attitude of surrender, but forged on with her argument. "I know it sounds weird. But Charlie loves me. I can explain it to him. I can paint it so that he *has* to save me, and that means saving Lucy. He can help us through the legal stuff. He might be able to contribute with a side-investigation of his own. At the same time, if we get into trouble, he can tip us off. I mean, it's golden. My boyfriend's a cop. Right now, that could be the motherlode."

Lucy sighed and shifted her weight around. "He's not exactly a big-shot cop."

"He's not exactly *big*," Andy put in, hoping to add a touch of levity.

Both Lucy and Camille did laugh, a little.

Camille took them up on their criticisms, using their points to her advantage. "That's what I'm saying. He's a cop, but not true blue. Nobody likes him on the force, they think he's a little guy with family connections. So he'll work on our side, I'm sure of it, because he doesn't give a damn about other cops. He's no hotshot, Lucy, but he has rank. He has—what's the word? *Latitude*, you know? He can help."

That night they couldn't resolve the issue, despite talking it through repeatedly. A few days later, Lucy finally relented. She was willing to let Charlie Painchaud help them out, hoping that he would guide her through the legal entanglements and keep her out of trouble. Almost any gambit seemed worth a try— doing nothing irritated her the most. Andy hated the idea, but when he brought the notion on the sly to Werner Honigwachs his boss advised him to go along with it. He explained that they'd have an inside track on what the cops were thinking. Sooner or later, he forewarned, cops would be involved. In the long run, it was better to have one around that Andy could befriend. Reluctantly, Stettler agreed—he had little choice—and Charlie Painchaud became part of the counter-conspiracy.

At his first meeting, on the following Sunday night, again above Lucy's garage, Charlie listened to their stories. He was appalled to find his girlfriend in such a serious jam, one with monumental repercussions. He assured both women that when the time came and they cooperated with the authorities to bring the real culprits to justice, they could probably leverage their testimony and walk freely away. What counted most was making absolutely certain that the men behind the crime were brought to justice. Otherwise, their own necks were seriously on the line.

Lucy liked that. She appreciated the leadership role that Charlie assumed.

He went on to say that his own department was a morass, a cesspool, that he himself was not the most experienced detective in the world, certainly not with a crime of this magnitude. He suggested that they lure a frontline cop onto the case, that they get a major detective to snoop around, that that would go a long way toward getting the job done. He did not believe that they could go it alone.

Lucy was again impressed, although Andrew and Camille were fit to be tied.

"Who?" Lucy asked.

"Sergeant-Detective Émile Cinq-Mars, from the Montreal Police."

They all knew the name. He was famous for both his integrity and his skill. His reputation was such that neither Andy nor Camille could object without generating suspicion.

"Let's do it," Lucy weighed in. A hesitation she had had with Charlie was his close association with Camille and his insignificance as a cop. Now he was offering a legendary detective independent of everyone in the room. "Let's go for it."

Neither Camille nor Charlie joined in her enthusiasm.

"We've got to be careful," Charlie cautioned. "We'll arouse his interest in the case. He won't have jurisdiction. Give it to him piecemeal, educate him slowly, entice him. We need Cinq-Mars to learn to respect and trust Lucy and Camille. That'll take time. Lucy, you'll call him. Camille, we'll use your fishing hut on the lake for the meeting. No, better—we'll ask him to rent his own fishing hut and meet him there."

Camille could not sustain an objection, not when she'd been the one to invite Charlie into their group. Andy had nothing to say, except, "All right."

"What's your problem?" Lucy asked him. "Speak up."

"He's a cop. Cinq-Mars is a cop. It's habit. I'm sorry, Charlie, but I don't like cops. Hello! I'm an ex-con, remember? Cops come around, I feel queasy."

He had no argument to defeat the suggestion, and after a discussion they agreed to set up a meeting with Cinq-Mars if they could for the following Sunday morning.

"How do we get him to come, without a reason?"

Charlie pondered the matter. "He fishes on the lake. I've seen him there a few times when I've been with Camille. As a matter of fact, his photograph is up at the diner for catching a big *doré*. That'll interest him, being invited to his own fishing hole. That's one reason why I chose the lake. Also, I can dig up his home phone. He'll notice that, too. With those two curiosities, he'll show."

"Sunday," Andy repeated.

"Sunday."

"Finally," Lucy enthused, "we're doing something."

Camille was not happy. The famous detective was not the timid lover she could control, and this hotshot cop was being invited practically next door to her fishing hut. But she was stuck. She couldn't define her concerns without implicating herself. "All right," she agreed. "Let's do it."

"Cops," Andrew Stettler muttered, shaking his head. "First one. Now two. Any cop gives me the shivers. Even you, Charlie. I don't know what it is." He'd been outvoted. He had no way to put the brakes on this development. He wondered how Werner Honigwachs would react. His employer had wanted the first cop around, would he also approve of the second? The others were gazing at him, wondering if he had a point to make. Andy shrugged. "Cops," he repeated, as though that explained everything.

After dinner out, and a few drinks at a bar downtown, Andrew Stettler returned home. Along the way he parked the Chevy he was driving and picked up his regular Oldsmobile for the remainder of the trip. He entered his duplex as quietly as possible, hoping not to arouse the attention of his mother. Upstairs, he took off his shoes and walked softly on the carpeted floor.

He phoned Werner Honigwachs on his cellular.

"There've been some developments," he told him.

"We should meet," Honigwachs snapped. "No more phone calls."

"When and where?"

"Tomorrow. At work. I'm free at eleven."

"See you then."

No sooner had he hung up than his mother's coded knock thumped his door. The wonder of that woman. She should have been the spy, he thought.

Stettler went into the bathroom and turned on the shower, then answered the front door.

"Home alone?" she asked. His body blocked the doorway.

"Not exactly," he lied.

"Andy."

"What?"

"Is she someone special or just a floozy from the bar."

"A bar-chick, Ma, and no, you can't meet her. She's in the shower."

"At least she's willing to wash. The two of you snuck in here like a couple of cat burglars, Andy. I thought you were a thief!"

"You thought no such thing. I didn't want to disturb you, Ma, because I don't want you coming up here bugging me."

"Why, are you ashamed of her?"

"You could say that," Stettler said.

His mother shook her head, smiled, then sighed heavily as she ventured downstairs. "The life you lead," was her parting remark.

Andrew Stettler closed the door.

Yes, he was thinking, *the life I lead*.

The phone rang, disrupting that brief reverie. The call display did not reveal who was calling, indicating that it probably originated from a pay phone. Andy picked up. "Hello?"

Honigwachs. "Change of plans. I'm worried about security."

"That's my department."

"Then get a handle on it, Andy! We'll play squash. Talk there. I don't want you showing up at the office for a while."

"What time?"

"Eight."

"All right. Sounds cloak-and-daggery," Andrew Stettler said.

"That's the way it's got to be, Andy, from now on. See you then."

Stettler put down the phone. His boss was rapidly becoming paranoid. He usually appreciated paranoia in a client. Fear created opportunities he could exploit. There was, he knew, much to fear. He wondered, with some anticipation, how Werner Honigwachs would react if he learned that the celebrated city detective, Émile Cinq-Mars, might be bumped off.

He was thinking about it. It would be a big step, knocking off a cop. A famous cop, especially. There'd be shit to pay for that, so the benefits would have to be large.

Stettler turned off the shower, then went to his fridge and helped himself to an individual-sized raspberry yoghurt. He retrieved a spoon off the dish rack by the sink. In his small living room, he slumped down in a big comfy chair, his legs slung over the armrest, and ate slowly, thoughtfully. He was tempted to see what was on the tube, but his mother might seize the opportunity. If she thought all he was doing was watching television, she might invite herself up to meet his date. Instead, Stettler sat in the dark and thought things through. He already had something in mind, but he needed to look at the benefits and weigh the consequences. His best option from various perspectives, he was guessing, and convincing himself by the minute, was to order the assassination of the Montreal detective, and tell Honigwachs about it in advance.

That's what he would do. At his meeting with Honigwachs, he'd let him know that a new cop was on the scene, none other than Émile Cinq-Mars. He'd listen to the man fulminate and fret. Then he'd tell him that he was going to have him killed. He'd make sure that Honigwachs understood that he had no say in the matter. Just to keep him in his place, to keep him apprised of how the real world—the world in which he found himself—worked.

Andrew Stettler licked the last of his yoghurt from the container with his tongue. It had been a long time since he had exercised the full power at his disposal. He anticipated that his associates would object to the victim being a cop. He'd have to talk them through that. He'd have to demonstrate that too much was at stake. Tons of money, for openers. Not millions—billions. That would impress them. He'd point out that the time was right, for the gang had no particular grievance against Cinq-Mars at the moment and therefore would invite no suspicion out of the ordinary. His gang always got away with murder anyway. The last time anyone had been convicted of a gang hit was way before anyone's time. If they used their media and internal police sources to protest that they weren't involved, they might not have to endure excessive heat. In terms of convincing the gang members, it wouldn't be hard to summon an array of grievances against this particular cop. That being the case, Andrew Stettler was confident that, through tact and strong argument, by measuring the payoff against the hurt they'd have to go through, he could persuade his people to dispose of the legendary detective.

He needed the spectacular hit. An end move to corral his prey. The drug project had proceeded as planned. Soon, money would be flowing into BioLogika in unprecedented amounts. He needed to implant more than mere paranoia in the brain of Werner Honig-wachs. He needed the company president to tremble at the sight of him. Now was the time to seize full control of the entire operation, and the best way to do that was through a show-crime. See, fella? This could happen to you, too. Honigwachs would also fear the police, know-ing that he was loosely attached to a cop's murder. He'd be broken, fearful, compliant, anxious to protect himself and willing to cooperate. But for his own good, his own enlightenment, he needed to be removed from his exec-utive suite and have his nose swished around in a cesspool, and he needed to have his natural cockiness surgically removed, as if it were a malignant tumour. Honigwachs needed to be convinced of the true might and the absolute authority of his colleagues. Time to turn down the lights on his party.

As for the cops, Stettler theorized, they'd get over it. Various departments would be in an uproar for months, but where would they look? All the obvious suspicions would lead nowhere. If anything came out about the drug deaths in the United States, if anything led investigators north, the local cops wouldn't take much of an interest, not when they had a cop-killing on their hands.

Stettler smiled. There were more benefits. The death would give Lucy and the others pause. They'd not connect it to their own enterprise—why should they? But a doubt would fester. They'd move more fearfully. They'd be increasingly distrustful of one another. Their petty counter-conspiracy would disintegrate, going nowhere, accomplishing nothing.

As an added bonus, he believed that he might be saving Lucy's life. Given the money at stake and the personalities involved, Honigwachs might be foolish enough to eliminate Lucy. If he was smart, if he had the nerve, he should do it. He probably had it in mind, it would only be a matter of figuring out how. Honigwachs was probably just waiting for the opportunity. One hadn't come up, as Lucy was defending her home on Indian land with a shotgun and not going out in public. Stettler believed that if he informed Honigwachs that the police detective was going to die, and the president subsequently read about the killing in the papers, the man would not presume to act independently. He'd leave Lucy alone, or get permission first. He'd be putty, Play-Doh in Stettler's hands. He'd tell him to leave Lucy alone, which would only help to keep him nervous.

The time had come to put the BioLogika Corporation under foreign ownership, and the aliens in charge would be the mob.

Returning to the kitchen, Andrew Stettler dropped the yoghurt container in the trash, then washed his hands. This would be a major play for him, the biggest of his career. He was pretty sure that he had everything covered.

8

DARK IS THE GRAVE

The following weekend,
Saturday night into Sunday morning, February 12–13, 1999

Andrew Stettler believed that the meeting had gone well. At the squash club, he had let Werner Honigwachs know that his universe was to be guided differently from now on, that the planets would be altering their orbits. He had told him that the policeman would have to die.

"Look up," he instructed Honigwachs in the change room.

Sitting with his pants off in front of his locker, the company president did so.

"No, sir," Stettler corrected him. "That's down for you. Now look down."

Confused, Honigwachs stared at the patch of floor between his bare feet.

"Wrong again. That's up for you now. Don't worry. You'll figure it out."

Honigwachs phoned him later on. He invited him to come out to fishing shack on the lake, near BioLogika. Andy was both suspicious and wary. He had told Honigwachs that the meeting with the Montreal cop was to take place nearby the very next morning, and he questioned the wisdom of visiting the lake that night.

Honigwachs appealed to his sense of mystery. "There's stuff you should know that you don't know yet, and the best place to find it out is on the lake. You don't want to meet that cop in that fishing shack without talking to me first."

He didn't like it, but he had to accept the terms. "All right."

Honigwachs knew what he had to do. Had Stettler not betrayed them? He had told Lucy, through Luc, about the drug cocktails being lethal. Perhaps he could be forgiven for that, but there was no discounting his latest threat. Andrew Stettler had taunted him and promised the death of a policeman. He had vowed to turn his world upside down. When Honigwachs had reported that news to Camille, she'd told him, "He's trying to scare you."

"He succeeded."

"No, you don't get it. He's trying to scare you once and for all. Why would he tell you about something like that ahead of time? He wants you in his pocket."

"Oh, God, what a mess."

Camille had tried to soothe him over the phone. Before long, they had agreed to meet at a bar halfway between BioLogika and Hillier-Largent.

The room was windowless, with a plethora of TV sets tuned to yesterday's hockey games and six-month old golf, all that was being broadcast on a dull day. Camille was waiting for him when Honigwachs strode inside.

"I didn't think it would come to this," she said. She was declining to look at him, but he knew what she meant.

"It hasn't," Honigwachs said.

"Stettler has to go."

"Don't be a drama queen, Camille."

She scooped up her purse then and started to slide

out of the booth, but Honigwachs grabbed her wrist. "Sit down, Camille," he said calmly.

She did. This time she stared at him across the table. "Stettler has to go," she repeated.

"Why?"

"He's part of the mob. Andy knows we're sitting on a fortune. He knows about all the necessary stuff we had to go through to get where we are today. Killing a cop is stupid, unless you see it for what it is. He's out to get you. Now that you've done your work and made your strike. As BioLogika stock rises he'll own you, own us, own this operation. You have to strike first, Werner. I can't believe it's come to this point, I can't believe I'm saying this, but there's no alternative."

"What makes you so sure?"

"He told you he's killing the cop. What killer, what mob guy, would say that unless he had a reason to say that? What's his reason, Werner. Damn it! Think!"

Honigwachs gazed at her awhile. Their waitress came and went and returned with their drinks, and he continued to stare.

They did not exchange another word at that meeting. He departed soon after finishing his drink, and they did not speak again until after Honigwachs had commanded Stettler to meet him in Camille's shack. The next time they met was to concoct a plan for which everything was already in motion.

And now, after asking Andy to wait in the car, he was calling Camille to check that she was prepared and to build up his courage.

He dialled the company cell phone he had lent her.

"I'm bringing him over."

"I'm ready," Camille said. "Are you?"

The phone shook in his hand. "I'm ready," he testified, sounding as though he was trying to convince himself.

"This is the only way we can go, Werner."

"That's what you keep telling me."

"Werner, you have to be sure. You have to be absolutely certain."

"I am."

"Do you have the guts, Werner?" she asked him quietly.

"Watch me," he whispered.

"Shoot straight."

"He'll be an inch away."

Honigwachs drove Stettler down to the lake and parked at the nearby strip mall, then the two men walked the short distance onto the ice. Under a full moon, the lake with its blanket of snow shone in the dark, the fishing huts gently emitting smoke from their tin chimneys in the snapping cold. Arriving at a hut, Honigwachs opened the door, his smile having expanded to a broad beam. As he stepped inside, Andy was in for a surprise, even while a lurking suspicion was being confirmed—the hut belonged to Camille Choquette, and she was there to greet him.

"Come on in, Andy. Take a load off."

"What's this about?"

"Come in first."

There wasn't all that much room for the two men to remove their outerwear without bumping into one another. When they sat down on opposite bunks, they found the cabin quite toasty.

"I've had a problem," Werner Honigwachs announced. "This is my way to solve it."

"What problem's that?" The president had called him away from a quiet night at home. Andy's shirt was an earth-tone green, something he usually put on only around the house. He'd dropped his good jeans into the laundry his mother had going and so had thrown on an old pair with frayed cuffs and holes worn in the hip pockets. The denim was thin for the cold, and he appreciated the stove's heat.

"Tomorrow, you and Camille have a meeting with Sergeant-Detective Émile Cinq-Mars."

"That's right."

"The two of you should go into that meeting with the knowledge that you're on the same team. That's what I think." Honigwachs himself was casually dressed for this occasion, as if he had just come from putting his kids to bed. He wore a bulky wool sweater and corduroy pants.

"We are?"

"You are."

Andy put a hand to the back of his neck and gave himself a gentle massage, as if he needed to relieve a pent-up tension. "Sir, I can see by your grin that you're feeling pretty pleased with yourself. Like you just swallowed a canary."

"I put one over on you, Andy. Admit it!"

"But anytime you want to compromise my identity to anyone, I might suggest that you check that out with me first. You told Camille about me?"

"Now listen, Andy—"

"No, asshole! You listen! *Don't* go around telling people who I am or what I do! Is that absolutely crystal clear?"

"Andy—"

"Is it? Crystal?"

Unaccustomed to being dressed down, Werner Honigwachs needed time to come around. He sighed heavily and looked around the cabin, anywhere but at the two people in it, and finally he conceded that he had missed a step. "I'm sorry about that, Andy. You're right. You're right. I should have checked first."

"Of all the harebrained—"

"I should have checked first. You're absolutely right on that."

"Okay. All right," Andy said, tamping down his rage. "So. Camille. You're in the loop."

"You're good, Andy. I'll give you that. You're really good."

He accepted her compliment with a wry smile. "You're not so bad yourself."

"Tell me …" Camille asked. She closed her hands over her crossed knees, shaking the dangling foot.

"What?"

"Your thing with Lucy. Is that for real? Do you love her? Or are you just, you know, stringing her along?"

Andy laughed lightly. "As you said, I'm good at what I do. That's the kind of detail that you will never know, Camille. You'll have to guess."

"You're the master."

"If you say so." He turned to face Honigwachs again. "What's this about?"

Honigwachs smiled and opened his hands in a gesture of conviviality. "I thought we'd fish, Andy. And, of course, discuss tomorrow's meeting."

"All right," the younger man agreed. "We can do that."

"Good. Camille? You're the expert. Show us how it's done."

She opened the floorboards for the men and saw to it that they both had lines with hooks and bait. Andy insisted on hooking his own minnows.

"Tell me something, Camille," Andy said. "I always wanted to ask you. I just never found the right … moment. You're a scientist, right?"

"I know my way around a lab."

"You're educated?"

"Is that such a shock?"

"Not at all. I know you're a bright woman. But, you know, you and me, we can both tell, we're from the same kind of background. You know? More or less." He paused to concentrate on hooking a minnow. "I think it's great that you got an education, I'm just curious about it, that's all. I don't mean to insult you."

The question struck a chord. Camille was interested in answering. "I liked science. That was one thing. When I was a kid. But probably I never would've gone to school, to university, if I hadn't had a benefactor."

"A benefactor?"

"Yeah."

"Now be careful, Camille." He lowered his hook through the ice into the water. "You know what some people would call a benefactor."

"No. What?"

"A sugar daddy."

Having gotten the men settled away, she spooned coffee into a pot for perking over the stove. Camille laughed lightly. "Nothing like that. I never actually met our benefactor."

"What do you mean, 'our'?" Honigwachs asked, getting interested in the story himself.

"My dad and me."

"Why did you and your dad have a benefactor, Camille?"

The way Andy posed the question startled her. She stopped what she was doing in mid-motion and stared at him, her spoon hovering above the pot. "You're kidding me," she said.

"How's that?" Andrew Stettler bobbed his line in the water, as though nothing else could interest him at the moment.

"You know. You bastard. You *know.*"

Honigwachs looked from one to the other and back again. "What are you talking about?" he asked finally. "What does Andy know?"

Camille continued to wait, and stare. Abruptly, she broke off her gaze and finished what she was doing.

"What do you know?" Honigwachs asked Andy.

"Camille had a brother." Andy looked at her at last

to gauge her reaction. "He was killed in his youth. Gunshot. Tragic. Wrong place, wrong time, that sort of thing. Well, associates of mine—"

"Hell's Angels?" Honigwachs wondered out loud.

Andy shot him a stern glance. "You can't expect me to answer that."

"I understand. I'm sorry. Go on. Your associates—"

"—felt sympathetic."

Camille made an odd sound, a kind of snort.

"You don't agree?" Andy asked her.

"Guilty, I would say. They felt guilty."

Andrew Stettler stared down at his fishing hole for a few moments, and then began to nod. "You could be right about that. Associates of mine—I mean the older crew, you know?—they felt some guilt for the incident. Nobody wants to see the innocent die. It's bad public relations. They contacted the dead boy's father and, as I understand it, offered to pay for the education of the family's remaining child."

Again, Honigwachs looked from one young person to the next. "That other child," he asked finally, "that would be Camille?"

"That would be me," Camille concurred. After putting the coffeepot on the stove, she stood with her hands on her hips. "Did you bring a bottle, Werner?"

"Oh, shit." He slapped his forehead. "I left it in the car."

"I don't need a drink," Andy said.

"I do," Camille barked out.

"All right," Honigwachs offered. "I'll walk back and get it. It was my own fault."

"Just give me your car keys. I'll take the Ski-Doo. Be back in a second."

Honigwachs put the little stick-holder for his fishing line down, stood, and went through his coat pockets in search of his keys. Camille put on her one-piece snow-mobile outfit.

She was going out the door when she paused and shut it tightly again. "We don't agree with you," she said, "about the cop thingamajigger."

"Camille," Honigwachs protested. He put his coat back down but remained standing.

"What thingamajigger?" Stettler asked.

"You know," Honigwachs said.

Stettler glanced between the two of them.

"The murder thing," Camille specified.

"You told her?" Stettler was clearly angry again.

"She's in the loop."

"Not my loop, she isn't. You told her about a cop-killing? Are you crazy?"

"I wanted her advice," Honigwachs demurred.

"Here's my advice. Shut the fuck up. Now I'll have to rethink. Too bad I already gave that order."

Honigwachs was mortified. "You did?"

"Call it off," Camille suggested.

"Yeah?" Stettler asked her. "That helps you out how?"

"We're all in this together."

"No we're not. I'm not in this with you. I didn't ask this asshole to blab to the whole world about my plans."

Honigwachs appeared offended. "It wasn't the whole world—"

"It was a big enough chunk!" Stettler told him. *"Jesus H. Christ!"*

Camille had said her piece, and so she went outside in search of alcohol. The two men who remained behind sat in a glum mood.

"Un-freaking-believable," Stettler mumbled.

Honigwachs took a stab at changing the mood. "That's quite a story," he said, while he continued to search through his pockets for something. "About Camille. I guess that's one way to get an education."

"There was more to it than that."

"Oh? Hey, just grab hold of my line there, Andy. Thanks. I wouldn't want a big one to slip away."

Outside, the snowmobile sputtered, then roared.

Andrew Stettler leaned across the hole in the water to retrieve the other line. From the pocket of his winter coat, Honigwachs pulled out a pistol.

The Ski-Doo revved louder.

The barrel of the gun grazed the back of the young man's neck and the older man's hands shook and Stettler jerked slightly.

"Oh shit," Stettler said under his breath. He bolted up.

Honigwachs fired.

He shot him through the neck.

Stettler fell face forward. His body continued to flex and thrash. Honigwachs slumped down onto the floor, suddenly unable to stand. He was breathing heavily and erratically, and outside the snowmobile continued to roar. Stettler's feet started kicking.

"Oh God, oh God," Honigwachs said.

Suddenly his voice was loud as the snowmobile was shut down.

The door opened, and Camille Choquette stepped back inside.

"Oh God. Oh God."

"What? Werner, what's wrong?"

"He's not dead. He's not dead yet!"

His head at the rim of the fishing hole, Andrew Stettler flopped like a hooked walleye.

Camille Choquette shut the door quickly.

"Damn it! Did you miss? How could you miss?"

"He's not dead," Honigwachs said.

Stettler's legs trembled and kicked, but there was little life in him.

"You missed? From an inch away?"

"Start your Ski-Doo again," Honigwachs ordered, getting a grip on himself and breathing deeply. He struggled up to his knees. "I was nervous, all right? I'll shoot him a second time."

"Don't be an idiot!" Camille scolded him. "You can't attract attention. Do something else. Drown him. Drown him like a kitten. Do something, Werner!"

"Camille, my God."

She shook him. "You have to do it! You can't stop now!"

He took a deep breath, then stood and moved above the trapdoor, stepped down onto the ice, and, without any further hesitation, pressed his boot onto the back of Stettler's head. He shoved his face into the water where it flooded up into the ice-hole, and he held him there while his arms flapped and his legs trembled. All the while, Honigwachs just looked up at the ceiling. He held him there until the young man moved no more, and after that continued to keep his face buried underwater.

Camille held her chin in her hand and stared.

Then Honigwachs raised his boot and the body below him remained motionless.

"He's done," Camille said, and Honigwachs finally looked over at her. He still held his gun.

"Shit," he said. "Ah, shit, he didn't die."

"What's your problem?"

"Camille!"

"Werner, pull yourself together. We have work to do."

He stared at the body awhile, then nodded. He stepped out of the hole onto the floor of the cabin, drawing himself up to his full height, as though assuming his place in all of this and shaking off the shock of his own action. "All right," he said. "Let's get it done."

Together they pulled Stettler's face out of the water and turned him over onto his back. He lay on the ice with his knees and lower legs perched on the cabin floor. They dragged him to one side of the ice-fishing hole and arranged him out of their way, then Camille went outside and fetched a few tools.

She carried in a block-and-tackle attached to a hook and a length of chain.

She went out again and returned with an ice-block carrier.

Then she closed and locked the door.

By the light of the full moon and a single candle the two applied themselves to the task at hand. First Honigwachs, then Camille, chipped away at a crack in the ice. They had previously sawn out a block around the ice-hole with a chainsaw, which, as they had anticipated, had refrozen to the lake's ice. They laboured to break it free once again. Camille always kept a crowbar handy to shatter ice, and she used it now to attack the fault lines around the block, and it was partially freed.

They worked steadily, methodically, calmly. Honigwachs utilized his strength and conditioning as both a squash player and a horseman, pacing himself but refusing to rest. He needed another hour to separate the block from the frozen lake.

On his back on the ice, Andrew Stettler's body froze. The cabin went cold.

The huts were constructed of debris taken from job sites, and for this one a hefty frame supported a stout roof beam. Camille wound the heavy chain around the beam. She attached the block-and-tackle to the chain and placed the ice-carrier on the hook, lowering it to the water. She had to fuss with it, but eventually they managed to grip the block of ice with the carrier and raise it higher, with Honigwachs pulling on the rope and Camille working the crowbar to good advantage. When the block dangled above the lake, swinging slightly on its apparatus as the old timbers creaked with the strain, Honigwachs spun a knot and the two sat down to rest.

"The fire's gone out," Honigwachs noted.

"Nobody needs to see our smoke."

"Let's move the body a bit. I don't want him freezing to the ice."

"Right."

They shifted Stettler a little, until they were certain that he wasn't stuck.

"Bastard," Honigwachs said, still emotional. "He blew the whistle on us."

"Organized crime, my ass. He was weak. He found out his friend was being treated so he blew the whole operation, then tried to finesse his way out. I still say the dumb prick fell in love."

"Don't take that organized crime thing too lightly, Camille. The last thing we want is to have those guys breathing down our necks."

"It's the perfect crime, Werner. Nobody can look at you for this."

"Hope so."

Camille stood and picked up the bait bucket half-filled with water. Ice had frozen on the water's surface and she broke through it with several light taps of the crowbar, then slid the minnows into a bowl. She stood the candle alongside the bowl to help keep the water warm.

"What did you do that for?" Honigwachs asked.

"I need the bucket."

"What for?"

"Wait and see."

The cold had penetrated the cabin, and it was colder still beneath the floorboards, where the ice in the ears, mouth, nostrils and lungs of Andrew Stettler continued to expand. Scant blood was evident, and what there was had congealed in the frigid temperature.

"All right," Honigwachs announced. "Let's get it done."

Together they hoisted the dead man up, and dropped him feet first into the lake, through the hole they'd cleared by removing the block of ice. His head bobbed in the opening. Using a plastic serving spoon, Camille held his hair and the top of his coat against the bottom of the ice, long enough for him to freeze in place.

"This way," she said, although they had already been through this, and she was merely confirming their agreement, "nobody will suspect I did it, not in my own shack. But that tramp Lucy will fear this. Fear she's next. That fancy cop they're bringing in, he'll have his hands full with this. He won't get around to much else."

"Imagine. Andy ordered him killed. A cop! He never consulted me. Wouldn't even listen to me when he told me about it."

"The cop might die anyway," Camille reminded him. "Andy being dead might not stop that. Not that I mind."

"Who knows? But we're not connected to it and we don't care. Not any more, that's for sure."

"Only Andy could betray us."

"He can't now," Honigwachs brayed.

"That's right." She stood beside him, holding his arm. She whispered, "We had to do this, Werner. You gave Andy the extra drugs for Lucy. He tied you to this. He was going to kill that cop and lord it over you. He was going to make your life miserable, squeeze the life's blood out of your company. What did he say to you about that?"

" 'Get it straight.' That's what he told me. 'Remember who's really in charge.' "

"Intimidation." She tugged his arm. "Who did he think he was? He was a sexy guy but, come on, he was a punk. Everything you've worked for should go to him? You're supposed to charge him an administration fee and be happy with that? That's a shakedown. That's not right, Werner. We had to do this. We had to test enzyme accelerators in order to discover their preferred script, and we had to do *this*."

Honigwachs nodded. "Funny. His last words were about you."

"Oh yeah? How romantic. What were they?"

"I can't remember. Something … I don't know."

"Come on. Relax. Think."

Honigwachs moved his arm around her shoulders and pressed her against his side. "Something about … that … there's more to your story than you told us. About your brother and your benefactor and all that. Something like that."

Camille put her arms around his waist. "I don't know what he meant."

Honigwachs sighed. "Andy could've made a link," he said, as though he still needed to justify the deed once again. This event put him close to the action. He was no longer safely ensconced in his suite while others performed his handiwork. "You know how cops make crooks talk. They threaten them with more jail time and the dickheads cough up everything they know.

"Once upon a time," Camille assured him. "Not any more. He's dead. He got what he deserved."

"He's out of the picture, that's the main thing. The one person nobody could trust is gone. We're in the clear."

"All the way, baby."

Satisfied that Andrew Stettler's corpse would not be floating away, Camille turned around. In a drawer she kept a hammer and chisel that she often used to chip away at the ice, and she did so now, down on her knees, this time to remove a coating of blood, hair, and frozen flesh. She gathered the contaminated shards of ice together in a heap, and used a cup to pick them up and drop them into the lake. Using the serving spoon again, she guided them under the ice-pack, away from the body.

She decided that the bullet must have gone straight down the ice-hole, as it was nowhere in evidence. *Good.*

Standing again, Camille worked on the block of ice dangling above the cabin floor, cleaning it of incriminating material and removing the shards. Then, with Honigwachs, she lowered the block back into place.

They sat on the benches, admiring their achievement.

Stettler's head bobbed in the dark aperture.

Camille stood at last and visited the minnows again. "I can use these tomorrow, make it look like I came here to fish. It's okay if they freeze. Once I put the stove on they'll thaw out." She slid them from one bowl into another, moving the water to stop it from icing just yet. Then she retrieved the bucket and leaned over the hole in the ice and, edging Stettler's head aside, filled it about a third full of water. She slowly poured the cold water over the old ice, filling the gouges she'd created to clean the surface of blood. She dug snow out from under the cabin floor and pressed that into the cracks as well, creating an old-looking patina. The fresh surface was smooth and quick to freeze. She and Honigwachs pulled the boards back into place and covered the corpse.

"That'll be some meeting tomorrow," Honigwachs imagined.

She kissed him.

Residual warmth continued to emanate from the stove, so Camille returned the minnows to the pail, which she then left on the stovetop. She'd let the candle burn itself out.

She took down the chain and packed the tools.

Having walked onto the ice, Honigwachs intended to walk off. First he'd mix his steps with hundreds of others. Camille would leave by snowmobile, so that neither person's identity or presence—nor Stettler's absence—would be noted by anyone, not in the dark, not out on the lake.

The last job in the cabin for Werner Honigwachs

was to take the pistol that he had used to shoot Andrew Stettler and wipe it clean of prints on a hand towel. When he was done, Camille, wearing her snowmobile mitts, took it from him. "They'll look for it underwater. I'll take it away from here."

She started up her Ski-Doo and roared off into the night, heading across the lake toward home. Knowing that she was defeating others—Lucy and Charlie and this new cop coming on the scene—gave her a sense of achievement, as though outwitting her foes was justification in itself. Charging across the lake under the bright winter moon she raised a fist in the air, shaking it with savage fury.

Approaching the far shore, in a part of the lake where the current was strong and where the ice broke up first every spring, she stopped her machine and buried the pistol deep in the snow. When the ice melted, the weapon would sink to the bottom of the lake. Until then, it would be well hidden.

Driving on, her satisfaction immense, and yet assailed by quirky spasms of guilt, Camille Choquette knew enough to kick off the negative feelings. She had planned a perfect murder. Honigwachs had done his job, even if he had missed slightly. At least he had pulled the trigger. Even better, Andrew Stettler had confessed to knowing associates familiar with the situation concerning her father and dead brother. That alone made her happy he was dead. He had said there was more to her story. Well, death had shut him up. "Yes!" she shouted under the roar of her engine. "There's more! You bastard! There's more!" Upon the pristine white of the frozen lake she was riding freely under an immaculate sky, observed only by the moon and stars.

Rather than dealing with the complication of hiring a babysitter, she had given her child a mild sedative and put her to bed with a brood of dolls, many of which were aged, raggedy and patched, left over from her own childhood and sewn together. Arriving home, Camille would have nothing more to do than tuck herself into bed and dream the dreams of the blessed. She was, she believed, home free.

She roared on.

THE INFLUENCE
OF DARK MATTER

9

JELLY ROLL

The next day, after midnight, Monday, February 14, 1999

Some fourteen hours following the discovery of
Andrew Stettler's murder, a blizzard that blew along
the Ottawa River Valley into Quebec crisscrossed the
Lake of Two Mountains and assailed the island city of
Montreal. Undulating like sand dunes, snow formed
ridges along the highways, where only the big rigs
travelled at that early-morning hour, and bore down
upon the Mohawk territory at Kanesetake and upon
the horse farms of St. Lazare. In the lakefront community of Hudson, yachts in their winter cradles lay
buried under a foot of fresh snow. Drifts swept across
the parking lots of empty shopping malls in the sleepy
outlying towns, and the storm advanced across the flat
suburbs of Montreal's West Island into the city proper.
Wind raged over Mount Royal, swirled above the
steep escarpment on the edge of downtown and along
the asphalt corridors between office towers, where the
homeless hunkered down next to heating ducts. Snow
scudded over the sloped rooftops of the English living
rich in Westmount and the affluent French asleep in
Outremont, blanketing the poorest streets of the south-
west and the East End. The storm played its brash
dance in streetlights, snow blanketing cars, piling

along sidewalks and over stairs, a nocturnal island city under siege.

Cinq-Mars slept peacefully in his country home, his wife beside him, their dog below the foot of their bed. If horses whinnied or stomped in their stalls they'd not be heard above the wind snapping at the outbuildings and trees and rooftops. Only the dog would look up as a gust shook a window for entry or yowled like the spirit of an ancestral canine in the chimney. Surfeited with their lovemaking, warm in one another's arms under a cosy duvet, the couple could only have been jarred awake by something as intrusive as a telephone's harsh jangle.

Which is what they heard.

As usual, Émile Cinq-Mars struggled up to answer.

He refused to keep a phone by his bed these days, having learned that the violence of calls in the middle of the night rattled him too deeply. He did not want the callous world in which he lived to also snooze alongside him. Cinq-Mars preferred to leave the room to take such calls, and now he was moving slowly, half-awake, staggering with the dog at his shins as if he were a blind man in need of guidance, shunting from one room to the other in a clumsy shuffle.

He cradled the phone to one side of his face, rubbing whiskers with his free hand, and sniffed his nasal passages clearer. "Yes?" he growled.

"Please. Detective—Cinq-Mars?—Sergeant? Help me." A woman's voice, faint, frightened, vaguely familiar, speaking English.

"Yes, this is Sergeant-Detective Cinq-Mars. Who's calling, please?" He and his wife used the small side room as a combination of office and study, a place to relegate bills that could tolerate delayed payment, scribble shopping lists or address Christmas cards. The walls had required no further decoration than shelves with books, and over time the space had acquired a worthy contribution of junk—maps, receipts, letters, to-do lists for the farm, paper clips, pencils, piles of magazines.

Faint, breathless, the woman was in distress. "I'm sorry. I'm so scared. I didn't know."

Wide awake now, he recognized the caller's voice. She was the woman whose anonymous, cryptic message had called him down to the lake during the daylight hours with an offer of information. "You never showed up, after promising you would."

"I was waiting for someone who never showed up either! Then cop cars were all over the place. Oh God. The guy I was waiting for, he's the dead man! I never thought he'd be killed! I just heard his name on the TV news."

"The late-night news, you mean?"

"Yes."

"That was hours ago. You took a while to call." Cinq-Mars stifled a yawn with his fist. He didn't know if he was grilling his caller about anything of substance but, out of habit, he persisted.

"I had to drive home first."

"So you know the dead man."

"I do."

"Who are you? First tell me who you are, then tell me how you got my home phone number."

"That's so complicated." Her tone suddenly changed from a whispered whimper to an expression of rage. "I'm scared, don't you get it? I'm scared!"

"Are you in danger?"

"Yes! I mean, I think so. They killed Andy, didn't they? If they know about me I might be next. I know as much about everything as Andy does … did. Maybe more. Maybe less, I don't know."

Listening, Cinq-Mars knotted his brow and spoke in a tone that was lower, and even more stern. "*Who* will kill you? Who killed Andy?"

"You don't *understand!*" she cried out. "Nobody knows for sure. I can take one mighty good guess, but I can't believe he'd *do* something like that."

"Calm down, all right? First things first. Tell me who you are." Cinq-Mars picked up the phone-set in his free hand and paced toward the window. He had to snap the cord to guide it around a table leg. For the first time, he noticed the blizzard, the fierce machinations of the wind, the snow flying horizontally to the ground. Outside, the porch light and the spot above the stable door illuminated the snow swarming over his brand-new vehicle, a Pathfinder, parked in the barnyard.

"I can't tell you."

"Why not?"

"I have to be careful right now. I can't be seen with you! If they think I'm talking to a cop ... Oh God. I'm so *scared,* and I don't scare easily. We have to meet in private."

"Why did you choose to call me in the first place?" The agitation in her voice convinced him that he had not taken her fears seriously enough, and his voice softened as he sought to gain her confidence. "How'd you get my number?"

"That's a secret. I can't tell you right now. We had it because we were planning to talk to you."

"Why?" Cinq-Mars pressed his mystery caller.

"Because you're famous! We heard about you. We thought you could help. We thought we could trust you, maybe."

"I'm sorry, I meant, what was it that you were planning to tell me?"

The woman paused, as though to consider if she should speak her piece now. In that moment of quiet Cinq-Mars stopped listening. He moved to the side of the front window that overlooked his horse farm and peered carefully out, concealed by the dark and by the curtain.

"I'm so scared now," the woman was saying, sounding as though she needed encouragement to proceed.

Cinq-Mars had covered the mouthpiece. "Sandra!" he called back into the house. "Sandra!"

Propelled by the urgency in his voice, his wife was quickly on the move. She hurried into the room, wrapping her robe around herself. "Émile?"

"Take this." He held out the phone to her.

"Who is it?" His alarm spurred a rampant fear of her own.

"I don't know. A woman. Keep her on the line. She's frightened. Try to calm her down. Get whatever information you can."

"Émile?"

"Stay away from the window!" he told her as he bolted from the room. "Keep the lights off!"

Sandra Lowndes picked up the phone, asking tentatively, "Hello?" As she had seen her husband do, she peered around the edges of the curtain to observe what interested him so much, to see what had suddenly made him fearful.

The family dog, Sally, a mix but largely a Labrador retriever, was excited by this rare nighttime expedition by her master and leaped around as Cinq-Mars dressed hurriedly in the dark. This was not a season to be out chasing bad guys without dressing properly. He would have to put on his winter duds or be seriously disadvantaged. Possessing the element of surprise, he did not want to neutralize that benefit by being underdressed for the blizzard.

His passionate collapse into bed with Sandra did not serve him well now. Cinq-Mars had to operate in the dark, and finding socks and shoes, pants and a shirt, all merrily tossed off earlier, was difficult. *Damn!* This was not supposed to be how middle-aged married people made love! He hadn't even brushed his teeth. To his dismay, he discovered that he still wore a drooping condom. He peeled it away and tied a knot at the top, felt for the wastebin and tossed it in. Cinq-Mars ruffled through his closet and dresser drawers to find darker clothing, wanting to wear whatever might camouflage his presence in the night. Although—he already knew—the intruder wore white, to conceal his advance across the pasture of blowing snow.

Cinq-Mars heard his wife uttering soothing phrases as he worked his way downstairs with the dog. The dark was more pressing there. He riffled through a cupboard, identifying objects by touch and pushing them aside. Back in the days when his situation with motorcycle gangs had been highly volatile, he had armed his wife with a shotgun for her protection while alone on the farm. That was his weapon of choice now. Cinq-Mars located the gun and pulled it from its lair, knocking over a collection of brooms and mops as he did so.

Shells were elsewhere, well hidden.

Down on his knees on the kitchen floor, Cinq-Mars had to keep pushing Sally off him while he reached behind the lazy Susan in a corner cupboard for the secret cache, knocking over spices and soup cans in the process. Finally, he grasped the box of ammunition and pulled it out.

He moved from the kitchen to the den.

Cinq-Mars blindly explored a side table for his cell-phone, certain that he had left it there, close to the TV. His hand finally retrieved it and his thumb hit the power button. Green lights glowed in the dark. Cinq-Mars punched the quick-dial number for his own office, loading the shotgun at the same time.

"Operations," a woman's voice replied.

"X-ray Yankee Zulu," Cinq-Mars chanted in an emphatic whisper.

In an instant a man's voice came on. "Identify."

"Sergeant-Detective Émile Cinq-Mars. Intruder on the perimeter."

"Number?"

"One known. Firepower unknown."

"Intention?"

"Intervention."

"Cinq-Mars, negative."

"He's wiring my car! He could blow my house!"

"On the way."

"Out."

Cinq-Mars quickly scampered from the den and back through the kitchen to the rear mudroom, where he encountered a problem.

His winter clothes hung in the closet there, but opening the door to fetch them would automatically turn on the closet light. The light also had a chain, but he would still have to spring open the bifold doors, reach very high, perhaps jump, and snare the chain on his first try. A momentary blaze of light could not be prevented, and he could only hope that the outside intruder wouldn't notice. Fat chance. He prayed that whoever was messing with his car was so preoccupied with planting dynamite that he would not see him awake and on the prowl.

Cinq-Mars counted down from three. He yanked the doors open and jumped. In that prolonged moment he felt himself hang in the air, as if suspended, while his fingers found, then lost, then relocated the chain. As he fell back to the floor, the light was switched off and blackness again stood fast.

Blackness, and the snow-white raging of a nocturnal winter storm.

Sally was jumping on him, wanting to wrestle.

Cinq-Mars snapped the shotgun closed.

He listened at the door. Heard only the wind's whistling clamour.

The dog posed a dilemma. She was a good watchdog for Sandra in the sense that she'd announce a stranger's arrival, bark an alarm. But in the uproar of the winter storm, with the windows sealed, she had detected no intruder, and if she spotted one she'd only prance about and yap, perhaps beg to play. Sally would not attack and responded to no such command. If he let her romp outside, she'd probably get herself shot. On the other hand, if he kept her inside and left the house without her, she'd bark to be let out, putting him in jeopardy.

At the closet, Cinq-Mars threw on his outerwear and boots. A John Deere baseball cap, gloves, a big eider-down coat. By the time he was ready he'd made a deci-sion about the dog. He located her leash by feeling around in the dark closet and fastened it around her neck. Sally was wagging her tail now. He'd take her out the back way, make her think they were off for a stroll in the blizzard, then tie her up. By the time she realized that she was about to be left alone, and protested, he'd be around the corner of the house. No intruder would expect him to be there, even after Sally commenced a ruckus, and he'd have gained an angle of attack.

With Sally firmly clutched, shushing her constantly, Émile Cinq-Mars departed the rear of his house and made his way around to the side. A stout maple there, about a foot in diameter, served as a hitching-post.

The wind was fierce and the cold bit into them. Sally was growing less enthusiastic about this excursion. The dog was unaware that she'd been tied until her master turned the corner of the shed. Then she started to fuss and whimper, and soon she was barking.

Cinq-Mars moved quickly to gain position. He slipped around the woodpile and was headed to the front of the house when his advance was met by a retort from way off to his left. Gunfire? Cinq-Mars was stunned and had to fight with himself to react. He didn't believe what was happening. He stumbled in his half-hearted retreat, rolled in behind the woodpile, and crouched down there in the snow in shock and amazement. He'd been ambushed. He took a chance to look up but saw nothing, only the white snow shooting sideways and beyond that, blackness. Sally was uproarious now and he believed that he heard, from way upstairs, Sandra caterwauling his name.

Then more gunshots, which he heard strike his woodpile and the garage at his back.

He punched the emergency number on his cellphone and quickly went through the drill, not waiting for a response. "X-ray Yankee Zulu. Cinq-Mars. Cinq-Mars. Officer under fire. Officer under fire. Crank it up. Crank it up. Out."

He heard a snowmobile's start-up roar then, muffled by the rabid wind, and it seemed to come from the same direction as the gunfire. Had it been four shots, five, six? It seemed to Cinq-Mars that he had actually felt a bullet miss him, then strike the garage, all before the sound of the blast had registered. He told himself that he must have imagined it. He thought to fire the shotgun in the general direction of the roaring, invisible snowmobile but feared that that might panic his wife even more. The last thing he wanted was to find her out in the storm searching for him.

Then a roar, and a faint blur, crossed to the front of his house, and Cinq-Mars moved from his hiding spot. He unfastened the double safety on the shotgun he'd had retrofitted for Sandra's sake.

Two shells to fire. Two triggers. His one chance to massacre these bastards.

Their escape route was away from his position and, cleverly, on a line passing between the corner of his house and his vehicle. Cinq-Mars had to scamper to the Pathfinder and crouch by the front tire there, listening to the diminishing bedlam of the machine. The snowmobile had been specially rigged to travel with its lights off, which was not normally possible. He still had a shot, but he worried now that his vehicle might have been wired so that the explosion could be triggered by remote control. What if the intruders were out there waiting for a sign that he was standing alongside it, breathing his last breath next to dynamite?

Having nothing more than retreating noise to fire upon, Cinq-Mars cracked the shotgun.

He jogged back around, collected Sally, and beat a full retreat into his home. He locked the doors behind him. Leaving the lights off, he ran upstairs, with the dog at his heels. In the side-room where he had left her, Sandra stood limply in silhouette, the phone in her hand held waist-high.

"Sand?" he queried.

She did not respond.

Cinq-Mars jumped to the window and pulled the curtain across. Only then did he consent to turn on a table lamp.

Before him his wife leaned against the edge of the desk with the phone in her hand. She was looking at him. At first she seemed shocked, dazed, but as her eyes focused, her expression turned to one of terror. "Émile," she said, as tears sprang up.

"Sand?" He took the phone from her and spoke into it. "Hello? Hello?"

Dead air on the other end, and his wife was shaking her head.

"They killed her," Sandra said.

"What? Who?"

"Somebody shot her. I was talking to her on the phone. Émile, I heard a pop. Like a shot. This small sound—a gasp—then her body hit the floor. I heard it!"

He moved across to his wife and held her, stooping to bury his face in Sandra's neck, kissing her gently. Cinq-Mars took a step back. He put the shotgun down on the desk and touched her face with his right hand while the fingers of his left located the digits to press on his cellphone.

"X-ray Yankee Zulu. Cinq-Mars. Turn me over."

Seconds later he heard, "Cinq-Mars, ETA two minutes. Status."

"Attack thwarted. Intruders, at least two, fled south-west by snowmobile. My vehicle could be wired with explosive. Haven't checked in the dark. Officer safe. Repeat, officer safe, intruders repelled."

"Wait."

Cinq-Mars hung on while the information was dispatched to the officers speeding toward his home at that moment.

"Roger that."

"Action—my home phone line is open to an outside number. Party at the other end believed to have been shot. Injured or dead. Find out the address of that location."

"Roger that."

"Give me a call-back on my mobile. Over for now."

The computer would give the officers his phone number, just as it had given them his address. Sandra hung on to his sleeve while he punched another number on his cellular.

"Hello?" The voice was croaky with sleep.

"Bill? Émile. Ready on. We've got something. I'll be back with the details."

"You all right?"

"Long story. Call you back." Punching that call off, he promptly sent another. "It's Émile," he said, upon receiving a sleepy response. He listened to the other person rouse himself with complaint and vitriol. When it seemed as though the other party was sufficiently awake, he said, "Forget about all that. Just tell me what's known about an SQ sergeant named Charles Painchaud."

Cinq-Mars was informed that not much was known but that the sergeant was considered to be a good man. Something was murky. Not much. Vague rumours about connections. Possibly, his rapid advancement was related to nepotism.

"That's the worst thing said about him?"

"So far."

"I need his home phone, AS AP. Call me back on my mobile only."

While he waited for information to come his way, Cinq-Mars held his wife in his arms. "What else did you hear?" he whispered.

"I couldn't tell. Odd sounds. Like they were moving furniture."

"They?"

"No voices, but I heard more than one set of feet. At times, they might've been on different sides of the room simultaneously. I heard heavy breathing, grunts, as if men were exerting themselves."

He reached behind her to pull the curtain open, and behind himself he switched off the table lamp. In the distance, at the edge of his property, Cinq-Mars spotted the flashing blue and red cherries of a squad car. The cruiser's slow speed suggested that the storm had completely obscured the driveway.

"Take it easy. It'll be all right," he tried to assure Sandra.

"She said her name was Lucy. She didn't give me a last name."

As much as she endeavoured to stifle her tears and sniffles, not much worked, and in the end Sandra slid down from her husband's embrace and clasped Sally by the neck. She sat on the floor and squeezed her dog instead. After kissing the top of her head, Émile Cinq-Mars returned downstairs, switching lights on along the way.

Fearing dynamite connected to the ignition, a method of execution favoured by local gangs, the detective was unwilling to start his Pathfinder. The young officer from the St. Lazare Police who'd been first to arrive on the scene volunteered to check it out for him and soon pronounced the car safe.

"How much do you know about bombs?" Cinq-Mars drilled him.

"Not a whole bunch." A red-haired, freckled, affable man, mildly plump, the officer stood in the mudroom with the outside door open at his back. Snow blew inside. The cold air mixing with the warmth of the house made the breath of the men visible and frosted the windows.

"Is it your particular area of expertise?" Cinq-Mars continued to press him.

"No, sir."

"They go *boom*, right? Do you know much more than that?"

The cop was accepting the inquisition with a sense of humour that Cinq-Mars could not quash. "Sir, your car was entered by the side door. Slick entry. Either that or your door was unlocked. Was it?"

"Could be." Cinq-Mars jutted his chin as if to accept a blow earned by his carelessness.

The officer nodded, gaining confidence. "The snow under the car is undisturbed, sir. On this side, there's the imprint where you crouched down. On the other side, it's easy to see where he got in and out by the passenger door. He was hoping you'd step into the car on the driver's side without noticing his tracks. Either that, or he expected the storm to smooth them over by morning." His words were underscored by a cockiness he didn't wish to hide, as though he wanted to impress upon the senior cop that he would not be intimidated by his reputation. "I checked under the door, sir, just to be safe. I checked under the car and around the wheel wells. I checked the motor. I checked the ignition and under the dash. I looked below the seats. Nothing's been disturbed. The trunk's clean. There's no bomb. No loose wires. You must've intercepted him before he had the chance to do anything. In the cold, in the dark, he was working slowly. When he ran, it's a good guess that he took the bomb back with him. If there was a bomb."

"A bomber, on the run, in the dark, takes his dynamite away with him?"

The cop shrugged. "Valuable stuff. His choice." He then coughed, and deliberately repeated himself, as though to introduce an alternative theory. "If there was a bomb."

Cinq-Mars wasn't interested in hearing any other suggestions. He'd felt a bullet whiz by his head. Five or so had been fired at him. That an intruder had dared penetrate his property, with the intention of killing him, had him more enraged than frightened. Keeping himself under control was a battle. This was a new level of combat and he did not welcome the escalation.

"So," he asked, relenting somewhat, "you believe my vehicle's safe?"

"Yes, sir, I do." The cop was a handsome young man, probably in his late twenties. Women loved him, Cinq-Mars suspected. He didn't look the type to marry young, or if he did, he wouldn't fare well in the role. He was a risk-taker, that kind of cop, not a homebody.

Cinq-Mars held up his keys. "Are you volunteering to start it yourself? Just so you know, you don't have to."

The cop laughed and accepted the keys from his superior's hands. "I'll be back in a minute, sir."

"Make a point of it."

Cinq-Mars watched. As confident as the officer had been with his preliminary investigation, now that his own life was at stake he double-checked everything. In the end he sat up in the driver's seat with a determined grin, stuck the key into the ignition, and boldly gave it a twist. The engine kicked over immediately, and the young cop revved it up high before turning the vehicle off.

By the time he came back to the house, other police-men were following the first set of tire tracks up the long drive. Local cops, *Sûreté du Québec*, and Montreal Urban Community Police converged. Without a Ski-Doo of their own they had no hope of trailing the culprits, and Cinq-Mars told them not to bother calling for one. Snowdrifts would hide the trail during the delay, and shortly the bad guys would connect to miles of intersecting trails, where their tracks would be indis-tinguishable from hundreds of others being covered over by the blizzard. Cinq-Mars asked instead that the SQ give him an escort, that the Montreal officers stay put to guard his wife until his return, and that the local cops drive the country roads and report any suspicious activity. All agreed.

Cinq-Mars returned upstairs to apprise his wife of the situation, to hold her, and to say goodnight. Although disturbed, Sandra was not fragile, and they hugged one another as though the strength of their squeeze was sufficient to ward off the world. He loved her and loved the scent of her, loved that they were getting along so well these days, and hated this turn, for marital pressures inevitably followed such an episode.

Back downstairs, he strapped on his holster and issue and retrieved his wallet and shield. Before he left the house he made and received several calls, including one to his partner and another to Sergeant Painchaud, now that he had his number. A call came in with the trace on the phone call, and he was given an address for a Lucy Gabriel, near Oka. Then he was outside in the blizzard again, starting his new vehicle for himself. He followed the flashing lights of the SQ cruiser onto the country road and, eventually, eastbound along the highway.

On the passenger side of the Pathfinder, snow carried in on the boots of the intruder slowly melted away, a reminder of his trespass that made Cinq-Mars angry all over again. Only as the cab warmed up and the snow vanished did he feel that he was alone in his vehicle, speeding behind the cruiser, headlights shining on the ferocity of the storm. The highway was difficult to discern. He drove hard. He assumed that if the cruiser ahead of him hit the ditch, or rammed a pole, that that would be his cue to swerve, brake, or prepare to crash.

Driving actually gave his nerves a chance to settle— he could reshuffle his anxieties, concentrate on the road—and he had time to think things through.

The cumulative effect of the events of the past fifteen hours indicated, if nothing else, that he was missing something. Apparently there was a gap in the spectrum of his knowledge that could be lethal. A woman had called offering information. He had travelled to the rendezvous. A man in the vicinity had been found dead, shot and submerged under ice. The woman had not shown up, but had telephoned again and, during the conversation, possibly or probably, had been gunned down herself. His property had been invaded, he'd been fired upon, his vehicle had been entered. No bomb had been planted on the Pathfinder—presuming that the brave young cop hadn't been duped in some way, that no remote-controlled *plastique* was under his rump at that very moment. But a bomb was still his first choice when ascribing purpose to the trespass. Most of the really bad guys on his turf, notably the biker gangs, were bombers. The woman had cited his fame as her primary reason for choosing to call him and not just any cop—whatever it was that she knew had gotten one man killed and perhaps her own life snuffed—but none of that explained a sudden interest the bad guys might have to want him dead.

Unless they assumed, or were worried, that the unknown woman, or Andrew Stettler, the floating corpse, had managed to divulge their secrets to him.

Cinq-Mars followed the cruiser off Highway 40 onto Côte St. Charles Road, which led into the town of Hudson. The route took him past farmland dotted with old and handsome rickety barns, then into an area of modest cottages on large properties. Before leaving home, he had arranged for others to meet him in different locales, and now he got back to Bill Mathers. They were travelling from opposite directions.

"What's your E T A, Bill?"

"Fifteen, twenty. I'm behind a plough. Which beats being in front of it."

"I'm ten, maybe fifteen minutes in this snow. The gatekeeper is being dragged out of bed as we speak. See you soon."

The street ended, and he turned east along Main Road. Here the homes were larger and occupied expansive waterfront properties. His cellphone rang. Charles Painchaud, coming from the northeast, was already on the opposite side of the Lake of Two Mountains, as he lived over there. "Trouble," Painchaud warned.

"What's up?"

"I'm searching for the house. I've left Oka. I'm now on Indian land."

Cinq-Mars swore under his breath. "Are you in a cruiser?"

"Personal vehicle, sir. Thank God."

"Uniform?"

"Civvies," Painchaud assured him. "Nevertheless."

"Right. Better call it in."

"Will do," Painchaud said. "See you when I see you."

So far, Cinq-Mars had four police departments involved in this escapade. M U C cops were guarding his house. St. Lazare Police were trolling the countryside, looking for a shooter and a mad bomber on a snowmobile. The provincial police were providing his escort, and Painchaud, also a member of that force, was operating on the opposite side of the lake. He had asked the Hudson Police to alert the gatekeeper for the ice-bridge. Now there'd be a fifth police force involved. The Kanesetake Mohawk Peacekeepers would not take kindly to foreign officers on their territory.

Something was going on. He couldn't quite smell it, he couldn't put any of it together, but his intuitive and intellectual senses were definitely being stirred.

He drove hard, keeping the lights of the cruiser ahead of him in view. Main Road in Hudson took him through the commercial centre of the village, then dipped and swerved as it ran alongside the Lake of Two Mountains. Earlier in the century, many of the homes here had served as summer cottages for the affluent of Montreal. Now, with the advent of fast cars, adequate bridges and express highways, the town was a bedroom community for those who commuted the other way and in all seasons. For more than a century, the lake had been circled by the three founding peoples of the country, native, French and English. Hudson was peculiarly English, and Émile Cinq-Mars was feeling like an obvious outsider.

At a quiet junction, he spotted the revolving blue light of a police cruiser where an officer from Hudson awaited his arrival. In summer, a ferry service operated from this location, small tugs shunting vehicles on barges between the towns of Oka and Hudson. In winter, the ferry operator used his private access on both sides of the lake to maintain an ice-bridge. The local police had awakened an employee to open the gate kept locked overnight. In turn, he had summoned a snowplough operator. The three men were waiting for Cinq-Mars as he pulled onto the property and stepped from his car into the teeth of a gale.

"Sir," the Hudson cop greeted him, in French. He seemed an amiable man, no doubt a job requirement in such a nice town. "Great night to be out for a drive."

"Couldn't have picked it better. Thanks for your help on this."

"No problem, sir. I have to warn you, though, the gatekeeper's feeling ornery."

At that point, the *Sûreté du Québec* escort who had followed Cinq-Mars from his house joined them. "Might as well call it a night," Cinq-Mars advised the SQ officer. "I'll take it from here. Thanks for everything."

"I don't mind going across with you, sir," the tall young man maintained.

"Think so? Turns out we're headed for a house on Indian land. Are you sure you want to drive a flashbulb cruiser over there?"

He was immediately less certain.

Apart from cheap American smokes, inexpensive contraband liquor and reserve-grown marijuana, native criminals had one other product they brokered with success. They provided armaments procured in the United States to interested parties. Grenade-launchers. Submachine guns. Automatic pistols. Rifles. Dynamite. The reserve was no place for outside cops.

As the SQ escort beat it, the ice-bridge manager trundled out of the warm police cruiser and, determined to have his say, expressed displeasure at being rousted from bed. "At least you got a four-wheeler there. Jean-Pierre, he goes across with you. We didn't plough yet. Don't get stuck. You go off course, hit a soft spot, me, I won't be responsible." He was a broad, short man who kept his hands stuffed in his pockets yet continued to gesticulate, flapping his lower coat.

"What'll Jean-Pierre do for me?" a sceptical Cinq-Mars asked.

"Plough. He'll clear the road ahead of you. He's got the keys to the gate on the other side. Me, I want to know who pays this bill."

"You're charging me?"

The owner shrugged. "What'd you expect?"

"You had to plough this road anyway," Cinq-Mars argued.

"Not this time of night. Jean-Pierre, he's gotta plough it again by morning. All this big raid does is cost me money."

"I didn't ask for the ice-bridge to be ploughed. I have a four-wheel drive. You're providing a service I never requested."

"Don't be so goddamn cheap! It's not your money! Me, I'm ploughing the road. The City of Montreal pays. That's that!"

"Fine. Send me an invoice. I'll get you a card from my car."

The three men drifted that way, the wind at their backs. A fourth, Jean-Pierre, on hand to operate the plough, sat slumped in his truck, his head over the steering wheel, looking dead to the world.

"Ready, sir?" the Hudson cop asked.

"Five or ten. My partner's on his way."

They waited then, Jean-Pierre in his cab, the ferry manager in the police cruiser where he tallied a bill, the cop beside him, and Cinq-Mars in his Pathfinder awaiting Bill Mathers. Heat from their idling engines kept them warm, but they were unable to keep tabs on one another, as snow masked the windows. Émile Cinq-Mars did not see Bill Mathers turn too quickly onto the unploughed drive, skid to his left, steer into the spin, right himself and pull over. The young detective locked up his car and came across to the Pathfinder, bent to the fierce wind.

"I heard you called in an x y z," Mathers said, clambering inside.

"Who told you that?"

"I called the office myself while I was thinking about something."

"Thinking about what?" Cinq-Mars spoke in his usual gruff tone. He rolled his window down and waved the truck on ahead of him. When that didn't work, he flashed his lights and honked.

"Booked tomorrow morning off. If I have to be out all night, I'm not going in early. So is it true?"

Cinq-Mars nodded briefly. "Some dickhead tried to wire my car. Can you believe it? I got shot at for intruding on his handiwork."

"No kidding." Mathers cleared his throat and rubbed his hands in front of the heater. His head was mussed, he wasn't clean-shaven—an unusual look for him. "Serious news, Émile. What's the story?"

"Hang on."

Jean-Pierre was climbing down from the cab of his truck. As he walked past the Pathfinder Cinq-Mars noticed the flare of the man's cigarette. The detective rolled down his window, admitting the blizzard, and scrubbed snow from his outer mirror. He rolled his window up again and watched Jean-Pierre go behind them and lock the gate after the cop car. As the man passed by on his return, Cinq-Mars opened his door to address him.

"How do I get back?" he asked in French.

"I'll wait for you."

"I might be awhile."

"I get paid by the hour. Not that it's worth it. This is a sonofabitch. I got to unlock the gate on the other side anyhow, so I'll wait for you until it's time to open up for the public. After that it won't matter."

"Well, you have a good night now."

"That's funny. Ha-ha. I'm laughing."

"Sorry about this. But it could be a matter of life and death."

"Yeah? Well, all right. Let's get you across."

Cinq-Mars filled Bill Mathers in on the scant details as they headed onto the lake behind the plough. It didn't take long to repeat what was pertinent, and after that both men were quiet. The events bothered them,

and initially made them solemn, their reticence
enforced by the eerie dimension of the drive. They
were out on the lake, driving on ice, following the
plough with its revolving lights, the storm arrayed
against them. They had to let the truck go farther
ahead as it churned up an avalanche of snow and blew
it onto their windshield. Winds funnelled down the lake
without obstruction, rocking the car, the snow flying
horizontally in a swirling maze. The Pathfinder had
entered another dimension, passed through a time
warp. Adrift upon an ice cap, isolated and cut off,
suddenly the men landed upon the opposite shore.

Cinq-Mars hailed Charles Painchaud on the cellular
and was guided down the main road in the direction of
the house. He crossed onto Indian land, but in the blizzard nothing could be seen. He had to find a driveway,
and that seemed impossible, until he was aided by a
Mohawk Peacekeeper waving a flashlight. What must
have been difficult for Painchaud was simplified for
Cinq-Mars. He and Mathers arrived amid a convoy of
police cruisers and stepped out of the car into the
hostile company of Indian cops. One accompanied
them upstairs, to an attic above a garage, where the
alleged crime had taken place.

Painchaud greeted Cinq-Mars as he and Mathers
kicked snow off their boots. "Sergeant-Detective," he
said.

"Sergeant. What've we got?"

"No victim."

"No? What else?"

"Check this out."

Painchaud and Mathers crouched down together to
survey the wood floor of the apartment. Cinq-Mars
preferred to get an overview first. A quick glance
confirmed that the room was well lived in, the tenant
being neither a notable, nor an atrocious, house-
keeper. Magazines—particularly *Vogue* and *Elle* and

old *TV Guides*—textbooks, a clutter of knick knacks and a scatter of clothes lay gathered here and strewn there, indicating someone at ease in her surroundings. A sense of cleanliness worked through the contained muddle. Whoever lived here had one large room, with the kitchen at the far end flowing into the dining and living areas. A bed was positioned along one side, next to a door that led to the bathroom. The kitchen sink and counter spaces were clean. The dining table was tidy as well, with a candlestick in the centre and a pewter incense-holder in the shape of a toad at one corner. A stick of incense had burned down, with only the ash remaining in a thin grey line on the tabletop. A desk between two windows sheltered a mishmash of papers along an upper shelf, although the surface of the desk was in reasonable order. The aging furniture appeared to have been well built in its day and to be comfortable still. The yellow-and-brown material for the sofa and large chairs was a tad threadbare and old-fashioned, but the cushions were holding up. There were two TVs, one aimed at the bed, another at the sofa. On one wall hung a banner that said "THIS IS INDIAN LAND," while on the wall opposite, with its four corners stretched taut, hung the flag of the Mohawk Warriors, a defiant golden male face on a red field. Cinq-Mars juggled conflicting impressions—controlled chaos opposed by a flimsy sense of organization. He was unsure which was the dominant sentiment.

"Sir?" Painchaud wanted him to study the floor. The stained oak showed a relatively clear area surrounded by a dusty, scuffed border.

Cinq-Mars stated the obvious. "A carpet was down."

"Until very recently," Painchaud concurred. "These foam bits look like particles of underpadding."

"If she was shot here, next to the phone, with the shooter coming in through the front door, blood and tissue might spatter—"

"—across the carpet," Mathers put in.

"Then they rolled the carpet up and carted her body away in it," Cinq-Mars concluded.

"Could be," Painchaud agreed.

"My wife heard them over the phone. They were moving furniture, that's what it sounded like to her." The men were quiet awhile, regarding the floor. "Roughly," Cinq-Mars judged, "a fourteen by eighteen. A carpet that large, plus the underpadding, makes for a heavy roll, even if the material's not thick. Difficult to bend. I'd look for a van, or a large station wagon."

"Let me introduce you," Painchaud suggested as both men resumed an upright posture.

Coming over was an officer in the blue uniform of the Kanesetake Peacekeepers. His name was Constable Roland Harvey. Painchaud undertook the introductions, and the man nodded.

Cinq-Mars told him, "Probably the woman was carted off in a van or a truck, bundled in a carpet. Can your people keep an eye out?"

"Not so many vehicles on the road tonight." The man, in his thirties, spoke with a deep throatiness at a measured pace. "We're stopping anybody going through the reserve. We ask them what they're doing out tonight. We check their trunks."

"Thank you. That's good. That's great."

The officer carried a considerable paunch. His face was pockmarked and quite dark—a wide, square Mohawk face. His was particularly distinguished by drooping jowls, and Cinq-Mars found him difficult to read.

"Her name was Lucy Gabriel," the Peacekeeper told him. "She lived here."

"What can you tell us about Lucy, Roland?"

"Good girl. Smart. She's Mohawk, but Lucy always blended."

"Excuse me? Blended?"

"With whites. She has a good job, everybody says. Drives a nice car. A Honda. An Accord, I think. It's still in the garage downstairs. She was on the barricades when we had that war."

One side's crisis was another side's war, Cinq-Mars noted. "Ever had any trouble with her?"

"No trouble, no. A few times we talk to her about her boyfriends."

"What about them?" Cinq-Mars could tell that Painchaud was hanging back, taking this in. Roland Harvey was more inclined to talk to a Montreal cop, such as himself, than to someone from the *Sûreté du Québec*.

"Nothing special. Those boys were all right. She dated white guys."

"Does that make it police business?"

"If they visit here, that's okay. That's up to her. They can stay overnight if she wants. If they move in, that's different. White people can't live here no more on the reserve. If you want to marry a white person, that's okay, all right, but you got to move off the reserve."

"She didn't want to move off?"

"Her boyfriends weren't that serious. That's what she told us. They weren't moving in."

Cinq-Mars nodded and paced a short distance. His demeanour made it clear that he had further questions on his mind, and the others waited for him to speak again.

Before he did, the senior cop caught a glimpse of his colleagues. In this light, at this hour of the morning, with a couple of them having been awakened from their beds, they appeared disgruntled and bleary-eyed. Mussed hair, whiskers, a poor choice of clothes, puffy eyelids. He was reminded that one problem with chasing down criminals was that the bad guys didn't always cooperate by working the same shifts as their pursuers.

Seeing his cohorts, Cinq-Mars was prompted to yawn—a gesture that expanded and took its own time. He imagined that he was their mirror image—maybe worse, given that he was the oldest.

"All right, sir, tell me, did she have a good relationship with the Peacekeepers? Did you get along, or was she afraid of you?"

"Got along, yup." Neither his blank expression nor his monotone speech gave anything away.

"Because she called me, you know. In the middle of the night. If she thought she was in danger she could have called you. You were closer. You were awake. You or one of your colleagues would've been on shift."

The cop nodded. "I don't know why she'd do that. I'd get here sooner."

"No doubt about it. Which tells me two things. She really didn't think anybody would be walking through the front door, and her troubles probably don't originate on the reserve. They got started off the reserve. She didn't expect local trouble or she would've called you. That being the case, I hope you don't object to our being here."

The officer looked rather slowly from Cinq-Mars to Painchaud and then back again. "Nobody wants SQ snooping around. What good does that do? Nobody's gonna talk to SQ. Ask the chief. He'll tell you we don't want SQ walking around."

Unsure whether he meant the Chief of the Peacekeepers or the Chief of the Grand Council, Cinq-Mars chose to hold his peace. The point had been made that the SQ was not welcome to investigate on the reserve, and if they came anyway, they'd be ineffectual.

"All right. Listen, Roland, we need your help here. We need you to talk to her friends. We need to know what her carpet looked like, what colours were in it, what was the design. We need to know whatever you can find out about her boyfriends. We need you to hunt the reserve for a girl rolled in a carpet, for a carpet tossed off by the side of the road somewhere. Lucy might have a gunshot wound. Something else, Roland. We need a forensics expert to scan this apartment with a microscope and a fine-tooth comb. You can't provide us with one of those, I don't imagine. I understand that you don't want the SQ. But if I clear it with Sergeant Painchaud, will you allow a forensics examiner from my department on the premises? I'll guarantee that the report will be shared around to everybody."

"Montreal cops." Roland Harvey mulled the news.

"No uniforms. No cruisers. Plainclothes and plain cars all the way, and your people can be on hand."

"They have to be," Harvey said. He didn't explain himself, but Cinq-Mars assumed that even Montreal cops would need local protection. This was going to be a tough working environment.

"Desperate measures, Roland. We believe that Lucy's been shot. She could be badly hurt. She may be one of your own but she could be anywhere. We'll have to scour Quebec. Off the reserve and on. Across the border to Ontario. Maybe down to New York State. We need to rely on you and you on us if we're to get a handle on this. Lucy is one of yours, Roland, but her troubles probably got started off the reserve."

Roland Harvey gave a nod. "Sure, yup. Bring your people on. No SQ."

"Deal," he said. Cinq-Mars turned to Painchaud. "Deal?" he asked him.

Painchaud didn't have a problem with the arrangement. He understood the situation. Cinq-Mars liked him more by the minute, liked him almost as much as he was puzzled by the guy. He was not accustomed to SQ officers willing to take a back seat in the interests of an investigation. "Done," Sergeant Painchaud agreed.

"Émile?" Bill Mathers had wandered over to the missing woman's desk and returned with a photograph and a check stub. Cinq-Mars took the picture, examined it, and showed it to the native officer.

"This her? In this photograph she looks native."

"That's Lucy. She's wearing her number-one tan in that one. I didn't say Lucy don't look native. She blends in with whites is all. She's got their culture, the way they talk."

"English or French?"

"Both. English for sure."

"Pretty girl. What else?" Cinq-Mars asked.

Mathers held up the stub. "Hillier-Largent Global. She makes a decent salary, with benefits."

The senior detective studied it for himself. Lucy Gabriel's paycheque bore marked similarities to his own. Suddenly the modest premises seemed odd. "What is this place, Roland? A garage? Is there a house that goes with it?"

"Used to be, yup. Burnt down years ago. Lucy's folks owned it. Lucy already lived here by herself from the time she was eleven years old, about. Her folks' house was thirty feet away. The foundation's still there, but that's all."

"She lived on her own from the age of eleven?"

"Not all the time since then, no. Her parents, they died in that fire. White people took her in after that. A doctor living on the reserve back then, he became her dad, but at one point he took her off the reserve. Lucy kept the garage as her private place. It's her property. Moved back when she was old enough for that."

"What does Lucy do?"

"Biologist," Roland Harvey explained.

"Excuse me?" The surprise Cinq-Mars expressed had more to do with Lucy's profession causing him to think about the laboratory at the head of the lake, BioLogika, and not, as Roland Harvey perhaps assumed, that a young native woman was a professional scientist.

"She educated herself," the Peacekeeper specified, his pride noted.

"A biologist. Is Hillier-Largent a pharmaceutical company, do you know?"

Harvey shrugged. Cinq-Mars flipped the check stub over several times in his hands.

"No address. Bill, find out where the company's located and its business."

"On it."

"Have you found anything, Roland, that can help us?"

"Bullet hole over here." The Peacekeeper nodded toward the far wall.

"Show me." Cinq-Mars followed him around the perimeter of the room to the kitchen, Painchaud trailing behind. A door under the sink stood open.

"We found it like this. The door ajar. But the door was closed when the bullet went through it. It went through the garbage can after that, then lodged in the wallboard. It's not so thick. Looks like it got buried in the insulation. Either that, or the shooter went and pulled it out already."

"These guys were probably looking to get it back, judging by the way they cleaned up. Let's hope they failed. Anything else?" When Roland Harvey shook his head, Cinq-Mars pushed him further. "How do you think this went down?"

"No forced entry," Harvey mentioned. "No big surprise. Probably she never bothered to lock up. Not here, on the reserve. Not on a night like this one."

"She told me she had to get home after the evening news. Which means she must've been in the city, that accounts for the time. A slow trek on a night like this. Somebody might have followed her home, or they were waiting for her."

"So they walked in and shot her," Painchaud concluded, shaking his head.

"I doubt they came here to shoot her," Cinq-Mars told them, which caused both men to jerk their heads up. How he could be promoting theories with nothing to go on struck them as odd. "If that's true, they'd have left her where she lay. I think they sneaked in here, their arrival camouflaged by the storm. Probably turned their engine off and coasted down the grade to the house. Lights off, for sure. I think they came here to abduct her. When they heard her on the phone, about to say something, that's when they shot her."

Painchaud appeared sceptical, his head bobbing around.

"What's wrong?"

"It's a possibility, sir. But I don't know how you can put that together."

"They shot her, and never said a word after that. Two men. They didn't have to discuss what to do next. They rolled her in a carpet and hoisted her out of here and never said a word. My wife told me they were mute. Probably they taped her mouth to keep her quiet as well. If she was conscious. Question: how did they know what to do without talking? Answer: they had planned that part ahead of time. They expected to come in here and find her in bed. Or, if they had either followed her or waited for her, they expected to find her getting ready for bed. That's why they waited awhile. They expected to tape her mouth, tie her up, wrap her in the carpet and haul her out. Because they came in here and found her on the phone, they shot her first instead. They needed her instantly mute. They weren't going to cross the floor to hang up that phone."

Painchaud shrugged. "It's a possibility."

Sergeant-Detective Cinq-Mars had a matter of tricky diplomacy to conduct. He motioned Painchaud over to a corner and placed a fraternal hand upon his shoulder. "Charles, I want to thank you for granting me some leeway here."

"No problem, sir."

"You know that I don't have jurisdiction—"

"Sir, I'm not that kind of cop." He had that wonky mouth, and his words carried a slight inflection caused by the distortion of his lips. "Keep the lines of communication open, that's all. I don't want to look bad. It's clear to me you're involved. People call you up, next thing you know, they're a missing person. That's more important than jurisdiction. This moves around you, so I want your input. Besides that, we both appreciate that I can't operate on the reserve without you. You've got your problems with the SQ—"

"There's been some history," Cinq-Mars acknowledged in a confidential voice.

"—but I'm just a cop trying to do the best job I can."

"I can see that, Sergeant. Speaking of which, how did you make the ID on that body in the water so fast? Was he carrying a wallet?"

Painchaud smiled, his mouth showing its deformity again. The left side of his lips seemed paralysed. "We got lucky, sir. Down deep in the hip pocket of his jeans was an old credit card slip, for gas. Under a microscope we got a read on the name and number. We ran it down, visited his place in the city. That confirmed it was our guy. Andrew Stettler."

"Good work." Cinq-Mars straightened, as his weariness and the late hour had caused him to stoop. "Sergeant, we need to find this girl. Dead or alive. If she's dead, she could be anywhere by morning. We need the SQ to cover the countryside. We need Peacekeepers to scour the reserve. I'll get my people to hunt Montreal."

"Do you think she's in a ditch?"

"It's possible, but I have my doubts. If they wanted to dump her, why take her away from here? Shoot her, get it over with, beat it. If she's dead, they wanted the corpse for a reason, and I can't imagine what kind of reason would qualify. Why would they want to take a corpse? They knew she'd been on the phone. They knew somebody heard her die, so they couldn't keep this a secret. They knew cops would investigate. Why roll her up in a carpet and haul her away with them? That's high risk. A risk that big has to give them a reward. For the life of me, I can't think what it could be."

"She could identify them."

"There's that. But only if she's not a corpse and they have no intention of making her one."

Painchaud nodded. "Makes sense. Okay. Let's assume she's alive. What do you want to do in here?"

"Nothing. I'm too afraid to disturb the dust. They didn't hang up the phone. That tells me they did their best to touch nothing. They opened the cabinet door to get at the bullet hole. So they tried to retrieve it, and they probably succeeded. They showed an interest in cleaning up. There won't be much to find so I don't want to mess what's here. It's not like we've got anything to go on. Let's seal it, have the Peacekeepers sector it off. Wait for the crime scene technicians to do their thing. Then give the Peacekeepers first crack."

"That's political."

"I suppose it is."

Painchaud gave it some thought. He failed to arrive at a worthwhile alternative.

"I guess we go home now," Cinq-Mars decided.

"No argument there."

First, Cinq-Mars gathered his colleagues for a summation. He cleared his dry throat. "Gentlemen, why would they want to dispose of a corpse? Most killers have no use for the body unless they want it hidden, but this shooting was done while she was on the phone, so it was no secret. Why, then?

"My first guess," Cinq-Mars continued, before anyone had a chance to answer, "—and maybe I'm only being optimistic—is that this girl is not a corpse.

Alive, she's worth something to someone. She was peddling information. Somebody took an interest in what she had to say and to whom. So let's agree. There's a good chance that a young woman is out there wrapped in a rug bleeding from a bullet wound. With that in mind, let's do our jobs well. Make sure our respective departments are aware and active. Gentlemen, thanks. Good night."

Outside, Bill Mathers clambered into the Pathfinder beside his partner. He'd been on the phone awhile. "The firm—Hillier-Largent Global—is located in Saint-Laurent," he told him, referring to a suburb of Montreal north of downtown.

"Thank goodness. Finally! We have a piece of this on our own turf."

"Their business is pharmaceuticals and biotechnology."

Cinq-Mars was letting that sink in when he yawned hard and realized that his body temperature was dropping fast. He turned on the ignition and let the engine warm up before blasting them both with heat.

"So," Mathers suggested, "do we start tomorrow at Hillier-Largent?"

His partner shook his head. "BioLogika first. Then there."

"Why BioLogika?"

"Get there before anybody figures out we don't belong. We want to be the first cops to show, not the second or third wave. You might want to think about sleeping at my place tonight."

"Sounds good, actually. You're closer."

Cinq-Mars put the car in gear. Wipers, front and rear, strained to clear a patch of visibility.

The partners drove down the small highway that would take them back through the Indian reserve to Oka. A snowbound night. Bill Mathers raised their department to sound the alarm about the missing girl.

After he was done, Cinq-Mars told him what Charles Painchaud had said, and asked what he thought of the other man, given that they were both about the same age.

Mathers mulled the question awhile. Hauled out of bed by the events of the night, he carried himself differently than usual. His attention to grooming thwarted, he seemed less composed, less in control of himself. Often he was overly concerned with how his opinions were being received. He was a man with a resident softness to his body and limbs, despite his broad shoulders and deep chest. He was not a man to bulk up, which disguised an above-average strength and a strong constitution. He preferred to look serious, responsible. On this night, with spiky hair and bristles and droopy eyelids, he was failing, and somehow that let him throw caution to the wind, speak more freely.

"At first, I thought he was cooperating to see what that did for him. That's all he's got to trade—cooperation, nothing else. God knows it's a rare commodity. I thought he might be coattailing you. We've seen that before. Now, it sounds like he's making a contribution. I might come around to your side, Émile. Maybe he's a cop who wants to get the job done."

Émile Cinq-Mars uttered a gentle grunt. He generally concurred, but he would have preferred being beaten off that position. "I heard he's connected, moved up through the ranks that way. We don't have time yet, but when we do, I'd like him checked out."

"Meaning by me?"

"Preferably."

"You're the one with the insider connections, Émile."

"That's why I'm asking you. I want to know if he's left a clean trace, or if his story's been buried."

"All right. I'll do your dirty work. Nothing unusual there." He wasn't complaining. He was content whenever Cinq-Mars trusted him with a specific duty.

At the edge of the lake, Jean-Pierre, the snowplough driver, was nowhere in sight. The engine in his vehicle was not running. This was not a night for him to be taking a stroll, or going far for a pee.

"Check the cab," Cinq-Mars told his partner, "maybe he's sleeping." He had an odd, eerie feeling. Drivers didn't turn off their diesel engines in weather this cold. He watched as Bill Mathers climbed up to the cab and opened the door, but he could not determine what he was doing in there.

Mathers came running back, lumbering through the snow, and threw open the passenger door. "He's unconscious, Émile."

"What!"

"Bleeding from the back of the head."

"He's alive?" Cinq-Mars opened his car door.

"No question. Looks like he was pistol-butted, something like that."

"This means whoever it was waited for us to cross over, then they crossed back."

"I'll call for an ambulance," Mathers said, squeezing himself into the seat.

"Do that. Then alert all forces on the other side. I'll go have a look."

Hands in his pockets, head bowed to the wind, Émile Cinq-Mars walked through the blizzard to the truck, where the groggy driver was beginning to stir. He already assumed that the man had seen nothing of significance—given the weather, it was unlikely that anyone would have been able to provide a useful description of anyone else. He felt that way himself, an indecipherable shape in an immense void, weary of this world, ghost-walking. The wind was particularly severe around the truck, as if nature herself was incensed by all that prevailed in this place and in these times.

Worse than being shot was being mummified in the carpet.

Her arms had been pinned to her sides. As she grew more conscious, Lucy was sure she'd suffocate, and she inhaled each dust-filled breath with desperation. *It hurts!* Her mouth was taped. She could not shout warning, she could not indicate that she was losing it. She had only one choice. *Breathe. Don't vomit.*

Room light, between her feet. Down there, at that end—air. *Breathe.* Then she was being bumped around as they got her out the door, and the carpet bent to her shape as they jostled her down the stairs. The men dropped her a couple of times, jarring her bones. *Breathe. Keep breathing. Slow breaths, don't hyperventilate. It hurts! Don't panic. Breathe. Come on. Slowly. Breathe. Please don't panic. Oh!*

They dropped her down on another hard surface. Shoved her forward.

Car doors slammed. A van. The engine started up. The voices were indistinct. Between her feet—space, light, air.

She warned herself to stay calm. *Just breathe. That's it.* If she panicked she knew that she would never recover. She'd lose her mind.

She fought to stay calm as the van worked its way up the small valley of her property, climbing her driveway. She heard and felt the wheels on the snowy road.

Breathe. Slowly. Just breathe.

The van stopped and the men had a serious argument and Lucy listened. One was being blamed for shooting her. He had panicked, the other two were saying, and they were pissed off and even, Lucy thought, frightened of a reprimand.

Being shot had been a mistake, and Lucy took some comfort in that.

A long delay, then they were on the move again. The next time they stopped the men discussed attacking a snowplough driver. "Don't shoot anybody this time," one man was told. Lucy wanted to scream, shout warning, do something. When the man came back he said it had been easy, "He's out like a light," and apparently he had been vindicated because they didn't argue any more and drove on in silence.

Then they were stymied by a gate. "All right," a man said. "Now you can shoot something, if you're so goddamned trigger-happy. Shoot that fucking lock off."

She heard the shot, the retort muffled by the roaring wind. After that they drove for a long time.

When the van stopped and the motor was shut off it was still dark out. Cold air came up from between her feet. Rather than unroll the carpet, the men grabbed her ankles and yanked her out. Lucy Gabriel slid on her own blood. Other men were there to greet her, tough guys, one with a knife at her side, another with a pistol, and they made her walk between them out of the alley and across the street under the lights and over the deep snow that was still swirling, and she bled all the way to a door, her mouth still taped. She stumbled on the step and fell and she saw the drip-trail of her blood behind her. She did not know exactly where she had landed but the architecture placed her in Old Montreal. The men took her through the broad doors of a rundown office building, and together they climbed the stairs.

Her heart hammered in her chest. Lucy kept swallowing, her mouth dry, terrified that she might soon vomit.

They brought her into a large, open, empty room—a space that once might have accommodated a few dozen desks—and led her down to one end. A heavy, big-bellied man with the stench of stale liquor on his breath and an unlit stump of a cigar in his mouth introduced himself as a doctor and demanded to see her arm. Lucy sat in a chair by a kitchen island as he ran

the taps and cleaned the wound. She wouldn't look at
her arm as he worked on it. The slightest exertion
caused him to breathe more heavily. He hadn't shaven
and had probably been shaken from his sleep and
looked as though he belonged in bed. And yet, he
worked on her arm with tenderness. He examined the
wound and gently assured her that it was no big deal.
His fingers were pudgy and dirt rimmed his fingernails.
He placed the gauze and bandage over her wound with
a deft touch, and when he was done he smiled.

It hurt. Her fear had masked the pain, but when she
looked at the bandage she was suddenly aware of her
injury again and the pain stabbed her, and Lucy
moaned.

After that the doctor accepted a cash payment from
one of her captors and left. Lucy immediately felt less
safe.

A big man with long hair that was thinning on top, a
gold stud earring in one lobe, and small, black eyes
began the interrogation by punching her—once,
hard—in the stomach. She lay on the floor for several
long minutes trying to catch a single breath, gasping,
holding her tummy. The big man was talking to her.
"You see the trouble you caused here? You think we
didn't notice? You think you don't pay for that? Bitch.
Whore! You pay for everything in this world. Nothing's
free. You think you can walk away from this, you
skinny bitch? Eh? You think so? Well, change your
mind in one fucking hurry! We're not done with you.
We haven't even started."

When finally her lungs worked again and she had all
the air in the room, she still couldn't breathe. She was
too afraid.

The man leaned over her, pulled her hair back and
whispered in her ear. "One fucking little shit lie out of
you, sister, I'll finish you off personally. I will take my
time. Understand me? One tiny shit lie out of you. I

want *complete* answers, you got that? You fucking *hesitate* and I'll fucking tear your eyes out. Understand me?"

He still had not asked a question about anything material and she was unsure about everything he was saying to her. She just wanted to catch a breath so she could fight back.

Then the big guy made her sit on the countertop on the kitchen island in that large empty room in Old Montreal and he leaned into her with his hands on either side of her thighs and she could smell his sour breath, and a voice behind her and to her left asked, "Lucy? Tell us. What do you know about Andy?"

She couldn't speak. Her mouth was still covered with tape.

She gurgled.

The big man took out a hunting knife and sliced her gag away, then he gripped her jaw from underneath and the man behind her repeated the question.

"Nothing!" she claimed. "I heard he's dead. It's on the news."

"You know him?" asked the voice from behind.

"He's a friend of mine. So?"

Her answer caused two other burly men to grab her by the shoulders and they forced her down on the countertop. She kicked her feet and she thought they were going to rape her and she wanted to scream but she was too scared.

They turned her head sideways.

"Watch this," the voice from the man she hadn't seen yet said, and she could see him now. He was a pointy-faced man with a tan. He had deep ridges in his forehead and black hair that looked fake. Either it was heavily dyed or it was a toupee. He opened a test tube and held it above the plastic countertop, just held it there, and then he spilled a little of the fluid that was inside and it burned a patch of the plastic. She was overwhelmed with terror. She thought she was screaming but no sound was coming out of her, and she thought that she would vomit and her stomach convulsed but instead she only gagged.

"I'm going to ask you a question. You'll tell me the truth about it. If you lie, I get to splash your face with this stuff. Lie to me twice, I start on your body. First your breasts, then low down. Do I have to explain to you what I'm saying?"

The burly men holding her renewed their grip, pushing her shoulders down and each one clasped a thigh, and she was flat on her back and thrashing her head, turning her face away, then back, wanting not to see, then needing to see what was happening or what would happen next.

Lucy Gabriel could only gasp for breath. She could not answer.

" 'Cause what I'm saying is, go ahead and lie 'cause I don't mind."

He dripped the acid around the perimeter of her head. She heard it sizzle as she turned her face away. "Did you kill Andy Stettler?"

"No!" she cried out. *"No no, no!"*

He continued to drip acid around her head. She jumped each time the countertop burned. Then he held the test tube of scalding acid above her face. One of the others gripped her hair and made her look up at the tube of acid. She could see a drip, on the edge of it, trickle down.

"Think about this now. Don't answer too quickly." She was kicking her feet. Flailing her body. "Do you know who did? Did one of your friends kill Andy? You can tell me. You can save yourself here."

He was holding the tube above her face and she squirmed in the hands of the men holding her. She was making desperate little cries and she believed that her face was about to be scalded and she'd be scarred for life, and the pain, the pain would drive her mad. A large drop was forming at the base of the tube, preparing to fall.

"It's okay," the man soothed her. "Tell me who it was."

Lucy Gabriel looked right at him, right into his eyes. "I don't know who did it!" she screamed at him. She was desperate to believe that they wouldn't have arranged for the doctor to fix her arm if they were planning to maim her. That drop was going to fall. "I don't know who it was!"

The man continued to stare at her. He met her gaze. He poured a little of the acid just away from her neck and a speck of the stuff splashed up and seared her skin, and Lucy began to buck and kick on the countertop with all her strength and fury.

"You can tell me," he said. "Tell me, Lucy."

She reared up from the surface in the grip of her captors with her neck muscles straining and rage violent in her eyes and screamed at her tormentor, *"I don't know who did it! I just found out about it tonight, you asshole!"*

The man backed off, putting his test tube down.

Lucy kept after him. *"Go ahead! Burn me! Burn me, you asshole! I don't know who did it!"*

The man nodded to someone she couldn't see. She heard footsteps coming her way. She believed that whatever was imminent would be worse, worse than acid and worse than death, because death would be merciful now. She was trying to look up over her head to see who and what was coming.

"Nobody's gonna burn you, Lucy," a voice said, a familiar voice, an Indian voice. "That's not the deal. Come home with me now. We'll get you out of here."

Just like that, she was being rescued from oblivion.

This time she was not rolled in the carpet when she left in the van. The carpet had been tossed aside in an alley. Her wrists and ankles were tied, but she was permitted to sit on the floor of the vehicle. She could feel the miles clicking away, and believed that she was going home. At the very least, she was being driven by an Indian, and while she hated him and despised being tied down, she at least believed that her life was no longer in danger.

"Where are you taking me?" she asked.

"Need-to-know basis," the driver responded.

"I need to know."

He chuckled. "All right then, this works on a need-to-tell-you basis, and right now I need to tell you squat."

"Some days," she baited him, "I'm sick to death of Mohawk Warriors."

"This is not one of those days," the man told him. His name was Roger, she remembered, but she had never had much to do with him. They'd never dated.

"I'm not so sure about that," Lucy told him.

They were on a highway, driving fast.

"You think you'd be alive right now if it wasn't for the Mohawk Warriors?"

"Is that true?" That her captor might also be her protector was a difficult notion to grasp.

"You think you wouldn't have a burned-off face right now?"

Lucy challenged him on that. "I didn't hear you speaking up for me."

"You were spoken up for," the Indian told her. "You were spoken up for in advance. You're a pain in the ass, Lucy Gabriel. But you're still one of us, and some of us figure we still owe you. Just don't count on that forever."

She sat quietly while being jostled around in the back of the van. Road bumps shook her. "I'm not going home, am I?" she asked after a lull in the conversation.

The driver shrugged. "Need-to-tell-you basis," he said.

10

THE NATURE
OF THE BEAST

The same day, Monday morning, February 14, 1999

Contrary to his own expectations, Sergeant-Detective Émile Cinq-Mars fell asleep after he'd taken the trouble to lie down a little after four in the morning. By six he was up again, chased awake by Sandra's alarm. She had horses to feed and for safety's sake wanted to shovel the stable doors clear, front and rear, pending the arrival of their snow-removal man. A barnfire wouldn't wait for the exits to be clear first. Catching her husband forcing himself out of bed, she reproved him gently.

"Stay put, Émile. I can handle things. You're absolutely not working today."

"Who says?" He seemed genuinely disoriented. "Since when?"

"Me says. Since last night. Émile, *rest!*"

At four, he had crawled under the covers, craving sleep and hoping his adrenaline would wind down. That he had slept soundly since then, dreamlessly, seemingly without twitching a muscle, amazed him now.

"Not a good night," he conceded.

"So you said." As she recalled the reason for his nocturnal expedition, her voice quieted. She conjured again the fright of the woman on the phone, the bullet's pop, the sudden, surprised gasp at the other end of the line, and her own heartfelt terror. "You never found the girl?"

Cinq-Mars nodded with solemn emphasis. "She's missing. Could be she's all right—that's feasible. In any case, we didn't find a body."

Wearing a silky, sky-blue nightdress, Sandra was standing in the bedroom with a brush in one hand, hair tumbling down the left side of her face. Next to the snow-blasted window, her farm clothes had been carefully laid out across an oak chair, in case she had had to dress in the dark without disturbing Émile. Denim coveralls, a cotton undershirt, a man's heavy plaid shirt, a mauve woollen sweater, thick grey socks, but also a low-cut bra and high-cut panties. Decked out to shovel manure she preferred feminine underthings, and she moved so gracefully from one environment, and one fashion statement, to another, that Cinq-Mars never failed to marvel.

With violent strokes, Sandra commenced brushing her hair.

He waited.

"Émile, are we under attack?" Holding her hands high thrust her breasts upward against a lacy fringe, the tops visible to him.

"We don't know for sure. Let's take precautions, okay?"

"Meaning what? Do I go back to carrying weapons around the house? Do we hire Wells Fargo to take my dry cleaning into town?"

Cinq-Mars had envisioned a more drastic plan. "Sandra—" His voice caught in his throat.

She moved across to sit on the bed beside her brooding, naked husband. "Émile, as your other partner might say, run it down for me."

He still didn't speak, but took her right hand in both of his.

To Sandra, the solemnity of his mood struck her as

being carefully deployed. She couldn't stand it, and gently slipped a hand down his thigh and indelicately squeezed his testicles. He bent double, laughed, hugged her, kissed her temple.

"Happy Valentine's Day," she whispered.

"Oh, yeah?"

"Yeah."

"Happy Valentine's to you. Sweetheart," Cinq-Mars suggested, "we can farm out the horses. You can return to New Hampshire for a while, spend time with your cousins and your old pals."

"Oh, like that's an option. No, Émile. No. As you say in French, *point final.*"

Cinq-Mars nodded, getting the message. "All right then. This next part is not negotiable. I want you under guard. Until we find out who was behind last night's assault, officers will be posted around the property. Most of the time you won't notice them. Take a body-guard to town, whenever you go. If you need to pick up the dry cleaning, send a cop to do it."

This time, she took one of his hands in both of hers. "How bad is it, Émile?"

He lowered his head, his shoulders already slumped. "I'm in the dark. I honestly don't know what's going on."

After the trauma of the previous night, Sandra was not inclined to argue. She took a deep breath and consented to the loss of privacy. She nodded. "Émile, do we get through this?" Her eyes searched his for at least a measure of the truth.

They kissed gently, as though to give one another courage. Sandra lifted her nightdress over her head and was about to return to the bathroom when Cinq-Mars stood up behind her and pulled her against him. He nuzzled her soft brown hair. He whispered that it might not be wise to step beyond the bedroom door without first putting something on.

"How come?"

"Bill slept over. He's on the couch downstairs."

"Émile! Good job you told me! I might've gone down there!"

"So? I'm tempted to show you off."

"Beast!" She was wriggling out of his grasp. He loved her youth at times like this, the slipperiness of her skin and the lithe wonder of her. Seventeen years his junior, she'd always be young to him.

Tickling him, Sandra fended her husband off, laughing. To allow their worries to slide for a moment felt good, restorative, optimistic. She threw on a lavender silk housecoat while Cinq-Mars stretched and yawned and pulled on a ratty old maroon one. When he stepped out to the hall, Sandra was standing by the front window at the head of the stairs wearing a quizzical expression on her face. The sun had not yet risen. She was looking down on their front yard illuminated by the exterior lamps of the front porch and barn. She saw only Mathers's car there.

"Émile?"

"What?" he grunted.

"Where's the Pathfinder?"

Standing in the doorway, he explained, "The ambulance got stuck in a snowdrift so I let the medics use the Pathfinder." The night had gone from bad to increasingly worse. For a while he'd thought he'd never make it home.

"What ambulance?" she asked. "Who needed an ambulance?"

"The snowplough driver. Long story. I'll tell you over breakfast. Wake up that lazy, good-for-nothing detective downstairs, will you? Tell him to milk the cows or something."

"Émile, we don't have cows."

"Does he know that? Wake him. Tell him. Put the fear of God into him, where it belongs." Cinq-Mars leaned over the banister and shouted downstairs. "Bill! Wake up! The cows need milking! Bill! The cows!"

Smiling, Sandra went on down the stairs. Cinq-Mars heard his partner ask her, "What's he bellowing about?"

"The cows, Bill," she said. "Émile thinks you should milk them." Knowing that she could not keep a straight face for long she skipped through to the kitchen to start the coffeemaker.

"Cows?" Bill Mathers was asking.

Cinq-Mars rustled up breakfast, adding hash browns and rye toast to four eggs and five strips of bacon apiece. Mathers eyed his feast as though gazing upon an ethnic cuisine unfamiliar to him. "Is this what country living does to you?"

"No appetite?"

"My limit is two eggs a week."

"Hold on!" Cinq-Mars boomed in his rowdiest early-morning voice. "Are you telling me that you're already conscious of your cholesterol level and you're only thirty-five years old?"

"Émile, the idea isn't to get interested after it's too late. But that's not the point. I can't eat so much. I'll bust a gasket."

"Did you sleep last night?" trumpeted Cinq-Mars.

"No more than you."

"It's one or the other. Eat or sleep. No sleep? Then eat, it's the only remedy. We've got a day ahead of us, me and you."

Obediently, Mathers dug in, and to his surprise managed to clean his plate. "Must be the country air," he concluded.

"For me, it's getting shot at," Cinq-Mars countered. "That'll do it. Adds to my caloric intake like nobody's business. I'll gain ten pounds. Don't be surprised if I polish off a tub of ice cream before lunch."

They said goodbye to Sandra as she was returning from the barn, and in the wind Cinq-Mars kissed her. He could feel the tension on her lips. He watched as she gave Mathers a hug also and warned him to take care. "Look out for each other," she whispered, squeezing his elbow.

"We will. Try not to worry," Mathers said.

The two men remained quiet as they drove down Highway 40 with Mathers behind the wheel. Snow-ploughs had done an admirable job but the wind kept the conditions treacherous. Although he nodded off a few times, Cinq-Mars was sufficiently on the ball to direct Mathers to take the cutoff to Vaudreuil-Dorion.

"We're not going fishing," Mathers stipulated.

"Head for that tall building, Bill. BioLogika."

When they pulled up at the gate and flashed their badges, they found their authority unchallenged. The guard merely required that they register and declare whom they'd come to see. With the guard sitting up high in his glass booth, Cinq-Mars, on the passenger side, had to duck low and talk across his partner's lap. "What's the name of your president?"

"Mr. Honigwachs, sir. Werner Honigwachs."

"Write it down," he instructed Mathers.

"In case you forget?" His partner's incapacity to absorb names that were not French never failed to amuse Mathers, as did his irritation on the subject.

"Is he in?" Cinq-Mars snapped at the guard.

"His car went through twenty minutes ago, sir. You here about Andy?"

Carrying weight compatible with his years, which must have been about sixty, the guard possessed an extravagant white moustache wound to waxed points and a broad, reddened forehead. They were speaking French, but he had the rugged look of a Scottish highlander, which might easily have been part of his heritage. The cross-fertilization of Scottish, British and

Irish soldiers with farmer's daughters centuries earlier had influenced the lineage of many French in Canada. "You knew Mr. Stettler?"

"Of course."

"Why of course?" Cinq-Mars countered. "This is a big company."

"He's my boss."

"How was he your boss?"

"What do you mean? Andy's in charge of security. Ah—*was* in charge, I should say."

Cinq-Mars sat up straight then, mumbling something to himself that nobody caught. He asked Mathers, "Did you get the spelling on that name?"

While it was being verified, Cinq-Mars surveyed the grounds. The twelve-story building appeared immense, being the only structure of more than two stories for miles around. Its black glass, grey concrete, and monolithic posture made it appear aggressively imposing. The stance of the building was reinforced by the chainlink fence, crowned with barbed wire, that defined the acres of property. Maples and a few evergreens had been planted close to the buildings and drives, but the vast expanse of the perimeter had been cleared of trees. No one could leave or enter the premises without either breaking through the fence and crossing the open exposure, or announcing himself at the front gate.

Outbuildings—one a low sprawl that covered about five acres—had been constructed next to the tower and were identified, in large block letters, as labs. The fence, the moat of open property, the guards at the gate and doors, video cameras positioned like gargoyles to ward off whatever version of evil spirits the modern age spewed forth—all this indicated that security was an issue at BioLogika. Especially so, Cinq-Mars imagined, now that the Head of Security had been murdered.

They drove around to the back of the building and Mathers parked in the massive lot there, which was only spotted with a few other vehicles. "You got a plan?"

Cinq-Mars remained mute a moment and rubbed his freshly shaven chin. In the end he chose to state only the obvious. "I'm so tired. I'm wiped."

"Me too, partner."

"Do you know what happens when I get tired?" the senior officer demanded. He slouched down in the car seat as though intending to snatch an impromptu nap. "I grow irritable."

"You don't say."

"It's hard to believe, I know, but I grow irritable. I become crabby." Cinq-Mars folded his hands across his stomach and burped. "Excuse me. I ate too much. That's what happens when I get crabby and irritable, I eat too much. This is wrong, Bill. The bad guys should not be out hunting cops. The bad guys should be the ones in hiding, not me and my wife."

"Can't say I've noticed any difference to your irritable nature, Émile. You seem like your usual self to me."

"Very funny. You won't be laughing as time goes by. This is wrong, Bill, that's what I'm saying. We should not be the ones running and hiding. I'm taking offence. I'm way down the road to being royally ticked off."

"I'm with you there, partner."

Cinq-Mars sprang the door latch but still didn't move. He yawned, and the great gape of his mouth remained open awhile. Mathers noticed how truly worn down he was. He had to remind himself that his friend had at least twenty years on him, and what was tough enough for him was certainly more wearing on Émile. The older man conducted himself with an erect bearing, a sense of eminence, which gave the impression that he was immune to fatigue or boredom. Mathers reminded himself that that could not always be true.

"I'll take on the president," Cinq-Mars announced. "What's his name again? Hog-walks?—works? Hogginworks?"

"It's easy. Honigwachs. Here's the spelling." Mathers tore off a page from his notebook for him. "What do you want me to do?"

"Locate Andrew Stettler's office. Look through his desk. Check out his staff. Learn what's there to be learned. Snoop your ass off, but keep in mind that we have no right to be here. The next time we come back we probably won't be admitted, so this could be our only chance. At some point, go where you should not go. Find out what level of security responds. I'd be interested in that. Generally, make a pest of yourself."

"Same old routine," Mathers mentioned. "I mingle with the riffraff, you kow-tow to royalty. I choke on cigarette smoke, while you have coffee with the big shots."

Climbing out of the car, they were both dragging their bodies up, staggering a little on their feet. Cinq-Mars leaned against the vehicle to steady himself. "How am I supposed to do my job on next-to-no-hours' sleep?" he brayed, then burped. "Whoa." He stretched his spine to resume his upright posture. "There. That's better."

"You're ready to meet the Prez."

"Four eggs. Five slices of bacon. What got into me? Talk about a heart attack on a plate."

"Getting shot at, Émile. It made you feel young again."

Cinq-Mars chuckled. "Right. This morning I was pushing twenty-five. By the time we quit tonight I'll be slurping Pablum for dinner."

Lucy Gabriel was driven to a low-slung, broad cabin deep in the woods on the Kanesetake Reserve. The smoke billowed from a chimney in a steady white plume until it cleared the trees, then grazed eastward. She knew where she was. She had been inside the cabin before, and had dated the guy who lived there.

She had slept on the bed across from where she was now made to sit on the floor.

Her captors kept her ankles bound but they untied her wrists and passed her a plate of pork and beans for breakfast. She ate. She was famished.

Eventually, Constable Roland Harvey arrived home. He knelt in front of her and used a hunting knife to free her ankles, neatly slicing through the rope.

"Usually you're in it up to your hips, Lucy."

"Tell me something I don't know."

"This time, you're in a pile up to your eyebrows."

She was interested. He seemed to know more than she'd expected of him. Then again, he was not merely a Mohawk Peacekeeper, but also a member in good standing of the Mohawk Warriors. Just about everybody knew that. Compromises were necessary in the rough-and-tumble world of domestic politics, and if the bad guys wanted a least one cop on the force to look after their interests, then things were bound to be that way.

He helped her to stand.

Other men were sitting around the cabin, and Roland suggested, "Let's take a walk, Lucy."

She put on her coat and the two went outside. They followed a path around behind the hut, through the woods over the snow. For Lucy, it felt good to be fed, freed, and walking again. Her gunshot wound was not giving her much trouble, just a steady dull throb.

"You got people upset with you, Lucy."

"What else is new, Roland?"

"What's new? You got every police force in a few provinces and states out looking for you. I don't know what you been doing, so you'll have to tell me yourself. Do you want them to find you or not?"

She had to think about that. "Not particularly," she replied.

Roland Harvey nodded. "The bad boys know enough to ask our permission. We're the ones who negotiated to keep you alive, Lucy. That's what we all have in mind right now. Everybody wants you alive."

"What are you saying?"

"You can't go home. You can't be seen anywhere without being taken into custody. Maybe killed, that might be on the radar screen too. It's a rock-and-a-hard-place kind of thing. You'd be safe in custody, but I think I'm hearing maybe you'd rather skip that experience. Yup?"

"I don't want to explain it, Roland, but I can't go to jail right now. That's what we're talking about. Jail time. A good long stretch of it."

"All right then. I can offer you a compromise. You'll go into hiding. We've got a place for you. Yup. You'll be all right. Just don't cause nobody no trouble."

"On the reserve?"

Roland Harvey shook his head. "Too dangerous. You know that. Cops will look for you here. The Peacekeepers are out looking for you right now, and I can't exactly tell them to stop."

"I understand. Where, then?"

"The monastery. It's all arranged."

"Oka?" She knew of no connection between the Mohawk Warriors and their quiet neighbours, the monks.

Roland's breath was vaporous in the air. He hadn't put on a heavy enough coat and now he'd stopped walking, shivering, wanting to head back. "They got a whole wing that's empty. Not so many young men become monks any more. One of the brothers looks after the building during the winter, takes care of the maintenance and stuff like that. He'll take care of you too. But you got to agree."

Lucy didn't have any mittens and hugged herself, her bare hands under her biceps. "So I just stay there."

"That's right."

"For how long?"

"For as long as it takes, I guess. We'll wait for the cops to get less interested in you. The bad guys, they have to forget you exist. You tell me how long that takes."

Lucy turned with him and they walked back toward the house. Before they'd gone halfway, she told him, "All right. I'll stay there. Thanks, Roland."

He put an arm around her shoulders and they walked in that manner. "You're welcome, Lucy. Hell, we owe you. You know that."

Cinq-Mars ascended to the top floor of the BioLogika Corporation in a quiet elevator distinguished by soft mood lighting and black surfaces trimmed with reflective stainless steel. Subliminal New Age music provoked violent fantasies in him. The exhausted detective imagined himself emerging with a speaker in each hand trailing strands of spaghetti wire, the music shorted out in mid-chord and squawking.

At the top floor the doors swished open, and Cinq-Mars stepped out onto plush mauve carpet. The brushed softness underfoot caused him to feel sleepy again, as if inviting him to nap. His joints felt rubbery. Immediately ahead, a marble wall that travelled three-quarters of the way to the ceiling appeared suspended off the floor, adorned in its centre by a small scrap-metal sculpture vaguely suggestive of a Swiss Army knife gone berserk. Giving the artwork a quick study, he decided that, in a pinch, it might be useful at an office party as a communal bottle-opener.

He did a tour around the marble slab and on the opposite side found the receptionist's desk, unoccupied. He'd arrived before business hours. Cinq-Mars patrolled the corridor, made use of the men's room, then sorted out his bearings. As the president of such a company, would he not choose an office with a view of the lake? The detective strolled down to the north side of the tower, located the most imposing door there, and knocked.

"Come!"

Opening up, he stepped into an opulent office, large enough for nine holes of mini-putt. Behind the president's desk, floor-to-ceiling windows looked out over the Lake of Two Mountains, with a bird's-eye view of the fishing shacks where Andrew Stettler had been found dead. The carpet was deep, a dark grey with meandering lines of purple, and on it the company crest, a shooting star, was detailed in gold. Four chairs followed the sweeping curve of the broad cherry desk, and the wood cabinets and panelling that were prominent along three walls picked up the concave theme. Above the cabinets, an impressive array of sailing, golf, squash and equestrian trophies indicated an athlete on the premises, although Cinq-Mars had yet to locate the recipient of these accolades in the flesh.

To his left, a door opened wider. Bathed in light, a man in the executive bathroom was drying his hands on a towel that he hadn't bothered to remove from its rack. His sleeves were rolled up, revealing hairy and muscular forearms. Poking his head out, he called through, "Yes? You are?"

"Sergeant-Detective Cinq-Mars, sir. Police."

"Cinq-Mars! Of course. At long last we meet. Have a seat. I'll be with you in two secs."

The man returned to the depths of his cubicle without bothering to shut the door behind him, and Cinq-Mars sauntered farther into the office. He waited with his hands behind his back, trying to articulate what impression this opulence made upon him. What did it signify? He had expected an office dusty with scientific studies, perhaps Bunsen burners flaring on cabinet tops, walls of bottled pills and assistants frantic in white lab coats. He had expected—illogically, he realized now—a wild-haired biologist with rat feces on his sleeves, strange plants from the Amazon gobbling insects on the windowsills. He had not prepared himself for this display of corporate excess.

His host reappeared, doing up the cufflinks on a light-blue pin-striped shirt as he approached. The detective noted that the panes of mirror in the bath-room behind him were fogged with condensation.

"Detective? Werner Honigwachs. Sorry about the circumstances. I caught you on the evening news last night. What a shock. We haven't adjusted to the tragedy yet, not at all."

Cinq-Mars shook the proffered hand. Honigwachs looked dapper, regal. Cinq-Mars ticked off a mental list of the man's fashion accessories, noting the rings, an expensive watch, and a gold bracelet. The suit was blue.

"Please," the man offered again. "Have a seat."

Cinq-Mars was glad to accept. Conditioning himself to a lack of sleep was part of his job, but this morning his breakfast seemed rowdy, bent on payback, torment-ing a body that had not taken proper care of itself.

"Interesting design," he mentioned, indicating a free-standing sculpture of the solar system to one side of the presidential desk. Planets circled the sun. The earth's moon revolved in its traces. Orbs were connected to the centre by stiff silvery wires as thin as gossamer. In the stone base, a digital readout told the time.

"It's a clock," Honigwachs noted. He quickly waved his hand as though to dismiss the obvious. "You can see for yourself that it tells the time, but it's also a cosmic clock. Remarkably, it simulates the location of the planets at any one moment. Over the course of one year, the earth orbits the sun. Uranus takes seven years. The moon goes around the earth every twenty-eight days, that sort of thing. I had it commissioned myself."

"You're an astronomer?"

The question caused Honigwachs to smile, perhaps with more than an ounce of conceit. He had been speaking with the passionate intensity of a hobbyist. "Not my science, Cinq-Mars. My little toy reminds me of the great quests of our time. It's a reminder to nurture the broadest possible view. Here, at BioLogika, our preoccupations have to do with understanding and manipulating the body's immune system. Elsewhere, physicists are hunting for the origins and composition of the universe. One journey is connected to the other, I suspect."

"How so?" The conversation was drawing Cinq-Mars to a heightened level of wakefulness, which was useful to him, as potent as coffee. In the department he rarely had the opportunity to philosophize about the nature of the species or time's arrow. In Honigwachs, he sensed a peer, although for no particular reason he was not warming to the man.

The president leaned back and swivelled a trifle in his chair. "I wouldn't want to bore a man like you."

Cinq-Mars smiled. "Am I to take that as an insult?"

Honigwachs hesitated, then released a burst of laughter. "It's not intended that way, Detective. I mean only that I don't want to take up your valuable time."

A rumbling in his stomach provoked Cinq-Mars to stand, and he moved over to the window, drawn by the view. Fresh snow made the panorama exquisite, the settlements below him mere outposts in a vast wilderness. He focussed his eye on the bright orange hut where Andrew Stettler had been found beneath the floorboards in the icy water. "Cosmology is a pursuit of mine, sir. Yesterday I was out on the lake with a fishing line going down through the ice. By raising and lowering the line, I moved moisture from the frigid water of the lake, to the cold air under the floorboards, and to the warmth of the cabin. Fascinating, really, to watch the ice crystals form and expand. Simple minds are easily entertained, perhaps. You'll pardon me if I'm rambling, sir, I'm suffering from fatigue this morning.

Yesterday—it was fascinating—as if watching a galaxy form in miniature. Something you said interests me, Mr. Hogginworks—"

"Honigwachs," the president corrected him. "It can be tricky, I know."

"My apologies again. No excuses. I'm hopeless with names. Though it seems that I've heard yours before."

The executive smiled. "I'm curious now. What did I say of interest?"

"You said, as I came in the door, 'At long last we meet.' I find that curious. As if you believe that we should have met previously."

"We move in the same circles, you and I."

Cinq-Mars tilted his head slightly, looking down the slope of his nose at the man in his leather seat, in the saddle of his success. "I don't think so."

"Ah, but we do. You are the great Cinq-Mars, horse trader *par excellence*, known to produce the finest polo ponies in this part of the country. I, on the other hand, play. It's a wonder we haven't met, actually, from my point of view. I've seen you around. I already know you by reputation."

Cinq-Mars shot a glance at the trophies on top of the bookshelves and cabinets. He was so weary, it had not struck him that the equestrian silverware might be for polo. He kicked himself for being so obtuse. He looked back at the man and studied him with keen scrutiny.

"Imagine me with a helmet, Cinq-Mars, in my gear, on horseback."

"I've seen you. The name comes back to me now. I just never knew how to pronounce it. You're a two-goal player."

"Ah! I'm flattered," the man said, and he did seem pleased. "You've placed me. This spring we must talk horses. I'll need a fresh colt to start developing."

"We'll talk." Cinq-Mars returned to the chairs in front of the desk, settling into a different one this time.

"Tell me, I'm curious—how do you connect cosmology to the biological sciences?"

With his elbows on the arms of his chair, Honigwachs touched the fingertips of both hands together, a meditative posture. "I thought you were here to discuss poor Andrew. The sciences! Yes, they seem to move in tandem, have you noticed? Throughout the ages, if one area of science advances, then progress also occurs in other disciplines. At least, that's my shorthand version."

Cinq-Mars nodded as though he expected, and wanted to encourage, more.

"We live in a time warp, Cinq-Mars. That's my theory. That's the meat of the matter. Do you know how a star—our sun, for instance—sinks into the time-space continuum?"

"Yes," Cinq-Mars said. Which was true, he did.

"I believe that we haven't come to terms with what this really means, with how it confines us to a condition in which we live out of time. That warp, that gravitational bend in time—that's the realm we inhabit. It pulls us into the past, keeps us there. What will be will be, I suspect, because it has already been. We don't have a future, only the perception of *future*. The secrets of the cosmos are being revealed, Detective, the secrets of the biological sciences are rapidly being discovered, more or less in tandem, because the time has come— we are passing through the appropriate space—for such revelations. It's inevitable. All these things are already known, and have been known ahead of time. It's just a matter of stumbling across the appropriate information. Of catching up to time."

Crossing a foot over the opposite knee, the man gave his ankle a scratch through his sock.

"A simple theory, really," Honigwachs continued. "Sufficiently outrageous that I tend to keep it to myself. Essentially, the space traveller who does not age relative to those left behind on earth is living in real time.

It's the aging and dying on earth who are caught in the time warp, out of sync, muddled in the ignorance that comes with being strapped to the past. That will not change, but it seems to me that on rare occasions humanity passes through a grid where we do manage a paltry catch-up, a smidgen of progress, so that we live closer to the speed of light. Now appears to be one of those epochs, or spaces. More accurately, space-times. Best understood if we can agree that there is no *now*, only a *then* which carries the appearance, the artifice, the conceit, of being *now*. Sometimes we stumble onto *then*. We find ourselves on the threshold of an extraordinary age of discovery. Everything on earth—customs, cultures, politics, everything—is on the brink of change during such times. I know that you're here on serious business, Cinq-Mars, so I'll leave you with that."

Cinq-Mars liked the theory. While it was flaky, and could easily be reasoned into submission, he admired the mind willing to deploy the rational in service of the outlandish, to see what might float free. The theory was also, Cinq-Mars intuitively recognized, married to the ego of its progenitor. "Mr. Horningwachs—" he began, then paused.

The man allowed his smile to fade slowly, uncertain if he had been sideswiped or not. "Honigwachs," he corrected him again. "It's not *that* hard."

"Sorry. Honigwachs. I'll remember that now. Mr. Honigwachs, forgive my memory. Last night I got shot at. Getting shot at makes me lose sleep and losing sleep makes me irritable. When I'm irritable I eat too much. It's an old habit, a bad one. Eating too much puts me out of sorts. When my stomach goes out of whack, my brain follows suit. I hope you'll forgive my rudeness."

Honigwachs touched his fingertips to his chest. "There's nothing to forgive, I assure you."

Cinq-Mars jumped to his feet at that, suddenly a jack-in-the-box of energy and motion. "There is! If I were on the ball I'd discuss your theories of the universe. See how you melded those together with polo and horses. I'd question your use of the grey colt as your second horse when clearly he gets winded early—though, like you, I admire his initial speed—and I should be asking about the security concerns at BioLogika now that your Head of Security is dead. Instead, I can't even keep your name straight."

The president rose as though to see him to the door. "Everybody can have an off day."

"On the other hand, since I'm here, let's get to the bottom of this. Are you not alarmed that your Head of Security has died a violent death? Alarmed, I mean, for the welfare of your company."

Cinq-Mars was glad that the president did not know what to make of the interloper in his office, what to take seriously or how much he should dismiss. Honigwachs was a man given to command, and to control, and yanking that scaffolding out from under him amused the detective. His tired state didn't help, an upset stomach was certainly a nuisance, but Cinq-Mars was a great believer in turning liabilities to work in one's favour, which he was doing now.

"I was so shocked by the death, I just never gave it any thought. I assumed that it was unrelated to BioLogika," the president admitted.

"Why would you do that? What else could it be related to?"

Honigwachs shifted around a little. "I don't know. I assumed, I guess, that it was either a random act of violence, or maybe something personal. We have security concerns, yes, but never anything that's attracted violence."

"Do your security guards wear guns?"

"I suppose they do," Honigwachs admitted.

"So you do allow for the possibility of violence, for a possible need to resort to physical force."

"The guns are a deterrent, I suppose," Honigwachs argued.

"A deterrent to whom, may I ask?"

"I don't know. Mischief-makers."

Cinq-Mars smiled. He was only too happy to take him up on that one. "Armed mischief-makers?" he asked.

"You know what I mean," Honigwachs contended.

"I don't." Cinq-Mars took a deep breath, then said, "I have a better use for your grey, your second mount. He'd be superior on the hunt, able to pace himself, and yet still make good use of his speed on a dash. As it happens I believe I can put you next to a buyer. Then you'd need a replacement. But here's a coincidence! I have an animal, a four-year-old filly, who's not going to be sold to anyone less than a two-goal player."

"So that's what this is about," Honigwachs caught on. "You're selling me a horse. I've heard that horse-men have to keep their wits about them around you."

"Everything in life is a horse trade, sir. Are you a scientist?"

"That's how I was trained. My role has evolved over the years."

"How so?"

"Early in my career I grew frustrated with the slow pace of research funding—and the precariousness of funding—so I became involved in that aspect of the work." The lilt of his voice was rising, becoming more animated, as though talking about himself had launched him on a speech. "Years later, I still haven't gotten back to my research."

"I see." Cinq-Mars stood and roved around the room, admiring in particular the sports trophies placed on high. "What sort of security matters would involve your Head of Security, sir?"

"We're a biotech concern, Detective. We have a variety of issues."

"Educate me. Your Head of Security has been

murdered. Shot through the throat. Dumped in the lake. Not a pretty sight. I need to know who might have an interest in penetrating your security."

"So you *are* here about Andrew. Yes, I can see where these matters might become your business." The president shook his chin slightly, gazed upward and pulled his hands apart. "They're numerous." He brought his hands together again, knitting the fingers as though to diagram the complexity. "Any biotech firm must be wary of forced entry. We have drugs here, and the ingredients for drugs, desired by the illegal drug trade. We have dangerous materials. For instance, we wouldn't want some dumb crook releasing a virus into the atmosphere. In addition, any biotech firm has to be vigilant about special interest groups. Specifically, animal-rights advocates can be a nuisance. But our primary concerns, Mr. Cinq-Mars, revolve around internal and external espionage."

"Meaning?"

"Meaning that we are on the leading edge of biotechnology. We develop and hoard secrets. Our research into cancer and A I D s will be beneficial to mankind, and will also create wealth. That's the nature of the beast. We have competitors, Mr. Cinq-Mars, who'd dearly love to learn what we are doing. They try to keep tabs on our progress. They'd like to have access to what we know. Our information, our research, our knowledge is an exceedingly valuable resource. Combating espionage is the number-one priority for anyone who heads up our security department. Now that we have a vacancy, maybe I can interest you in the job."

His hands thrust into his pants pockets, Cinq-Mars rattled his keys. He did not acknowledge the offer, which he assumed to be in jest. "Is Hillier-Largent Global a competitor, Mr. Honigwachs?"

The man turned at the sound of the name as if Cinq-Mars had scraped chalk on a blackboard. "*Global.*

Hillier-Largent is about as global as my left buttock. Both those clowns worked here, Sergeant-Detective."

"Who?"

"Hillier *and* Largent. They broke away and took scores of my employees with them. They stole secrets, people, data, information, and departed with a reputation they'd earned on my dime. They turned that reputation into research funds, contacts and contracts. Yes! They're competitors. For certain kinds of minor issues. Murderers, no, if that's what you're thinking. They didn't kill Andy. Nevertheless, they are Class-A scumsuckers."

"If they didn't kill him, who did?"

Rising also, Honigwachs was unsure whether to treat the question seriously. "If I knew, Detective, I'd tell you."

"I see. This is not a secret the time warp is releasing at the moment."

"I presume you're pulling my leg." He was coming around the broad curve of his desk. "Bear in my mind that science has put the kibosh on countless scoffers."

"In my opinion," Cinq-Mars stated flatly, as though this had been the only subject on his mind, "if your second horse had similar speed to the one you use in that position now, but more stamina, you could move to being a three-goal player. Without that advantage, you may have reached your threshold."

Honigwachs laughed. "In other words, I must buy your horse. Do you always have half a dozen topics on your mind at once, Cinq-Mars?"

The detective was slowly shaking his head. "No, sir." He held out his hand. "There's only one matter on my mind. Thank you for your time, Mr. Honigwachs."

The president shook the proffered hand, looking him in the eye as though to unravel meaning there. "Thanks for coming in. It's a nasty business. I hope you'll keep me informed concerning your progress. If there's anything that we can do—"

"We?" Cinq-Mars inquired sharply. Honigwachs had used the word before.

"BioLogika," Honigwachs explained.

Cinq-Mars nodded. "I could probably use an antacid."

Opening the door to guide him out, Honigwachs enjoyed a laugh again. "There's a pharmacy in the strip mall up the road, sir."

"I see." Cinq-Mars raised a finger, as though a light in his head had suddenly switched on. "Darkling Star."

Honigwachs appeared to blanch as he took a step back. "What?"

"Darkling Star. That's the name of your grey colt." Regarding him curiously, the detective spoke slowly, for apparently his words possessed a power of which he was unaware. "It just came to me. Remember, I've got a buyer for that animal."

"And the one matter on your mind is?"

Cinq-Mars's response was a mild grunt and a slight wave goodbye. But he turned and stepped back into the doorway. Honigwachs hadn't moved. "Tell me about Andrew Stettler. Was he married?"

"Andy played the field. He was a fine young man. Bright. Ambitious. Charming when that worked for him. Aggressive when he had to be. He performed his job well. I considered him a friend, at least within the limits imposed by our professional relationship."

"He kept you protected?"

"I'd say so."

"Perhaps he did his job too well. Have you thought of that? Stettler might have died for the sake of your company, sir."

Honigwachs nodded with a certain gravity. "That hadn't actually occurred to me, Detective. I can't imagine that he came up against murderers. Conspirators, yes. People willing to accept a bribe in exchange for secrets, of course. But killers? I can't imagine that our society has come to this."

Cinq-Mars huffed, throwing up a hand. "It's the old time warp thing again, isn't it? We live in our primitive past. You, for instance."

"What about me?"

"You called Stettler a friend."

"I considered myself his mentor, to a degree."

"And yet, one day after he's dead, you're taking a shower in your office. You showered before I arrived, didn't you?"

Honigwachs was growing impatient. "I usually do in the morning."

"In your office, not at home?"

"I just came from playing squash, Detective."

"I thought so. I noticed the trophies. In the building?"

"At my club. I prefer to towel off there, shower and change here. I'm not partial to men's locker rooms."

Cinq-Mars gave a little burp of laughter. "You needn't explain yourself, sir. I'm not interrogating you."

Honigwachs cocked his head with curiosity and some misgiving. "Then why the questions?"

"To make a point. One day after your friend dies—a man you consider to be your acolyte—you're playing squash. You're not experiencing such sustained grief or upset that you are willing to break with routine."

"Mr. Cinq-Mars—"

"I neither condoned nor judged you, Mr. Honigwachs," the detective stressed, briefly throwing up his hands. "I'm just pointing out that our society has come to this, and it's rather silly to express surprise. We live in a world—don't we?—where people die and their friends play squash. We live in a world where a company dedicated to alleviating the suffering of the sick and the dying is in it for the money. As you said—

your words—it's the nature of the beast. You cannot imagine that Andrew Stettler came up against murderers. Perhaps we don't move in the same circles, you and me, despite what you said earlier, because I can't imagine that he didn't. In any case, he did. I saw the body. That proves it. So, I have to imagine what for you is unimaginable, Mr. Honigwachs, that's my job. I have to imagine that killers were involved in the life, not to mention the death, of Andrew Stettler, not just white-collar thieves trading secrets. But listen to me, are you playing this winter?"

"Playing?" As if punched on the chin, the president's head jerked back with the surprise of the question.

"Polo."

"Have you looked outside, Detective?"

The detective smiled and nodded. "Not here, sir. Boca Raton. Florida."

Honigwachs jogged his head from side to side a little. "Depends. The demands of work, Cinq-Mars. They can never be predicted. Why do you ask?"

"Because, sir, if you are going down there this year, we should talk. You might want to borrow my filly. See the difference for yourself. I warn you, though. Try her and you'll want her, and the price—now that I've seen your professional digs—has gone up. Good day, sir."

"Have a good one, Detective."

The building was populated with office staff now, noisy with activity and conversation, the buzz of telephones and fax machines. The detective waited for the elevator to rise, contemplating the dynamics of time warps and murder in the dead of winter, and what was it about this man that he remembered, on the pitch, his grey colt thundering, eyes wild, losing ground to a horse he often beat, the grey gasping for air at the end of the chukker, the rider's mallet swung high. And there, then, seeing the rider's eyes, pleasant enough, common enough, but galvanized that day on the ball and on driving the other horse off, despite his own animal's obvious fatigue, and swinging, the mallet exquisitely controlled, and patient despite the rampage of the moment, the click upon the ball, the herd swinging right to chase it down, then—yes, that was it—the rider not bothering to join the new pursuit, knowing his animal was winded, but holding his colt back to observe what commotion his play had created. That's how he remembered Honigwachs on the polo field, observant, cunning, a player who put things into motion and waited for others to beat themselves into the dust before he took the offensive again. Not a great player, but slyly effective, and tough when he had to be.

Nevertheless, the man would definitely have to change his second mount if he expected to improve his game.

In the lobby of the BioLogika Corporation, Bill Mathers was waiting for his partner. He was expecting flak from him, and promptly received it when he showed up.

"You've covered this place from stem to stern?" Cinq-Mars brayed. "That was fast. Take your shirt off."

"Excuse me?"

"Show me the bright red S on your chest."

"Émile, settle down. Take a peek. I picked up an escort." He nodded toward two gentlemen in trench coats. The one sporting a crewcut struck a sullen, threatening pose. The other was bearded, with a full growth of curly hair. Both stood with their hands in their pockets, watching the policemen. The bearded guy was the older of the two, around forty. The glasses he wore could not overcome his drained, sallow, slack-jawed appearance to make him look intelligent. He did not look particularly ornery. The other guy, if mistaken for intelligent, would probably take offence, and his crewcut cast him as mean.

"Who wears a trench coat in winter?" Cinq-Mars wanted to know.

"Sometimes they walk outside between buildings. Beats wearing a warm coat inside all day. I know because I asked."

"I see. So they attached themselves early?"

"Swarmed. Get off on floors three through five and you better know what password to punch or the Green Berets come running."

"You got nothing?"

"Approximately. You?"

Cinq-Mars moved toward the main doors. "I don't waste my time, Bill. I learned we're living in a time warp. I got offered a job. The Big Boss will let me take Stettler's position, with benefits. I'm sure I can wangle an increase in pay and a longer vacation. If I get that job, and people like you show up? I'll have your ass hauled off the premises." Cinq-Mars suddenly stopped walking. "How old was he?"

"Who?"

"Stettler."

"Twenty-eight."

"How do you know?"

"I asked."

Cinq-Mars grunted as they went through the doors and were struck by the cold outside. "Twenty-eight. He was young. Long hair. Something of a ladies' man, I hear. Let me in on this one, Bill. How does a twenty-eight-year-old long-haired stud get to be in charge of security in a place like this? What's his background? How did he acquire his expertise so young? Why him and not either of those two goons, for instance, apart from the fact that they look mentally deficient?"

"Quality questions," Mathers surmised.

"I'm interested in quality answers."

Walking to the car, they bumped into each other when they both headed for the driver's side. Cinq-Mars corrected himself, remembering that he had lent out his vehicle, and went around and waited for his partner to get in and lift the lock, then climbed into the passenger seat.

"Where to?" Mathers asked.

"Hillier-Largent Global," Cinq-Mars told him. "You can stick with me this time. Make yourself useful for a change."

They were driving off the grounds when Mathers's cellphone twittered. He fished it out of his overcoat and answered, one hand on the wheel. Saying little, he listened to the message and, when he'd signed off, told Cinq-Mars, "Hillier-Largent will have to wait. We're going to Old Montreal."

"What for?"

"The SWAT has cordoned off a block. We found the rug, Émile."

"The girl's carpet? Already?"

"Blood-stained," Mathers confirmed, "ditched in an alley. A blood trail leads away from it."

"Bill, *damn it!* Don't you carry a cherry in here?"

Mathers sighed, for he'd been through this a million times before. "Private vehicle, Émile. This is not department issue. A private vehicle does not require a flasher any more than it needs a siren."

"You don't have a *siren?* Damn it, Bill, are you or are you not a cop? Make up your mind. Now step on it. Go! Just don't get us killed. We've got a blood trail, partner. Who can ask for more than that?"

11

A BLOOD TRAIL

A short time later, Monday, February 14, 1999

Nine years before the *Mayflower* landed on Plymouth Rock, the future city of Montreal existed as a fur-trading post founded by the French explorer Samuel de Champlain. He wanted to make the island a centre of commerce, to exploit the trade in beaver pelts with Huron tribes to the west while driving the Iroquois far enough south that they could neither disrupt his trade routes nor sabotage his flank. Unwittingly, he was interacting with the geography and the natives in a way that would inscribe the nascent border between Canada and the United States.

Champlain would propose to the Huron that they intermarry with the French to form a new race, an idea considered, and eventually discarded, by the Indians, although unions between individuals of the two races were common and accepted. That original settlement on the island failed, but about thirty years later, in 1642, the next wave from France arrived with motives other than commerce, and this second adventure succeeded, never to be vanquished.

Greed, business, and beaver pelts did not constitute the backbone of the second fledgling settlement, not immediately. The newcomers represented a more

tenacious force. As in Plymouth to the south, where
the Pilgrims persevered, the basis of their rigor was
piety. From the dawn of its conception, then,
commerce and religion were the quarrelling progeni-
tors of the unborn city.

Old Montreal traces its origins back to that second
French settlement, on a flood plain by the riverside
adjacent to the current harbour. The adventure to
create a community in the New World had been
undertaken by a secret Catholic sect known as the
Order of Saint Sacrement, distinguished by the wealth
and privilege of its members. A particular obsession of
the Order focused on the conversion of heathens and
heretics—for them, the stunning opportunity to
convert an entire continent was too enticing to resist.
An agency was formed in France called The Association of Gentlemen for the Conversion of the Savages in
New France on the Island of Montreal, which recruited
men and women for the cause. Subsequently, a
company of warriors and saints, labourers and misfits,
crossed the Atlantic to bide among the Iroquois on the
island of Montreal.

Upon landing, the first item of business was to erect
an altar, where the company's nurse placed a glass vase
in which she'd trapped fireflies that flashed and glowed
in the gathering gloom, a moment, perhaps, that initiated the city's penchant for poetic expression in
perilous times. What had also commenced was the
enduring friction between religious orders and the
mercantile class, between secret societies and, if not a
savage, then an obstinate public, one not so easily
converted to anything.

Not much had changed, not in essence, Cinq-Mars
was thinking as he and Mathers sped into the old town.
Here the city showed its European heritage. The stone
of the aged buildings proved its mettle in winter, a
fortress against the elements. Narrow, cobbled streets

dated back to a time before the automobile had been imagined. Archways leading to the rear of stout buildings had been constructed high so that the riders of horse-drawn carriages would not need to duck. The vast expanse of the New World had not yet inspired the early architects to use the space, the more important influence being the need for warmth and the protection gained by close proximity, a buttress against both winter's severity and tribes of warring neighbours. On a cold, snowy morning, particularly, the beauty of the old town came into its own, reasserting its place in history.

In contemporary times, the conflict between piety and avarice had been replicated by the agitation between political and commercial forces. The drumbeat of Quebec nationalism, possibly to the detriment of a sporadic economy, had replaced the covert agendas of religious sects. On occasion, at least in the view of the minorities, the historic conversion of the savages found new voice in politicians rankled by the failure of ethnic populations to see things their way. The more things changed, the more they stayed the same, and this was especially so, in the opinion of Émile Cinq-Mars, when it came to secret societies. Terrorist cells would come and go. And while restrictive religious orders had lost their hold, occult groups filled the void to a minor, and perplexing, degree. Hydro-Québec— the largest supplier of electricity in the world, the company that dammed northern rivers and flooded huge tracts of native land to run the summer air-conditioners of New York City—was for a time riddled with members of the Order of the Solar Temple among its employees. The Order was a suicide sect responsible for scenes of mass death in both Quebec and Europe. As well, the work of secret societies was most conspicuously represented by warring gangs, the Mafia and the West Enders, among others, having yielded to, or been absorbed by, rival biker gangs—such as the Hell's

Angels, the Rock Machine and their new confederates, the Bandidos, who were moving up from Texas—all battling with dynamite and Uzis and chainsaws for their criminal turf.

As if that weren't enough, Russian coalitions were also flourishing. Jamaican youth gangs peppered the mix, following their wave of immigration. And organized crime syndicates from Hong Kong were finding a niche following communist China's reclaiming of their city.

For the same reason that Champlain had wanted the island of Montreal to be a fur-trading post, to do business in the west and guard against the south, criminal gangs also found the city ideally situated. An inland harbour leading to the oceans of the world helped with the import and quick distribution of narcotics and other contraband. The easy access between Toronto, to the west, and New York, south, both six hours away by car, assisted with cross-border commerce and the movement of guns, drugs, money and people. Often it was helpful to shunt enterprises across the relatively open frontier, keeping activities beyond the reach of even the most interested law enforcement agencies. By obliging police agencies from different jurisdictions and countries to cooperate one with the other, criminals discovered that they could retard investigations for years, and foil many forever.

That Montreal had become an international banking centre helped the criminals as well, and that the city was renowned for pharmaceutical research created a surplus of scientists willing to work at the behest of the gangs on illicit drugs in exchange for substantial remuneration.

The first leader of the island outpost, the tall, soldierly de Maisonneuve, had declared that if every tree on the island of Montreal proved to be an Iroquois warrior he would sail forth and build the New World anyway. True to his word, he had voyaged to Montreal and, like the others, discovered beauty that first evening on a wilderness altar illuminated by fireflies. He would build his community. He'd combat floods with faith and arrogance, and cause the river to recede by planting a cross on the mountaintop—or at least get lucky with that move, for the water did subside. He'd convert natives and engage in the Iroquois wars. He'd contest starvation, disease, death, and mosquitoes with prayer and fortitude. As had been the case at its conception, the city thrived with joy and high spirits while also undertaking brutal battles.

For the most part, Montreal was a pleasurable city—fun, peaceable, pleasant, safe, interesting, lively—usually ranked with New Orleans and San Francisco as the most distinctive on the continent. But a side of the city had become a war zone, the death count mounting. It had been that way at the beginning, and Cinq-Mars believed that little had changed.

Mathers's car rumbled on the cobblestones of rue St. Paul, then turned the wrong way down narrow St. François-Xavier. Traffic had been halted throughout a radius of several blocks, and Mathers parked behind a line of police cruisers. The rest of the way would be managed on foot. Their gold shields weren't necessary. Cinq-Mars was universally recognized, and they walked with the brusque disposition of cops on the job. Uniforms watched from doorways as the pair of detectives strode down the sidewalk to where the s w a t marshalled forces. Cinq-Mars noticed that the rooftops were occupied by police snipers while, behind cars, cops readied themselves for heavy weapons fire. If the action was gang-related, a cop never knew what degree of force might greet him. Smart ones expected the worst.

A colleague signalled Cinq-Mars to an alleyway and gave the two rumpled detectives a bemused smile. Lieutenant-Detective Remi Tremblay, tall and angular

with an academic's demeanour, shifted his weight from
side to side to warm his feet. He nodded to his friend.
"Heard you had a bad night. Looks like it, too."

"You're out of place, Remi. Where's your desk? I
haven't seen you this far south of a coffee machine in
months."

"If I'd known you were getting out of bed, Émile, I
wouldn't have bothered."

"What've we got?"

Tremblay displayed the carpet, partially unrolled
over a bulwark of trash cans. A modern design, Cubist-
influenced, with irregular blocks and rectangles of
colour and bold black lines. A yellow patch was stained
with blood. "We're guessing the vehicle stopped in this
little alley to unload. Somebody dripped blood halfway
down the block and crossed the street."

"No van?"

"No van."

"Who found the carpet?"

"A janitor. This is somebody's parking spot, a
tenant in an office. The janitor clears snow in the
morning. He came down, found the carpet, says he
unrolled it to check if it was worth keeping. The bloodstains were warm enough to come off on his gloves. So
he called it in."

Things went your way sometimes, Cinq-Mars
mused. He studied the block. Cops were everywhere
but he saw no action. "What's our situation?"

"The blood trail disappears on the sidewalk, outside
that wood door. Uniforms are inside, room to room.
We'll hear back soon."

Cinq-Mars sighed deeply. "Let's hope," he said. "I
appreciate your getting the news out."

"A cop was shot at, Émile. Just because it happened
to be you doesn't change our approach. Have you been
pissing people off lately?"

Cinq-Mars smiled, then beckoned his friend closer

for a whisper. Both officers were tall, half a head above the others around them. "Remi, this could be real enough. Gut feeling. This could be bad."

Tremblay nodded emphatically, as though he had already reached the same conclusion himself. "I'd say so. Attack on your house. A murdered young man, that's not friendly. A native woman kidnapped."

Cinq-Mars signalled his superior to incline his ear again. "The point is, we need good people inside that building, Remi. I don't want dead air. I want live radio."

Gravely, Tremblay nodded with understanding. "That's the word I gave out, Émile. I didn't say it lightly. Not much we can do about it now. Do you want to wait in the car? Warm up? You really look a mess."

Detective Bill Mathers quit the wait and headed back up to rue St. Paul, where a coffee shop had remained open despite losing its morning business to the police action. He ordered a coffee to give his system a jolt and after a sip stepped across to the public phone situated in a cramped corner. After three rings his wife picked up.

"Bill. Oh, Bill, where are you?"

"I'm downtown."

"Don't kid me. You're in Old Montreal, aren't you? I heard the traffic report. You're messing up the rush hour. Is there a gunfight?"

"I'm in a coffee shop, actually, having a conversation with my wife. I'm the only customer and the chef's not shooting anybody yet. How're you doing, Donna?"

"We're okay. Kit's coming down with something. I hate to say it but she's so cute when she sneezes. You?"

"Bad night. You can imagine. I miss you, sweetheart."

"Do you?"

"Oh yeah. I'm tired, sweetie. I'm beat."

"I bet. So what is it?" Donna pressed him.

"What's what?" The man behind the counter had caught his eye and gestured to indicate that he'd carry over his coffee, which he'd left on the counter, if he liked. Mathers agreed, and stretched out his hand to receive the cup.

"The missing-me-sweetheart bit. What do you want to say?"

She'd make the better cop, he believed. Perhaps he really was hopeless at disguising his intentions. If tempted, however mildly, by a flirtation, Mathers would cut it off quickly, knowing that he'd never be able to hide the truth when he got home. "Have you talked to Sandra, by any chance?"

"This morning? I called. No answer. Why?"

"Busy with the horses, probably. She'll call when she gets a chance."

"Bill?"

"What?"

"You're stalling."

He'd like to have her on his side in an interrogation room. "I'm just drifting, sweetheart. I'm so tired."

Her silence felt weighted.

"What?" he asked.

"Don't 'sweetheart' me," she warned him.

Mathers reminded himself to keep some things in perspective. The next time he was toe to toe with a gruesome con he'd remember what was really difficult in life. Compared to explaining to his wife that they might have to go into hiding, breaking down a homicidal gorilla goon was child's play.

"Sweetheart—"

"Stop that! Don't do that, Bill!"

"All right. All right. Listen. There was an attack on Émile last night. He came through unscathed but, you know, it was at his house."

"Oh, God. Bill. Sandra must be frantic!"

"Their place will be under guard for a while. Donna, it might be a good idea if we vacate the apartment for a bit."

"What?"

"Not for long. It shouldn't be for long."

"What? Bill!"

"It'll be wise to take precautions, too. There's a possibility—however remote that is—that we could also be in danger. Nobody knows why."

Now her silence felt altered, as though time had elapsed, as if the hands on a clock had rewound. The quiet was lighter, airier, as if what had been compressed had suddenly been released, taking flight.

"Where will we go?" Donna Mathers asked her husband in a hushed voice.

"My sister's, I was thinking."

"Bill, does Janice have two extra rooms, or a double bed?" she chided, as though his organizational skills were deficient. Bill Mathers waited, allowing the implications to sink in, grateful in a bizarre way that his wife, finally, was not getting the better of him. "Oh, God," she said, catching on. "You're not coming with us?"

"For Kit's sake, for yours, it's too risky."

"Oh, William. Bill!"

"I'll still see you. I'll still slip by. This shouldn't go on for long, sweetheart."

"I can't take this!" she finally blurted out. "Not again. This is not a life."

"Donna, come on, I'm a cop."

"You're a cop. Fine. I signed on for that. But *you* signed on to be Émile's partner, and nobody said that *that* was for life. You can get a new partner and give yourself back a normal cop's life. God knows that's bad enough."

Mathers still held the coffee cup in his hand and he took a second sip. He exhaled with exasperation. "Donna, you know I can't bail out on him now."

"That's the difference between me and you, Bill. Because I can."

She hung up.

He stood there, beat, and wondered why in the movies when someone suddenly hung up the other person would keep on talking. "Hello? Hello?" the actor would say into the phone. Who would do that? Who would talk to that persistent buzz which told anyone with a brain a fraction the size of a pea that he'd been disconnected? Mathers gave her a minute, sipped his coffee, then dialled again.

"Donna, don't do this."

She didn't speak for awhile, and he hoped that what he detected in her breathing was resignation. "All right. I'll take Kit to Janice's. But you and I have to talk, Bill."

"Good. Take the bare minimum with you. I'll pass by later to pick up what you need. Now listen. When you go, take a cab to the shopping centre. Step inside for a few minutes. Go out a different exit and grab a cab to Janice's from there. Okay?"

He heard the intake of breath, the dawning awareness of danger. "All right," she consented.

"Good girl. Don't worry. Things will be okay."

"Things have to change, Bill."

"Just let me get through this case."

"Émile's been saying that to Sandra for as long as they've been married. During every slam case he says it."

"Donna, we'll talk it through when we're out of this one. I promise."

"Think hard about leaving Émile, Bill. Don't think you're going to wriggle out of our talk. Now, goodbye, and please, please, take care of yourself."

He waited. She didn't hang up on him this time. "Bye for now. Take care. I'll be in touch."

"Good thinking. You do that."

As he hung up the phone, he noticed his cup trembling in its saucer.

The feet of thirty cops thundered on the hardwood floors as uniforms, detectives and s w a t moved on the double. The all-clear had sounded, but no one dared trust the news, so cops were checking doorways and swarming apartments, confirming "Clear!" as they shunted through rooms previously gone through by the s w a t, up stairwells and along corridors.

By the time he reached the top floor, Émile Cinq-Mars, like anyone else over thirty, was puffing, running on the memory of an athletic youth.

Wearing a vest and hoisting an automatic rifle, a cop gestured him down to an end room on the fourth floor and Cinq-Mars walked over with Tremblay and Mathers in tow and stepped inside. The office space was bare and dusty, with an atmosphere of long-term abandonment. The air tasted stale on his lips and the corners of the room were propped up by cobwebs. Windows wore the oily grime of the city as a second skin. A kitchenette, an area that now interested those cops first on the scene, was separated from the expansive main room by an island counter. The new arrivals quickly discerned the attraction. The sink and countertop showed fresh bloodstains, and bloody balls of gauze and cotton batting littered the floor. Mathers pointed with his toe to a syringe. Tossed against the radiator lay an empty i v bag.

"Some of it's recent, some of it's old," a s w a t sergeant offered.

"An operating table," a second officer confirmed.

"Check this out," the s w a t guy said. "It's definitely recent." Each man, including Cinq-Mars, Tremblay and Mathers, bent over the countertop to closely eyeball an unusual pattern. A semicircle and, off to one side, a burned splotch marred the surface.

"What do you make of it?" Tremblay inquired.

"Acid," an officer replied. "Burned right though to the wood."

The room grew quiet with the news.

"Blood's caked," Cinq-Mars mentioned. "They got out before we got in."

"Forensics?" Tremblay called out.

"On the way!" brayed a uniform from the doorway.

"Émile?" the Lieutenant-Detective asked quietly.

Cinq-Mars shook his head, despairing. "They want her alive, that's the good news. The bad news is, they've got her alive and we don't know why, we don't have a clue what they're after. The acid—I don't want to contemplate what that means. We have to find out what she knows that others want to know so much. We have to do it sometime soon."

"All right," Tremblay decided. More detectives were coming into the room and awaiting orders. "Canvass the neighbourhood for anybody who saw that van arrive or depart, or for anybody who noticed a young woman walking away in the company of men. We need to run down possible physicians, starting with any sawbones connected to a gang. Filter through the usual hacks after that. Then think about legitimate doctors, maybe in the neighbourhood. There might've been a few vehicles coming and going—ask if anybody noticed traffic. Émile?"

"She lost blood. They might be wanting some."

"Bikers have their own supply." Worried about AIDS, the warring gangs maintained private stocks.

"Doesn't matter. They still need a lab to make the match. Nobody knows for sure that it's a biker action anyway. Run down the hospitals and the labs, look for emergency requests."

"Done. Get on it," Tremblay told his men, and as they were rushing out he moved across with Mathers and Cinq-Mars to the broad windows for a private chat. "Do we have a next move?"

"Her name is Lucy Gabriel," Cinq-Mars told him. "She's native, from Oka. We know next to nothing about her, except that she works at a pharmaceutical company called Hillier-Largent Global. Bill and I are heading there now. I'd like background information on her and on the dead man, Andrew Stettler. Can you put some people on that? I'd really appreciate it, because after we do this interview, Bill and I will need personal time. I'm whacked. Last night was no accident, Remi. The bull's-eye on my forehead might not scrub off anytime soon."

Nodding, Lieutenant-Detective Remi Tremblay placed a hand on his friend's shoulder and left it there a moment. "Go," he said. "I'll have the background checks done. You take care." He nodded deliberately at Mathers to include him, and the partners left the room, their footsteps echoing off the stained oak flooring.

Mathers hurried ahead at a fair clip down the stairwell until Cinq-Mars called him back. He was moving stiffly now, his calves and thighs having knotted following the sprint up the stairs. "Is there a horse race I don't know about?"

"Sorry, Émile. I'm pent up."

"Not enough gunfights for one day? You're hoping to take somebody out?"

Cinq-Mars was leaning to one side and holding the banister as he stepped down on one foot, tilting in the opposite direction for the other, as though his knees and hips were locking up. Lack of sleep sometimes did that to him, old horse-riding injuries acting up in his joints. As he moved, though, his muscles slowly relaxed again and he began to find his rhythm.

"That's not it. I talked to Donna. She's not too happy."

"Did you wish her a Happy Valentine's Day?"

"What? No."

"There you go. That's half your problem right there. You can't continue to make these huge blunders in life, Bill. They'll cost you."

"I don't think candy and flowers will cover this one." As Cinq-Mars reached him, he turned and they walked down together.

"Maybe not, but it won't hurt. This isn't easy for her."

"How do you handle Sandra, Émile?"

The Sergeant-Detective's short burst of laughter was so loud that it echoed down the stairwell. "That's a good one, Bill. Me—handling Sandra. Thank you for that. I needed a good laugh right about now."

The two men descended the stairs and returned to the street. To anyone watching, the elder appeared amused, the young one glum, so that no bystander could ascertain whether the raid had gone poorly or well. Cinq-Mars carried on as though he had places to go and people to contact. He acted as if he might be onto something new, on the chance that among those looking down from their windows or from behind police barricades were people with a vested interest in having him fail. The way the investigation had gone so far, he wouldn't discount the possibility that a spy had him in his sights.

Dressed in a brown habit, the cowl lying loosely around his neck, a monk used a plastic ladle to transfer soup from a stainless-steel pot to a heavy porcelain bowl. He repeated the action twice, filling the bowl, pouring with extreme care. With each scoop he swilled the soup around, sure to catch a rich complement of vegetables and lentils. He placed the bowl upon a tray. Alongside the steaming broth, the monk arranged an assortment of cheeses and bread. He poured hot water into a small green teapot and dropped in a single bag, leaving its string to dangle on the outside. Then he sliced thin squares of butter and placed them delicately upon a plate, and added a napkin and cutlery. The monk picked up the tray in both hands and departed the broad kitchen with the high ceilings and old, chipped enamel sinks, and started on his trek.

Officially, this wing of the monastery was vacant.

The monk walked down a sombre, cave-like corridor, his soft steps creating a trace of an echo off the stone walls. Forty yards along he was bathed in refracted sunlight angling through the high window. When he reached the end of the corridor, he placed the tray on a shelf while he opened the doors to a dumb waiter. The monk then placed the tray inside and pulled a rope with both hands, which lifted the tray to the floors above. As the counterweight for the dumb waiter descended on its rope, it signalled what floors the rising tray had attained with old, hand-drawn signs. The numeral nine appeared, indicating that the tray had reached that floor, and the monk fastened his rope with a quick and expert hitch.

Then he commenced to trudge up the stairs himself.

He was not an old man, despite the weariness of his walk and the ample streaks of grey throughout his wavy hair. He had to lug a considerable paunch around with him, and so he paced himself, stopping briefly on the third and fifth floors before climbing higher. At each level he was washed anew with sunlight.

At the ninth floor, the monk removed the tray from the dumb waiter and shuffled on down that corridor, away from the window light, toward the gloomy interior.

Eleven doors down, he balanced the tray in one hand and knocked.

"Come in," a woman's voice responded.

The monk opened the door and entered.

"Hey, Brother Tom, how are you?" Lucy Gabriel inquired brightly. She wanted him as a friend.

Brother Tom smiled, nodded, and placed the lunch on the simple wooden desk beneath the room's window. This was a spartan enclosure, with a cot for a bed, the mattress no more than two inches thick. Next to it stood a table and two ladderback chairs.

"Beautiful day," Lucy offered.

Mute, Brother Tom nodded, and bowed slightly on his way out.

"Have a great day, Brother Tommy!" she called as he was closing the door.

Lucy did not immediately fall upon her food. She stood by the window next to her desk, the steam of the soup bowl rising to touch her wrists and the bandage on her upper arm, then lifting higher, to touch her chin. She gazed out the tall, narrow, castle-like window, with a view of the blue winter sky, and if she stood on tiptoe and angled herself over the desk she could look left, south, to the Lake of Two Mountains, where the snow-covered ice reflected the sun.

She sat down, and in the austere quiet of the monastery's empty wing Lucy began to eat her lunch, her first as a secret novitiate. Her first meal, she thought, as a damsel in distress tucked away in what might as well be a medieval turret.

Before heading to Hillier-Largent Global, Sergeant-Detective Émile Cinq-Mars and Detective Bill Mathers commandeered an unmarked cruiser. Émile's Path-finder, pressed into service the night before as an ambulance, had been returned to the station, and Mathers parked his Ford alongside it.

They made their way up the Décarie Expressway trench. The highway was dug deep below ground level, with ramps ascending and descending, and few drivers heeded the speed limit of forty-five miles an hour unless forced to do so by heavy traffic. Mathers was doing sixty-five and still waiting for a chance to slip into the fast lane when a call came over the two-way radio.

SQ Sergeant Charles Painchaud had left an ASAP call-back request and a number where he could be reached.

"Morning, Charles," Cinq-Mars said into his cellphone. "Are you living on coffee too?"

"Slept like a child, sir. But, unlike you, nobody took a shot at me earlier in the evening. Don't have your celebrity status, I guess."

"What's up?"

"Heard you were on a blood trail. Anything come of that?"

Cinq-Mars paused while Mathers undertook a highspeed, somewhat risky manoeuvre to duck in behind a Mercedes, pass two trucks on the right, then scoot back out to the fast lane. "Gone before we awoke. We found the rug from the girl's place. It could use a dry cleaning. Interesting thing is, it looks like she received medical attention."

"That's great news! Sounds like she's among the living. I re-interviewed Camille Choquette this morning."

"Who?" He covered the mouthpiece and whispered to his partner, "Who's Camille Choquette?" Mathers could only shrug.

"You know, the woman who rents the shack where the body was found," Painchaud reminded him.

"Ah. Never did catch her name. What's the story there?"

"She can't explain what the body was doing there. Says she wasn't there. Hadn't been around for several days. Says the lock on her cabin was intact when she arrived, and nobody else has a key."

"Hang on," Cinq-Mars instructed the SQ detective.

This time he buried the mouthpiece against his coat. "What's wrong with this picture, Bill? The woman who rents the shack full-time where Stettler was found—"

"What about her?"

"—she told Painchaud she hadn't been there for days."

"Days?"

Cinq-Mars nodded.

Mathers caught on. "Then why wasn't the ice thicker?"

"Charles," Cinq-Mars said into the phone, "do you remember the heavy bar on the floor of that cabin? It looked like a railway lining-bar, some kind of crowbar."

"She cracks the ice with it," Painchaud explained.

"Sure she does—when the ice is thin!" Cinq-Mars roared back. He switched ears and spoke more softly. "When it's thin she cracks the ice. When it's thick, she uses an auger, like everybody else, or a chainsaw. If she hadn't been there for days, how could she *crack* the ice?"

Painchaud went quiet a moment to contemplate the point. "I'll have to re-interview. She's gone to work. I'll catch her there maybe."

"One more thing. A minnow bucket was on site. Minnows were swimming beneath a thin layer of ice. Categorically, that shack was *not* unoccupied for days. Hang on a second," the senior detective requested. The car was heading off the expressway, where the road diverged in different directions, and Mathers chose the quiet streets of Ville St. Laurent. Cinq-Mars needed a second to think this through. He asked Painchaud, "Where does she say she's been lately?"

"Home alone," the SQ sergeant replied.

"This is what you do." As Bill Mathers looked across at him, Cinq-Mars caught himself. "Sorry. This is what I'd do if I were you."

"I'm open to suggestions," Painchaud assured him.

"Talk to her husband."

"She's not married. She lives alone."

"Better still. Find out who babysits her daughter. Talk to the sitter. See what that tells us about her schedule. Then do the re-interview. Compare her schedule with the babysitter's version."

"Good thought. I'll take care of that. There's something else that'll interest you. The woman works at Hillier-Largent Global."

"You're kidding! Does she know Lucy Gabriel?"

"Yes. I told her about Lucy and the news upset her. Ms. Choquette used to work at BioLogika, also, but that was long before Andrew Stettler showed up."

"She works at Hillier-Largent, and used to work at BioLogika," Cinq-Mars repeated to Mathers, the phone in his lap. "I'm declaring a pattern as of right now."

"What was your first clue?" Mathers asked, tacking on a grin.

"Do me a favour, Charles," Cinq-Mars requested into the phone. "Delay your re-interview. Don't talk to her inside Hillier-Largent. Keep it external."

"You're on. I'll keep in touch."

"I owe you, Sergeant."

"Balances out."

"All right. Thanks for all this."

Émile Cinq-Mars shook his head as they turned down a residential street, a mix of parks, duplexes and individual homes. Snow clearance was usually tardy in this district, and the street had narrowed. Sidewalks were engulfed by snowbanks and parked cars intruded into the traffic lanes. Vehicles travelling in opposite directions had to wend their way around each other with care, the traction slippery. Although Bill Mathers drove with authority and ease, his older partner kept one hand on the dash as though a crash were imminent. Cinq-Mars was not distressed, merely distracted by his fatigue and the intermittent churning of his digestive system.

"Go figure. Charles Painchaud is one cooperative cop. I wonder about him."

"You two should partner up, Émile. Cross the great divide. Get married."

"What's with you?"

Mathers shrugged. He checked his mirror to make sure the car behind him was capable of stopping as he pulled up to a red light. He told Cinq-Mars, "Donna suggested that I cut you loose. You're trouble, Émile."

"Donna," Cinq-Mars advised, "is a delight. Tell her we'll talk things through as soon as we're off this case. We'll see what's what. We just have to get out from under this one."

"Nice try, Émile. I think that's what I did say to her. She mentioned that that would be your usual line. I think she's on to you, partner."

Émile Cinq-Mars offered up a grunt, as though it expressed an opinion.

Hillier-Largent Global Incorporated was situated in an industrial park beyond a large shopping mall. The company did not occupy the vast space that its competitor, BioLogika, commanded, and managed as well to cope without fences, barbed wire or guards. Once inside, the detectives found that the building was more secure than at first glance, in the sense that any visitor entering the premises was prohibited from passing beyond the receptionist without an escort. All doors leading from the lobby were electronically locked. Employees had to show their identification or have their faces verified by the receptionist, then punch in a password, with the entire process recorded on videotape.

"You don't carry a weapon?" Cinq-Mars asked as he displayed his badge and, for the first time in his lengthy career, had the information off his shield written down.

The receptionist was black, exceptionally attractive, and her voice carried a Caribbean lilt.

The woman appeared nonplussed and managed a smile without responding. "Whom do you wish to see, sir?" she asked sweetly, finally.

"Lucy Gabriel. I believe she works here."

She checked her computer, then announced, "I'm sorry, sir. Miss Gabriel didn't come in to work this morning."

"That doesn't surprise me somehow. Who else is here?" Cinq-Mars inquired.

"Excuse me?"

"Hillier? Largent? Either of those guys? What about Global? Is he around?"

"Both Mr. Hillier and Mr. Largent are in, sir. Whom would you prefer to see?" She was finally aware that she was dealing with an ornery caller who had not arrived on the friendliest of terms.

Cinq-Mars appeared to give weight to the question, rocking his head slightly. "Tell you what, set up a meet," he decided. "I'll talk to both of them at the same time."

Mildly befuddled, the woman put in the call to Mr. Largent, notifying him of the policeman's request. She was attentive to instructions. "If you'll have a seat, sir," she informed Cinq-Mars after hanging up, "someone will be down shortly to escort you upstairs."

Comfortable on a pair of Naugahyde loveseats under flowering tropical plants, both detectives were tempted to nap. Cinq-Mars appeared to nod off for a second, only to be awakened by a random burp. Their escort arrived, a young, curly-headed, arrogant trainee with his sleeves rolled up and tie slackened. His glasses were thick. In one hand he carried a clipboard. In the other he drummed a pencil against the door he held open with his foot, with more than a hint of impatience, as though to suggest that he didn't have all day, that this interruption was probably retarding science. The hour was coming fast, he would have liked to announce, when he'd achieve a station in life that would allow him to speak his mind. In the meantime, he'd serve up fake smiles. "Follow me," the young man instructed. He took them around the corner to an elevator, earning the ire of the senior cop.

"Is there any particular reason why we're running?" Cinq-Mars asked him. On a good day he could keep up, but this was not a good day. His escort smiled at the rebuke. The youth struck him as bored, as if meeting someone from the outside world for the first time in months had proven, yet again, that the species remained as he remembered it—indolent, dull, dumb.

The elevator travelled just three floors to reach the top. Cinq-Mars and Mathers followed their guide to the office of the company's Chief Executive Officer, where he scurried away to save the species. *Randall Largent*, said the imprint on the door opened in their honour. Inside, two men were waiting.

As Mathers quietly closed the door behind them, the impression he shared with his partner was that they had entered a photograph, a portrait of two gentlemen frozen in time. The man who posed at the side of the desk was strikingly bald, his pate made especially prominent by his thick, black side hair, which he combed straight down. Although he tried to carry himself erect, he stooped. His partner, who was seated, had wild, Einstein-like white hair. Both returned the gaze of the visitors, until the man who was standing announced, "I'm Harold Hillier, sir. To my friends, I'm Harry."

"Randall Largent," the seated man said. He did not extend an invitation to be called 'Randy,' and remained seated behind the desk.

"Gentlemen," Cinq-Mars replied.

"Sir," Randall Largent began, "what can we do for you?"

Cinq-Mars curtly introduced himself and Mathers, then demanded, "What positions do the two of you hold in the company, please?"

"Officially," Largent explained from his leather chair, "I'm the CEO and Harry's President. What the titles mean can change on a whim. Essentially, we're equal partners. We're both men of science, only Harry's the genius. His bailiwick is the lab. I try to make myself useful in management. Now, what is this about?"

"One of your employees has been abducted from her home," Cinq-Mars declared. "We're here to investigate."

Air rushed from Harry Hillier's lungs. "What?"

"Who?" Randall Largent, still seated, managed.

"Lucy Gabriel."

"My God, *Lucy?*" Hillier slowly drew a hand across his shiny pate, to mop sudden perspiration there, then ran it down the back of his black hair.

Largent moved his swivel chair closer to his desk, as though to signal a different stage in their discussion. "Please, gentlemen, be seated."

"Lucy," Hillier repeated. "I can't believe it."

"Well," Largent declared, "I can."

"Her abduction is understandable to you, Mr. Largent?" Cinq-Mars asked. He and Mathers helped themselves to the twin chairs facing the desk. Neither man wanted to be on his feet too much today.

"Don't get me wrong, Lucy's a fine young woman. Not that I know her well, but she's upstanding, a good worker. You know how it is, she lives on a reserve. With Indians. Who knows what goes on out there? During the Oka crisis we lost her services for weeks. I'd go home at night and there she'd be—my employee—

on the evening news, taunting soldiers along the barricades, wearing feathers in her hair and war paint and those awful tie-dyed T-shirts. Can you imagine? Instead of being at her station and collecting a salary, she was behaving like a renegade. Okay, that's Lucy. We're tolerant. It's the times. But things like that, kidnappings, abductions, I expect they happen out there as a matter of routine, am I right?"

"I doubt it," Cinq-Mars told him, having stared at him throughout his discourse.

"She might have been shot as well," Mathers added.

"Good night, don't say *that!*" Harry Hillier stormed. He spun his body halfway around, then wound himself back again and shoved both hands down into his pants pockets and paced. "Coming on the heels of yesterday, this is *très* bizarre. I thought you'd come here to talk about Andrew Stettler."

"Why would you think that?" Cinq-Mars inquired, finally breaking his eye contact with Largent.

"I watch the news. I heard your name mentioned. You found the body. When your arrival downstairs was announced, I assumed you'd come about Andrew."

"Why would I?"

The partners looked at one another, as though they each needed the other to confirm their astonishment. "Sorry?" Largent asked. "Andrew was murdered. Doesn't that interest the police?"

"That investigation is being conducted by the SQ. I'm city. But I meant something else by my question. I meant, why would the death of Andrew Stettler interest the police, any police, in *you?*"

This time, in checking each other's reaction, the partners determined the source of their confusion, and the officer's ignorance. "Sergeant-Detective," Largent explained, and as he spoke smoky plumes of his white hair shook, "perhaps you're unaware that Andrew Stettler worked here."

Mathers and Cinq-Mars shared a glance.

"He doesn't mean now," Harry Hillier qualified.

"No," Largent assured them. "He worked here, after a fashion, very briefly, but he's not with us now. Pardon me, I don't mean because he's dead."

"He's with BioLogika."

"That's right. Well, *was*, poor soul."

"You're aware of that."

"Yes, sir," Largent confirmed.

"We were instrumental in finding him a job at BioLogika," Hillier pointed out.

Cinq-Mars noticed that Largent might have wanted to censor that remark, his head snapping around rather abruptly, his wild hair flying, but he didn't speak.

"Really? That's surprising."

"Why's that?" Hillier asked.

"I don't know what this has to do with anything," Largent stated irritably.

"After talking to Werner Honigwachs over at BioLogika this morning," Cinq-Mars continued, "I assumed the three of you weren't on speaking terms."

"Business is business," Largent explained. "It doesn't mean we have to like each other."

"Lucy Gabriel, now she does work for you," Cinq-Mars stated.

"Yes," Largent confirmed.

"Currently?" Mathers double-checked.

"Yes. She's been with us for a while now."

"And Camille Choquette?"

"Camille works for us," Harry Hillier spoke up. "Why are you asking about Camille?"

"Did she know Andrew Stettler when he was here?"

"I doubt it," Hillier said.

"I'm rarely down in the labs. I wouldn't know," Largent said from his chair. "Is Camille all right?"

"I saw her this morning," said Hillier, hands still deep in his pockets, still pacing. "She's fine."

"Mr. Largent," Cinq-Mars asked, "are there any other connections between Lucy Gabriel and Andrew Stettler?"

"Connections?"

"Were they friends?"

Simultaneously, Largent replied, "I don't really know," while Hillier said, "Yes."

Cinq-Mars looked at Harry Hillier.

"Lucy found Andy," Hillier explained. "She hired him as a lab rat, as someone to undergo tests for our research. She's the one who discovered he had talents. She was pleased when Randall got him the job over at BioLogika."

"That was nice of her."

"Lucy's a sweet girl."

"That's right," Largent concurred, "I remember that now. She spoke up for Andy. Lucy's always looking out for the underdog."

"In Stettler's case, what talents did she perceive in him? He was here doing—what? What does a lab rat do? Ingest drugs?"

"He would've done something like that, I imagine. I can't remember now."

"What talent would show through?"

Largent shrugged. "I expect they talked. I expect she took a shine to him. She's in the business. She knows where jobs are available. He ended up in security over at BioLogika."

"Tell me," Cinq-Mars inquired, "why don't you use monkeys or rats for your tests?"

"We do. Of course. But there comes a time when a study must progress to humans. Give a cat morphine, Detective, it'll climb the walls. Give a man morphine, he'll relax and be immune to his suffering for awhile. Every drug has to be tested on people at some point."

"You don't have trouble finding these people?"

Hillier, still standing, sighed. "I'm not saying there's

an endless supply. We need people, usually, who are healthy. Generally speaking, your skid row derelict, or your drug user, they won't do. But we do have a supply, Detective. Sadly."

"Since it's your livelihood, sir, I can't imagine that your regret is too severe." Cinq-Mars leaned forward to impress his next question upon them. "Yesterday, Andrew Stettler was found dead. He was killed the previous night, we suspect. At the time of his death, he was a young man in his late twenties and the Head of Security for a relatively substantial company. Are you telling me that he started in the field as a guinea pig— a lab rat, as you call him—and, what?—a short time later, he held a high position? I don't know what needle you stuck in his arm, but I might want a shot of that myself."

He took a breath. "Tell me, do you routinely take these unfortunates, these men and women at the bottom of society's ladder, just trying to get by—let me get this straight now—do you routinely see that they're promoted to the executive suite in competing companies? Do they come in one door, destitute and grim, then go out the other as middle-management types who have a president's ear? Does that happen often, Mr. Hillier—sir?"

Hillier shook his bald head, confirming the oddity of the situation. "I would agree, Detective," he mustered, "that Andrew Stettler was indeed a phenomenon."

Avidly nodding as well, Randall Largent apparently concurred.

Cinq-Mars stood and picked up his overcoat, which he had slung across the arm of his chair. Surprised, Bill Mathers jumped up beside him, also clutching at his coat.

"That's a story that'll be revealed," Cinq-Mars declared, "in due course. But I suspect it's a long tale, and my time at the moment is precious. I take it that neither of you knows what's happened to Lucy Gabriel?"

They both vehemently shook their heads.

"Concerning the death of Andrew Stettler—" With his coat slung over his forearm, Cinq-Mars suddenly sat back down again. Mathers didn't know what to do with himself at that moment. "Is his death as much a mystery to you as it is to us?"

"Indeed," Hillier concurred.

"We're in shock," Randall Largent stressed.

"Shock? Really? Over someone who worked for you for—what?—a weekend? He must have made an impression. Tell me, what sort of work did Lucy Gabriel do? Was she working with four-legged rats, or with the sort of lab rat who walks in the door on two legs and actually expects a check for his misery?"

Largent deferred to Hillier, an indication that his realm was the executive suite, while his partner was more likely to keep his eyes and ears tuned to the lab.

"Lucy's specialty is plasma, Detective," the bald-headed man, Harry Hillier, explained. "She takes blood. Analyzes it. Reports on her study. She's very good at what she does. But, yes, she works with the guests we hire. We discovered early on that she's naturally sympathetic with these people, so she does both jobs."

"Plasma," Cinq-Mars postulated, leaving his hosts in the dark as to his meaning. He shifted in his seat, folded and unfolded his arms, and crossed his legs. "The blood trail continues. Gentlemen, I'm off! We'll visit again. Cover some ground. I'll want a quick tour of your lab, with your permission. And I'll want to speak with Lucy's co-workers—her lab rats, as well. Perhaps today. Gentlemen, I'll see you later."

He took his leave with a flourish, and Mathers rushed to catch him. In the corridor he reached out and clutched his elbow. "Émile!"

"God help me—diarrhea," the senior partner explained, his facial muscles contorted in a fierce grimace. "Quickly! Bill. Damn it! A toilet!"

Although he had handled it with aplomb, Werner Honigwachs remained agitated by the visit from Sergeant-Detective Émile Cinq-Mars. He had not expected to be interrogated at the start of his day about Andrew Stettler's death, and had not expected aggressive questioning on the matter at any time. Part of the whole point of putting the body under the ice and creating a mystery around the death was to sidetrack the investigation and wrap the famous detective in a knot. The cop was not supposed to be on his doorstep first thing Monday morning with an attitude, that had never been the plan.

Honigwachs mentally replayed the conversation a thousand times, confident that he had not slipped, and yet confounded by the direction of the officer's inquiry and his tenacity. Cinq-Mars had had the look of a man who didn't believe him. No doubt it was a practised art, a voodoo developed over a lifetime of inquisitions. He could not allow the cop to faze him, nor could he let him push him into a blunder.

Honigwachs used his willpower to refrain from calling Camille Choquette. That would be the kind of mistake he could not afford.

Something else vexed him as well, a feeling that was difficult to identify. Not conscience, exactly. Good Lord, he was responsible, some might argue, for the deaths of dozens of people in the drug experiment program—how could he feel a pang of conscience over shooting just one man if he didn't care a whit about them? Andy hadn't been a worthy man, either. He'd been a twerp and a traitor, and although it was easy to forget it around him, he had also been a gangster, a low-life. Killing him was probably doing society a favour. He felt

no remorse for offing Andrew Stettler. And he had seen
blood before, and corpses, and had carved dead bodies,
human and animal, and gone inside the bellies of
monkeys and dogs and cats and rats with his bare hands
to examine the results of lethal experiments, and a
couple of times he had done so while the animals were
still breathing, their frightened, teeny hearts palpitating.
Gore was not the problem. And yet, he was fixated on
the moment of Andrew Stettler's death. The roar of the
snowmobile outside. The explosive blast of the pistol in
his hands. Shooting someone was a different kind of
killing. The way his head had exploded forward, dashed
against the ice as if walloped by a sledgehammer. The
body suddenly in spasms.

He was not feeling remorse. He was not feeling
revulsion. He wondered what it was, why he could not
kick the images from his brain. He couldn't stop thinking about it, he couldn't stop being *fascinated*. He
reviewed the murder because he wanted to revisit the
moment, not to do it again—he was no goddamned
maniacal killer for heaven's sake—but because he
regretted that he was not still right there in the
moment. That sensation as the second neared, the time
to shoot, to pull the trigger, knowing that the very next
second he would do it, get the job done, then Stettler's
head flinching as he fired, the instant before he fired,
the pistol jumping in his hand, that joy, the body slam-
ming down, and for that nanosecond, for that magical,
amazing flash, he knew power. And a certain cosmic
connection he could not explain, as if the stars had
taken notice. The moment had been an occasion. An
experience to remember. Again and again he'd sift
through it in his mind. Honigwachs logged minutes lost
in the maze of the instant, frozen in time, out on the
ice, entranced.

In the shower he had found himself thinking of
those precious seconds, his hand on his soapy, erect

penis. He knew he'd have to stop, square himself, claw back to reality. Reality, as it turned out, was an early-morning visit from Émile Cinq-Mars, and an impending visit from people and forces he would rather not see right now.

His secretary piped them in with her usual cheerful, singsong voice.

The first man who stepped into his office smiled and held out his hand, although he was still wearing gloves. He had very black hair that could have been dyed and was unnaturally stiff and greased back. Honigwachs knew him only as Jacques, and he had often wondered if his hair was real or a toupee. You didn't see that too often, a greaseball's toupee, but in this world you never knew. The visitor and Honigwachs shook hands, and the two guys following behind took up positions at the door. They closed it and stood on either side, each holding a wrist with his opposite hand just above his genitals, saying nothing and looking at no one.

Honigwachs offered him a chair. The man smiled again and positioned his rump on a corner of the broad desk instead. "You know why I'm here."

"Not exactly," Honigwachs told him.

The visitor was not impressed by his answer.

"Andy, he was working for your company. He was in your care, if you follow my drift. Do you think one of our boys gets blown away and me and my friends, we don't take an interest? Is that what you think, Mr. Honigwachs?"

With the man posted on the corner of his desk, the company president did not want to take a lower position by sitting in a chair. He remained standing. "I'm sorry. I didn't catch your meaning, at first. It's a big shock, to all of us."

"Is it?"

"Yes, certainly. I never expected anything like that."

"That's good. Because if you'd expected something

like that you would've mentioned it. Isn't that right?"

"That's, that's absolutely right," Honigwachs concurred, but even as he spoke he could feel the jaws of a trap closing, like a fierce, ungodly hand crushing his skull.

"How would you do that?"

The man was shorter than him by a foot, and as well dressed. He had pointy shoes and a pointy nose, high cheekbones and dimpled jowls. The lines on his forehead were wavy and deep, and his skin colour suggested that he visited southern climes regularly during the winter. His black hair, whether natural or synthetic, was slicked back close to his scalp. He was not the muscle on this crusade. Honigwachs knew him to be a spokesman of some standing. That he was here in person and hadn't sent a lower-grade goon was encouraging, a sign of respect. Of course, Honigwachs held responsibility over many tens of millions of dollars that belonged to close associates of this man.

"How do you mean?"

"How would you get in touch?"

Honigwachs had to shake his head. "You're right. You're right. I don't know how to do that. I could only get in touch through Andy, and—" He briefly held up his hands as a sign of helplessness.

"So, what, you were just going to forget about our association?"

Honigwachs tried to smile himself. He was having difficulty. "No, I assumed, I guess, that you'd be in touch."

"So you're glad to see me?" the man suggested. He had one foot on the floor, and the other swung freely back and forth.

"Yes, of course. You could say that."

"We're not going to forget about you, you know that."

"Of course not. No."

The man nodded, looking down at the floor a moment. Finally, he looked up and said what was on his mind. "Was it you whacked Andy?"

"No," the president objected, "no—"

"Because if you did, maybe you had your reasons. Sometimes people have reasons. Maybe we could talk about those reasons. Maybe Andy got out of line—"

"No! No, Andy was, Andy was great, actually. He was. He was great."

"That's true, in my opinion," the visitor emphasized. "Andy was great. He had talent, you know. He could be different people. Maybe you didn't know that about him. He could see things in ways different from other people. He could see things the rest of us missed. He was quite a guy, Andy."

"Yeah," Honigwachs said.

"Don't you think so?"

Honigwachs answered with greater conviction. "Absolutely. He was quite a guy. I liked him. A lot. Andy—he was a great guy. Really."

The man stood. He held his arms out from his body, and one of the men from the door came over and helped him out of his coat. Then Jacques removed his gloves and placed them neatly on the desk, one exactly on top of the other. He used the index finger on his right hand to draw a line down his left cheek. "If you didn't whack our Andy, Mr. Honigwachs, who did?"

"I don't know."

"You don't know. He was in your care."

"Well, I wouldn't say that necessarily. He worked for me."

"No, no, Mr. Honigwachs." Smiling again, but with only one side of his mouth, as if it was a strain to do so, Jacques came alongside the company president and, gripping his arm above the elbow, twisted it back. He hurt him. He steered him toward the window for a look at the view. When he spoke again, he lowered his voice.

"Andy didn't work for you. *You* worked for Andy. You work for me, and you work for anybody I send out here. You understand that? You're in my pocket. See this?" Reaching into a trouser pocket, he pulled out a quarter. "This is you. This is you, Mr. Honigwachs. You're in my pocket. Maybe you had a misunderstanding about that. Maybe you thought Andy worked for you, like you just said, maybe you had some kind of miscommunication like that. Maybe Andy set you straight and you got carried away with your response. Maybe you wasted him."

"You can't believe that."

"Why not? Somebody did. I see you had cops here this morning. Maybe they're thinking the same thing."

Honigwachs was stunned that this man knew about the other visit. What else did he know? "No, no, they're not thinking anything like that."

"Maybe they should," Jacques said.

"No, I, I didn't shoot Andy. I'd never do that. Even if I wanted to, which I *didn't*, I'd never have the guts for something like that. I'm not some kind of Rambo." He tried to laugh, and to get Jacques laughing along with him. "Besides, I mean, I had no reason." Honigwachs wished that he could just shut up. That would be the preferred strategy. Take charge of this conversation through reticence and disdain. He'd be more convincing that way. Sit back in his swivel chair and scoff at this man, as he had scoffed at Cinq-Mars, let him know how preposterous he was being. He also knew that he could not pull off that pose right now. He was too nervous. He had to hang in there, he had to keep talking, he had to keep denying and denying until the message got through. "I'd never shoot Andy. He was like a son to me."

"A son!" Jacques boomed. For the first time, he looked back at his men waiting at the door. They smiled, encouraged by his glance. "A son. Well, you wouldn't be the first father to bump off his kid, now, would you?"

Honigwachs declined to answer.

"Would you?" Jacques slapped the back of the larger man's head.

His head bent, Honigwachs gasped from the shock of the blow. "No," he admitted, panting. "I guess not."

"You shoot him?" He whapped the back of his head again.

Honigwachs was unaccustomed to humiliation. The burning feeling that was building in his head was partly his rage and partly his fear. "No, sir. I did not."

"Were you in that shack at the time?"

Honigwachs flinched even before the hand came up to hit him again. After he had flinched, Jacques smacked the back of his head. "No, sir!" Honigwachs said.

"You weren't there?" He hit him, the back of his fist thumping his temple, hard.

"No, sir."

"Where were you?" He hit him with a closed fist behind the right ear, three quick, solid punches that caused Honigwachs to lift his shoulders to defend himself and try to hold his head away.

"I don't remember."

"You don't remember?" Jacques smacked the back of the man's head again. "You don't remember where you were when the man who was like a son to you got whacked?" He gave him a karate chop across the back of his neck.

Honigwachs was reeling, blood throbbing in his brain. "At home, I guess."

"You guess?" He gave him a harder chop across the neck again.

"I was home. Stop hitting me." He heard a ringing in his ears. His vision had become obscured, as if tears had sprung to his eyes. He hoped they hadn't.

"You're telling me what to do?" Jacques rammed the heel of his palm into the man's ear and Honigwachs grunted with the shock of it. "You don't get to do that," Jacques warned him, then smacked his temple again. "All you get to do is take it." He slapped the top of his head again. "All you get to do is hope maybe I get tired." He punched him behind the ear again. "Not so tired that I don't just whack you, because I'm inclined to do that. Maybe you did it, maybe you didn't, maybe I'll whack you in case you did. You ever think about that? You ever think I might whack you *just in case* you were the one?" He did not hit him again, but Honigwachs stood curled against the window, waiting for the smack.

Jacques backed away and put on his leather gloves, as if this was a ritual that carried meaning, as if it indicated a change in procedure.

"I can have you whacked just by thinking about it, Mr. Honigwachs. Don't forget that. Right now, I'll keep you alive because you might help me find out who did Andy, and because I need you to take real good care of the funds that've been turned over to you for your safekeeping. I hope you take better care of that money than you did Andy, who, as I recall, was also turned over to you for you to look after. At all times, remember, all I have to do is think about it. I don't even have to change my mind. All I ever have to do is just get a look in my eye, then Jesus Christ, you're gone, you're done. All you can do then is pray the job gets done by somebody who does it properly, who keeps it neat. Some guys, you know, are sloppy about the work they do. When they do a whack it can be a mess. Keep that in mind."

Honigwachs nodded, as though consenting to the terms.

Once again, Jacques lifted his arms away from his body and one of his associates came over and helped him on with his coat. "Any suggestions? Give me a name. Tell me maybe who might have done it, who maybe was thinking about it in some kind of delirious moment."

Honigwachs shrugged. He was so thrilled to see him putting on his coat.

Jacques chuckled. "I'm not leaving here without a name."

"I don't know. He was friends with Lucy Gabriel. She's an Indian girl."

"Naw, it wasn't her."

"How do you know that?"

"That's my business. Why are you giving me the name of somebody who didn't do it? That's what guilty men do. You're looking and sounding to me like a guilty man, Mr. Honigwachs. I might do some careless thinking about you if you don't watch out."

He put up his hands as though to defend against a physical barrage. "I'm sorry. You asked for a name. She popped to mind. I wasn't saying it was her."

"It wasn't."

"So I don't have any other names."

"Just give me the name of somebody I can talk to. Because let me tell you something. Andy Stettler, he was a friend of mine. So give me the name of somebody I can talk to, and we'll see where that leads. Give me that name."

"I don't know—"

"Give me a name!"

"I …"

Honigwachs stopped talked because Jacques had reached under his coat and taken out a gun. He held it down by his side in his gloved hand, and he told him to take off a shoe.

"What?"

"Take off your right shoe, Mr. Honigwachs. Quickly, please."

Standing on one leg, the president undid his shoelace, then kicked off the shoe.

Jacques moved close to him. "Pull off that sock."

Honigwachs obeyed.

"Put your right foot forward."

"Please." Honigwachs pointed his right foot forward. The big toe sunk into the plush, dark-grey carpet. It trembled.

"Now I'm going to shoot off your toe or you're going to give me a name."

Honigwachs started hyperventilating as Jacques aimed the pistol at his toe.

"Camille Choquette," Honigwachs said.

"Who's that?" Jacques continued to aim along the barrel of the gun toward the other man's foot.

"She works at another drug company. I think they went out. They knew each other, I know that."

"So? He knew lots of people." Jacques pulled back the trigger.

"It was her hut!"

"What?"

"It was her hut! Where Andy was found. That was her hut."

Jacques looked up at him then. He nodded, and put away his gun. "Put your shoe back on," he said. "I wouldn't want you to stink out the joint."

Honigwachs fumbled with his sock, but his hands were shaking too much to get it back on his quivering foot.

"God, what's that stink? Did you shit your pants, Mr. Honigwachs?"

"No."

"I wouldn't blame you if you did. It can't be a nice thing to contemplate, your toe blown off, all that blood, not being able to walk again except with a limp. You got a fear-stink all over you."

He just couldn't get his sock back on, he was trembling too much.

"I'll look up this Choquette. See where that leads. Meanwhile, you don't have to worry about contacting me. That's never going to happen. But I'll be in touch. I want you to know that, Mr. Honigwachs, that you can count on me being in touch."

Jacques and his well-dressed toughs opened the door and went out.

Werner Honigwachs was finally able to put his sock back on, and he stood there holding his shoe. Time had stopped for him. He could not keep track of his thoughts. He turned and faced the Lake of Two Mountains again, looking out on the ice-village where the fishing huts stood as multicoloured sentinels in the sun. He remained still like that for a while, and he did not move until some time later when his secretary came in to ask him if everything was all right. She wondered why he was standing there, not moving, not saying anything, just holding his shoe and staring out the window like an imbecile.

Throughout the spasms and volcanic indignities inflicted by his body, Émile Cinq-Mars sat with a bemused resignation, too weary to indulge his misery much. Upon emerging from the cubicle into the large employees' restroom he noticed that he was pale, and washing his hands, he sank into a stupor of indifference, the swirl of water consuming his full attention. Honigwachs had talked about the planets in their traces, this spinning, this spiralling downward, a distortion of time. Straightening, he felt his feet glued to the floor, his energy sapped.

Mathers pushed open the door and, seeing him at the sink, came inside to commiserate. "Head home, Émile. We can cover this ground another time." The young cop leaned against a sink while Cinq-Mars dried his hands slowly. "You look like hell, and if you're a time bomb I don't want you going off in the cruiser."

"I've got another question to ask those two." His voice had a gravelly, weary timbre. "But I'll keep it to myself for now. This is a story, Bill."

"What is?"

"How an unemployed, destitute guinea pig, a lab rat, became Head of Security in no time at all while still in his twenties, and all that got him was a premature and violent death. I want to know why. Come on. Let's get out of here."

Bill Mathers took the elevated Metropolitan eastbound from near the industrial park where Hillier-Largent Global was housed. As they drove, they could easily see the mountain, ten miles away. On the other side was downtown. They passed the edge of an affluent suburb and turned onto the l'Acadie circle where a congested immigrant quarter began, and they got bogged down in the usual snarl of traffic there. Pedestrians and cars moved to and from a busy shopping centre. Cinq-Mars was tempted to join the hordes himself and hunt down a hit of Kaopectate, but the congestion deterred him.

"Scary," he mentioned, without any particular reference.

"What is?" Mathers was thinking about his wife, wondering what she was feeling now, trundled off to his sister's house. Perhaps she was at the shopping centre at that moment, walking through in order to change cabs, so that no single cabby could connect her point of origin to her destination. Following the line of his partner's gaze, he took in the pedestrians, an immigrant crowd, the colours and hues and languages of the world mingling and shuffling along. They were neighbours, as his apartment was located nearby, a few blocks up.

"It's scary that people sniff nose-sprays and swallow pills and allow serums to be injected into their arms to see whether or not they'll have a bad reaction. It's a game of Russian roulette."

"I've heard of worse."

"I'm not making comparisons, Bill, I'm just saying. It's amazing that this is routine. If you advertise in the paper for guinea pigs, they'll line up and actually hope to be selected."

Traffic moved a hundred feet before stalling again. "In the States," Mathers went on, "I think in Chicago, men volunteered to get AIDS."

"Excuse me?"

"I kid you not."

"For what purpose?"

"So they could be experimented on later."

"Hold it."

"That's what I heard."

Cinq-Mars had to mull that one over. "You mean that people have volunteered to be injected with HIV so they could be useful guinea pigs for a cure? How much does that pay?"

"Nothing. It's a public service. You know, men who had lost lovers but didn't get the disease, they agreed to get the disease to help with the cure. Other kinds of idealists. It's an epidemic, Émile. Some people have lost dozens of friends. Some people are willing to lay down their lives."

"Meanwhile," Cinq-Mars observed, "some scientists are willing to postpone their research until they've been assured a better cut of the profits. They say it's the nature of the beast. What do you make of that?"

"Medicine is money," Mathers postulated. "Health is big business. Medical research is a growth industry. You know how things go when money's involved."

"I've seen a few things."

"I heard that if the big international drug companies sold heroin and crack on the streets, they'd have to take a cut in their profit margins. Imagine that."

Cinq-Mars whistled at the comment, then paused to stretch in the limited confines of the car. "So far we've worked this case top-down, Bill. Sooner or later we'll try bottom-up. Trace the life and times of Andrew Stettler. How'd he win friends and influence people? How does a lab rat get to be the job-boss? What's up with Lucy Gabriel? Where does she fit in? Honigwachs and Hillier and Largent can enlighten us with their view from on high, but what's life like down in the lab, where most visiting rats get injected except for one, one special rodent, who gets promoted? I'd like to know what the technicians think."

"About what?" Mathers asked. With any luck he'd make the next light and be free to scoot up Boulevard l'Acadie. The route separated the rich from the poor, and immigrants from established residents. To further divide the classes, the boulevard was guarded with a chain-link fence down one entire side, the contemporary mansions behind it having perfectly manicured, treed lawns, while on the opposite side were row houses, scruffy apartment buildings, and scarcely a blade of grass.

"About their bosses. About life in the biological sciences. Are they idealists or skimmers? Are they devoted to antihistamines or the cure for AIDS? What do you think about the nature of the beast?"

He didn't make the light, but his would be the first car out of the chute on the next green. "You're right. We don't know the environment. Bottom-up it is."

"There's a blood trail and it's still fresh. I got a feeling we need to know what's on the ground. I bet some people are stepping on monkey poop and rat feces, and we've got to find out what's in it for them."

"Then there's Lucy," Mathers reminded him.

"That's true, there's Lucy. Did you notice? We told Hillier and Largent that she'd been kidnapped, and both of them neglected to ask the big question."

"Which is?"

"You should know."

Mathers thought for a moment. He was about to complain about his weariness when the obvious struck. "They didn't ask if there was a ransom demand."

"The first question on anybody's lips after they hear about a kidnapping, what do the bad guys want? What's the ransom? How many bucks. File that one away. Hillier and Largent didn't ask. Maybe it's because they know why somebody would want her."

"Are we going to ask?"

"Bottom-up, Bill. I want knowledge first. Then I'll ask."

Mathers shot forward on the green light as if giving chase. Pushed back in his seat, Cinq-Mars braced his abdominal muscles against an impending turmoil.

"What's next?" Mathers wondered.

"Drive us to the station. I want to pick up my car. I'm going home. Visit your family at your sister's. Just make sure you're not followed."

"We're knocking off?" Mathers doubted the apparent good fortune.

"Not quite."

"Ah, here we go. What do I have to do while you're home napping?"

Cinq-Mars tilted his head back, as if to bring his partner into clearer focus, and stared down his impressive beak at him. "Youth is not an achievement," he preached, "it's a responsibility. While I am napping, pup, you will be finding Camille Choquette's address for me. You'll also find Andrew Stettler's. Then tonight, while you're enjoying Valentine's Day with your wife, I will be talking to Ms. Choquette. Tonight, while you are making your wife feel better, I will be taking a stroll through Andrew Stettler's residence. Tomorrow morning, there will be no excuse for you to be late for our rendezvous."

"What rendezvous?"

"The ice-village, for breakfast, let's say, eight? We'll have a thorough look at the crime scene after you've had a good night's sleep. I, on the other hand, will be feeling no less ornery than I do right now."

Mathers thought about fighting back. He knew that his partner had problems. Today they were partly physical, but also he had a father who was dying, and his own home had been attacked the night before. Now was not a time to get crotchety himself and tell him to stuff his crankiness.

"I'll do my part."

"One more thing. Let's drop by your place. Surely you have some Kao in your medicine cabinet? Or, like everybody else, will you send me down the block?"

Mathers had reached his limit for one day. "We'll pass a pharmacy along the way, Émile. You can buy your own damn Kaopectate."

Cinq-Mars glared at him, astounded. "I should have known. You're like all the rest. You're a thoroughly unworthy sort of man, Bill."

Mathers chuckled. "You know where you can shove that, Émile. But before you do, let's find you that Kao."

12

PERILOUS LIAISONS

Later the same day, Monday, February 14, 1999

From a small portal in the thick stone wall, the young woman gazed down at the lake and the twinkle of lights surrounding the expanse of ice wherever cottage windows reflected the sun. Her loneliness swelled and yawed and settled inside her. From her precipice, Lucy Gabriel cast a light of her own, felt her spirit float free and rise on a sunbeam. She sensed a kinship with damsels in distress from olden days, fair maidens locked in towers awaiting rescue by a knight. She hated the association, for despite her depression and anxiety, and her aching, warring loneliness, she was a woman who wanted to act. She had every intention of slaying her own dragons and assailing her own castle walls. Her favourite fairy tales might derive from English lore, she might be a native steeped in the myths of her culture, but she also knew that she was a woman who lived in different times, modern times, one who moved across borders and communities. She worked among scientists and native activists. She had hobnobbed with criminals. While she enjoyed the nightlife of the city, she would never think to permanently move off the reserve and away from her people, for she was committed to their causes. She was off the reserve now, though, she admitted, unable to hide among her own, a refugee in a tower, hidden from the world, frightened by forces unseen and persons unknown.

Turning, she looked at the man behind her. Brother Tom checked on her regularly, although only for a few minutes at a time. As he had taken a vow of silence, their conversations would travel in one direction only.

"I need to get out of here, Bro'."

He raised only his eyes when he looked at her, the angle of his chin tilting downward slightly, perhaps denoting disapproval of the enterprise.

"I'm serious. I can't defend myself stuck in here. It's not a question of my freaking safety, it's a question of finding out who did what to who when. And then proving it. I'm the only one who can really do that."

The monk was sitting on one of two ladderback chairs. She pulled the other in front of him, sat, and leaned closer to him. Whenever he shifted his weight, the chair squeaked.

"In my house, in the garage under my house, I have a car. I have a guy who ploughs the snow. He doesn't know I'm here, he'll just keep ploughing until I tell him to stop. The point is, Bro', if we go get the car, we'll be able to get out all right." Perhaps because she was off the reserve, she deliberately wore a shirt with native embroidery and decoration. She had many shirts that carried Mohawk symbols, but over the years she'd also gone to meetings and public powwows where native crafts from all round the continent were sold, and she had acquired both jewellery and clothes from other Indian nations. The white shirt she had on now was Navaho, while the beading on her denim skirt was a Sioux creation.

"There's plenty of spots to park it down below. With our own car, we could slip out when we needed to— you could come with me, Tommy, if that helps. I don't mind. But I can't sit around on my ass all day—I'm sorry, my rear end all day—while people are messing with my life!" She had her elbows on her knees and implored him with her eyes. "Tommy. Brother Tom. I know—I know you think you're saving me from harm. But if I'm not out *there*, harm is being done to me, and you're not helping *at all*. You're hindering. I have to be out there. I'm the only one who can solve my own problems."

She made eye contact while speaking, talking as though her words flowed into the monk's eyes. She liked people to see the intensity behind her thoughts. She declined to take her eyes off Brother Tom's. Seated alongside a little pine table, his hands folded in front of him, he was squirming around a little under her gaze, his chair noisily complaining about each movement as though the wood might snap.

He appeared to be contemplating her words. She had not expected to make much headway, but with her eyes locked on his she did not detect any denial there, or any particular restraint. When she eventually chose to have mercy on him and relinquished her claim to his eyes, it seemed to Lucy Gabriel that the possibility of her request being accepted was somehow vibrant in the air.

"Brother Tom?" she stated simply, without looking at him. "I need your help."

He nodded, but she did not know what that meant exactly, or if they had agreed upon anything of substance or not.

While her husband slept into the afternoon, Sandra Lowndes fed and groomed her horses. She was glad to have him in the house during the day, even if he was in bed, and even if he had warned her that he'd be going out again that evening. She felt a certain comfort, following their eventful night, in having her husband at home.

From an early age, Sandra had known that her life

would revolve around horses. Her love for the animals
was not dissimilar to that of her school chums, but she
was convinced that her parents' assumption—that one
day her interests would break out along the predictable
paths—was mistaken. Her folks had hoped that horses
would inspire a sense of responsibility in their daughter,
that the sport would equip her with a healthy lifestyle
and a rounded education. Equestrian discipline was
supposed to be preparatory to something else—a law
degree, perhaps, or medical school. Although it was
never stated, growing up she'd come to realize that,
bereft of sons, her father imagined an important career
for his outstanding daughter. Sandra secretly discarded
his aspirations as being far too time-consuming. If his
plans were going to take her away from horses, she
wasn't interested.

As it turned out, her father did not live long enough
to be disappointed, suffering a stroke while she was in
her junior year at Brown studying American literature.
She was glad that she never had to stand up to him,
never had to refuse to carry on into law or political
science. She would have defied him. She had rehearsed
speeches to break the news and had auditioned a few
with her mother. Now, the dramatics would not be
necessary. She held his hand and whispered to him
while he gurgled in his hospital bed. He withered away.
Two months after his stroke she received the news,
before going into an exam, that her father had died.

Upon graduation, Sandra Lowndes returned to New
Hampshire to run and expand the family farm. What
had been a hobby for her father would be her life, her
passion. Although she was an experienced and accom-
plished rider, competitive events were not her primary
interest. Just as she had known that she would never
step away from horses, she had also accepted that there
would always be a better rider or a more tenacious
competitor, if not in her county, then in New Hamp-

shire, and if not in the state, then across state lines. What was more important to her than riding was the nurturing, training and, ultimately, the breeding of horses. These interests would command her devotion, and in these matters, over time, she would excel.

The death of her father had afforded certain opportunities for the young Sandra Lowndes. Her essential financial needs had been met, and she had further room for risk-taking. With experience, she would learn how to make a business work, but in the early days mistakes were common and funds were squandered. Her mother was enjoying a merry time with her share of the inheritance, travelling the world. When she died nine years later without much left to pass on, Sandra's business was in recession. The entire region was hurting, money was tight. She had to parcel off land at low prices, and that was painful, but she muddled through the bad patch and managed to keep herself afloat. She'd had to govern her expectations. Ingredients she'd counted on to give her business an eventual boost—such as a sound economy and a second inheritance—hadn't panned out. Her long-standing relationship with a local sporting goods retailer failed to result in marriage. She had put him off for years, then he had begun putting her off, and suddenly he was simply gone, off to open a new branch in Massachusetts where, he said, the opportunities were limitless.

"Opportunities," she had asked aloud, "for what?"

A light dawned. Throughout her life, she had been somewhat cavalier, and not particularly adept, in her personal relationships.

Although inclined to settle down, Sandra would no sooner get close to a man than she'd begin to analyse what benefits he'd contribute to horse-rearing. Could he bring income onto the farm, or expertise, or contacts? Could he be transformed into a salesman or a veterinarian, hired hand, something useful? Could he mend a fence or put in a well or fix a windblown roof? On one blind date, a disaster from start to finish, she had been tempted to check the guy's teeth. It took a while, but she finally understood that men did not simply stop going out with her. They'd leave the county. Or vacate the state. One scrammed all the way from Maine to Missouri—*and who, who goes to Missouri?*—and another vanished altogether.

Around the time that she met Émile—a few loves and half a dozen years later—she had begun to rethink. She'd given her life to horses, and they weren't providing much in return. Perhaps her father had been right, horses should only be a phase in a young woman's life, or a sideline that validated one's place in society. To actually raise the beasts and devote yourself to their welfare was not so much a life as a life sentence.

As the business sagged once more, the local economy again in tatters, Sandra Lowndes looked around for fresh opportunities. She discovered a growing, reasonably lucrative niche breeding polo mounts. A good polo pony could be sold to the rich. She didn't have to depend upon a young girl's ability to implore her father to spend money to buy her a pony, nor did she have to limit herself to local buyers. She could speak directly to men with deep pockets, and get her price whenever it was warranted. As well, anytime she was lucky enough to have a special horse, she could readily tap into an organized international market.

Polo put her into contact with a mysterious, unmarried, not-divorced-exactly, French-speaking, older, Montreal *police detective, for heaven's sake,* who knew horses, who dropped by her farm one day scouting ponies for a friend. He was tall, he was austere, he was knowledgeable and articulate and astute. He had bearing. He could bargain hard, yet do it with a smile. She was intrigued. He was definitely not on any map she'd drawn for herself. He lived outside her geography. He was *French!* He was from a city, he was *old! Well, older.* But no matter how she ran down his dire traits for her best friends—*He has a big nose! It's the size of Rhode Island at least. What a beak!*—he stuck in her head.

Émile called, without pretence or preamble, offering no deals. This time around he was not buying horse-flesh, although he did know someone who might be in the market. Then why was he calling? To talk to her. And he asked, *Would that be all right?*

"Tell me something, Detective, what does 'not-divorced-exactly' mean?"

"I'm Catholic."

"So?"

"My first wife was fragile. I was much younger then. I found the trait endearing. In my youth, wanting to protect people was a weakness, a character flaw. She'd stay up worrying while I was on the job. She couldn't take it. She had a breakdown. I guess she was even more fragile than I'd realized. Being Catholic, I didn't believe in divorce. I didn't believe in hypocrisy either, but a choice had to be made. We had our marriage annulled."

Did I mention, she'd recite to her confounded friends over the phone, *that he's religious? Religious!*

So it began. Leading to the dangers, the lonely nights, the worry, calamities and stress that left her feeling fractured. Had she known that she'd depart New Hampshire, give up the farm, move to a city, become lost among people she not only didn't know but could not address in their own language, be scared half the time and half the time not get along so well with her husband, then she might not have altered her life's course. But she had not perceived the downside, or how bad it might be. Neither had Émile. She trusted him, and only later did she learn that that was a mistake. He was completely trustworthy, of course, once she understood the ground rules, which were that he was wholly committed to crime-fighting, totally absorbed in chasing down the bad guys, and consumed by a desire to undermine the machinations of criminals, foil the syndicates, disrupt the alliances and hurt the organized operations. Émile had not fully appreciated that things would get worse from year to year, or that he'd become more deeply involved. Organized crime was not his official bailiwick—more often than not the gangs operated outside his jurisdiction—but increasingly he came up against them, and they against him.

In Montreal, when Sandra arrived, a war was just heating up between rival biker gangs that within four years would claim ninety-eight lives with no sign of stopping. There'd be another ninety attempted murders, a hundred bombings and a hundred and twenty flash fires, and to those who were counting it was only the beginning. No cessation was in view, no genuine hope of a truce, no hope at all for victory by the police. At times, Émile found himself in the midst of the conflict, putting his life in jeopardy and, by extension, hers.

Then last night they had been attacked.

They were getting along well these days, and they'd come through so much. Three years earlier, she and Émile had moved out of the city and back to the country, and she was raising horses again, doing what she loved. With Émile's guidance she was more businesslike, an aspect of her enterprise that she could now appreciate. She wasn't a young girl with an expensive hobby anymore, she was a savvy, small-business woman making her way in a foreign land. Émile was there to lend his practised eye, speak French for her, help her negotiate better deals, offer a second opinion on an animal. In the end she had found what she had been looking for in the beginning, someone who could help out with the horses—she had just never calculated or imagined the complete package.

She loved him. Desperately. More than ever now. She'd learned to manage the stress, and they'd learned to communicate more directly. He had lived with suspicion as a companion for so long that it had taken him a while to express trust. He'd been cynical and doubtful for so long that he did not readily drop the pose upon arriving home. In the early days he'd keep his major worries to himself, thinking to protect her, succeeding only in keeping her at a distance. But crises that could have destroyed them brought them closer, and they had become closer still as Émile's father's condition had deteriorated. Sandra was wholly confident now that her odd union with this *older! French! religious! cop!—a detective yet! With a beak!* as she'd regale her old friends on the phone, long-distance, *who snores a little!* suited her well.

She returned to the house from the barn, bone-weary and famished. Before making herself tea and a snack, Sandra went up to check on Émile, and observed him from the bedroom doorway. His rest was fitful. He appeared to be dreaming, and the dreams were not tame. Then she saw his arms and hands move under the covers, and feared that her presence had awakened him. But no, he might still be asleep. She looked closer. What she saw startled her, for her husband's face appeared to be wincing with pain. "Émile?"

He opened his eyes, as if awake all this time. Sandra approached the bed and when he saw her, he tried to turn away, but the pain he was experiencing prevented him from covering up his agony. Sandra gently pulled the tops of the covers off him and watched, terrified, as her husband slowly unbent the fingers on one of his hands, then on the other. The softly curled fists seemed benign, but clearly he could not unfold the fingers without applying external pressure, and doing so in even the gentlest way hurt him enormously.

"Oh God, Émile, what's happening?"

"I forgot to take my Aspirin."

"Émile! How long has this been going on?"

"Months. It's only when I sleep."

"Oh, honey. Haven't you seen a doctor?"

"I don't have one."

"The department—"

"—would boot me out if they knew."

"Émile." She moved against him, kissed his head, cradled him and made him rock. "Sweetheart." She bundled both of them up in the blankets again. "You should've told me, you bastard."

"I didn't want to worry you."

"Instead you've been worrying yourself senseless. Hey, Mister Man, you don't think I've dealt with arthritic horses before?"

"Yeah. I do. Some of them you've put down."

She laughed, although she was half weeping. "I'll put *you* down if you don't see a doctor. Come on, baby, if Aspirin's been working it can't be that bad. You don't hurt during the day?"

"Only when I walk."

She laughed again.

"I'm serious. On long walks, my hands hurt. Otherwise, I'm fine."

"Oh, baby, we'll get you through."

"If I can't hold a pistol—"

"Shhh. Shhh. I know. We'll get you through, baby. We'll get you through."

Werner Honigwachs timed his arrival at Hillier-Largent Global to coincide with Camille Choquette's afternoon break. She ran outside without bothering to throw on an overcoat and scurried into the front seat of his Mercedes-Benz.

"What's up, Wiener. You look like yesterday's bacon."

"I've had visitors."

The anger underpinning his tone was difficult for Camille to fathom. She did know one thing. He had no business being angry at her. "Like who?"

"That detective. Cinq-Mars."

"I know for a fact that he doesn't have jurisdiction. Charlie mentioned it."

"Well, mention to Charlie for me, will you, that he's been coming around," he scolded her.

"Come on, relax. If he comes by again, blow him off, Wiener. He's not allowed to talk to you."

Honigwachs took comfort from that option. If a city cop had no right to talk to him, he would not stand on ceremony. Next time, he'd eject Cinq-Mars. "All right. Good. He didn't get far with me anyway. But then I got a visit from guys I can't blow off so easily. The mob showed up, asking questions about Andy."

"What'd they want?" Camille had no personal experience with such people, but they'd been around the periphery of her life, and they scared her. The mob represented the rogue wave in their entire operation, the one group she could not control and might legitimately fear. When she had pitched the idea of doing away with Andrew Stettler to Honigwachs, that had been the element most difficult for her to assess. "We won't try to bury the body," she'd told him. "It'll be under water, under my hut. I'll announce finding it. Nobody will think it had anything to do with me. The mob will assume some other punk did it. One of their own. Aren't they always killing each other?"

"They wanted a fucking name!" Honigwachs was storming. "They're not reasonable people, Camille. They expect me to know who killed Andy. They asked me if I did it."

She kept her eyes on him, noting his agitation, his upset. "What did you tell them?"

"I told them to check out Lucy Gabriel."

"That was good. That's what I would've done."

"Yeah, well, it was not the right thing to say."

The motor was running, the car's heater keeping them warm. "Why not?"

"Because they already know it wasn't her. Don't ask me how."

"So what did you say?"

He gazed down the road and declined to look at her. "Nothing in particular."

She studied his profile, the tension in his jaw and around his eyes. "Werner," she asked softly, "what did you say?"

"I didn't say anything. It's no big deal."

"You stood up to the mob?"

Honigwachs shook his open hand in the air. "This asshole was going to shoot my foot off!"

"Why didn't he?"

"He said I had to give him a name for his list."

"What list?"

"He's going down this list of people. The idea is, everybody he talks to has to give him another name."

"So he's threatening to shoot your foot off, and you talk him out of it? You're a brave man, Werner."

"I don't think he really wanted to do it right there in my office. He was bluffing."

"I never knew you were so brave. You called his bluff," she said coldly.

"What? You don't believe me?" Finally, he spun his head around.

"Are you here to warn me, Wiener?"

"What do you mean?" He looked at her for a few moments only, then stared down the block. She saw his Adam's apple bob as he swallowed.

"Did you give him my name, Wiener?"

Werner Honigwachs glanced at her quickly. "I didn't have to," he told her.

"What does that mean?"

"He already had your name. It was on his list."

Camille weighed his words a moment. "How did my name get on his list?"

"How should I know? Fuck! Out of the newspapers maybe. Your name got mentioned. It was *your* hut. That's where *you* wanted to do it. Maybe Andy said your name to somebody sometime. I don't *know*."

"You don't know," she said.

"Your name's on the list, that's all I know."

Camille nodded. "All right," she said. "Okay. We can work through this one."

Honigwachs was not so sure. "These are tough boys."

"They want a name, don't they? All I have to do is give them a name."

"Whose?"

This time, it was Camille Choquette who was looking down the block, although nothing of interest was there to be seen. "It had to come to this."

Honigwachs was confused. "What do you mean?"

Camille shrugged. She put a hand on the doorknob, preparing to leave. "I've got a problem in my life. It's time to get rid of it."

"What does that mean? These are tough boys," Honigwachs reiterated. "You have to be serious about this!"

She looked into his eyes. "I'll give them a name."

Honigwachs put a hand on his chest. "Not me," he threatened. "You won't give me up."

Camille smiled sweetly. "No, Wiener, I won't give you up. How could you think that? You're not my problem. You're my pipeline to fast cash. You're my walking, talking ATM. But I'll give them a name. If Lucy's name is no good, I'll give them another one."

"Whose?" he asked, puzzled.

"I know the perfect name. You would, too, if you had the guts to think about it. After I give them a name, the mob won't be pressuring you. That's all that counts."

First, she had told him how to get rid of Cinq-Mars. Now, she was saving him from the mob. "How? What will you say?"

She opened the car door. "Don't worry about it, Wiener. I'll convince them. In the meantime, keep your shit together. Don't sell out your friends or loved ones."

"I wouldn't do that, Camille."

"Yeah, right," she said.

Honigwachs watched her walk away. How had he gotten involved with this woman? He could hardly remember. He did remember watching her walk away from him once before, after the first time they'd had sex, which had been in the front seat of his car. She had taken his penis into her mouth and driven her fingernails into his thighs until he bled, then she had walked away and he had watched her go, thinking, *I can do better. She's not so fine. She's not so pretty.* The next day, he was calling her up, wanting to meet her again. Already back then, by their second date, she'd been laughing at him. She never stopped laughing at him, and he always kept calling.

About to enter the building, Camille turned, and Honigwachs expected her to wave goodbye. Instead, she seemed to look right through him, as if neither he nor his Mercedes crossed her field of vision. Rather than wave, she pushed the door open with her rear end, spun, and vanished into the building.

That's what got me. That, that shadow in her.

Honigwachs bore in mind that Camille was a woman who could hold the hands of men who were dying when she herself had participated in their deaths. She had watched him step on the back of Stettler's head and hold it under water and shown almost no outward emotion, except, perhaps, rage at the victim for being uncooperative, or at him for having missed with his bullet. *That shadow.* In bed, she'd consume him one day and demand to be devoured the next, and in the early days it wasn't perfectly clear to him if he liked that or not. But he had always called her back, and after a while the addiction had taken hold, she had taken hold, and now he believed that he liked it, that he had probably liked it all along. He knew that he needed what she did to him, he needed her intensity, the danger, her wildness, the savagery of her kisses, and only rarely had he thought that he might want out. Now he knew, through experience and the change in their circumstances, that there would be no getting out. That time had passed. There'd never be any getting free of her or free of the shadow she emanated.

As he drove away, it still wasn't perfectly clear to him if he liked that or not.

Later the same day, Monday, February 14, 1999, after dark

Feeling fine and having enjoyed a pleasant dinner, Cinq-Mars drove back into the city. He stayed north, and carried on into a neighbourhood he had not visited in a long time.

Little had changed here, and he took some comfort in that. North Montreal had long been home to Italians, and they kept their language active on the streets, in the restaurants and stores. As a cop on the beat, Cinq-Mars had worked this neighbourhood during the Mafia heyday, when the bad boys operated out of an ice-cream parlour where they decided who would live and who would die and masterminded international drug deals. In uniform, Cinq-Mars would walk right into the parlour on a hot summer day and the place would go quiet. Only the big whirring fans and the squeaky refrigeration units made noise. Card players cut the deck with an exaggerated slowness. Mirrors on each wall multiplied the eyes watching him as he'd order a double praline on a sugar cone, then sit in the coolness of the shady store, the big fans blowing, licking his ice cream and consuming the cone while Frank "Ice Cream" Vanelli himself, rotund, sleepy-eyed and sullen, slouched against the doorjamb, his usual post and posture.

Vanelli was the number-two man, and Cinq-Mars knew that, although for a long time that theory was in dispute. When the number-one guy lived in high style among the rich, the police brass had a hard time believing that the number-two hung out with working lugs scooping ice cream. Cinq-Mars tipped off the anti-gang squad about the Mafia's one and only weakness. Ice Cream Vanelli was cheap. Even though he was doing hundred-million-dollar deals, he maintained his ice cream parlour on a budget, keeping ancient refrigeration units running forever. Several times a year, usually on the hottest days of summer, technicians were called in for emergency repairs. On one of those occasions, the technician left listening devices behind, a tap that would provide information to the authorities for five years. Having been promoted and assigned to a different neighbourhood, Cinq-Mars was out of the operation when he saw the photo of Ice Cream Vanelli—who, awaiting trial, had been lounging in the doorway to his parlour in his usual style—face down, bullet-riddled, on a hot August day. That's what being cheap cost him. That was the cost of his negligence in allowing bugs into his parlour.

Cinq-Mars had enjoyed his time in the neighbourhood. The summers had been festivals of chatter and noise, with groups of old men playing *bocce* and kids rampaging with the joy of being young. He did not have language or culture in common with these new arrivals to the city, but he did have religion, and he appreciated how the rituals and feast days so common in his own childhood were faithfully observed by Italians. He knew the Mafia to be a warring spirit tucked amid an effervescent and industrious people, and he considered himself, in his youth and naiveté, to be a protector of the faith and of the old virtues in their midst. Cinq-Mars had made it his personal mission to keep as many of the troubled street toughs out of the clutches of the Mafia as possible.

Since those days, the Mafia's authority had waned. That might have been good news, but the new criminal alliances were worse—better organized, richer, more vicious. He was pleased, though, seeing the storefronts again, getting a sense of the vitality of the place, though it was dormant now on a winter's evening. He drove to Andrew Stettler's house.

He walked up the inside staircase. The key, Charles Painchaud had told him, had been left by SQ officers above the door on a small lip, right side, which Cinq-Mars located easily.

He entered without expectations. Police had already scoured the premises, and if they'd come across anything of interest, they'd presumably taken it with them for further study. As he had told Painchaud, his point was not to show up other cops, but just to get a feel, an impression of the dead man, who he was, what he was about. Essentially, he wanted to sense why the man was dead.

The apartment was remarkably nondescript. Closets and drawers were of interest though, for they housed both a working man's clothes and those belonging to someone who was prosperous. He had a squash racket, for instance, and tennis whites. Several suits. A variety of ties. Half a dozen pairs of black shoes, as well as a collection of winter boots that would be in fashion at any exclusive ski resort. The furniture was also a grade higher than Cinq-Mars would have predicted. While Andrew Stettler might have shown up at Hillier-Largent

Global as a destitute lab rat, and while he was living in a modest duplex in a modest neighbourhood, clearly he was not impoverished and had not been for a while.

His reverie was interrupted by a gentle rapping, almost a signal, on the front door. Two taps, a pause, two more taps, a second pause, one final hard knock.

Curious, Cinq-Mars chose to answer.

The woman on the other side of the door was wearing a gaudy, multicoloured cape, sprinkled with beading, and a skull-fitting cap of a similar design. The predominant background for the cape was white, giving her the appearance of a priestess, an impression enhanced by the tufts of wild, grey hair poking out from under her cap.

"You are?" Cinq-Mars inquired.

"I am who I am," the woman responded. "Whom would you be?"

"Excuse me?"

"What are you doing in my son's apartment?" she demanded. "Is he here?"

The apparition before him took on a different aspect. On first impression, she'd been an eccentric neighbour. Now he understood that he was being presented with a difficult situation.

"You're Andrew's mother?" he needed to confirm.

"Yes."

"Andrew Stettler?"

"That's right."

"And no one has spoken to you?"

"About what?"

"Come in." Mrs. Stettler entered the apartment and Cinq-Mars closed the door gently behind her. "Has no one told you what's happened to Andrew, Mrs. Stettler?"

The woman moved away from him and took a gander around the rooms, looking through each door from a distance. Her great cape swirled with her turns, and in the end she faced the stranger again. Her eyes were reddened, as though she'd been weeping. "I know that Andrew has passed on. I was told about that."

Now Cinq-Mars was confused. "I thought you asked me if Andrew was here?"

"Have you seen him?"

"No," Cinq-Mars answered cautiously.

"I've been trying to contact him," the woman explained. "His soul is still restless. He hasn't settled down on the other side. His soul is straining to make contact with me. Death has been a shock. He'll be in touch soon, I'm sure."

Was she using a telephone, or, Heaven forbid, e-mail? "How are you trying to contact him, Mrs. Stettler?"

"I'm in touch with the dead on a regular basis. Seance. For me, it's no different than picking up a phone to call someone in Manitoba."

"I see," the detective replied. At least now he had a grasp of what was going on here. He smiled to assure her that he meant no harm. "Before moving on, did Andrew live here a long time?"

"Who are you?"

"Sergeant-Detective Émile Cinq-Mars, Mrs. Stettler. I'm a police officer."

She nodded. "Are you interested in his death?"

"Yes."

"I am too. I'd like to know what happened. I'm going to ask him who did that terrible thing to him. If you give me your number, I'll let you know what he says."

"Thank you. I'd appreciate that. I'll leave questions of his death to you and Andrew. But I was wondering, would it be possible for you to tell me about his life? I'd like to know more about him."

She said that she did not know much, and would have little to tell him—a statement that proved untrue.

Mrs. Stettler rattled on for more than an hour about
her son, about his problems with the law on one occasion, when he had been "wrongfully accused" and
"picked up by the police" and "hustled off to prison like
some no-account hooligan." Her boy was a good boy,
she explained to him, and she backed up that accredi-
tation by telling Cinq-Mars how good her son had been
to her. "He had a goofy mom, he was not advantaged
in life," she explained plainly and honestly. "He could
have turned his back on me and no one would have
said boo about that, including me." Instead, Andrew
had looked after her necessities, given her an allowance
each month, made sure that she had everything that
she needed in her apartment, and lived right above her
so that she would not be afraid "when bad spirits ring
the buzzer at night."

Her voice was excitable, as if she was on the verge of
being frantic, and her head wagged along with her vocal
rhythms. How her son had earned his living she did not
know, but it was clear to her that he had friends, or at
least a lengthy list of acquaintances. In summer they
would sometimes come by on their motorbikes, "And if
you think I look silly, let me tell you about those men!
With their tattoos! And their badges and crests! Hell's
Angels! Glory be! I have spent my life in communication
with Heaven's angels! I've barred the door to the Devil's
agents! You would think—wouldn't you think?—that
nobody in their right mind would want to attract an
angel from *Hell?* If there are such things. I told Andrew
often, devils are from Hell, angels from Heaven, but
he'd only just laugh at me."

So Andrew Stettler was connected. To the bad guys.
This was news. Even if his mother failed to deliver the
name of her son's murderer straight from the lips of the
deceased man himself, at least he had gleaned this
tidbit. Cinq-Mars knew that the case had taken a
deeper, menacing turn.

"Did Andrew ever mention the name Lucy to you, or Lucy Gabriel?"

She shook her head. "Who's she?"

"She's missing. I'm trying to find her."

"When he checks in, I'll ask him if he knows her. If he's not too busy, maybe he can look around for her from up in Heaven. He probably has a view."

Cinq-Mars gave her his card, patted her shoulder, and led her back to the front door. "I'll look forward to hearing what he has to say on that subject, Mrs. Stettler. Thanks."

He wandered through the house some more after she'd gone downstairs. He found a writing pad inside a side table by Stettler's bed. Three pages were covered with notations concerning bill payments and dates for credit cards and utilities. The amounts had been added up and ticked off as if they'd been double-checked. On the top page, the name *Jacques* was inscribed in the upper-left corner. On the next, again in the upper left, the author had written *Paramus, New Jersey*, in full. On the third sheet of domestic financial notes, Andy, presumably, had written, *lips lips lips*, and underlined the words three times.

Cinq-Mars stared at the writing for a while, then flipped the page. There were no more financial notes, but again there was writing in the top-left corner: *C-M.* Beside the letters was a tick mark.

The detective felt his hands go cold, as if the woman downstairs had summoned one of her ghosts. He put the notepad back in the drawer. Locking up, he left the building to its mysteries and ghosts, and to its last, sad inhabitant.

The signal was the most common of covert codes, generic to television and movies. A car drove into the parking lot and backed into a spot as far from the building as possible. The engine was shut down, the lights turned off. The occupants waited awhile in the dark, then flashed their headlights at the building once, twice, a third time. Another pause. On the second floor in a darkened office window, a desk lamp was switched on and off twice in response.

The occupants of the car continued to wait. They remained silent. Watching. Suddenly, both front doors sprang open and a man, from the passenger side, and a woman, scrambled out. They moved with alacrity. The man wore a brown robe, each of his hands tucked in the sleeve of the opposite arm. The woman pulled her collar up as she walked, either to deflect the night's cold air or to conceal her identity.

The pair did not enter the premises of Hillier-Largent Global by the front door, nor did they choose the loading ramp or the side access to the parking lot. Rather, they waited by a small fire door, which did not have a handle on the outside. In a minute, a young woman opened it from the inside, her form visible in the red glow of an exit lamp, and the visitors—Lucy Gabriel and Brother Tom—stepped inside.

Their accomplice eased the door shut, making sure that the latch did not click too loudly. The door was connected to an alarm, but the woman inside had the key, which she inserted into a wall device that armed the system again. She then placed the key in a gap under a built-in radiator and pointed at it.

Lucy understood. She was to replace the key in the same spot when she was done. Lucy touched her forearm lightly. "Thanks," she whispered.

"Shhh," the other woman dictated, putting a finger to her lips. "You're on your own from now on, kiddo."

"I owe you."

"Big time." The woman opened the door to the lower floor, listened a moment, then went through it.

"This way," Lucy whispered, and she led Brother Tom up the stairwell.

Whenever they passed a window, Lucy insisted that they duck. They moved at a pace Brother Tom could manage, and, accustomed to climbing stairs, he diligently kept going. At the third floor they paused while he caught his breath, then Lucy opened the door and listened to the hush of the nearly vacant building.

An empty building at night is never quiet. The thrum of its heating and air-filtering systems, the underlying hint of electrical buzz, can be boisterous. Furniture and doors might squeak, or shift, or sigh, or suddenly release a *crack*.

There'd be security guards. The possibility of scientists or managers working late could not be discounted.

Brother Tom was breathing like a violent locomotive, every little sound exaggerated.

Lucy heard her first step out onto the corridor carpet and was terrified. The carpet was an industrial, heavy-duty fibre with a bland checked design of browns, yellows and pale reds. The material was so thin that their steps were not muffled unless they stepped lightly, and what sound they made echoed along the empty corridor. Lucy crept alongside the wall, Brother Tom following, until he clutched her wrist suddenly and made her start.

"What!" she whispered hotly. "What!"

He could not explain except in sign language.

"You want us to walk down the centre? Why?"

He put his hands out as if the answer was obvious, but Lucy wasn't getting it. She acquiesced only because she wanted to get on with this and not waste her time arguing with a mute.

She understood before long. Creeping along the walls was suspicious and made them no less visible. Walking naturally, as if they were going about their business, would not immediately give them away if they were spotted by a security camera or by a guard.

They walked on.

The lighting was dimmer in the executive area. Lucy guided her companion to an office where the name *Harold Hillier* was imprinted on the door.

The door was locked when she tried it.

She crooked her finger and signalled Brother Tom to keep following her.

The next door down opened, and they entered the office for Harry Hillier's secretary and clerks. A door led from that office into Hillier's, and in a secretary's desk she found the door key in the top left-hand drawer, her hand going to the correct spot immediately. Harry himself had told her where to find it, but that had been a long time ago, when they had worked together on a different project.

He was such a cute little man, with his shiny head and big smile, and he had always been so fond of her. Harry was also brilliant. They'd had fun in the past whenever she had assisted him on his research. She'd known why she had been chosen for certain tasks. She never complained about the long hours, but mainly she was pretty and she could be good company. Her job had been to keep Harry entertained, to keep him in good humour and thereby keep him awake and working, and she really hadn't minded doing that at all, especially as she had learned so much and become a better technician because of it.

She opened the door to his office, entered, and she and Brother Tom shut it behind themselves.

Brother Tom turned the lever on the vertical blinds to close them, and only then did Lucy switch on a table lamp. In the large maple executive desk, Lucy quickly located a key to a filing cabinet. To her surprise, however, she found that the cabinet had been left unlocked. Opening it, she went straight to the files under "D" and sorted through them. Almost immediately she came across a file marked "*Darkling Star.*"

Camille Choquette had told her the name, and here it was. Pulling it out, she stood bent over the drawer, reading intently.

The file contained a typed report, a series of notes in Hillier's outlandish handwriting and tossed in at random—a filing procedure that had always given her headaches—and a collection of material photocopied from scientific journals and added to the hodgepodge. This was Harry's way of working—to bring intuition and evidence and experiments together, throw everything into the mental mix and see what jelled.

Lucy wanted to exploit any advantage she might have. Her friendship with Harry Hillier, and her belief that he was a good guy, were avenues she wanted to investigate. She did not believe that Harry could knowingly be involved with the deadly aspects of *Darkling Star*. She had always been told not to mention anything about it, or their other illegal experiments, around him, but she also knew that whatever was learned from their covert work eventually had to be sifted through him. He was the bright one, the affable, unassuming genius. Sooner or later, in some disguised way, the knowledge had to be passed to Harry.

Lucy did not know what she was looking for, but she found it anyway. In the formal report, certain passages had been highlighted by a yellow marker. In the margins next to these sections was scribbled the word "human," followed either by a question mark or a frantic series of exclamation marks. Lucy picked up the telephone receiver.

Dialled.

A woman answered.

"Good evening. Is Mr. Hillier there, please?" she asked.

"One moment, please."

In a moment she heard Harry's voice. "Hello?"

"Harry? It's me. Lucy."

"Lucy! My God! I've been worried sick! Where are you?"

"I'm in your office, Harry."

"What! What do you mean? What are you saying?"

"I'm in your office, Harry, and guess what? I've found the file. *Darkling Star.* I know what you've done, Harry. Harry? Harry? Are you listening to me? I know what you've done. I know whose side you're on. I'll be in touch."

She hung up, tucked the file under her arms, and switched off the light. "Let's go," she said to Brother Tom.

At the door from the secretary's office she froze—a cleaning lady was coming down the corridor. They waited, wondering where they could hide. The woman opened a door a good distance from them and went inside another room. Still, they were no longer alone on the floor and would have to move carefully. They would also have to pass the room where she was working.

Lucy indicated that it was time to move. They crept away, and this time they did cling to a wall and work their way down, as if somehow that made them invisible. At the room where the woman laboured, Lucy stole a glance inside, then skipped across the open space. She took another look, and signalled to Brother Tom to jump across as well. *How*, she wondered, *do I explain the monk if we get caught?* But she didn't want to have to do that, she didn't want to get caught.

Downstairs, they found the key to the alarm where they had left it, shut it down and opened the door. Brother Tom held the door while Lucy ditched the key under the radiator, then the two of them scurried off.

Lucy Gabriel took the file called *Darkling Star* away with her.

Running behind schedule, Émile Cinq-Mars decided to stick to his plan and make another visit. While it was a little late for a social call, this was business, and the business at hand was of more than trivial importance. Painchaud had been doing a good job, and was proving to be cooperative, but in the long run Cinq-Mars preferred to receive his information straight from the source. While he would, no doubt, be disturbing a woman who was raising a small child by calling on her so late, that could not be helped. The detective chose a rural route that followed the north side of the Back River, then the forested north side of Lac des Deux-Montagnes. Camille Choquette rented the hut where Andrew Stettler's body had floated to the surface—a good enough reason to ask her a few questions. She had testified to Sergeant Charles Painchaud that she had not been up to the hut for a while, testimony brought under scrutiny by the minnows found swimming in a bucket of water not wholly frozen. She also knew people—Lucy Gabriel, and maybe Andrew Stettler. So the interview had to be conducted.

The woman lived in the small community of Lac des Deux Montagnes, on a street of modest cottages. For Cinq-Mars, the village was only slightly out of his way home, as long as he could make the ice-bridge before it closed for the night. He had to ask directions at an all-night gas station but found his way soon enough.

Two cars were parked in front of Camille's house, one in the short driveway, which did not lead into a garage, the second, on the street. Cinq-Mars recognized the second vehicle, so he parked farther down the block. To make certain, he called in the license plate number, and was informed that the vehicle belonged to Sergeant Charles Painchaud of the SQ. So the other man was also pulling long hours—a credit to his profession. Cinq-Mars elected to wait, perhaps talk to Painchaud before he interviewed the woman. That way, any contradictions could be worked to their advantage.

His bones ached, his eyelids were heavy. Cold, and huddling inside his coat, the city detective nodded off. He woke up frigid in his car and immediately started the engine to generate heat. Painchaud must still be inside, his car remained at the curb. Cinq-Mars did a slow drive-by, to see if there was anything to pick up. He observed a light being extinguished in the living room. He parked and walked by on foot. Lights were on at the back of the house, which was strange—not customary procedure for a police interrogation. Two options presented themselves. Painchaud could be in danger. Unlikely, but conceivable. Or—but the second option struck him as absurd.

Cinq-Mars walked up the drive. He hated to go around to the side or rear of the house, as his footprints would be well marked in the snow. Instead, he went up to a window in the front door, which didn't have curtains, and peered inside. He was patient, glancing in from time to time, then ducking his head out of sight. He saw nothing.

Then he did see something.

Charles Painchaud emerged from the bathroom. He was out of uniform.

Camille Choquette bounced up to him and gave him a peck on the lips before she entered the bathroom herself.

The police officer disappeared down a hall, turning left.

Émile Cinq-Mars returned to his car.

On his cellphone, he called his partner. "Bill? Before we meet on the ice tomorrow morning, I've got a couple of things for you to think about."

"What's up?" Mathers asked. He was wary about losing his night off.

"Andrew Stettler was connected to organized crime.

It's tenuous, but it's real enough for me. His buddies are Hell's Angels."

"That opens up the floodgates. What else do you have?"

"Camille Choquette, the woman who discovered Stettler's body—"

"I remember who she is."

"—and Charles Painchaud, remember him? They're lovers." After listening to dead air awhile, Cinq-Mars added, "Kind of takes your breath away, doesn't it?"

"How do you know?"

"I saw it with my own eyes, Bill. Good thing, too. I might not have believed it otherwise."

"Émile," Mathers said, "something's going on."

"Tell me about it. Do you know what else?"

"There's more?" Mathers asked.

"We don't have a clue what's up. What do you think about that?"

He could almost hear Mathers shaking his head, trying to put something together, but coming away more dumbfounded than before.

"That's what I say," Cinq-Mars told him. "My sentiments exactly."

13

PICKING BONES

The next day, Tuesday morning, February 15, 1999

Close to the appointed hour, at seven minutes past 8:00 a.m., Detective Bill Mathers joined Émile Cinq-Mars on the frozen lake for breakfast, near the hut where Andrew Stettler's body had been found afloat. He parked on the ice between his partner's Pathfinder and the makeshift white trailer that had the word RESTAU-RANT emblazoned in bold red letters. At one end, the diner served up bait, and at the other *perchaud*—grilled fresh perch served on a hot dog bun with tartar sauce. A full breakfast was also on the menu, and during the day the diner did a brisk business in hamburgers and hot dogs. The restaurant opened at six each morning, catering to fishermen who had slept in their huts overnight. Snowmobilers dropped in as well, along with commuters on the lake road bound for their jobs in the city. As these patrons had to get going early, the detectives were arriving after the usual morning flurry, and, for a little while at least, they had the place to themselves.

Awaiting his bacon and eggs, Bill Mathers studied the wall of fame—fish photographed with the proud men and women who had made the catch. One man he recognized. A large, hefty walleye was held aloft by a straining, smiling Émile Cinq-Mars. "You never told me."

"I'm a modest man, Bill. But that was one impressive fish."

"Maybe that's how she knew to call you down here."

"Who?"

"Lucy Gabriel. When all this began, she asked to meet you here, didn't she?"

He hadn't considered the possibility before, that his honoured place amid proud anglers had compromised his anonymity. "It's not that good a picture," Cinq-Mars grumbled, his usual surly morning self.

"It must be a likeness, Émile. I picked you out."

Their coffees came up first, and each man was anxious for a gulp.

Bacon and eggs, hash browns, toast and jam followed. The men devoured their food with wanton appetites, although they took care this time not to go overboard. Counters ran along opposite sides of the trailer, and they sat in chairs that offered a view of the lake. Although the room was warm, the knowledge that they were on ice caused both men to keep their coats buttoned up.

Cinq-Mars filled his partner in on the strange news from the previous night's reconnaissance.

"What now?" Mathers wondered.

"Let's study the shack again."

"Hoping to find out what, exactly?"

Cinq-Mars nodded slowly, as though he'd been asking himself the same question. "We'll keep an open mind. So far, the hut has been thoroughly inspected only by Painchaud, and we don't know if he did a proper job. It's his girlfriend's hut. We thought he was a good cop. Now that we're thinking he's not, it gives me an incentive to double-check his work. He might've been covering up."

"That man has some explaining to do."

"I'd be interested in hearing how he'd even begin."

After breakfast, they learned that the crime scene had been placed under police lock, and that the hut's proprietor had not been furnished with a key. He was a squat, cheerful sort who owned the farm on the opposite side of the road from the lake. His wife and daughters managed the leasing of the fishing huts and ran the bait shop and the restaurant, while he controlled public access for vehicles driving onto the ice. The farmer had met Cinq-Mars when the policeman had come to fish, and had often read about him in the papers.

"Do you have bolt-cutters?" Cinq-Mars asked the man.

"You'll sign a paper?"

"Happily."

The detectives waited on the ice, away from the restaurant and just beyond the parking lot, stamping their feet and gazing across the vast white expanse. "You look tired, Bill," Cinq-Mars observed.

"I had my line checked for bugs. Then Donna and I talked half the night. She's not thrilled about all this, Émile."

Cinq-Mars nodded. "We'll get our lives back."

"What are the odds on that?" Mathers didn't expect an answer. He sounded, if not bitter, fed up. The prospect of living a bachelor's lifestyle again did not appeal to him.

"I'm churning a few thoughts," his partner told him, as though that vague notion ought to be sufficiently soothing.

They continued to gaze across the frozen lake.

Both were dwelling on private matters. Cinq-Mars reminded himself to call his father. Mathers reflected on his wife's upset. Together, they toed the snow, drawing doodles, their hands stuffed in their pockets, collars up to ward off the breeze.

Cinq-Mars broke the silence, bringing them back to the task at hand. "Bill, why?"

"Excuse me?"

"Why trouble yourself putting the body under the ice? Ice is heavy. Bodies are cumbersome. The night was cold, freezing. Why put yourself out? Most killers prefer to get away from the corpse, beat a retreat. As it turns out, the corpse was discovered, and it hasn't told us a whole lot. Why go to the trouble?"

Mathers stretched in the blinding sunlight, working a morning tension out of his joints. Driving out from the city at dawn had stiffened his muscles. "We don't know where the body went in the water. Maybe it was easy. We don't know if the killer expected the body to be found anytime soon."

"Maybe it went in where it was found, and that wasn't easy at all."

"Why, though?"

Cinq-Mars shook his head. "Didn't I just ask that question?"

"All right then, how?"

"Ah," he acknowledged, "that's a better question. Or at least as good."

The farmer drove back from the huts in his big four-wheeler and got out and walked through the loose snow to where the policemen were standing. "It's open. When you're done, I'll snap on my own padlock."

"Appreciate that."

The two walked onto the ice-road and made their way to the scene of the crime. Inside, the hut was frigid. They shut the door to keep out the breeze. The windows were small, with individual designs etched on every pane by frost, but adequate light filtered through, and each man examined the room with care. They handled the objects they found—the toys, the tins of fruit and vegetables, the cooking utensils and the extra clothing—with a detached interest. The pantry had been emptied of perishables but was otherwise undisturbed.

"She slept here, obviously," Mathers stated.

"That night?"

"Who knows? This winter though, definitely, at least from time to time. The bedding's not dirty, but it's not exactly fresh from the wash either. Either someone slept here on occasion or—"

"—other activities kept Miss Choquette warm."

While Mathers continued to examine the everyday objects, Cinq-Mars folded his arms across his chest and stood still, just trying to get a feel for the place.

"Open the hatch," he directed after a bit.

Mathers did so. The black hole where Stettler had been found, and the cavity created to remove him, had frozen over while the cabin had been barricaded. The surface was depressed like a spoon's where new ice had formed.

"I imagine the original hole had been cut out with a chainsaw," Cinq-Mars stated, "the same way they widened it to free the body."

"You can still see the outline of the old hole."

Cinq-Mars grunted, for no particular reason. "Painchaud and Choquette are lovers. On the day the body was discovered they kept that juicy tidbit to themselves. What else were they hiding? Did they know the victim? Camille works where Stettler got started in his new career." He gazed at the ice while his partner, weary of that contemplation, looked up instead. After a few moments, Mathers stood on the grey wool blankets of the bed to examine the central roof beam.

"What are you doing?"

"What if?" Mathers mused. The beam was scraped, gently gouged in an area directly over the hatch.

"Wrap a chain around the beam and hook it to a block. Use a five-part, or a seven-part block-and-tackle to handle the weight."

"What weight?" Cinq-Mars wondered. He put his hands on his hips.

"Chain or cable," Mathers continued, "wrapped around twice, maybe three times. I'd say chain. Then the upper block is hooked to the chain, and *voilà!* You have leverage."

Cinq-Mars was catching on. He crouched down, resting a forearm across a bent knee. "You'd need some kind of grapple hook to handle the ice."

Mathers jumped down beside him. "That's not a problem, because they already have a hole in the ice. After a second block is cut out, you could lift it, put a body under, then freeze it back in place."

"Making it look like the death occurred elsewhere." From his crouch, Cinq-Mars gazed up at the ceiling again.

"It also means that the body was not meant to be hidden. The opposite. It was meant to be discovered."

"In a controlled environment. But they made mistakes."

"Such as?" Mathers was feeling animated again, gaining a sense that they were understanding what had been elusive. Like a jack-in-the-box, he bounded back onto his feet.

"The minnows were swimming. The Investigating Officer and the so-called innocent witness are sleeping together."

Both men listened to the quiet. They heard their own breathing and the periodic creak of plywood and timbers in the cold.

"We have something on Painchaud," Cinq-Mars mentioned after awhile.

"Yes," Mathers concurred. He made a fist of his right gloved hand and covered it with his left, then shook them together in a gesture of determination.

"It would be nice to go after him. But he doesn't know what we know. We could play from that position.

It's the only advantage we have." Cinq-Mars rose to his feet again.

"Or, we could haul him in and see what he has to say." Mathers still held his right fist in his left hand, as though eager to strike a blow.

"Whose side is he on?"

"Not ours."

Cinq-Mars returned his hands to his hips. "You're sure?"

"The facts, Émile. What else can I do with the facts?" Mathers finally unclenched his hands and stuffed them in his coat pockets.

"What facts? That he's in love? That he wants to keep it a secret?"

"Why? He's not married, Émile. Neither is she."

"True, but still, facts are in short supply." Cinq-Mars turned partway around and sat down on the bed. He bounced on it slightly, as though testing the foam. All right. We'll ask him nicely to meet us downtown, then put his nuts in a vice, see if he hollers. If he squirms, if he can't explain his lover, we'll arrest him. I don't see him wiggling free, do you?"

"I can't see it. Sleeping with a witness, that's one thing. Pretending she's a stranger, that's something else."

Cinq-Mars stared up at the beam where chain had been looped to support a block-and-tackle system to lift a wedge of ice. The ice had contained the black hole where Andrew Stettler would be deposited, inert, dead, shot, frozen. Who, he wondered, would want to raise a hole? *Why?* Why did someone go to the trouble to slip the body under the ice, only to have it discovered? Had the killer hoped for dramatic effect upon discovery? Or did Painchaud and Camille Choquette need to get rid of the body in their hut, and the only way they could do it was to put it under the ice? Then Painchaud put himself in charge of the investigation, and the two of them waltzed home. No other scenario made sense.

"Émile? You coming?" Mathers asked him.

Suddenly, Cinq-Mars jumped up, still looking at the ceiling. He thrust out his arm and gripped his partner by the lapel.

"Émile? What? Do you see something?"

Cinq-Mars glared at him. "Remember this! That was a big fishing night. The night of the full moon. No way did anybody come out here after dark and cut the hole bigger with a chainsaw. Every fisherman in the village would be banging on the door telling him to shut up. The ice was cut out ahead of time."

Mathers nodded, agreeing, as he gently pried his partner's fingers free of his overcoat. "Émile?"

"Sorry." Cinq-Mars let him go.

"As soon as they cut the ice earlier it would start refreezing," the younger man pointed out. "It was cold out." His objection was not intended to dispute his partner's logic, only to see if it could be expanded.

"They'd be aware of that. But once the cut was made, it could then be broken loose again later if it refroze. It would be a fault line, weak. After that it could be patched with water and snow. All they had to do was lift it a little. Slip the body under. Drop the ice back down. Clean the surface of blood and tissue and use water to make a new surface. The perfect way to clean up a crime scene, and we're left playing guessing games for the rest of our lives."

"Is that what they wanted?"

Cinq-Mars shrugged. "When they came back at night the blocks had refrozen, to a degree—they'd have to pry them apart again, but it would be doable. Do we have Stettler's time of death?"

"It came across my desk: 10:30 p.m., if I recall."

"According to Painchaud. But it's from his department so he probably didn't lie. It explains the body freezing in the cold air, before being in the water. It

could've taken some time to float him. Bill, this was a
thoughtful murder. The grave was prepared before the
killing. Remember that, and don't let me forget it
either. The killer, or killers, prepared their method of
body disposal *before* they disposed of the body. Anybody
wants to argue that this was not premeditated, hang
him by his toes until that lie spills out of his maw."

They stepped from the cabin into the bright sunlight
again, and Cinq-Mars observed the sparkling windows
of the monolith at the head of the bay, the BioLogika
Corporation. "Let's go see Honigwachs," he said. "I've
got a bone to pick with that man."

"Émile—"

"Damn it, Bill! Follow me!"

Camille Choquette noticed the white stretch Cadillac
fall in behind her Mazda 626 on her way to work. She
thought nothing of it for a while, in the maze of the
morning rush hour, until she made a favourite turn to
cut through suburban streets to Hillier-Largent Global.
The Cadillac followed, and her breath caught in her
throat. She felt her fear, the tightness in her buttocks
and stomach, but told herself to handle it, to get a grip.

Near the end of a block, the car surged past her, then
stopped in her path, and Camille had to jam on the
brakes. Two men jumped from the car, running up to
her. She gave out a little cry and held her hands to her
mouth. They were on her before she could think how
to react.

One man opened her door and pulled her out. The
other jumped in behind the wheel and began backing
her car up. She was pulled by the hair and she
squealed, and the man rammed a towel into her open
mouth, and she remained on her feet until she was
thrown onto one of the facing back seats of the Cadillac. The towel fell onto the floor. Another man was
inside, smiling, and the man who had hustled her into

the car grabbed her shoulders and propped her upright. The big car was already moving.

"Good morning," the man who was smiling said.

"Who the *fuck* are you? *What are you doing!*"

The man nodded to his assistant and suddenly a knife appeared at Camille's throat. "Speak with respect, or don't talk at all. You understand, Miss Choquette?"

She nodded and managed to gasp, "What do you want?"

"That's better. Tell me why Andrew Stettler's body floated up under your hut."

Breathing heavily, she just looked at him with incomprehension.

"Didn't you know him?"

She tried to twist away but the big man beside her pushed her back hard against the seat and showed her the knife again, right in front of her eyes. She was facing forward, her inquisitor directly opposite in the plush leather interior.

"The body was just there," she whined. "I don't know how it got there."

He smiled again. "Miss Choquette, let me introduce myself. My name is Jacques. I give you permission to call me by my name. Now, my friend is going to cut out pieces of your tongue, bit by bit—"

She cried out.

"—for every lie you tell me," he said, raising his voice to drown her out. "Soon you will never be able to lie to me or anybody else again. Now, start over, and this time get it right. Did you know Andy?"

She did not speak, but nodded.

"That's all right. You don't have to open your mouth as long as you answer with the truth. Did you kill him?"

"No. Of course not. No!"

"Who did?"

She panted, and struggled on the seat.

"My friend will now cut out a piece of your tongue."

"*Nooooo!*" she screamed. "*Noooo, please! Noooooo!*"

"Do you want another chance? Is that what I'm hearing?" Jacques demanded.

Camille nodded.

"All right then. Tell me. Who killed Andy?"

She was breathing heavily, shoved down into a corner of the seat. Her skirt had risen almost to her waist, and her immodest disarray infuriated her. She tried to push her hemline down. Camille spoke the name, but no one could hear her.

"What?"

"Charlie," she whispered.

"Who the hell's Charlie? Why did he kill a friend of mine who was like a brother to me?"

The big man beside her yanked her up to a proper sitting position and she arranged her skirt.

Camille Choquette was panting and her voice was very quiet. Her eyes flooded with tears and fright and her lips and chin trembled. "Charlie's my boyfriend. Me and Andy, we had a thing going, you know? And Charlie, Charlie, he got jealous."

"What's his full name?" Jacques asked. Reaching behind himself, he tapped his driver's shoulder.

"Sergeant Charles Painchaud."

"Sergeant?"

Camille nodded. "He's SQ. Charlie's the Investigating Officer on this case."

The men in the car regarded one another. Then Jacques clasped his hands together and leaned forward. "A cop killed Andy?"

Camille whispered, "I don't know. Maybe. Probably. I don't know."

"And he's the Investigating?" Although he was asking a question, it was clear that he had already accepted her reply as valid. The car was slowing down.

After it stopped, everybody waited for Jacques to speak again. Finally, he addressed Camille. "Don't tell nobody about this. Especially, don't tell this Charlie guy. Forget about him. He's a dead man anyways. He's a whack-job. If he hears about our conversation, I'll assume you decided you got no further use for your tongue, or for your ears, or for your fingers, or for your little girl. That's right. I know all about her. If this Charlie gets wind, I'll deduce you were the one who told him. You understand me on this?"

She hated playing the role of a frightened ninny, but Camille Choquette said, "I understand you," and her voice was breathless, faint, afraid.

"Get out."

Wobbly, Camille Choquette stepped onto the street. Parked alongside the curb, her Mazda was waiting. She walked to it and got in, and the man who had backed it up returned to the Cadillac. She crawled in behind the wheel, too nervous to drive, and she watched the white stretch Caddy speed away, scarcely slowing down at the stop sign.

The encounter had gone well, Camille believed. The bad guys had their name. The cops would discover one of their own dead, and they'd probably correctly link the murder to organized crime. That would put the blame for the Stettler killing onto thugs, so it could go into the books as a settling of accounts between gangs. No big deal. Soon to be forgotten. Nobody would know any better, and after that they'd be more interested in the cop-killing. Nobody would bother her or Werner again.

Camille took a deep breath. She smiled. Turning the key in the ignition of her Mazda, she drove on.

Werner Honigwachs had to leave a meeting of middle managers to receive Sergeant-Detective Émile Cinq-Mars in his office. He had left his jacket slung over the back of his swivel chair and he put it on before sitting, to govern the conversation with formality. Having waited for him for three minutes, the two cops were already seated.

"Sir, this is Detective Bill Mathers."

"Pleased to meet you, etcetera." The man leaned forward in his chair, tapped his right middle finger three times upon the edge of his desk, and offered a thin smile. He gave Mathers nothing more than a glance. "Any progress?"

"I'm not at liberty to say. Since speaking to you yesterday, matters have become distinctly more complicated."

A man accustomed to having his questions answered, Honigwachs freely exhibited impatience. He did not quite rock in his chair, rather, he set up a slight side-to-side motion. His moon face was impassive, grim, as though he expected others to speak up for themselves while he revealed nothing. His tightened eyebrows, the scrunched lines of his forehead, indicated both his tension and his contempt for the men in the room. "What can I do for you, Cinq-Mars?"

"Mmmm," the detective murmured. His attention seemed momentarily lost to the maze governed by the astronomical clock on the president's desk, where the planets and the earth's moon continued to revolve in exact formation to their actual orbits. "When we talked yesterday, sir, I hadn't had much sleep."

"You looked rough. I remember."

"The reason for my lack of sleep had to do with a kidnapping—a shooting and a kidnapping both—that had occurred overnight. Perhaps you know the victim. Her name is Lucy Gabriel. She works for Hillier-Largent."

Honigwachs shook his head slightly, dismissively. "Doesn't sound familiar," he said. "In my business, I meet a lot of people."

"I'm curious about something," Cinq-Mars stated.

"So am I," Honigwachs interrupted. He leaned back in his chair. "What right do you have to be here?"

"Excuse me?" the policeman asked.

"I understand that the SQ is investigating Andy's death. I've been led to believe that Montreal detectives have no jurisdiction with regard to this matter. Therefore you have no reason, not to mention no authority, to be talking to me."

Cinq-Mars loved it when the bad guys chose to be smug. No one ever taught them that pride shows up before a fall. Nor did they understand that their attitude gave away a range of inner emotions and proved they were not in control. Smiling, he brushed imaginary flecks off a trouser leg, a gesture that told the person he was questioning who was in charge, who knew where he was going and exactly how he was going to get there, and who was enjoying the experience so much that he intended to take his time.

"This is a friendly visit, sir. That's allowed."

Honigwachs snorted slightly. "That's all very nice, Detective, but I was in a meeting. I happen to be a busy man. So if you'll excuse me—"

"We could call it a business visit, if you'd prefer. Let's pretend that I'm here to sell you a horse."

"I don't have time for your games, Cinq-Mars. I'd like you and your *partner*," he spat the word out as though referring to a diseased rat, "to go now."

"I could arrange to have my questions asked at a stockholder's meeting, if you'd prefer that, sir."

Although he knew that it was a desperate ploy, that he was being baited, Honigwachs found the tease difficult to resist. "What questions are those?"

"Why it is that your Head of Security, Andrew Stettler, was closely connected to organized crime? He was friendly with the Hell's Angels, sir, the most notorious and violent gang around. Stockholders might take an

interest in your reasons for hiring a convicted felon to
look after security, without first checking if he had a
criminal record. If you did check, and knew that he'd
been convicted, why did you hire him?"

At the outset, Bill Mathers had been unclear on why
they were re-interviewing Honigwachs, but now the
line of questioning was beginning to make sense. Once
they'd got Camille Choquette and Sergeant Painchaud
on the hook, Honigwachs had seemed to drop out of
the picture. Mathers reminded himself that the president of BioLogika was connected to the victim, and the
nature of that connection had never been fully
disclosed. Cinq-Mars, it seemed, had a point.

"As stated," Honigwachs demurred, "I don't have to
answer your questions."

"Bill," Cinq-Mars directed, "make a note. Buy one
share of BioLogika, and mark the date for the next
Annual General Meeting."

Shaking his head and chortling a little, Honigwachs
said, "You're incorrigible."

"Count on that," Cinq-Mars warned him.

"Andy had talents," Honigwachs explained. "I
decided to use them. As to his past, I was convinced
that he had reformed. You know, sometimes the best
security personnel are the ones who know how to beat
security systems because they used to do it for a living."

"I see." Cinq-Mars looked across at Mathers and
fiddled with his tie a bit, as though a thought had stuck
in his craw and he needed to shake it loose. He also was
not sure why he was here. He had been hoping that
Werner Honigwachs was involved in this case, because
he knew he'd enjoy the pleasure of the man's arrest. But
he had other people at the top of his list now, and so, if
he was going to arrest Painchaud for Stettler's murder
and take this guy off the hook, he'd at least like the pleasure of worrying the arrogant company president one
last time. "Sir, you told me during my previous visit that

pharmaceutical firms are interested in your secrets. In part, Mr. Stettler's job was to protect against espionage, is that correct?"

"That's right." Boredom evident in his sigh, Honigwachs put a hand through his hair as if tempted to pull a fistful out by the roots. Then he sank with resignation into his chair again, preparing himself for a lengthy discussion similar to the one he'd endured at their first meeting.

"What about *your* business, sir? Does BioLogika engage in espionage? Do you spy on other companies and scientists to see what they're up to? Did Andrew Stettler involve himself in that line of work? Was he, in fact, a company spy, someone who did illicit work on your behalf?"

Honigwachs shook his head and calmly checked his fingernails, as if to determine whether or not it was time for a manicure. "We've never felt the need, Detective. At BioLogika, we lead. Others follow. Others want to know what *we* are doing."

"Weren't you interested in what Hillier and Largent took away with them when they formed their new company? You entered into a legal wrangle with that firm, did you not? Didn't you want information on them?"

"I'm not afraid of Hillier-Largent, Cinq-Mars." He was refusing to look at the policeman now, and his voice had adopted a dull monotone, as though the discussion was too mundane for a man of his intelligence.

"Who else left BioLogika with Hillier and Largent? Surely they didn't go alone."

"I don't recall at the moment."

"Anyone?"

He rapped his hands against his armrests like a horse's galloping hooves, as if he wanted to speed the other man along, as if the progress of the slow and poky was a great cross for a man such as himself to bear. "A few might've thought twice about the move. I'm not sure we cared."

"Scientists leave and you don't care?"

"Scientists," the president scoffed. "Hillier was the best of the bunch and he wasn't returning, obviously. He'd burned that bridge. The remainder are a dime a dozen. Cheaper than that, some of them. If they're not loyal, then good riddance."

Cinq-Mars looked over at Mathers, then back at Honigwachs. "I have to think that you couldn't allow Hillier-Largent to establish itself without knowing what they were doing. Perhaps that meant hiring a man like Andrew Stettler, and sending him in. I happen to know that he was in contact with people at Hillier-Largent."

His hands folded across his stomach now, the president offered up a nod of concession. "Maybe he had contact with individuals. Big deal. As I recall, the people at Hillier-Largent did him a favour and sent him over to me."

"'Yes!" Cinq-Mars enthused. "That still puzzles me. I don't see why your arch-enemy would send you personnel. Unless, of course, Andy was *their* spy? Now that's a thought. Here's another question—why would you hire somebody sponsored by your rivals? That makes no sense, unless you thought that maybe Andy could help you penetrate Hillier-Largent's security."

"Really, Sergeant-Detective, you're living in fantasyland." Honigwachs was sitting straight up now, inadvertently acknowledging that Cinq-Mars had trapped him. He had raised questions about his relationship with another company, and questions about Andy's role. The president had not wanted that.

"Think so? Do you know Camille Choquette?"

"Who?"

Cinq-Mars did not bother to repeat her name but sat still, waiting.

"Her name's familiar. Didn't she work for me at one time? I think she did. She might have gone to Hillier-Largent, now that you mention it."

"Actually, I didn't. Mention it, I mean. Not with reference to Miss Choquette."

"Anyway," Honigwachs said.

"What about Lucy Gabriel? Do you know her?"

He shrugged.

"Is that a no?"

"I don't recall the name. But thousands of people have worked for me. Who is she?"

"Just your average run-of-the-mill kidnap victim. She also worked for Hillier-Largent. Strange, your employees are being murdered, your competitor's are being abducted. I keep trying to put two and two together, but nothing adds up."

"I guess you have a problem there."

Cinq-Mars shifted his weight around. He caught a glimpse of his partner observing him, and it was evident that Mathers was amused. The younger man liked to watch his senior in action, that was one thing, but Mathers was also tickled by the evidence of his partner's rancour. Cinq-Mars shot a little smile back at him, as if to confirm their little sport. He didn't like Honigwachs, and even if he was innocent of any crime, he wasn't going to leave him alone without first making life uncomfortable for him. He believed that his presence alone made Honigwachs uneasy, so he was in no hurry to depart the man's company. "Sir, on the night of Saturday, February twelfth, into Sunday, the thirteenth, the night that Andrew Stettler was murdered, where were you?"

Honigwachs was still a moment, mildly smirking. Then he rubbed a finger just over his upper lip, to dry a thin line of perspiration. "Here," he answered, smiling more broadly. "In my office. I had work to do. I often come by when the premises are empty. A job like mine, Cinq-Mars, isn't nine to five."

"Who saw you here?"

"The security guard, I suppose. No one else was around. The building was pretty much empty."

"So you were in the vicinity." Down the great length of his imperial nose, Cinq-Mars studied the man under duress.

"What do you mean, vicinity?"

Cinq-Mars nodded toward the lake. "That's the scene of the crime, sir. You'll have to agree, it's not far. By your own admission, you were in the vicinity."

"I wasn't on the lake."

"You were in the vicinity." The detective's beeper sounded. He clicked it off and passed it to Mathers to answer. Both the senior detective and the executive watched the junior policeman leave the room. Cinq-Mars stood and retrieved his winter coat from the back of the chair. "Thank you for your cooperation, sir. We'll be in touch."

"You're supposed to be a hotshot cop," Honigwachs protested. "If you're accusing me of the crime, you're nowhere near solving it."

"I have not accused you of the crime, sir. We've had an exchange of views. If I had accused you of murder, you wouldn't be sitting comfortably in your chair. You'd be handcuffed and in a state of agitation. I know. I've arrested many people. You'd hear the charge loud and clear. You'd want your lawyer on hand for the occasion, sir, if for no other reason than to help you believe your ears. For now, I'm off."

"You're barking up the wrong tree, Cinq-Mars."

"Then who killed Andrew Stettler?"

"Not me."

"That's not what I asked."

Honigwachs shrugged again. "Your guess is as good as mine."

"Maybe it is," Cinq-Mars mused, and shifted his overcoat over his shoulders. "Or maybe it's not as good. Maybe it's better, there's always that possibility. Not that it matters. In my work, I try not to leave matters to guesswork. Do you think that Andrew Stettler was involved, perhaps, in illegal activities—corporate spying, for example—that cost him his life? Is that not a possibility?"

Honigwachs held his ground. "I don't see it."

Cinq-Mars didn't want to leave this man with his confidence intact. He crossed to the corner of the desk where the astronomical gizmo was located, the one that kept distracting his attention.

"The event horizon," Cinq-Mars mentioned, inviting the question.

"Pardon me?" Something in Honigwachs appeared to stir. He straightened, as though he'd suddenly been prodded with a stick.

"Seizes the imagination, doesn't it? That plateau in space-time where objects—planets, stars, light—drift before falling into a black hole. The most terrible wonder in the universe, don't you think? Here, on earth, people die, enemies die, while the knowledge they carried with them continues on. But a black hole bends light into itself. Deflects time. Consumes everything, and the knowledge of the material, of matter, is crushed within its sphere."

"Do you have a point, Cinq-Mars?" Honigwachs inquired.

"This. Andrew Stettler was shoved down a black hole."

Honigwachs twisted an impressive topaz ring on his left index finger back and forth repeatedly, until he seemed to decide consciously not to do it any more. He put his hands on the surface of his desk with all the digits closed together, then he spread only his thumbs apart before returning them to their original position, hands closed. People talked with their bodies, Cinq-Mars knew, with their gestures and postures, and the movement of the thumbs seemed to admit his question, then close on any possible response. "The metaphor escapes me," the president of BioLogika admitted.

"Someone took the trouble to open up the ice to shove him down the hole. Not *through* the hole, but under it. Peculiar, don't you think? I have to wonder why."

"You have so many questions, Cinq-Mars. As do I, in my business. But my business demands answers. I would think that yours does as well. Let me tell you, I'm disappointed in your lack of progress." He folded his arms, with his elbows on the desk. These were all self-conscious gestures, Cinq-Mars believed, orchestrated to try to make him look relaxed, when clearly he was not.

"Do you really think we haven't progressed?" Cinq-Mars narrowed his gaze slightly, as though trying to peer inside the president's head, read his thoughts, worry him.

"What evidence do I have to the contrary?" Honigwachs asked. He shook his head, dismissing the detective's opinions. "If you think that I was somehow involved in this crime, then I know you're fishing."

"Fishing, yes, as I was on the day we found Mr. Stettler. You're right, sir, our businesses are alike. You allow a theory to evolve. You give it great thought and develop a formula that should work to suit the theory. You test the theory in the lab and on the computer, but at some point you must test your formula on people, see how they respond. That's very much what I do. I can work an issue to death inside my head and among my colleagues, but at some point I must see how people react."

"Then let's conclude that your experiment today was

a failure, Cinq-Mars. It's back to the drawing board for you."

The detective raised a finger to the air. "I beg to differ."

"How so?" Smiling, Honigwachs seemed to be enjoying the gamesmanship once again. "Have I compromised myself in some way, by your scorecard? I'll admit, I was, as you say, *in the vicinity*. But that's true of thousands of others, anyone who lives around here, anyone who was visiting. Anyone on the highway. That sort of information doesn't allow you to convict the innocent, Cinq-Mars."

The detective was smiling also, nodding slightly, as though to concede the point. He moved, ever so slowly, little more than a shuffle, toward the door. "There were subtle moments of interest."

"Care to confide? Your mind is an attraction to me, Cinq-Mars. Clearly you're out of kilter here, but I appreciate your intellect. I'm conscious of my innocence in this, so go ahead, enlighten me with your *subtle moments of interest*."

Cinq-Mars put on his coat, and turned the collar-flap the right way out. "Thank you, sir. I appreciate *your* intellect, as well. I believe that what you do not say might be as significant as what you choose to confide. For instance, we know that Stettler was connected to bad guys. He was never an out-of-work bum. So why did he show up at Hillier-Largent as a lab rat? Why did you hire him? He was working for somebody. If he was working for you, he might have double-crossed you, sold out secrets, something like that. If he was working for Hillier-Largent, then you'd have an obvious reason to want him dead. Either way, I mentioned today that you had motivation to kill Andrew Stettler, and do you know, sir? You didn't even blink. Which tells me that either the news came as no surprise to you, or you were relieved that I haven't properly figured it out yet.

Either way, I appreciate, to use your words, our time together."

"If that's all you've got—"

"I agree, sir!" Cinq-Mars interrupted. He was through listening to this man. "Mere speculation. Nothing I can take to a court of law, but we are discussing *subtle* moments of interest. We've agreed on that. For instance, I revealed to you something that no one knows. Andrew Stettler was shoved down the same hole he was found in. No one knows that. No one's even thought that. And yet, you greet the news with scarcely a ripple. As if, sir, you knew it all along."

Honigwachs wetted his lips, and his chin did a small, involuntary jerk. When he spoke again his tone was modulated, controlled, as usual. "Always a pleasure, Cinq-Mars. Now if you will excuse me, I have to get back to more serious matters."

The cop nodded. "Finally! I am being dismissed. Don't you think that it's a lot like being on an event horizon, flowing toward the black hole?"

"What is?"

"Premeditated murder." Putting his head back, Cinq-Mars used majestic hand gestures to underscore his words. "The killer feels the presence of a black hole ahead and commits his victim to being crushed, to having the totality of his knowledge and light extinguished. A fearful thing, don't you think, to be poised above that precipice before the murder? Equally fearful, you must agree, is the realization *after* the murder that the victim has not yet gone over the edge, that the victim has not yet been wholly consumed but continues to emit erratic light and issue blips of knowledge. In the meantime, the killer discovers that he is upon an event horizon himself, inextricably drawn into the clamour and weight and awesome gravity of a black hole—his view of the justice system."

Sitting cockeyed, leaning on one arm of his chair as

though in danger of toppling over, Honigwachs maintained a bemused expression that the detective, for all his dramatics, could not vanquish. "I take it that you're a frustrated actor," he replied.

"Priest, some would say. Good day, sir. Thank you for your time."

He departed with a flourish, closing the door firmly behind him.

In the corridor, Mathers was waiting. "Painchaud," he said, indicating his cellphone. "He's agreed to meet for a conference, so he thinks, downtown."

"I don't want it to be Painchaud," Cinq-Mars admitted.

"Yeah," Mathers agreed. "Nobody likes busting cops."

"That's not it," he told him brusquely. He jerked his thumb over his shoulder. "I want it to be this guy. I don't like him." Cinq-Mars noted his partner's expression. "What are you grinning about?"

"You want it to be the guy you first thought it was. You don't want to admit how much you've confided to the real killer."

"Don't jump to conclusions, Bill. We don't know it's Painchaud."

"It's how we're betting," Mathers pointed out. He punched the call button for the elevator.

Cinq-Mars again aimed his thumb in the direction of the president's office. "He's hiding something," he decreed. "Mark my words. That man's seriously worried."

The same day, mid-afternoon, Tuesday, February 15, 1999

Cinq-Mars slipped into the squad room and headed for his cubicle. He hadn't been here much lately—he'd been taking days off at random to visit his father—and he missed the place, although nothing had become any neater in his absence and yet more paper had accumulated. News of his arrival got around, and he was called in to see Lieutenant-Detective Remi Tremblay, who asked if his caseload was going to remain untouched forever.

"I've got a murder to solve," Cinq-Mars told him.

"Really. Let me see." His friend took a quick glance at the shift rotations. "Nope. Nobody put you in Homicide."

Cinq-Mars chuckled and took a seat, putting his hands behind his head and stretching his legs. He and his boss might be close, but he would still have to explain himself. "Whoever attacked my house put me in Homicide. The two events are knit together."

"You know that for a fact?"

"Remi, it's a perfectly valid hunch."

Tremblay picked up his ballpoint pen, a sign that he was about to get serious. "Émile, it's an SQ case. They don't inspire you with confidence, I know, but—"

"I'm working very closely with the SQ. They're happy to have my input."

Tremblay doodled a few circles on the file folder lying in front of him. "That'll be the day," he stated.

"It's true. It's a good thing, too, because the prime suspect in the case happens to be the Investigating Officer from the SQ."

Tremblay threw down the pen. "Oh hell. Émile!"

"He's coming in shortly for an interview. We'll see what's left of him when I'm done. Expect the shit to hit the fan, Remi. I'll let you know in advance so you can contact your buddies in the SQ, break the news to them gently."

"That's all they need right now. A rotten officer."

Cinq-Mars stood, preparing to depart. "Run this one through your head, Remi. A rotten officer, but with high-level family connections—political connections. Yep, when I'm done here, you'll probably wish you'd never come to work today."

Tremblay tilted his head to one side and rested it on a palm. "Get lost," he instructed Cinq-Mars. "Don't come back. And remember," he hollered to the detective's retreating back, "you've got no jurisdiction!"

Cinq-Mars shrugged, then turned. "What about those profiles on Lucy Gabriel and Andrew Stettler?"

"They're on your desk—if you'd bother to look!" Tremblay admonished him.

Cinq-Mars had a sandwich quietly by himself in his cubicle, taking in the chatter from the squad room, while he read through the briefs. Just about everything on Lucy was taken from the public record. She'd been arrested at the end of the Oka crisis but not held, and eventually the charges had been dropped as the police focussed on a few criminal Indians rather than on half the reserve. Stettler's brief was curious, in that very little jibed with what he had learned about the man so far.

After reading the reports, Cinq-Mars called through to his father, and the nurse picked up. His dad was resting. Things were quiet. He was breathing well but talking less, she said. He was eating less, also, but drinking tea, and she was giving him nourishment intravenously as well, just to keep his strength up. *Strength up,* Cinq-Mars wondered, *for what?* He was not in pain, thanks to medication, and the drugs he was taking appeared to be slowing the progress of his cancer, although he was failing, a little more every day. He thanked her and hung up, both grateful and disheartened. He supposed that it was necessary to keep up the strength of a dying man, if the issue was dignity or clarity of mind. He wondered how he himself would handle dying should the event also come to him slowly, piecemeal.

Cinq-Mars wished he could be there all the time, holding his father's hand.

The call he was waiting for came through from downstairs, and Cinq-Mars asked that Painchaud be escorted up. The SQ sergeant arrived in uniform, looking eager, happy to have the confidence of the famous detective. He sat in the cubicle and wanted to talk about the case, for he had had a discussion with Camille Choquette and with a few of Andrew Stettler's fellow employees at BioLogika.

"What did they give you?" Cinq-Mars asked. Mathers joined them, bringing coffee for everyone, and he pulled up a chair beside the visitor.

"That's the strange thing. He had a title, Head of Security, but nobody knows what he did." Painchaud tore open a packet of sugar and poured it into his Styrofoam cup, then used the plastic stir-stick while he continued talking. "He had the ear of Werner Honigwachs, they spent time together, but the night watchmen and the guards at the gate, and the guys who looked after keeping information confidential, they never talked to Stettler. The computer guys, forget it. A couple of them paid him a visit when they had a problem. Guess what he said."

Cinq-Mars shrugged.

"'I don't know anything about that shit. Figure it out for yourself.' That's what he told them." Painchaud looked from one man to the other with wide eyes, wholly expecting them to share in his amazement.

Taking a moment to swallow a hot sip, Cinq-Mars suggested, "That's the kind of advice I'd like to hear from executives more often."

Painchaud looked over at Mathers, who gazed back at him without helping him out with his partner's point of view. "Well," he said, weakened, "it sounded like strange behaviour to me."

Cinq-Mars grinned. "Come on," he invited. "Grab your cup. There's something I want to show you."

Leaving his own cup on his desk, he led the officer from the *Sûreté du Québec* upstairs to the interrogation rooms. He took the steps three at a time, and while he did not wear the younger man down, his long strides forced Painchaud to jog at a quickened pace while trying not to spill his coffee. For reasons he did not comprehend, his joints had stopped bothering him, and Cinq-Mars felt energetic, even twentyish.

"What's up?" Painchaud asked as the door to the sparse room closed behind the three of them. He was flicking his fingers dry.

"This is where we bring our tough guys."

Painchaud remained confused. The paralysis of his facial muscles seemed more evident when he wasn't smiling or avidly talking. "Who're you bringing in?"

"Sit down," Cinq-Mars told him.

"I don't get it."

Mathers seated himself, putting his own coffee down. "Would you mind sitting on the other side of the table, please?"

"I'm sorry," Painchaud declared, "what's going on here?" He had a pinched, offended look on his face, as if he were being bullied and had suffered similar abuse in the past but would tolerate no more of it.

"Please, sit down, sir," Cinq-Mars instructed.

The use of the word "sir" impressed Charles Painchaud, and he proceeded to the opposite side of the table in the dull room where paint was peeling off the walls, and he put his coffee down, spilling some more. He seated himself, his chair scraping the floor. He looked from one Montreal cop to the other. "What's going on?" he asked tersely.

"You tell me," Cinq-Mars suggested.

"I don't understand."

"Yes you do."

"No, I'm sorry, I don't."

Cinq-Mars signalled to the officer behind the one-way mirror to roll the tape recorder. "We'll record this conversation, if you don't mind." He looked back at

Painchaud, who appeared ashen and stunned. "I can start you off, Charles. However, it would be better all around if you just told me everything."

The younger man folded his arms across his chest. The gesture did not seem particularly defiant, rather, the man appeared to be settling in, as though he assumed that this was going to take a while. "Start me off, Émile, because I don't know where you are."

Cinq-Mars identified himself and the other two men in the room for the sake of the recording. Then he declared that, "Andrew Stettler was killed in the fishing hut where he was found—"

"He was?"

"—a fishing hut that belongs to your girlfriend, Camille Choquette."

Gradually, his chin fell, his gaze shifted downward. When he lifted his head again, he did not make eye contact. He looked higher, over Mathers's head, as though scanning his brain for thoughts. "If I'm not under arrest—" he said finally.

"Not yet," Mathers qualified.

"—then we are in this room as equals. As fellow police officers."

"That could change in a hurry," he was warned.

"Until it does, I have a proposition for you."

"What's that?" Cinq-Mars was willing to give him a little latitude, as the man had not denigrated himself either by denying the charge or offering up an inane lie.

"I will tell you something pertinent to this case that you don't know, and then you will answer a question of mine." He looked at Cinq-Mars. "You can cut off the discussion if you decide you're not interested."

The deal was a good one. "All right," Cinq-Mars began. "Tell me something I don't know."

"I put you on this case."

The older cop checked with his partner to see if this made any sense. Mathers shrugged.

"You know yourself that I could have blown you off the ice the day that we found Andy. And incidentally, Andy was a friend of mine. Did you know that?"

Cinq-Mars spoke slowly. "You knew the victim and you're telling me that that information is incidental?"

"Think back, Émile. I allowed you to stay on the lake. For what it's worth, I was behind getting you to be there. After that, I allowed you to stay in touch with this case. I fed you information."

"What information?" Cinq-Mars corrected him. "You left out pertinent facts!"

Painchaud tilted his head as though to concede that much. "What I'm trying to tell you is, I was the one who told Lucy Gabriel to call you. How else do you think she got your home number? I used my connections to get it. I'm the one who put you on the ice that morning."

The two men stared at one another. Mathers's gaze drifted between the two.

"Why?" Cinq-Mars asked.

"It's time for you to answer a question of mine," Painchaud determined.

"Don't push my buttons, Charlie. I might be charging you with murder today."

"Answer my question. How could Andy die in the hut and end up under the water?"

Cinq-Mars sat back. To answer the question was to put Painchaud on a different plane, removing him from the status of a suspect and restoring him to that of cop. He didn't like the shift, but believed that he could move him back at any moment. "Ice was cut out and raised using a block-and-tackle attached to the roof beam, which was stout enough. Stettler's body was tossed in. The human debris and blood was scraped off the surface, then the surface was re-formed, and the ice was frozen back into place."

Painchaud mulled the information awhile. Maintaining one arm across his chest, he rubbed his face with his

other hand. Interestingly, for Cinq-Mars, he rubbed the
side of his face that was paralysed, as though trying to
awaken something that had atrophied within him. "How
did Andy get in?" he asked. "He didn't have a key."

"Maybe not, but he has a background. I checked his
record. It wouldn't have been the first lock he'd ever
jimmied. Or, you let him in. Or, Camille let him in.
Or, he had his own key."

"I asked Camille. She told me he didn't have a key.
So maybe you're right. He has a background. Maybe
he didn't need a key." He seemed dazed.

"Camille's your girlfriend?" Mathers wanted
confirmed.

As a small man, Painchaud felt somewhat compromised behind the large table. He leaned forward,
putting his elbows on the table and folding his hands
together. "You have to start with this one point, Émile.
I brought you onto this case. Andy Stettler, Lucy
Gabriel, Camille Choquette and me, we were all working together, and together we brought you onto this
case."

Cinq-Mars copied his posture, except that he raised
both his forefingers to form a point, steeple-like. "All
right," he told him. "I've got that. I admit that it's
interesting. Now I need you to sell me on it. I need you
to tell me why."

"I was involved in a case I couldn't handle by
myself."

"Why not invite the SQ to join you?"

"I can't trust my department. Not with something so
big, or, from my perspective, so sensitive. My
colleagues don't trust me any more than I trust them. If
I had suggested to someone that I wanted to spare my
girlfriend, I'd probably have been arrested along with
her on the spot. Even if I'd found people I could trust
and who would trust me, we'd probably still have

botched it. I needed somebody good, Cinq-Mars. I needed you."

A compliment wasn't going to weaken his aggressive approach. "Why keep your relationship with Camille Choquette a secret?"

"For starters, I've had one friend murdered and another abducted. I kept Camille a secret because I believed that her life might depend on it. Also, and this is not a small point, she's in trouble with the law. The law doesn't know it. I've protected her to give us time to get at the real culprit in a terrible conspiracy."

"Lovely." Cinq-Mars let his hands fall hard upon the table. "Just what I need. A conspiracy theory. Is the world in danger, Charlie?"

The smaller man would not accept the abuse. He continued to stare at Cinq-Mars, and he did not relent until the other man did so first.

"Who's the real culprit?" the detective asked at last.

"Werner Honigwachs."

Cinq-Mars looked across at Mathers. "Bingo," he said.

"Your lucky day," Mathers replied.

"All right," the senior cop decided, addressing Painchaud. "Convince me."

To his increasing astonishment, Sergeant Charles Painchaud managed to do so. He had been brought into the fray because Camille Choquette and Lucy Gabriel were in trouble, and the nature of that trouble horrified him. Painchaud had a story to tell, and the pair of Montreal policeman absorbed it all with trepidation. If the SQ officer was wiggling out of things, he was doing it awfully well.

The three men sat in the stillness of the room awhile, each gazing at the table or at a wall, until Cinq-Mars finally signalled the recording to be stopped. He made a cut sign with his hands to indicate to the officer in the booth to leave them in peace, and a moment later he asked Mathers to check that they had been left alone. When Mathers came back with the all-clear, Cinq-Mars addressed Painchaud.

"Tell me more," he demanded. "Details."

Painchaud told him Lucy's story about the motel clerk in Paramus and that Camille had said that she had found him dying. He had died in her arms. He told stories of the men who were Lucy's friends, and that Camille had reported on which ones had lived and which had died, and that Lucy had wept at the recital of names.

"I'll need to speak to Camille," Cinq-Mars pointed out.

"She's not the one we're after," Painchaud attested. He took a sip of coffee.

"I need to talk to her."

The officer conceded as much. "All right."

"You both live on the other side of the lake. I'll pick you up this evening, after her working day is done, let's say seven, then we'll drive to her house."

"We can meet at her house, if you like. Or she can come to mine."

"No. I'll pick you up. I'll have a few more questions for you by then."

"All right."

"You don't know what's happened to Lucy Gabriel?"

"Not a clue. I fear for her."

Cinq-Mars nodded.

"We have to protect the two women, Émile. They're not innocent, but they were both used as pawns in this."

Cinq-Mars continued to nod. "Why didn't you tell me sooner?"

"I had to involve you, Émile. I had to get you onside. I couldn't say to you, here's Camille Choquette, she's partly responsible for the deaths of forty-two people. That's the final body count, as far as we've been able to determine. The woman you're hunting, Lucy Gabriel, she administered the drug cocktails. So I tell you that, and then I'm supposed to say, 'Oh, by the way, I want you to watch out for these women, and look after them, and see that they go free.'"

"No one's been granted their freedom yet," Cinq-Mars emphasized.

"I had to involve you in the ramifications of this case first, Émile. I'm sorry about that, but I had to work you. I had to arouse your interest."

The older man clenched his fists and tapped them on the table lightly. He had to reprogram his thinking. One part of him was judgmental, but that attitude warred against a part of him that understood the benefits of compromise and the need for mercy. "You can go," Cinq-Mars said. Painchaud left without saying goodbye, and several minutes later Mathers tapped his partner on the shoulder to break the spell, to draw him out of his trance.

"What do you think?" Mathers asked.

"When we go onto Indian land, what do we do?"

The answer surprised him. His partner had moved on to a different subject, it seemed. The younger man had to think about his response. "We notify the Mohawk Peacekeepers."

"What do you think the bad guys do?"

Mathers thought about that. How the question was connected to the matters under discussion he did not know. Again, he had to think hard before answering, and even then posed his reply as a question. "Do they call the Mohawk Warriors?"

"I don't know, but it makes sense to me. I'm going out to the reserve before heading home. I'll pick up Charlie as planned this evening. After we talk to Camille, I'll give you a buzz. We'll thrash this through."

"What do I do in the meantime?"

"Do what you do best, Bill. My dirty work."

"Meaning?"

"Follow me out there. I'll take the ice-bridge to Oka. I want you to take the land route around. Arrive ahead of me in some beat-up old crate. Wear grubby clothes. As soon as I find out where my meeting takes place, I'll let you know. After I leave the meeting, tail whoever's behind me. Find out where he goes, stay on him until he moves again. Very important, Bill. You'll be on Indian land, so don't get caught. As a precaution, I'd take your badge out of your pocket. Hide it under your seat. But keep your gun."

Mathers nodded. "What are we looking for?" he asked.

"Knowledge. It's been in short supply around here lately." Cinq-Mars patted his shoulder as they vacated the room. "Better get down to the costume room, Bill." Mathers nodded but didn't appear to be in any great rush, as though the news of the afternoon had left him stunned. "Hickory dickory," his senior admonished him.

14

COMMEMORATION

The same day, Tuesday afternoon, February 15th, 1999

Crossing the lake under a bright glare intensified by the sparkling snow, Sergeant-Detective Émile Cinq-Mars put in a call to Constable Roland Harvey of the Mohawk Peacekeepers. Even in broad daylight, and driving an unmarked car, he preferred to cross onto Indian land with the acquiescence of the local constabulary—and preferably with their protection. He and the constable arranged to meet at Lucy Gabriel's house, and Cinq-Mars told him that he would be there shortly.

He then put a call through to Bill Mathers, who confirmed that he was deep in a driveway, buried in the woods, but with a sightline to Lucy's house. He had already seen Constable Harvey drive onto the property. Cinq-Mars warned him to stay alert.

While listening to Painchaud's story, Cinq-Mars had grown increasingly convinced that he needed Lucy Gabriel alive. He was desperate to find her. If she still walked among the living, he had to make contact. But how could she have been allowed to live while in possession of such terrible knowledge? What had impressed Cinq-Mars in the story's detail was the involvement of Mohawk Warriors providing access to and from the United States. If they'd been involved at one stage, they might have continued to play a part. Whoever had abducted the young woman had wanted her alive, presumably for questioning, and after the interrogation had taken place in Old Montreal they had not left her corpse behind. On the contrary, a physician had attended to her. Why? Had Warriors intervened? Had the bad guys thought to make contact prior to an incursion onto Indian land? That would have been the wise thing to do. Had a deal been struck? Could Lucy's life have been a concession granted to the power and, ultimately, the authority of Mohawk Warriors on Indian land?

Possibly.

He had to contact them. But how? He was white, he was a policeman, he'd be mistrusted at every turn. He had met only one Peacekeeper, and he'd have to go with him, to try to convince him to help.

As he drove across the ice, wearing sunglasses to protect against the brilliant shimmer off the snow, Cinq-Mars succumbed to thoughts of his ailing father. His dad had apologized for wishing that he could have been a priest. If matters in his father's life had not gone awry, Émile would not have been born. The child, then, from one perspective, was a poor substitute for a thwarted ambition. Émile was ashamed that the statement had been necessary, for indeed he had lived with the burden of his father's lost purpose. Perhaps it was that subliminal message, complete with its secret and hurtful underpinning, that had prevented him from fulfilling his father's ambition in his stead. He had resented that his dad would have preferred the priesthood over fatherhood, and he was not going to devote his own life to the calling that would have denied him a chance at life itself. To have become a priest would have been tantamount to nullifying his life, correcting the mistake of his existence. He would not do it.

Cinq-Mars had talked these things through with his

father's priest, the one he had found for him. Some psychological murkiness had crystallized during the discussion, and now he had to come to terms with what he'd learned.

For many years, he had been burdened by a sense of error, as though his own soul was intransigent, as though he was repudiating his appointed destiny. Shaking off the shroud of his spiritual failure had taken awhile, longer still to acknowledge that he had found his proper work in life. He was doing what he was meant to do. As he had told Father Réjean, and not without a certain anger, his work was every bit as precious, every bit as ordained, every bit as *consecrated* as a life in the priesthood. This case had again demonstrated the truth of that viewpoint. A horrific tragedy had occurred in which many people had died. Their lives and their deaths moaned for justice. His reputation was like a beacon, and Charles Painchaud had drawn him into the fold to protect the women he cared about, and protect them also on behalf of those who had died.

Cinq-Mars reached the far shore and stepped hard on the gas pedal to ascend the snowy ramp into the village of Oka.

If a priest in the name of God called upon angels and saints to transform the world and defeat its devils, then the detective called upon his colleagues to institute justice. Devils or bad guys, he didn't care about the terminology, he had forces to defeat and moral judgments to discern, and he was willing to take it upon himself to do both. The women had committed crimes. As a police officer, he had an obligation to drag them before the courts. As a police officer, he also believed that he had work to do apart from the everyday, separate from the routine, and beyond the purview of the law. As a police officer who carried with him a sense of the world's need for redemption, and not merely justice, there were times, and this was one of them, when he would act on his own, preferring to answer to the angels and the saints, whether or not they watched or cared, rather than superior officers or prosecuting attorneys. His father had wanted to be a priest, and failing that he had wanted his son to be one. What he had not perceived or acknowledged was that both of them had become priests, minus the garb and rituals, each in his own way. That awareness had taken Cinq-Mars some effort, and some time, both to comprehend and to accept.

Turning the corner toward Lucy Gabriel's house, Émile Cinq-Mars called upon the powers of the universe to lend a hand with the scheme he was about to put into play.

What Painchaud had told him had changed everything—almost. What had not changed was Andrew Stettler. He remained dead, but he also remained the one person in this case who had made things happen. He had not been fully consumed by a black hole, but continued to emit blips of light, squawks of information. Having talked to his mother, Cinq-Mars now viewed him somewhat differently, and certainly more deeply. What he had dredged up from the brief that Lieutenant Tremblay had passed on to him was interesting in that nothing fit with his recent involvement with BioLogika. Cinq-Mars believed that he had good reason to focus on the man. The more that he uncovered about the case—and he had uncovered a lot in a short time, thanks to Painchaud—the more he realized that he had been launched among conspirators of every description, a phalanx of shooting stars. Honigwachs liked to dabble in cosmology and ponder the possible origins and fate of the universe. In those interests, they were alike. For Cinq-Mars, every aspect of the case, every turn, was complicated, not unlike trying to figure out the grand issues of time and space. Black holes and comets and the influence of dark matter and galaxies collapsing and red shifts of light—in his personal constellation he could rely upon one thing only. Anything that had happened of any consequence, any planetary rotation, had revolved around Andrew Stettler.

After interrogating Painchaud, while he was waiting for Bill Mathers to put on a disguise, Cinq-Mars once again read the report on the ex-con. He had been raised by a single mother, the wacky apparition encountered the night before, in some kind of spiritual cult. Cinq-Mars imagined that the boy had learned to be secretive from infancy. Probably, he had never been allowed to bring friends home or talk about his life. He began to build a sense of the man as a divided mind, someone who could bring down the curtain on one part of himself and seal it off from another. The record showed that he had begun his troubled youth in a spectacular fashion. He'd never been known to rob or do violence, but one day, at the age of sixteen, he had advised a few young friends that he felt like killing somebody, nobody in particular. That night at an amusement park a youth was knifed, his life taken, and Andrew Stettler was arrested for the murder. He got off, pleading self-defence, but the jail time that he served during the trial, and the nature of the crime, attracted the attention of the Hell's Angels, who were always on the lookout for talent in the prisons they controlled. After that, he'd suffered a few minor busts for burglary, then dropped off the radar screen. Had he reformed?

Given his connections, his smarts, his ability to live a covert life with ease and, apparently, with conviction, Cinq-Mars readily imagined that Stettler had proven to be an asset to one gang or another. From what his mother had said, the Hell's Angels were his associates. He was not a full-patch member—all of these were known to the police—but he must have developed talents that the gang could use, which would have made him a valuable entity. As he had enjoyed a mete-oric rise inside the BioLogika Corporation, it stood to reason that BioLogika, and, by extension, Honigwachs himself, were also involved with the Angels.

Andrew Stettler was the go-between.

Now men were dead by the dozen.

Coincidence?

Émile Cinq-Mars turned down the drive onto Lucy Gabriel's property, which was much easier to find in the daylight than it had been on the night of her abduc-tion. Roland Harvey's patrol car was parked there, although the officer was not in sight. He resisted the urge to see if he could spot his partner, as the act of looking for him could compromise their situation. Instead, Cinq-Mars searched for Roland Harvey, which led him to take a peek through a garage window. Then he noticed tire tracks leading into, or out of, the garage, beneath a light dusting of snow. He also discov-ered footprints going one way only, upstairs, to Lucy's loft. Cinq-Mars climbed the stairs himself, but, before he had a chance to knock, the Mohawk Peacekeeper opened the door for him.

"Hey! Good to see you again, Roland. How've you been?"

"Not bad. You?" Although the uniformed officer was being civil, his tone indicated wariness.

"Not too bad. Obviously, you have a key to this place."

The officer nodded and looked around. "I thought I'd see what there is to see. Nothing much here, I guess."

Cinq-Mars surveyed the premises himself. He liked the apartment, for often crime scenes gave no clue to an occupant's character. The general tone of the place defined Lucy's personality in his mind. The apartment spoke of an active, engaged, interested, casual, intent, whimsical, probably talkative and well-informed, probably complicated and somewhat troubled individual. The subdued chaos of the room alluded to her free spirit, and it was that innate spiritedness that had gotten her into trouble, no doubt, as Painchaud had implied.

Cinq-Mars faced his native counterpart. "Advise me on something, Roland. If I wanted to set up a meeting with the Mohawk Warriors, how would I go about that?"

The constable's eyes shifted away, then back again. "Anybody in particular?" he asked.

"Ones who count. Men who make decisions. The leadership."

"What about?" Roland Harvey asked him.

"Personal matters," Cinq-Mars told him.

The thermostat had been turned down. Cinq-Mars stood with his long overcoat buttoned in the cool room, while the zipper and the snaps were done up on Harvey's police bomber jacket .

"Not police business?" the Mohawk constable inquired.

"Personal matters," Cinq-Mars reiterated. "You'd be welcome to attend the meeting yourself, Roland."

The two men were gazing at one another. Harvey had the wide neck and big chest of someone who used to lift weights, the muscles having fallen into fat now that he had quit working out. His stomach was quite immense. Cinq-Mars crossed his hands in front of him. A softness to the eyes of each man indicated that they were not staring one another down, but making an evaluation.

"You're assuming that I'm on speaking terms with Warriors."

"In my department," Cinq-Mars countered, "guys in the anti-gang squad are always on speaking terms with the bikers. It's only normal. I figure it can't be much different here. I want you to know, I don't mean any offence by that."

Roland Harvey put his thumbs in his gun-belt and thoughtfully nodded. "I could arrange it," he agreed, "if the Warriors are willing. They might say no."

"No is no. I'm just asking for the meeting to be proposed."

Roland Harvey had sagging jowls and a flat face, and when he shook his head his double chin trembled like jelly. "I might need more to go on than 'personal matters,'" he pointed out. "Nobody knows what personal matters you got going with the Mohawk Warriors."

Cinq-Mars did a little tour around the room. "Roland," he said, "I want to be straight with you." He opened a couple of cupboards and gazed inside at the plates and cups, glassware and pans. Lucy didn't stick to patterns with respect to her dinner service, and had accumulated mismatched pieces throughout her life. "Lucy Gabriel's in trouble with the law, but I don't give a damn about that. All I care about is that she's safe, and that the trouble she's in doesn't get pinned on her. She has information. That makes Lucy a valuable commodity in this world. I think she's doing the right thing to be in hiding—"

"Who says she's in hiding?" the officer interrupted. "The last I heard she'd been kidnapped."

"Well, now, Roland, there's kidnapping and then there's kidnapping. I don't know for sure if she's being held against her will, but it's not a big concern of mine. Tell the Warriors that, in case they're the ones holding her."

"What makes you think so?" Harvey didn't move from his position, just followed Cinq-Mars around the room with his eyes.

"Come on, Roland, do you really think the bad guys came onto this reserve without first getting permission from the Warriors? It's common sense. If the Warriors gave their permission, do you think they'd also give them permission to do whatever the hell they wanted? I don't think so. Warriors would look out for a woman who fought alongside them during the crisis, or the war, or whatever you want to call it. I think they'd take an interest in her safety, just like I'm doing. Especially because recent information which has come my way indicates that the Warriors were a party to her present difficulty."

"What does that mean?" Harvey asked. He led only with questions, never responses, but the nature of those questions allowed Cinq-Mars to trace an outline of the man's knowledge.

"I mean she was crossing the border at Akwesasne and the Warriors over there assisted with that. I know this to be true. I don't believe they'd just abandon her to some white gang. Do you know what I mean?" Cinq-Mars caught Roland Harvey nodding for a split second before the man altered his demeanour and merely shrugged. The visiting cop continued to browse through cupboards and drawers and wound up doing a full circle of the room before returning to Roland Harvey's side. "Well," he concluded, "it's not in here."

"What's not?" The officer was genuinely puzzled this time.

"Her Honda Accord. It was in the garage downstairs two nights ago when she was abducted, but it's not there now. Do you know where it is, Roland?"

He had caught him off guard, Cinq-Mars guessed, but he didn't know what to make of that. "No," he confessed, "I don't."

"Neither do I. Do you think if we find the Accord we'll find Lucy?"

The Indian cop made a questioning gesture with his hands. "I don't know."

Cinq-Mars found it curious that he was finally speaking to him about matters beyond his awareness. "Neither do I," he admitted. "That's something else I'd like to talk to the Warriors about, Roland. But understand, this is strictly personal. I won't be going into that meeting as a cop. I'll be going into that meeting as someone who wants Lucy Gabriel alive and, as soon as it's possible, I want her out of hiding also. Do you want that, Roland?"

The question was trickier than it might have sounded, for to answer in the affirmative Roland Harvey had to agree on some level that Lucy Gabriel was in hiding and was not being held against her will. Cinq-Mars would not have pilloried the man had he missed that subtlety, but the constable appeared to be giving his reply all due consideration, which suggested that he might be fully cognizant of the ramifications. Constable Harvey said, "Sure."

Cinq-Mars lightly patted his shoulder.

In his car again and driving away from the meeting, Cinq-Mars called Bill Mathers on his cellular. "Track him, Bill. And listen up, we're looking for a relatively late-model Honda Accord. I don't recall the colour. It's missing from Lucy's garage. I'll get that information and a plate number for you. Lucy could be mobile."

That was interesting, he was thinking. If Lucy Gabriel was driving around, what would she be up to? Mischief, most likely. From all that he knew about her, she wasn't a woman to be kept down for long. As a captive, she wouldn't make a model prisoner, and if she had chosen to be in hiding, probably she stunk at it. Either scenario, Cinq-Mars mused, suited him.

Sergeant Charles Painchaud was feeling excited and confident. All along, he'd planned to coax Cinq-Mars onto the case, keeping him interested long enough to learn the players and draw the right conclusions. He'd succeeded in that. The celebrated detective had made no promises, but he seemed inclined to adopt a favourable attitude. He sympathized with the women and reviled Honigwachs. Now, he had only to wait for the detective at home, and they'd be going over to Camille's house, where his girlfriend would continue the eminent police officer's education.

Charles Painchaud's life and career had been an ongoing frustration to him. As a child, he had been regarded as unpromising. People thought less of him because he had fallen victim to polio and his mouth was partially paralysed. Early in his life, dyslexia had been wrongly diagnosed as a lack of aptitude. That he was too small to compete with his older brothers in anything athletic confirmed that he would be the underachieving, ordinary son. By the time that he was ready for university, his reading disability had been diagnosed, and Charles successfully clawed his way through classes by recording lectures and playing them back until he had them all but memorized. Although reading remained a chore, he managed some plodding improvement, enough to graduate, but Charles would not be able to prove himself by following his brothers into law, or his father into politics. Law enforcement interested him, however, for surely he'd be looked upon differently in a uniform.

Diminutive, Charles had to lean on his father to coax the police department to make an exception to the rules. The process was humiliating on several levels. He had to plead with his father. He had to listen to his father get on the phone to beseech high-ranking officers in the department. When he was finally awarded a hearing, he had to point out to a panel of officers that the SQ was finally hiring women, and that many of the women were no bigger than he was. It seemed a mortifying position to take—*my daddy's powerful and I'm no smaller than most girls, and they're no stronger than me*—but he so desperately wanted in.

Promotions would come at regular intervals—no one could say for certain why, but most officers were

willing to guess, and the word went around that
Charles Painchaud was connected. His old man looked
after him. Having begged his dad to get him onto the
force, he couldn't suddenly ask him to butt out, and the
young man was obliged to accept promotions he knew
he did not wholly deserve.

Happy enough being a cop, he was happier still that
the khaki-green uniform had brought Camille
Choquette into his life. They both lived on the same
side of the lake, she in a small village, he in the countryside. From time to time she had noticed him shopping for himself in a local supermarket. She had
discerned the bachelor traits, particularly a predilection
for frozen dinners to augment a diet of chips and beer.
Camille made the first move.

"It's not that I love cops," she cooed. "I don't know
any cops. It just seems to me that a man who straps on
a gun to go to work in the morning has to be more
interesting than some toad who checks to make sure he
has his comb and calculator."

Painchaud was not going to argue the point. Accepting his elevated status above mere toads, he smiled, and
conceded that she might be right.

Camille made the relationship amazingly easy for
him. Initially wary, he understood the situation soon
enough. He was no prime catch, but she was an unwed
mother, which limited her options and opportunities.
Everybody carried baggage, and if he possessed liabilities—not too tall, not particularly charismatic, a wonky
smile—well, so did she. Love was a guessing game for
him. Camille made him happy, and he offered her the
convenience of an established man with a regular job
and a natural affection for children. He was someone
to take her to dinner and a movie on a Saturday night.
Love? Maybe. She offered him intermittent compan-
ionship—she didn't seem to want him around *too*
much—and aggressive sex. They were a fit.

Painchaud showered, shaved, and put on his uniform. He'd pulled a half-shift in the morning and planned to record his meeting with Cinq-Mars and Camille as being his second half-shift of the day. As he geared up for the meeting, his excitement intensified. His purpose in all this was to save Camille, and that thrilled him, for it would make him look good, possibly heroic, in her sight. He also hoped that he could save Lucy. While his primary interest was to help the two women, he knew that if he succeeded he'd reap personal benefits. If he continued to work alongside Cinq-Mars and crack this case, his own reputation within the department might soar. Suddenly, he'd be looked at differently. He did not require the adulation that consistently befell Cinq-Mars, but he was hoping that, finally, he might earn simple respect from his colleagues.

That would be nice.

Emerging from his bedroom, Painchaud heard the cranky buzz of his doorbell and checked his watch. Too early for Cinq-Mars. He crossed through his small living room to answer the door and neither saw nor heard either of the two men who emerged behind his back, crouching, moving silently forward, one from the kitchen, the other from behind a bookshelf. Opening the inside door, he saw the back of a man's head outside the locked storm door, then white light as a blow to his scalp drove him to his knees. Too late, he resisted, grasped a leg, but he had lost his bearings, his strength was gone, his coordination. Vaguely conscious, he remained unresponsive while he was dragged back across the living-room floor. He wanted to kick, or flail, but he could not. Through his daze he tried to make out the man who had rung the bell and who had been admitted into his house, and at first he saw only that he wore a suit and tie. Something was wrong with the guy's face. It looked grotesque.

Suddenly, Painchaud understood, and he was terrified. This attack was not the work of drugged thieves or juvenile hooligans. The man who had entered through the front door was wearing a nylon stocking over his face.

Simpler to blindfold him. Simpler still to knock him out cold. Apparently, the men in his house wanted him to see what was coming next, and so had disguised their identities.

Mathers stayed behind Roland Harvey at a safe distance. The rolling, wooded terrain allowed him to catch sight of the squad car ahead of him through the trees or on the crests of hills while simultaneously providing camouflage. In his rickety wreck he remained inconspicuous on Indian land.

They crossed into Oka, then left that town behind.

Suddenly, he lost him. The road skirted a hill with broad views of the valley sweeping down through parkland to the lake. The vehicle was no longer ahead of him on a straight run. Mathers did a U-turn and slowly headed back, watching for side roads and drives. This time he spotted the squad car as he passed the Oka Monastery.

He continued on by and turned again, and he was passing the monastery a third time when he pulled off into a visitors' parking lot, close to the store where the monks sold their cheese, maple syrup and sundry farm products. Famous for their cheese, the monks had sold their operation to Kraft, but they continued to maintain small cottage industries. From the lot, Bill Mathers strolled down through the snow and the trees to lower ground, and there, in a much smaller parking area, were two cars—Roland Harvey's squad car, and a blue Honda Accord.

His cellphone vibrated in his pocket. Behind a maple tree, Mathers answered. "Hello?"

"Bill?"

"Émile, give me the number."

"Excuse me?"

"The license plate for Lucy's car, do you have it yet?"

"Hang on." Cinq-Mars read the plate number back to him.

"I've found her, Émile. The car, anyway, but I bet she's here. I bet she's in the east wing of the Oka Monastery. Harvey led me right there. How about them apples?"

His partner whistled at the news.

"What should I do?"

"Beat it. Don't be seen. Knock off for the day. I'll call tonight."

"Take care, Émile."

At the monk's store he purchased a pound of cheese, then headed back to the city. Along the way Mathers passed Charles Painchaud's house—out of curiosity, he'd looked for it on the way out—and noticed, beside an SQ squad car and a Dodge Neon, a white stretch limo parked in the front yard. Some cops, although not too many, lived charmed lives. Mathers assumed that Painchaud's big-shot father was paying his son a visit, and he continued the drive around the frozen lake toward home.

The impact of the first blows to his gut was thunderous, robbing him of air and strength, and Charles Painchaud was reduced to gasping on the pinewood floor. As a skinny kid he'd been bullied often, and he knew that he had to keep his mind together, he couldn't panic, he'd have to start talking soon. But this was already different, he felt paralysed, he couldn't breathe and he was scared for his life. The men were waiting for him to recover, and nobody had pulled a knife or a gun. That gave him hope. Then a big man commenced beating him again, raising his fist back and smashing whatever part of him Painchaud could not protect, and the policeman cried out and groaned.

The gorilla started methodically kicking him. Painchaud buckled with each blow and he was moaning now continuously as blood filled his mouth and nostrils and a horrendous pain in his groin made him scream, and he was spitting blood when he was skimmed off the floor and thrown against one wall and picked up again and thrown against another. He crashed through furniture and blood blinded him and suddenly he was tossed back up on the arm of his sofa.

"Sit up," a voice instructed him.

Painchaud groaned and held his arms wrapped across his chest as though holding himself together, and he tried to concentrate on breathing.

He looked up through the blood in his eyes.

The three men who faced him wore nylon stockings over their heads.

"Sergeant Painchaud," said the man who had been at the door, as he put on a pair of leather gloves, "call me Jacques. I answer to that name if you speak to me in a civil tongue."

"What do you want, Jacques?" Painchaud's own voice was faint, breathless, it sounded far away to him. Breathing hurt. One of the punches had probably cracked a rib and the pain had begun to overwhelm him now. He saw that the goon who had done most of the damage had huge hands and wore a massive set of brass knuckles that dripped blood. His blood.

"Explain to me why you killed my good buddy, Andrew Stettler."

"I didn't."

That was the wrong answer. A fury of blows drove him over the side of the sofa onto the floor again where he was kicked and stomped and the policeman sheltered his eyes in the crook of an elbow and curled up to protect his groin. Painchaud was spitting up blood now and he was delirious, wanting to get away, wanting to be released from the hammering punches and the scrum of boots, and when it was finally over he wanted to crawl away but he could not, he could only curl up with the pain and moan.

His assailant pulled him off the floor again as if he were weightless and propped him up on the sofa's armrest once more.

He could see through only one eye now and breathing caused sharp pains in his chest.

"Now that's a shame," Jacques commented. "I was hoping we could get along. You're a professional, I'm a professional, I thought we could conduct business in a professional manner. In a practical way. You know what I mean? If you killed Andy Stettler, say so. I'd like to discuss that with you. Find out what happened. Just don't bullshit me, Sergeant. That's all I'm asking of you right now."

He wobbled on the armrest. He tried to look at his inquisitor, but had trouble raising his head, and when he did he only glimpsed that nylon stocking through his one undamaged eye.

"So I'll ask you again. Why'd you whack Andy?"

To answer honestly would be to receive another drubbing. In his misery he was tempted to lie, to confess to the crime. He had to believe that they were beating on him because they were not sure of their facts and wanted things confirmed. If he was going to prove his innocence in this courtroom, he would have to convince the judge and jury through the crucible of punishment.

"I didn't do it," he said.

The thug held him up with one hand and slammed blows to his midsection with the other. With every punch, Painchaud emitted the last of his air and spittle, and his body convulsed and he moaned aloud. He fell to his knees and the man punched his face then. He heard his nose break and felt teeth pop loose, and his jaw cracked, and that punch turned him around and dashed him to the floor again.

He was being raised up once more, but now the pain and the shock and the misery raged inside him, and he was seated once more on the armrest, where he tottered.

"My man will keep whaling on you until you learn to speak truthfully. I know you think you're Camille Choquette's boyfriend, I know you were jealous that Andy was giving it to her the same time as you, and I know you killed him because you're a jealous little prick. Now hold your head up and look at me, Sergeant!"

Fearfully, Painchaud managed to do so.

"Do you want me to take off my stocking? I'm asking you fair and square. Do you want me to take off my stocking?"

He knew what that meant. "No," he mumbled.

"That's the first smart thing you've said since I got here. I'm not going to knock you around for that. See how it goes? If you make sense, we leave you alone. We'll listen to what you have to say. If you want to be an idiot and waste my time, then I'm sorry, but my partner's going to work you over. Understood?"

Jacques was speaking rapid-fire French. Painchaud wanted to plead with him. He resisted, knowing that it would do him no good. With every unbroken bone in his body he wanted to reason with this man's good nature, because with every pore of his flesh he wanted to believe the man had to have a good side to his nature—his life depended on it.

"I'll ask you again. Do you want me take off my stocking?"

"No, don't take it off," Painchaud insisted, slurring his words as his tongue, which he had bitten himself, and his swollen lips no longer functioned properly.

He suddenly vomited blood, and the men waited for his retching to cease.

"Why'd you kill Andy?"

The thug was already raising his fists, the knuckles dripping blood. Those hands could do him serious damage. "I think I know who did it," Painchaud managed to murmur. "But it wasn't me."

The man's fist seemed the size of Painchaud's head, and he raised it back with the brass glinting in the light as though to unleash a horrendous blow. The policeman cringed and was trying to back his head away when Jacques dropped an arm across the goon's chest to deter him. "I'm listening," he said.

"Werner Honigwachs," he gasped. Painchaud winced as he tried to draw a decent breath.

"Look at this!" Jacques yelled at him as the third man in the room came over with the policeman's holster and pistol. "We've got your weapon. We'll use your own weapon! Now, do you want me to show you my face or not?"

"No! No! Don't show me your face. I'm the Investigating Officer on this case." He had to talk without moving his smashed mouth. "I believe it was Honigwachs!"

"Prove it."

"I can't! Yet."

"I'm taking off the stocking now—" Jacques threatened.

"*No! No! It wasn't me!*"

The next punch came right across his jaw, his head spun out and back, and Painchaud flew up and landed hard on the floor. The three men stood over him and he was breathing in pain and he was in shock and not wholly cognizant of his circumstances any more.

Then the two larger men came around to where he had fallen and between them they kicked him awhile.

Jacques bent down beside him when the other two

had stopped. "Your own gun," he said in a low, soft voice. "Think about the indignity of that. That's gotta be the worst thing for a cop. Everybody in the SQ will know it. They'll say, poor bugger, he bought it the worst way there is. That's a stinking way to die, if you ask me. Me, I'll take my mask off. I'll let you see my face. Then I'll blow your brains out. But your buddies? The cops? They'll kill you a thousand times over. Poor little shit, they'll say. Took it up the ass with his own gun. Oh yeah," he whispered. "First I'll blow your brains out, as a kindness, then I'll shoot one up your ass. For posterity, you know? You'll be remembered that way. The cop who took it up the ass from his own weapon."

He shifted his weight around to rest one of his bent knees. "Hand me his pistol," he said to an associate. He took the gun in his hand. Jacques snapped the safety off. He pulled back the hammer and placed the cold steel of the barrel's tip against Painchaud's temple. He began to tug his stocking up and off.

"It wasn't me," Painchaud coughed, and with his words he spit blood.

"Why'd you kill Andy? Just tell me why, that's all, and I will leave you."

"It wasn't me," he pleaded.

Jacques tugged the stocking higher, revealing his chin and then his mouth. "Why?"

"It wasn't me!" He breathed out heavily and a tooth that had been rammed through his lower lip tumbled out, pulled from its socket by the effort of speaking.

"Why'd you kill Andy?" The policeman's head lolled around and Jacques followed it with the pistol.

He was weeping now. Painchaud sputtered quietly. "I didn't. It wasn't me."

Jacques pulled the stocking up to his nose.

The cop dropped his head down and he found the strength to raise his hands and cover his eyes. He awaited death.

Jacques held the gun to his head.

Then he said, "Shit," and he pulled the stocking down. He stood up. "The goddamned system gives us a reasonable doubt. I've gotten off on a reasonable doubt myself once or twice. Maybe it was three times. So I'll do the same thing for you. This is your lucky day, asshole. I won't do no cop-killing if I got a reasonable doubt." He tossed the pistol onto the sofa. "Beat on him awhile," he told his confederates, "just in case I'm wrong and he killed Andy. I wouldn't want him to think he got away with something here."

The two other men beat him with their boots and their brass-covered fists, and the only sounds in the room were the terrible thuds into the man's body and the grunts emitted by his attackers. Finally Jacques said, "All right. Now wreck the room." His goons went around the room smashing things until Jacques called them off.

The three left by the front door.

Long after they were gone, Painchaud was awakened from his stupor by the buzzing of his telephone. The instrument had been knocked from its table onto the floor, and the phone emitted a repetitive burring to alert the occupant that the receiver was off the hook. Painchaud gazed at the phone awhile. Then he crawled toward it. He had a little bit farther to go, although his body screamed to stay still.

Painchaud worked his thumb onto the small plastic bar that closed the line, then released it to get a dial tone. He had automatic dialling. The phone had been a Christmas gift from a brother who thought the convenience necessary for the proper enjoyment of life. Concentrating, Painchaud tapped Camille's code. One digit. The only speed-dialling numbers he had entered were hers. He intended to call her at work, but in his pain and delirium he'd dialled her home answering machine by mistake. "Camille," he stammered. "It's

Charlie." His voice was guttural, plaintive, slurred. "Need help. My place. Get help. Call someone. Hurry."

He never did hang up. The receiver fell at his side as he succumbed first to a tide of pain, then to a growing grey fog that seemed to rise from the floor like smoke and, entering through his skin and larynx, comforted him.

The same day, after dark, Tuesday, February 15th

Camille Choquette pushed her child ahead of her into the house, toting the groceries, yearning for the day when somebody else would perform these chores. *Freedom!* From the mundane, *from crap!* She was so close. She just had to get through these days, and she and Werner would be home free.

She'd had to pick up food for dinner, and something to serve Charlie and Cinq-Mars when they dropped by in the evening. She had had to dash to make it in from work, pick up Carole from her after-school babysitter, tidy the house, feed herself and her child, and plan what she was going to say and how she was going to say it. *Damn you, Charlie—springing this on me!*

And yet, she could not have refused. Cinq-Mars knew things now, Charlie had said, and it would be just like the little prick to have revealed those things himself! She planned to wring his neck. He had actually sounded excited when he'd called. She didn't think she had to worry, but things were moving so fast it was hard to stay calm. And she had to stay calm.

Andy was right to have wanted Cinq-Mars out of the way.

She was scrubbing up in the kitchen and yelling at her daughter to turn down the volume on the television when she reached out and punched the play button on her answering machine. Just one call. She froze with her hands under the taps. Then she spun the taps off, yelled furiously at Carole once more, and replayed the message from the beginning. There was no end to it. Charlie never hung up. She tried her phone and there was no dial tone. Was she still connected to Charlie's house? She said his name. Suddenly she was in a flurry again.

"Carole! Get dressed! We're going out."

"Mommy, I'm watching TV."

"Get dressed!"

Her tone scared the girl, and Carole, whimpering, complaining incessantly but only to herself, put her winter clothes back on. Camille dressed as well and held open the front door for Carole to scamper past.

Storming violently through the suburban streets, she hit the highway on the fly. Charlie's house was normally fifteen minutes away, but she was there in less than eight, fishtailing on the slippery slope that ran up between apple orchards. Both Charlie's own car and his squad car were in the circular drive. No lights were on in the house. She drove onto the lawn where snow had been cleared for the purpose, and parked.

Camille turned to her daughter. "Stay here. You stay put! If you step out of the car, young lady, I'll paddle your bare bottom until it bleeds. Do you hear me?"

"Mommy! Don't say that!"

"Shut up and listen to me! Stay in the car!"

"Okay!" She slumped back in her seat, pouting, on the verge of tears. Her curls fell in a cascade along the top of her forehead under her multicoloured wool hat, and she reached across and clutched her favourite raggedy doll. The doll had often been patched over the years, and its lips were sewn shut to keep its stuffing in.

As though to emphasize her command, Camille slammed the door shut getting out. She stomped up to the house and rang the bell, but when she tried the outer storm door, which was usually kept locked, it swung open. The inner door opened as well, and Camille moved cautiously inside.

"Charlie?"

Everything was in darkness. She flicked the pair of light switches by the door. One was for the porch light behind her, the other, for a standing lamp along the wall on her right. The lamp came on, and Camille gave a start, for it lay on the floor.

The beam shone across the carpet, creating spooky designs on the ceiling and walls, and at first Camille noticed only the chaos. She stepped over and around debris carefully.

"Charlie!"

Then she saw him—or a body, anyway—behind the end of the sofa. He was lying on his stomach, one hand on the telephone receiver, his head facing away from her. She moved closer, tripping slightly over a belt of some kind.

Camille moved forward with baby steps, as if the floor might suddenly give way. Closer, she could see a dark pool of blood around his head, and more smashed objects in the room. She pulled the coffee table out of her path, leaned closer, and confirmed that it was him.

Camille backed off and stood still, five feet away from him, panting, fighting her surprise, and trying to think.

Suddenly, she stepped quickly toward the kitchen. She turned on the light there and glanced at the room, then came out and went down the corridor to the bedrooms. She turned on lights, and when she came back she switched on a wall lamp at the edge of the living room. She was alone. Whoever had done this was gone. Camille assumed that Charlie was dead.

She moved closer to him then, and knelt down a few feet from the top of his head. She heard a faint gurgling sound. Blood clogged his throat but he was still breathing and Camille flew into a tantrum. She stood up and spun around. She wanted to get her hands on the man who had done this. *"I didn't want him beaten up!"* she railed. *"I wanted him dead!"*

She needed to cry. This was too much torment. She had hoped to get Charlie out of the picture and had assumed that Jacques was going to take care of that for her. She had told him that Charlie had killed Andy—shouldn't Charlie's death be the logical outcome? Now what? Had he talked? Had Jacques told him what she'd said? This was serious. She'd wanted him dead but now that he was both beaten *and* alive she was worse off, and Charlie was more dangerous to her. What did he know? What had he told Cinq-Mars? What did Cinq-Mars know? *Damn!*

Camille spotted the pistol lying on the sofa. At her feet was Charlie's gun-belt and holster, the one she had tripped over earlier.

Camille went to the front window. She could see Carole rambunctious behind the steering wheel of the Mazda, pretending to drive, as usual.

"Charlie," she said, and her voice was stern, filling the room. "Charlie. You're pathetic." She moved back into the room and sat properly, primly, in the armchair across from him. "Do you really think I loved you? Do you? Do you really think I cared? You're a cop, Charlie. You're a cop. Let me tell you something about cops. Are you listening to me, Charlie? Maybe there's something you should know."

Camille slumped back into the chair, her legs wide now, her body sprawling. She closed her eyes and touched the tip of her mouth with her index finger, while the other arm dangled across the armrest. "Aw, Charlie," she said, "aw, Charlie," and she was beseeching him, moaning, as a lover in the throes of passion might do.

"Andy knew," she told him. "He knew something. I don't know what. Andy knew something, but he couldn't know it all. Nobody knows it all but me." She brought her hands behind her neck, as though massaging a tension there. "My dad, he said I had to kiss my brother's lips. He watched me do it. My brother was in his coffin, and I leaned over him, and I saw that his lips were sewn together. I kissed him and I could feel the threads. His throat, too, was all sewn up. I saw it. I didn't like that at all. When everybody was gone, when the visitation was over, my dad asked the funeral director for some quiet time alone with Paul. He took me in there. Dad did. He whispered to me. My dad whispered. He said—real quietly, Charlie, I could hardly hear him, you know? He said, 'You killed him you kiss him you killed him.'"

Camille began to toss her head and she flapped her arms in a vague fashion. "Well!" she said. "Well, Charlie!" She stood up, and made several full turns, her arms flapping as if she were trying to shake off a swarm of bees. "I was upset! I know I sent my brother to buy me drugs, but I didn't pull the trigger! Charlie! It was a goddamned accident! I didn't kill my brother Paul. I loved my brother Paul. I loved my dad, too, but he said it to me again. He said it to me, 'You killed him you kiss him you killed him.' And my daddy, my daddy pulled me over to the coffin again and he was saying, 'Kiss him, kiss him again,' and I was screaming, Charlie, I was begging him, Charlie, I was saying, 'No no no, Daddy, nooooo!' And he was pulling me over and pulling my hair and he said, 'Kiss him, kiss him, kiss him again. You killed him, you kiss him.' And I don't know why he did that, Charlie, but he made me kiss him again. I kissed Paul, and my daddy, he pushed my head down and he held me down and I could smell the awful makeup on Paul and I could see his sewn neck under his collar and my lips were on his lips and his lips were all sewn together. Oh, Charlie! It was terrible, you know? Aw, Charlie."

THE INFLUENCE OF DARK MATTER

Camille stared at the ceiling for a few moments and then removed her winter coat. Charlie had a small corner table which had been undisturbed in the melee, and she placed her coat across it. She was wearing an ankle-length, floral print dress and she pulled it over her head. She was now in her flesh-coloured bra and panties, her short black winter boots and almost knee-high socks.

"Aw, Charlie," she said. "I never loved you. I just noticed you, you know? I thought it would be nice if Carole had somebody to look after her once in awhile. A decent kind of guy. I figured you might be a decent kind of guy in that uniform. I thought it would be nice to have an ordinary guy in my life for a change. You know? Somebody to go to the movies with. You must know yourself it wasn't working out. We were just playing house, eh, Charlie? Me and you? Until something better came along? One thing about you, you got that paralysed mouth. Know what? That attracted me, Charlie. What do you think about that? I was attracted by your freaky mouth. Ah, Charlie, maybe things could've been different, but you were a cop, you know? You know? You were a goddamned cop, Charlie."

In her underclothes, she sat on the armrest this time, placing her hands on her upper thighs. "Everything's gone nuts, you know? It wasn't supposed to work out like this. Aw, shit, Charlie. It's all a big mistake. One giant fuck-up."

She started to breathe heavily, as though she might be on the verge of retching, as though something was moving against her ribcage from within. The speed of her breathing increased, and she cried out once, twice, a pain overcoming her. Tears broke, she wiped them off her cheeks, and somehow that release seemed to restore her somewhat.

"A couple of days after we buried Paul," she told him quietly, "my daddy came home early. He took me

into my room. Told me sit down. I sat down. He said I
used to be a good student. He said I was going to be a
good student again. He told me that some men had
talked to him. They were sorry, they said, about what
happened to Paul. They wanted to show their sympathy, my daddy said. They were going to pay for my
education. So long as I was in school, so long as I didn't
quit or flunk out, they were going to pay for my education. They'd tell the press, too. Public relations. You
know, Charlie? I had to go to school. I had to be a good
student. It was like a prison sentence. When I got older
I had to go to university. The men were paying my
daddy. I got some of the money for that and he got the
rest. He smacked me over the head if I didn't do so
good. One time, when he was really drunk and mad at
me, he said he'd kill me if I quit, and I believed him.
You know? I believed him. He said I had to do it for
Paul. I had to go to school, Charlie. Do you understand? I had to go school and live off my brother's
blood money so my father could live off my brother's
blood money, too. Do you understand me?"

Camille stood and removed her bra. Her breasts
were small and the nipples dark against the stark white
of her skin. She carried the bra over to the desk with
her other clothes and tossed it on the pile. Then she
kicked off her boots and peeled off her socks and
panties. Naked, she walked back to Charles Painchaud.

"Let me tell you about the cops, Charlie. They were
fucking useless. They never caught the guys who shot
my brother. One guy smiled at me and he said that life
was tough sometimes. Well, what the fuck did he know
about it? What the fuck did he know? You listening to
me? Do you understand me now? Charlie? Life was
tough? That's all he had to say? Cops! Charlie!"

She walked around him and down the hall to the
bathroom and her heart was pounding now. This was
different. She had made love to this man. She had

kissed him and held him in her arms. This didn't feel so good. But some things had to be done. She was always telling Honigwachs that. Some things had to be done. She had to make it look like the men who had beaten him had killed him also. Nobody would be surprised by that. Bad guys shoot people.

She'd do it the right way. She'd shoot Charlie with his own gun.

In the bathroom she retrieved a washcloth. She would pick the gun up with it to conceal her finger-prints. She had to think of everything. That was always her job. She had to be meticulous with details.

This was so good. Nobody would ever think for a second that she could have inflicted the beating on Charlie, even if he *was* a pipsqueak. Everybody would assume the gunshot was the final act of the beating. In a million years, nobody would think that this had anything to do with her.

She slowed down now. She liked this part. What had been so good about New York and New Jersey was that she could take her time. She could talk to her victims. She could prolong the pleasure. Camille was not terri-bly surprised that she had killed two men herself in the States. *What an opportunity!* That's all she had ever desired, what she been longing to do for years. All she had needed was opportunity, and the dying AIDS patients had given her that. Weak men. Unable to resist her. She could go slow and enjoy the moment and she was free of the fear of being caught. From the beginning, from the time she had first pushed Werner Honigwachs to do the drug-testing in the States, she had expected the opportunity. To kill the dying. To snuff out the weak. To expel her rage. To sew the lips of each victim and then give his corpse a final kiss.

Camille returned to the living room. With the wash-cloth in her hand, she picked up the pistol and crooked two fingers around the trigger. Next, she positioned a cushion from the sofa against her biceps, and another against her forearm, and held both in place with her other hand and arm. The cushions would muffle the sound. The technique made her awkward, and she had to stoop over Charlie's body with care, anxious not to pick up any trace of blood. She looked at his pulverized face. The closed eye. The blackened cheeks. The blood dribbling from his mouth and nose, and seeping through holes in his puffy lips where teeth had come through.

"He touched my ass, Charlie. He did. I'm not making that up. I'm sure I remember that now. It's hard to remember some things. I try. I try. He was rubbing my ass. My daddy. I didn't want to remember that, I didn't want to think about it. He made me bend over Paul and kiss him and his lips were threaded and I had to kiss him and I went on kissing him because my daddy held my head down and he rubbed his other hand all over my ass. You see? You see, Charlie? How it goes?"

Camille asked him that question, then she shot him just above his bad eye.

The body convulsed and a small fountain of blood poured up for a second, then diminished, and blood ran down from his temple across his face onto the floor.

The shot had thrown Camille off balance. Her legs buckled, and a knee touched blood. She lost control of the cushions and one fell onto Charlie, while the other landed off to one side. There was blood on her ankles and Camille did turns again as if she had to catch something in flight behind her, catch a movement, or a presence that was stalking her. She spun in circles the other way, looking to put the gun down, wash herself, scream, do something. She kicked his foot. Then she kicked it again. "Stop it!" she hollered. "Stop it!" Meaning, perhaps, herself, or the invisible hand on her ass, the hand on her neck holding her down. She wanted to stop the eroticism and the horror of that kiss, the excitement and terror she had felt kissing the dead, her beloved brother, his lips sewn shut, which meant that he would never tell. Nobody would tell. Nobody would know. "Stop it!" She dropped the gun and it hit the coffee table and fell onto the floor, and Camille ran around Charlie into the bathroom to wash off the blood and clean up.

The washcloth seemed fine, there was no blood spatter that she could see. She rinsed it thoroughly under the hot water tap and wrung it partially dry, then dropped it into the laundry hamper after shifting a few clothes around to conceal it from view. She didn't imagine that the bad guys would've used a washcloth, so she wanted it hidden.

Better. You're doing better.

Camille used toilet paper to clean blood off her ankles and the tops of her feet. She noticed herself in the mirror. She stared back into her own eyes. *I can do this.* She'd been so strong when Honigwachs had shot Andy, this was no different than that. Both men were almost dead at the time. She had been merciful, putting them out of their misery. The same with the AIDS patients, they were half dead, too, she'd just been putting all of them out of their misery. Giving them a kiss. Dispatching them to the other side of life. She hadn't done anything so wrong.

The gun, the gun had been the shock. The force of it exploding in her hand. So that's what Honigwachs had experienced out on the ice. The gun. The power of it. The thrill. All she had done was squeeze a trigger. Big deal. But she felt strangely, oddly now, thrilled.

She bolted to the living room.

Watch where you step! Watch where you step, Camille! Don't leave a woman's footprints in blood!

She carefully checked the floor to see if she had done that, and was soon satisfied that she was in the clear. She put her clothes back on, facing Charlie and making sure that her panties went on the right way around, pausing once to notice that the pool of blood was still growing across the floor.

Run, Camille! Leave now! Get out of here!

She hesitated.

Camille stepped into the kitchen. She knew where to go. She wanted to escape this ritual but already knew that she would not, could not. She knew where Charlie kept needles and thread, and she brought out the box of goodies, sat down at the table, and calmly threaded a needle.

No need to hurry. She took her time.

This is what she had to do. Make this her own doing.

The bad guys wouldn't do this, Camille!

How do you know? How do you know that? How does anybody know that?

She put the box back and returned to Painchaud's corpse.

Maybe if his lips hadn't been pummelled by the beating, if they weren't cut and damaged, she could think only of her own safety and do what was necessary—run, escape. But she had to stay awhile longer. She had to pierce her needle along the edges of his cuts and draw the thread through. Camille did so. He didn't bleed as she sewed his wounds tenderly, lovingly. She sutured his mouth shut, a kind of commemoration.

As she was running out of thread she leaned over the dead man to cut what remained from the needle in her teeth, and knotted the last stitch.

Then she leaned forward and tenderly, tenderly, kissed him.

She pulled her lips away. Tasting his blood. Licking Charlie's blood off her lips. She had loved the kiss, and wished it could never end. *The others didn't mean anything to me, Charlie. I wasn't cheating on you, honest. They were just a glorious opportunity. Who could resist? You, Charlie, I want you to know, you're special. You're the best yet.*

Camille! Stop talking and get out of here! I don't like it here, Camille!

Her hands were all bloody now. She looked at them.

She walked around the body and returned to the bathroom, where she dropped the needle down the drain.

She had blood on her boots now. She'd left a trail back to the living room.

Everything's fallen apart. Everything!

Shut up!

She washed her hands, and used toilet paper to clean up her boots, flushing the soiled paper down the john. Then she went back to the living room.

Camille Choquette surveyed the damage.

She picked up the pistol and dropped it in her coat pocket.

Stop being such a fucking idiot!

Shut up, I said! I might need it. You never know.

Everything was perfect!

It'll be perfect again.

She had a vague feeling that everything was not yet over.

Leaving the house, Camille was struck by a sadness of heart, a heaviness of spirit. She walked quickly down to her car, where Carole stood up on her knees in the driver's seat, spinning the wheel to one side and the other. The front tires had burrowed a wide shallow hole in the snow. The doors were locked, the keys still in the ignition.

"Open up, sweetie!"

Instead, the girl honked the horn.

"Stop that! Open this door right now!"

Knowing that she was in for it now, the child crawled off into the back seat, but she would not release the door locks.

"Carole! I mean it! Open this door right now!"

She shook her head. Stuck out her tongue.

Camille looked quickly around. She ran up to the house and came charging back with a snow shovel held aloft like an ax. She slammed it down hard on the roof of her Mazda. "Open up! Open up right now!" She looked through the back window at her daughter. "Do you want me to smash your little head like this?"

The girl nodded no.

"Open up, Carole."

The girl cried.

Beside herself, Camille reared back and smashed the driver's-side window with the blade of the shovel. The glass shattered but held together like a jigsaw puzzle until she rammed the butt end of the handle against the window and it caved inward. She tossed the shovel away, unlocked the door, opened it, sat down on the glass, and started up the car. Camille spun her tires in the snow getting out of the driveway and never looked in any direction hitting the road. She drove hard, the cold wind blasting her, slowing down only when the house vanished from her rear-view.

"That's enough," she told Carole. "I don't have the energy to punish you so just stop your snivelling."

The child had not been making a sound. She sat with her head down, staring at the floor, her mouth opening and closing the way a fish breathes through its gills underwater.

"Quit while you're ahead, that's my advice."

She had to make sure the girl stayed quiet. Before long, Cinq-Mars and other cops could be on her doorstep. She had to appear shocked, play the grieved girlfriend whose car, coincidentally, had been vandalized. She had to be the warm, comforting mother. She'd try to farm Carole out for the evening. She had an excuse. Cinq-Mars and Charlie were supposed to be coming over for a serious chat, weren't they?

"Carole? How would you like to spend the evening at Minnie's?"

Carole raised her head up. She looked out the window, her mouth still opening and closing, and she was making smacking noises now with her lips.

"Carole! I'm talking to you! Do you want to go to Minnie's or not?"

"I don't like Minnie," the child said.

"She's your best fucking friend."

"I don't like her at all."

"Are you trying to get on my nerves? Are you trying to get on my nerves?"

"You broke the car, Mommy. It's cold in here now."

"You're going to Minnie's. That's that. I don't want to hear one whiny *word* out of you."

"I didn't say a whiny word."

"Just look at you. You're pathetic. Do you think I love you? Stop doing that with your mouth! Do you think I love you? Ask Charlie how much I love you."

"Mommy!"

"Ask him." She made eye contact with her daughter in the rear-view, her eyes blazing.

"Mommy—stop! Stop it!"

Maybe she could put a plastic sheet in her car window, pretend to be a victim of vandalism if necessary, but keep the car out of view so no one would ask.

"I'm a guppy," the child said. "I breathe through my ears. The water goes in my mouth and I breathe through my ears. Look, Mommy. I'm a guppy."

"That's right, honey. You're a fucking guppy."

"That's not nice that word. You broke the car, Mommy. You shouldn't say that not nice word."

"No? Well, I know what I should've done. I should've had a fucking abortion."

Camille drove into her town in the dark at a moderate pace. She had a lot to arrange, but she was confident that she could do it now. She'd get through this. Charlie was a dead cop, and murdered cops got all the attention. Who would be interested in her except sympathetic friends? She had a role to play, and she had to get on with it. She believed that she could do it now. Believed that she was all right. Suturing the lips had been a good idea after all. She'd got what she needed out of that.

Charlie had been a cop. The cops had been no help at all when her brother was killed. No help at all. The bad guys brought money, she got an education, and the cops did nothing. They deserved their punishment, and now she was ready for whatever came next.

15

MISSING MATTER

The same night, Tuesday, February 15th, 1999

Émile Cinq-Mars pulled into the drive at the home of
Charles Painchaud only slightly late for their appoint-
ment. Most of the lights in the house were on, and two
cars, including a squad car, were parked on a snowy
clearing. Sharply colder air had moved in with the fall
of darkness, and as he walked up the lengthy path the
detective's breath was visible in large billows. He
resembled a snorting dragon, but, bone-weary from his
long days and fitful nights, he felt considerably less than
mythological.

No one answered when he rang the bell. Moments
later, he knocked.

Cinq-Mars rang the bell again.

Out of good manners, he initially resisted peering
into the house, for he assumed that Painchaud was
either on the phone or in the bathroom, but when he
did finally glance through the door's window his
intestines clenched. He reached high on the outside
door with his gloved hands to open it, in order not to
leave prints or disturb those that might be there. The
inner door required that he turn the handle, and he did
so by placing two fingers on the inside of the knob,
where others had not likely touched.

Inside, the chaos proved to be widespread, and just as he was about to call out Charles's name, he saw him.

All that blood told him that he was too late. He circled the body, and from a distance noticed the bullet wound. Still, he had to confirm the man's death. The detective picked his way over debris, took off a glove and stretched his hand out to take the man's pulse. The body was still warmish, but he was dead.

Keeping away, Cinq-Mars circled the corpse, not wanting to step in blood or disturb anything, and for a moment he had to turn away from the evidence of the beating the young man had endured. The phone was off the hook. It looked as if he had made a call, or tried to. Strange, that. Whoever had beaten Painchaud might have left him alone long enough for him to dial, or at least take the phone off the hook, and only then had he fired the bullet. Maybe he had gone to find the gun. Painchaud's gun-belt was on the living-room floor, but the weapon was not in sight. The attacker could have beaten him, then shot him with his own pistol, and in between the victim might have managed to call someone.

Cinq-Mars closed his eyes. He was being professional. He was examining the scene of the crime, collecting first impressions, but he knew this man a little bit, he had liked him, and the savagery that had occurred was unspeakable.

He breathed deeply. His lungs ached with anger and sadness.

Then he opened his eyes again.

He kneeled, trying to see what there was to discern of the man's face. Cinq-Mars was taking out his cellular when he paused. He'd noticed something. He leaned in toward the man, but it was hard to observe him properly as his body was in shadow cast by the sofa and he couldn't get close enough. He backed away, stepping around the blood, and looked down one hallway, which appeared to lead to bedrooms, then headed for the other door to the room. This led him into the kitchen. Being careful not to alter anything, he opened drawers and soon found what he needed, a flashlight. He returned to the corpse and assumed his previous position, crouched on the balls of his feet and leaning as far forward as he could, this time shining the light onto the man's mouth.

Several cuts, and the man's lips had been stitched shut.

Cinq-Mars made the call to his department and instructed them to inform the SQ that one of their own had been gunned down, murdered in his own home.

Then he stood up. Walked away from the dead man.

He surveyed the room, noticing every detail his eyes would give him. The havoc in the room seemed to him somewhat perfunctory. There was no getting away from the fact that a police squad car was parked outside, that the man was in uniform—whoever had come in and done this knew who they were attacking. If it was professionals—and the ferocity of the beating had Cinq-Mars half persuaded that it was—then the ransacking of the room had been put on as a sign of disrespect, and as a means of mocking the investigators, forcing them to work ten times harder than necessary at the crime scene for no good reason.

After five minutes he returned to the kitchen and replaced the flashlight in its drawer. He would tell the SQ nothing of what he had discerned, as they'd only resent his opinion and give him grief. Nor would he tell them much about what he and Painchaud had been up to lately. Right now, the last thing he could endure was an intensive, days-long grilling from their officers.

He knew what came next. Muscle-flexing. A cop-killing provoked a show of extraordinary force. That this murder had been especially violent foretold an uprising among cops, a media circus, public outrage, and, possibly, political folly. If the crime was linked to the gangs, wolf packs would burst from their dens. In the midst of the anger and chaos, little time would be allocated for reflection and sorrow.

Cinq-Mars gave Painchaud that now. A prayer. A silent expression of grief.

He then went outside to clear his head in the night air and to think. Had Charles Painchaud been forced to talk? If so, what had he said? He'd been brutalized, which suggested that he had not been cooperative, but despite evidence of the young man's heroic defiance, every man had his limits. Charlie had probably talked. Either that, or he'd been pummelled for answers beyond his knowledge, his wretched pleas of ignorance, for mercy, proving futile.

The detail that especially nauseated and enraged Cinq-Mars was the sutured lips. Was this some kind of cynical torture he had endured for refusing to talk? What was that about? Suddenly, he stood stock-still, remembering the message that Andrew Stettler had written and underlined on a pad: *lips lips lips.*

Lips.

The horror of the killing made him shiver. Cinq-Mars walked back to his vehicle to start his engine and wait for the SQ out of the cold. Now that he knew he was at a crime scene, he was careful where he stepped, walking in light cast by the house. A shovel, which he had noticed coming in, now struck him as significant. Nobody leaves a shovel horizontal on the snow, ready to be buried by the next storm to come through. Very close to his car, twinkling in the light, he saw bits of shattered glass, many of the pieces clinging together the way a smashed car window often does.

Cinq-Mars sat in his Pathfinder, waiting, the engine rumbling. He took out a notepad, not wanting to forget any of the key details.

Lips. Stitches. Stettler was concerned about lips.

Pistol missing maybe. Phone call. Beating, then the call? Then shot?

Who'd he call?

Shovel in yard. Car glass.

Lights on. Happened after dark? Get time of phone call.

He called Mathers and told him the bad news.

From the height of land that Painchaud's cottage occupied, Cinq-Mars could see the SQ coming, their red cherries flashing. A cop-killing prompted a general response. The cars were speeding along at different points on the highway, often vanishing from his sight-lines and then reappearing again. He got out of his vehicle before they arrived and had his shield ready to show the first cops on the scene. He shouted his name the instant the driver jumped out of his patrol car, both hands in the air, his gold shield flashing in the head-lamps. "I'm police! MUCPD! I called it in. Sergeant-Detective Cinq-Mars!" You couldn't be too careful around upset, jittery cops.

By the time Bill Mathers arrived, the SQ had the investigation in top gear. He had to park some distance away and walk briskly through the gathering of reporters, television crews and a bevy of police and emergency vehicles to where Cinq-Mars, his chin downcast, leaned against the side of his Pathfinder, his hands deep in his coat pockets and his collar pulled up around his neck.

"I've answered the same questions a dozen times over," his partner told him before the young man could utter a word. "You can spare me."

They stood side by side, each content to be in the other's company and out of the way of the SQ officers. Mathers didn't speak until Painchaud's father arrived in a black Lexus. "Shit," he said.

"Keep your opinions to yourself, Bill."

"That's not it, Émile. I have to talk to the SQ. I'm a witness."

"What do you mean?"

"I just remembered. I drove by here today—after I followed Roland Harvey to the monastery. A white Caddy was parked in the yard. Émile, it could've been around the time. I thought it might've been his old man, just because, you know, it looked like wealth. But that's not the car."

Cinq-Mars nodded toward the SQ. "Go tell," he said.

That delayed them awhile, and when Mathers was finally released, Cinq-Mars suggested they visit Painchaud's girlfriend. "She's not here. I have to figure she hasn't heard the news. Maybe nobody knows to tell her."

"Is that our job?" Mathers pondered.

"As far as I can tell, Charlie didn't have friends in the SQ. It might as well be us. At least we know what he's been doing for us lately."

"How much of that do we tell?"

"None of it for now."

"Émile—"

"It's unexplainable, Bill. He was trying to save his girlfriend. I think that's the least we can do for him now, don't you?"

They left in the Pathfinder, with Cinq-Mars dropping his partner off by his car farther down the road. In tandem they continued on to Camille's house, where they discovered that the SQ had arrived before them, and in significant numbers. Half a dozen squad cars and a couple of unmarked vehicles filled her driveway and spilled out onto the street. A few neighbours had come out to have a look. Mathers followed Cinq-Mars past the house and parked behind him on another street. Before he had a chance to turn off his car, he spotted Cinq-Mars coming around to climb into the passenger side, so he left the motor running to keep them warm.

"That's a surprise," Mathers said.

"How'd they know to come here?" Cinq-Mars asked.

"Any ideas?"

"Two. Somebody in the SQ knows Camille and Charlie were going out. That's not hard to believe, he could've had a friend who knew about her, but why would they send so many people to deliver bad news?"

"What's your other idea?"

"Who did Charlie call before he died, if anyone? By now, the SQ must know. If it was Camille, then yes, they'd be here in force." Cinq-Mars had taken out his cellphone and was punching in a number with his thumb. "Is he in?" he asked whoever answered. After a moment, he said, "Yeah, I know. We're all busy. Could you get him, please? Tell him it's Jeremiah."

"Who?" Mathers asked.

Cinq-Mars did not respond, the phone pressed to his right ear. More than a minute passed before he spoke again. "Hi. Yeah. I heard. That's what I'm working on." He listened awhile. "Yeah, I'm sure they are. Listen. I need to know if Painchaud got a call through before he died. If so, what time, and to whom. *Noqua*." A moment later, he said, "Yeah. I'll wait."

"Jeremiah?" Mathers asked, while Cinq-Mars was silent.

"Any prophet will do," his senior told him. "I'm talking to my contact inside the SQ."

Mathers nodded. "*Noqua*, that's also some kind of code?"

"For 'no questions asked.' It could apply to you, too."

The younger detective had never met any of the famous Cinq-Mars contacts, although he understood the concept. Cops found like-minded and trustworthy colleagues on other forces. When it was necessary to bypass the bureaucracy, they did so, trusting one another to use the information wisely. He wished that he could set up his own pipeline inside these forces, but it wouldn't be easy. To start with, you had to be an excellent judge of character. As Cinq-Mars had done, he would have to find the right people, then assiduously avoid using them until they all got older and became well placed and trusted within their departments. Patience was the operative word. Bill figured that he would do one thing differently. If he ever put together a similar group, they'd never use the names of prophets to identify themselves. Rock singers, maybe.

"Yeah, I'm here," Cinq-Mars spoke up. "Yeah. Yeah. Thought so. Yeah. Really? Okay. Listen. I'll give you something. Tell your people this. According to you, Painchaud made the call during daylight hours, right? When I arrived, the lights were on. A lot of lights is hard to explain. No, no, you don't get it. He gets the shit kicked out of him. He makes a phone call. That happens in daylight. Somebody else shows up and turns on the lights. Maybe that person kills him. Or maybe that person sews his lips together. Somebody who shows up and runs away scared doesn't first turn on all the lights. Do you hear what I'm saying? Anyhow, the point is, pay close attention to the time of death and the time of the phone call. When you get the time of death, let me know. Yeah. Right. I got you. Okay. But, listen—find out exactly how long she listened to the tape. Okay. Right. Thanks."

Mathers sat up straight after Cinq-Mars signed off, anxious to know what was going on.

The senior detective put his phone away and moved his body so that he was sitting almost sideways on the seat with his knees up, facing Mathers. "Okay. The SQ is at Camille's house because Charlie called her. The call went through before dark. She says that when she got home there was a call on her answering machine, but no one said anything. She listened to a lot of blank air on the machine, then erased it."

"That could be," Mathers said, "if Charlie passed out after making the call."

"Makes sense. Or, if he was shot just as the call went through, she'd only hear silence. There'd be no gunshot on the tape. Apparently, she listened to the tape for a little bit, waiting for a voice, then she stopped it and pressed erase. So we don't have a record."

Mathers took a deep breath. "Where does this leave us, Émile?" he asked.

Cinq-Mars shook his head. "I don't know. I don't want to put myself in the middle of that hornet's nest." He jerked his head in the direction of Camille's house and the SQ. "I guess we knock off. Pick up the pieces in the morning."

His phone twittered, as though to immediately contradict him. After saying hello, he listened for awhile. Once he said, "God." Later he said, "Shit." At the end of the call he hung up without saying thanks or goodbye and tucked the phone away in his breast pocket. Then he slumped backward in the seat.

"You should have a hat," Cinq-Mars told his partner.

"Why's that?" He looked closely at his partner, who looked defeated, somehow.

"Because now would be a good time to hang on to it." He sighed. "This has gone dark, Bill. It's all pitch-black now." He spoke in a low voice.

"Émile? What's up?"

"Harry Hillier," Cinq-Mars recited slowly, trying to comprehend the words as he uttered them, "of Hillier-Largent Global. He's the bald one, right?"

Mathers concurred.

"He just blew up."

"Blew up?"

"Outside his office. Stuck his key into the ignition of his car, and the whole works exploded. Harry's history."

They were both on overload, and the information they processed cascaded into a darkened realm. Cinq-Mars hoarded a visual image of a black hole, where planets and galaxies were extinguished, where time itself was bent out of shape. Life seemed to be mutating. Whatever was not crushed became monstrous.

"What's going on?" Mathers begged.

Cinq-Mars failed to help him out. "Scientists puzzle over a problem of missing matter in the universe." He put up a defensive, gloved hand. "Don't worry, I'm not going to lecture you. I'm just tired. I'm just saying that the matter missing in the universe, Bill, doesn't compare to this. Everything that matters here is missing. We're nowhere. We're lost."

"His car, we're talking dynamite?"

"Or *plastique*. I keep forgetting that somebody tried to wire *my* car."

"I don't forget it. I'm not living with my wife because of it." Mathers gripped the steering wheel as though he wanted to rip it out. "What are we going to do, Émile?" he demanded, shaking himself loose from his own lethargy. "We have to *do* something. We have to respond."

Cinq-Mars nodded. He was tired, but the young man was right to remain aggressive. "You get the scene at Hillier-Largent. Find out what's there to find out. I'll talk to Roland Harvey."

Mathers was confused. "About what?"

"Harvey led you straight to Lucy, Bill. At least, he led you straight to her car, and I'm betting that that's pretty much the same difference. He didn't ask anybody's permission first. Either the Mohawk Peacekeepers are hiding Lucy, which is possible, or the Warriors are, and he's a Warrior, too. Either way, Roland's involved, and he's going to introduce me to

Lucy Gabriel. I'd prefer going to see her with an invitation. I'd like that meeting to be friendly."

Mathers wasn't so sure. "He might not feel inclined to do that, Émile."

Cinq-Mars grunted. "After tonight, he'll feel inclined. There's been a cop-killing. They know what happened the last time there was a cop-killing near here."

"The last time it was the Indians who shot the cop. Are you suggesting—"

"I'm not," Cinq-Mars assured him. "But they know that when a cop is shot dead the world goes crazy for a while. He'll lead me to Lucy."

The night was brightening, the clouds dispersing to reveal a half-moon. The detectives headed in opposite directions, intent on different situations. Bill Mathers would deal with the grisly aftermath of a car-bombing. Émile Cinq-Mars would enter a domain of cop-hating criminal Indians—some of whom might be cops themselves—hopefully to arrange contact with a young native in hiding, to see if they could find common ground.

Cinq-Mars drove back along the highway through the woodlands and farms that rimmed the north shore of the lake. He made a phone call, which gave him Roland Harvey's home address, culled from a phone book. He was then passed along to a police dispatcher who searched through her directories and gave him the necessary directions.

To pop in on Lucy uninvited was a temptation, but he didn't know what level of security existed inside the monastery, and he certainly had no desire to instigate a gunfight or to spook her, or anyone else. His best bet was to visit Roland Harvey first.

The directions took him onto Indian land and down a narrow, winding back road through a forest of pines.

Snow hung on the boughs, pristine in the moonlight. Initially, the road carried him uphill, but later it veered and descended into a clearing, where he spotted a smoking chimney before he saw the house. Cinq-Mars was unnerved by the number of vehicles parked in the driveway. Ratty pickups and high-priced four-by-fours. Rifles were mounted across the back windows. As he dimmed his lights and turned off the engine, he saw movement inside the house responding to the sound of his vehicle.

At least he wouldn't be waking people up or disrupting matrimonial intimacy.

His steps crunched snow as he walked toward the door. He made a point of remaining in the light from the living room, so that he was seen, to keep everybody calm. A fine, crisp night. A snapping cold. His breath visible in the night air.

Stars twinkled through the bare trees.

Cinq-Mars knocked on the stout pine door.

Roland Harvey waited a moment, then opened up. The two men regarded one another carefully.

"What's happening?" Constable Harvey asked. He was out of uniform, wearing jeans and a plaid shirt. The men behind him were standing, as though worried they might have to move quickly, and a couple of guys were keeping a vigil at various windows in case Cinq-Mars was not alone.

"Lucy Gabriel's at the monastery," the detective declared. "I want to talk to her."

Harvey continued to watch him steadily. Then he said, "Hang on," and closed the door. When he opened it again he had thrown on an overcoat and boots. Harvey came outside with Cinq-Mars and they walked a short distance away from the house, then stopped and faced one another. The Indian said, "You're asking me?"

"That's right. I'm asking you to take me to Lucy."

"I can't just do that."

"Why not? You went there after we talked today."

"You had me tailed?" The way he stuck out his chin underscored his hostility.

"I had you tailed. You're not going to trust me now?"

"That's right. I'm not going to trust you now. But I didn't before, not so much."

"Remember Charlie Painchaud?"

"Yeah. Sure." He hadn't buttoned his coat, and he flapped it impatiently with his hands in his pockets.

"He's dead."

Roland Harvey first leaned into the news, as though he could not trust his hearing, then leaned back, absorbing its impact. He took a deep breath and shook his head. Then he asked Cinq-Mars, "What are you saying to me?"

The Montreal cop took a step forward. He whispered, "I'm telling you that Sergeant Painchaud of the SQ was beaten in his own house and shot to death. I'm reminding you that he was working on a case that concerned the abduction of an Indian woman. A woman, incidentally, who happens to be living in the Oka monastery under your auspices. I'm pointing out to you that the dead man lives close to Indian land and there will be shit to pay for this all around."

"My people didn't do it," Harvey declared.

"You know what, Roland? That doesn't surprise me. But that doesn't mean that your people won't be considered. He's SQ, Roland. SQ. You know there's no love lost between the SQ and your people. He lives near Indian land. He was working on an Indian case. He was worked over and shot in his own house. Don't expect his colleagues to be reasonable about this. They're going to kick doors down first and ask questions later. I doubt if they'll need any particularly good excuse to kick down Indian doors, do you?"

"That'll be too bad if they do," Harvey warned defiantly. Again, he stuck his chin out as though to goad the other man into throwing the first punch.

"That's exactly what I'm saying," Cinq-Mars replied. "It'll be too bad if they do."

Roland Harvey had to ponder the situation. He kept his hands in his pockets to protect them from the cold. He looked around at the woods awhile. "I can't bring you to Lucy," he said in the end.

"Why not?"

"I don't have her permission. You've got to understand. Lucy is hiding out so she's protected from people who kill people in their own homes—"

"—and from people who might splash acid around her face if they want her to talk?" Cinq-Mars asked.

Harvey looked in his eyes. "Yeah," he said quietly, gravely, "from people like that." He continued in that tone. "She also needs protection from interested parties."

"From pharmaceutical executives who might wonder what she's been doing lately, what she's been saying. Is that what you mean?"

Roland Harvey nodded. "She also has to be protected from the police."

"I expected as much," Cinq-Mars told him. He looked up at the stars a moment, as though he needed help to construct his next proposal. "I was saying to you earlier today that I wanted to meet with Mohawk Warriors. Maybe your friends in the house are discussing that now, Roland? Maybe it's on the agenda?"

The Peacekeeper continued to gaze at him steadily and said nothing.

"In any case, you could bring the same news to Lucy. Tell her that I want to meet her on a personal basis. Not as a cop. As somebody who wants to keep her safe. You can tell her something else. I want her to stay in hiding. I think that's a good idea right now."

The officer cocked his head with curiosity. "You do."

"Yes, I do. Charlie Painchaud was a friend of hers. Let her know that he's dead. You can also tell her that Harry Hillier, one of her bosses, was the victim of a car-bombing tonight."

The news was sounding increasingly dire to Harvey. "He's dead too?"

"Oh yeah. He's a cherry pie."

The Indian exhaled a long breath. As he turned his face to the moonlight, Cinq-Mars could see the pock-marks on his skin and the fleshiness of his jowls.

"Take me to her," Cinq-Mars pleaded.

The Mohawk shook his head, holding his ground. "I'll talk to her. See what she says."

Cinq-Mars lowered his head, nodding. He had made progress, and he would have to settle for that, for now. "You have my number? Do you know where I live? She's mobile, Roland, she's got her car."

"She's made a solemn vow to stay put."

Roland Harvey was admitting to something with that remark, and Cinq-Mars looked up at him. He was saying that he was in charge of her, and admitting to it had been a concession, not a mistake. He was putting himself on the line. "Anytime," Cinq-Mars urged him quietly, "day or night. I need to talk to her."

The Peacekeeper nodded.

Cinq-Mars turned toward his car, as though by taking his leave he could change both his tone and the subject, and seal their professional relationship. "I like the scheme, Roland. The monks take Indian land for themselves. A century or so later, a new generation of religious man feels guilty about all that and seeks to make amends. Indians go to the monks and ask them to hide someone. The monks agree."

Although his expression hardly changed at all, Cinq-Mars believed he detected an inner smile cross Roland Harvey's face.

"Write them down for me," the constable instructed, "your numbers and stuff. I'll go see her, but I don't want anybody tailing me this time. You're not going inside the monastery without Lucy's permission."

"I wasn't suggesting that, Roland."

"Because my own people will be right behind me. I think you know what I mean by my own people."

Everybody would have their armies on the road tonight.

"Be careful, Roland. There's movement out there."

The Indian nodded solemnly. "You too," he said.

Starlight lit his way home. The clouds had moved east. The ride across the lake felt infused with an old, odd magic. The dance of the heavens, the soft fall of lights from homes along the shore and silvery moonlight across the snow. Another world, one that seemed far removed from danger. Cinq-Mars was not convinced, and twice after leaving the lake he stopped in a quiet spot and waited, checking that no cars were following him. Twice he doubled back, to verify his security. The roads on the south side of the lake proved to be clear, he was alone in the country under the moonlight, beneath the stars, skimming across bright, gleaming surfaces.

Sandra had left a light on in the kitchen. Turning the Pathfinder off and walking toward his front door, he heard his dog whining and scratching on the other side. As he opened the door, Sandra was coming down the stairs to meet him, having been alerted by the dog's excitement.

"I'll walk her," Cinq-Mars said. They kissed.

"We both will," Sandra offered, and she jogged upstairs to get dressed.

Outside, the couple played with their retriever awhile, chasing her off with showers of snow. She'd yelp and scamper away, only to bog down in the powder and desperately bound back to them. Finally she wearied of their nonsense and braced herself beneath the branches of a magnificent Great Eastern Pine to do her business. Then it was back to the comfort of the house.

And upstairs.

Cinq-Mars undressed his wife.

He supposed they were lucky. Her body remained an adventure to him. Familiar, yet also a surprise. He had been alone most of his adult life, and she was such a wonder to him, how she moved with him as he caressed her. There was weight to her flesh, and toil, and history. Tracing the contours of her skin with his fingers, his tongue, he revisited the years of her life, the times when he had not known her, making her laugh as a girl, or sigh with the ardour of a young woman in the early throes of passion. Sandra was a woman who had made her way, suffered setbacks, persevered, managed, struggled through, and when she turned under him on the bed, kissing him, drawing him down, she was his wife, here, now, in their home, in the middle of her life, anxious and content.

Sally lay at the foot of the bed, eyes open part of the time.

They moved together, intent now, and Sandra incited her husband with crude whispers, her mouth to his ear. She knew that the words were strange for him, for his priestly Catholic mind, but he responded with guttural fulmination and an increased tempo, and she laughed as she hugged him and squeezed and met his lunge with her hips, a lifetime's experience as a rider put to strong, athletic use. At the penultimate moment they were both perplexed, bewitched, straddling laughter and joy and a sense of sheer fun with an underlying and soon dominant need and lust and release. They broke the silence of their rural landscape, their outcry boisterous across the contours of fallen snow.

The couple nestled together awhile, then rearranged themselves to escape the cool breeze coming through the window, which was open a crack. They cuddled in a warmth of their own creation under the duvet. They might normally have tumbled into sleep, but the silvery, bright moonlight through the window, the eerie quiet, the particular joy of lovemaking on this night, and the anxiety of the day's news kept them awake. They lay, spooned together, listening to one another breathe against the backdrop of the night.

The wind picked up. They felt the cold air on their noses.

Trees made cracking sounds as they swayed.

Sandra remembered to pop an Aspirin into her husband's mouth.

As quickly as it came up, the wind ceased.

"I heard on the news about the policeman. Did you know him?"

"I've been working with him since Sunday."

"Oh, Émile."

"There was a bombing tonight, as well. That's also my case."

Gently, she reached behind her to touch his shoulder with her fingertips.

After a while, after she thought he had fallen asleep, Émile said, "I was standing outside Charlie's house tonight. He's the dead man. I found him. I was standing outside and I was thinking, it's death. That's my enemy these days. I'm fighting against death, and how crazy is that? Men have pills, drugs, that precipitate death, speed up the process of dying, because that might teach them something. My father is dying and I only want him to live longer. But I know, he knows, his life is over. Death. Death wins. Where in all this is life?"

She craned her neck, twisting her head around to kiss his shoulder with grave tenderness. After a while, she whispered, "Here."

He bound her closer to him then, and tucked in one another's embrace, they slept.

16

DARKLING STAR

The next day, Wednesday, February 16, 1999

Dawn found Émile Cinq-Mars invigorated, driving eastbound toward the city, connecting with the early commuter traffic that flowed from the rural communities on either side of the Quebec-Ontario border. Like him, his fellow drivers had chosen life in the countryside while holding down city jobs, and the price to be paid was late nights, early risings, and hard drives in the winter's dark along snowy highways. Frustrated by the slow pace, Cinq-Mars dug out his red cherry flasher from under the passenger seat, leaning way over and bobbing up again to check on the traffic until he'd rooted it out. He ran the wire to the cigarette lighter, opened his side window, and plopped it on the rooftop of his Pathfinder, where it would be held in place by magnets. That gave him some driving room, and he sped on through to downtown Montreal.

He had a jag on. His sleep had been beneficial, and now he felt that he was ready to take command of this case.

At Police Headquarters he primed himself with coffee. He had no room to stomp around in his cubicle, but when he stepped outside to the squad room he bumped into people and desks. So he invaded the lunch room and told the cops hanging around in there to get the hell out. By the time Bill Mathers arrived he was pacing, and taunting himself.

"Émile?" Mathers had had a bad night, beginning with his investigation of the car-bombing of Harry Hillier. When he had called his wife later, she'd been in a state, upset by the news that a cop had been beaten in his home and murdered.

Cinq-Mars stopped in his tracks, suddenly surprised to see him. "Bill."

"What's going on?"

"I have this case," the older man said.

"What do you mean? What do you have?"

"Nothing. Nothing yet," the senior cop admitted.

"You have this case, but you've got nothing. All right." Mathers sat down, willing to give his partner the benefit of the doubt.

Cinq-Mars turned and faced him. "I can feel it, Bill. I know that I've seen something. My mind, in my sleep, somehow, my mind thought things through and under- stands everything, or understands enough of every- thing, and I can *feel* that I've got this made. I just don't know what my mind knows. It's all—*right here!*" Cinq- Mars exclaimed, and he held both his open hands a foot away from his eyes.

Mathers watched his partner stomp back and forth. "All right, Émile, I don't quite know what you're saying. I've never seen you like this before."

Cinq-Mars stopped again, and sighed, and held out his open hands chest-high. "It's inside me, Bill. All right? I don't need more information. I don't need to interview anyone. My brain either saw something, or figured something out, but that information hasn't registered yet with *me*, you know? I don't have it in my conscious mind, but I do believe, I *feel*, that it's all inside me." In his pent-up frustration, Cinq-Mars pushed a hand through his slightly graying hair. He looked up at the ceiling for a moment, then said, "When I talked to my father's priest, Father Réjean, I told him that my job is to be ready. That sounded so foolish at the time. Except that a part of me believed it. And I still do. The only thing I can offer in this job is readiness. If something happens, I react, and I have to be ready to react. I woke up this morning, Bill, and I felt ready. I've trained myself for a case like this my entire adult life. I'm prepared, Bill. I just don't have all the synapses firing and connecting, not yet."

Mathers nodded sympathetically. "You're wired, Émile. Maybe you should try calming down. If you're waiting for something to float to the surface, you might want to relax."

He was right, of course, and Cinq-Mars conceded as much with an odd grimace. He sat down. They were interrupted by a cop coming in for coffee, and he brayed at the intruder, "Get out! Get out now!" The rookie beat a retreat.

After awhile, Mathers tried to prime him. "You have this case."

The senior detective nodded. "I saw something. That's what I think, anyhow. It must have been at Painchaud's house. I saw the answer, or the clue we need. In all that mess, something registered with me, but subconsciously. Damn it, Bill, what was it? I know it's important. Why can't I get at it?"

They were interrupted again, but this time, before he could yell, Cinq-Mars was informed that a call had come through to him from the Mohawk Peacekeepers. He and Mathers returned to his cubicle where he picked up his phone. "Cinq-Mars here."

"It's Roland Harvey."

He sat in his swivel chair behind his desk. "It's good to hear from you."

"I set it up with Lucy for this afternoon. Anytime after one, she said."

"I just show up at the monastery?"

"That's it. It's the wing on the west, the part that looks like a castle. Either Lucy or some monk will meet you, show you where to go."

"Any restrictions?" He slouched down, stretching his neck and legs. As he spoke he surveyed his desk. The clutter of paper was getting out of hand.

"I wouldn't bring in the SWAT. That might spook her."

Cinq-Mars appreciated the humor, as it showed that they were getting along, a trust was forming. "Thanks for this, Roland. Will you be there yourself?"

"Lucy said no. It'll be you and her."

"All right then. Thanks again."

He hung up, put his hands behind his head, and told Mathers the news.

"What're you going to ask her?" Mathers wanted to know. He stood, thinking about going out for a coffee.

"To be decided."

Mathers left and when he came back he was blowing the steam off the top of his mug. He put his coffee down to cool beside the computer—perpetually unused—and with his left hand played with the cord for the mouse, which hung off the edge of the desk. The day the department had furnished Cinq-Mars with a computer, the curmudgeon had installed an antique clock on a top shelf that tolled the hour and half-hour with a deep mellow chime. Most of the squad believed it was a message to the upper ranks to screw off. While the mouse dangled freely, advising anyone who entered not to ask for his e-mail address, the keyboard, Mathers noticed, lay buried under files on a side shelf.

"Spill the beans, Bill," Cinq-Mars said, noticing a worried look on his partner's face.

Mathers looked up at him briefly, but chose to remain silent.

"How's Donna?"

Mathers sighed. "The cop we were working this case with is dead. She noticed that, Émile."

Cinq-Mars nodded. "It is tragic. Today, every cop's wife is rethinking."

"I think Donna has done her thinking on this."

"Really? And?" He felt like another coffee himself, but knew that he had better not indulge.

"She wants me and you to split up as partners."

Cinq-Mars looked off to one side, taking that in, absorbing the sentiment on the chin. "Now?" he asked. "Today?"

"No," Mathers shot back, as if that idea was ridiculous. "Not today."

"When then?" Cinq-Mars kept his hands behind his head, taking his partner's measure.

Mathers tried a sip of coffee, and he could just manage the temperature. He cocked his head first to one side, then the other. "Tomorrow," he said. "Or maybe the next day." He didn't look at Cinq-Mars after that. He just stared into his mug.

Cinq-Mars sat straighter in his chair and clutched an armrest in each hand. He observed his partner a moment, then deliberately averted his gaze to spare him the severity of his disapproval. He wouldn't tell him that his wife had to understand that she could not dictate how he did his job, that she just didn't have the proper expertise. In the past he had been able to assure both of them that his notoriety gave them a kind of unofficial immunity—it was dangerous to kill a cop, extremely so if he happened to be famous. Recent events had pulled that argument out from under him. "Well," he said quietly. "That'll be a sad day. I don't look forward to it." He lowered his head a moment, as though to shift mental gears. "Bill, tell me about the car-bombing. What's there to know?"

Mathers told him about the crime scene. He was glad to do that, to be on a different subject. Harry

Hillier had been blown up in his car in the company parking lot upon his departure, after working long hours. The keys were in the ignition, and the bomb squad speculated that starting the car had ignited the explosion. The windows in Hillier-Largent were blown out, and residents for blocks around had been shaken off their favourite television sofas. Randall Largent, Mathers said, had arrived on the scene and was upset, even hysterical.

Cinq-Mars breathed deeply. "This is part of my problem. Maybe I can't process my information because I don't know what I'm trying to do. Am I after the people who killed AIDS sufferers in the States? Am I after Stettler's killer? Or Charlie's? What does this bombing have to do with any of that, or the attack on my house? How many people are we after? Deep down, I think it's a house of cards. I have that impression. If we can get one answer, we'll know them all. But which crime am I solving? I'm not even sure, and maybe that's what's gumming up my head. Partly."

Glad that Cinq-Mars had not roasted him for his announcement, Mathers nodded. The case was a puzzle, and it was getting more complicated as time passed.

They sat in the cubicle awhile, then Cinq-Mars excused himself to go to the john. While he was gone his phone rang and Mathers answered it. He talked to Lieutenant-Detective Tremblay, and when his partner returned he delivered the bad news.

"Tremblay says we have to stay in. Two New York cops are coming at 12:30. He wants us to talk to them."

"What for?"

"That he wouldn't say."

"Why not?"

Mathers took a swig of coffee before answering. "Émile. Guess what? The Lieutenant doesn't explain himself to me."

"We have to wait here?" He checked his watch. "That's two hours! The *hell* I'm staying here!" Cinq-Mars stormed from his cubicle for a combative tête-à-tête with his commanding officer. This was supposed to be his day. He had the case inside him, waiting to burst forth in a wild moment of cognitive illumination. He was not supposed to be playing babysitter to visiting cops. Mathers knew that the tirade Tremblay was about to hear would have very little to do with the content of the order he had given, and more to do with his partner's warring frustrations.

Camille Choquette kept her daughter, Carole, home from school. She didn't want her blabbing anything she shouldn't to a teacher or a friend, and word had probably gone around the community that the police had visited her the night before. Everybody would know by now that Charlie was dead.

While the child watched television by herself, Camille tossed and turned on her couch. She hadn't slept at all through the night, although she had survived the interrogation all right. Sticking to her guns had been the right strategy. Somebody had called her house—according to the SQ officers, it had been Charlie—but no message had been left. No cop accused her. Instead they prowled around her house, apologizing for being thorough. While it was true that Charlie had dialled her place, it was considered understandable, and he had been beaten so badly that no woman would be under suspicion for his murder.

For a while, she answered repetitive questions about the timing. When did she get home? Was it dark? Was she sure it was dark? Where was she before that? *At work.* What did you do at home? *Waited for Charlie.* Did she ever leave? *Yes.* Why? *To take my daughter to her friend's.* Why? *Because Charlie was coming over.*

In the midst of the Q & A merry-go-round, she had

played the role of the stricken girlfriend, and eventually her misery had mitigated the police onslaught. She'd arranged to have Carole stay where she was, at her friend's house, and after midnight she'd been left alone. Lying in her bed, she'd stared at the ceiling, praying that Honigwachs was having a miserable time also, in bed with his wife, fretting about the state of the universe.

The next morning she had picked Carole up early, as everyone in that household was going either to school or to work. Then shortly after noon, while she was serving Carole and herself lunch, Lucy called.

"Lucy! *Lucy!* Are you all right?" She couldn't believe it!

"Camille, oh Camille. Charlie's dead. Did you hear about Harry?"

"What about Harry?" At first, she couldn't believe that Lucy had called, and then she moved the phone from one ear to the other and wondered if this was a trap.

"He's dead too. He got blown up in his car. It's on the radio."

"Oh my God."

Who had killed Harry? It couldn't have been Honigwachs. He participated in murders but he didn't plan them. Why would anyone *want* Harry dead? Then she felt suddenly exhilarated. All the fuss would only make it more difficult for anyone to suspect her.

"How are you?" Lucy asked.

Camille spontaneously burst into tears. She wept, and sputtered, and told Lucy that they might be next, that somebody was probably hunting them down.

"I've got a real good place to hide," Lucy told her.

"You do?" She dried her eyes with the back of her hand.

"You could come here too."

"I could? But, no. I can't leave Carole."

"Bring her."

"What? Really? Where?" This could be a trap, or this could be the best thing possible, under the circumstances.

"I don't know if the phones are safe, Camille."

"Oh my God," Camille moaned. "Oh my God. We're not going to make it."

"Camille. Listen. Drive toward my house. I'll see you coming. I'll jump out at you, show you where to go. Come now, Camille. Come right now. Bring Carole with you. I don't want you to die too, Camille."

She hesitated, panting into the receiver. Then she said, "All right."

Camille put the receiver back down in its cradle. Then she went to work. She packed the kinds of clothes someone was likely to take into hiding, for herself and her daughter. The last thing that she tucked away into her overnight bag was Charlie Painchaud's pistol.

Cinq-Mars alternated between time alone, in which he tried to cull from his memory the answers he was looking for, and time on the phone, in which he tried to learn as much about the death of Charlie Painchaud as the SQ already knew, hoping that that information might help him.

"Maybe I have to think outside the box," he told Mathers, who looked at him in surprise. "What? Do you think I've never heard current jargon? Isn't that a new phrase, think outside the box?"

"Yeah," Mathers assured him. "It is. But what do you mean?"

"I keep thinking that I saw something at Charlie's house that I passed over. I didn't take proper note of it. Maybe that's wrong. Maybe what I saw, or heard, or remembered has nothing to do with Charlie's house."

"Maybe. Try to relax about it, Émile." He was trying to do something about the shambles on his own desk, or at least appear to be interested in his caseload.

"How can I relax? I've got two cops flying in from New York for no known purpose other than to waste my time."

Tremblay had been emphatic. He had to wait for the New Yorkers.

Mathers grunted and didn't go any further into that problem, not wanting to encourage his partner's rant. He hadn't told Cinq-Mars the worst of his own problems. Donna's demands had gone beyond Bill splitting with his partner. She was leaving him. The only thing that would make her stay would be the news that he had quit the department and was looking for another career. He had coaxed her into giving him more time, but first he had to quit the partnership with Cinq-Mars as an act of good faith. She hadn't given him a couple of days. He had to be off the case and out of the partnership when he came home, or their marriage would be irreparable.

"I've made this case, Bill," Cinq-Mars was muttering as he passed behind the room dividers into his office cubicle. "I know it's inside me."

Maybe Donna's right, Mathers was thinking. The man seemed half mad.

"New York cops!" he was raving, as if the indignity was too much to bear. "I have to waste my time with New York cops! Doesn't anybody around here know we've had a cop-killing?"

They were both quiet awhile, then Cinq-Mars blew up and shouted from behind his dividers, "They'd better show up on time! And if they do, they'd better have something interesting to tell me. Or else!"

Against his better judgment, Mathers replied, "Or else what?"

Cinq-Mars came to the entrance to his cubicle and stared down his lengthy nose at him.

"Sorry," Mathers apologized. "I didn't get much sleep last night."

Another time he heard Cinq-Mars ranting and got up to calm him down. "Apparently, nobody cares if cops are being shot," he was shouting, "or if key players are being blown up in their cars, or if witnesses are being stuffed under an ice cap or squirreled away from public view to keep them alive. I'm on assignment. I get to talk to New York cops. Whoopee!"

Mathers stood in the entrance and discovered that Cinq-Mars wasn't ranting to himself but talking on the phone, to his dying father, as it turned out. The morning was shaping up to be a long one for everyone concerned. For his own sake, he hoped that the New York cops arrived on time.

The same day, Wednesday afternoon, February 16th, 1999

They arrived late, escorted by Lieutenant-Detective Remi Tremblay.

"Explain it to me, Bill," Cinq-Mars whispered as, over the room dividers, he watched the men approach. "If the New York Police Department needs to communicate with us, if they have to do it in person, why are they sending *two* cops? Two plane tickets, two hotel rooms, double the meals. Either they don't have a single cop smart enough to keep things straight, or this is a boondoggle. I'll lay odds these guys brought their skis."

Standing next to him, buttoning his jacket, Mathers mentioned, "They're not wearing ski boots, Émile."

Cinq-Mars wouldn't be knocked off his soapbox easily. "They were lured here by the cheap Canadian dollar. They'll want our opinion on restaurants."

Three men entered the cubicle.

Tremblay undertook the introductions. Austere, he carried himself with a professorial countenance. Not a man displaced by the new wizardry of statistical analysis or computer-generated profiles of crime suspects, the lieutenant was a team player at heart, although for him that usually meant being the team leader. Before Christmas, Cinq-Mars had enjoyed ribbing Tremblay after the lieutenant had given an interview on television. "Crime is down except in certain pockets of the city where children are stealing automobile hood ornaments, which is a new fad, thereby creating a statistical anomaly." In department meetings, Cinq-Mars had taken to asking if they were going to put together a major task force to crack down on the scurrilous, hood-ornament-stealing, statistic-busting twelve-year-olds before it was too late, before all hell broke loose.

"Detective First-Class Recchi, NYPD. His partner, Detective McGibbon," Tremblay stated. "Gentlemen, may I introduce Sergeant-Detective Émile Cinq-Mars, the man I was telling you about. This is his partner, Detective William Mathers. You four have a lot to talk about. I have to run, so take care of our guests, Émile." He gave a little questioning nod, as though to indicate to Cinq-Mars that his best behaviour was being solicited.

They shook hands. They were all large men, Cinq-Mars the tallest, but the new arrivals had broad shoulders and chests and the necks of football linebackers. A black man, McGibbon offered a relaxed and cordial smile. Recchi, olive-skinned, dark-haired, carried himself with the chiseled head and loping, worried stance of a pugilist. Both men held their overcoats slung across a forearm.

"Sit down," Cinq-Mars invited. Mathers had already brought chairs in for the purpose. "What can I do for you?"

Seated, McGibbon straightened his tie. "I didn't know for sure if you guys spoke English up here." He smiled again.

"My partner's English," Cinq-Mars remarked. "He's dragged me down to his level." He wished they'd get on with it.

McGibbon braced his hands on his knees, his overcoat falling across his lap. "We have a situation in New York, sir. Men with AIDS have been dying prematurely. Unexpectedly. All at the same time. Before dying, a few talked about being on a secret drug therapy program—some kind of thing like that. They'd been undergoing treatment for years, that's what they told people, but this time, when the program changed, they didn't stay well or get better. They got worse. They slid downhill fast."

Cinq-Mars and Mathers shared a glance. Chickens were coming home to roost. "The reason that my superior officer charged out of here so quickly—"

"He explained," Recchi said.

"We have no jurisdiction on this case."

"He said something about SQ?"

"*La Sûreté du Québec*, the provincial police."

"Sir," McGibbon stated, straightening somewhat and lowering his voice, as though to sound conspiratorial, "obviously, we don't know the ins and outs of how things work up here."

"Frankly, we don't care," Recchi put in.

"The lieutenant, he said even though you don't have jurisdiction, the one person up here we got to talk to, that one person is you. To confer with anybody else would be a waste of our time. Maybe damaging. Would you disagree?"

Without committing himself, Cinq-Mars folded his arms across his chest. "What do you know?"

"One woman came to New York City and administered drug cocktails to AIDS patients," McGibbon recited. "The patients thought they were getting the latest deal, experimental drugs on the leading edge, not yet approved. That woman's name was Lucy. She's native, attractive, long-legged, black hair. We have a decent description. A week later a second woman appeared on the scene. She checked on the health of those taking the first woman's medication, to see how they were doing. She's referred to as Camille. Her name, and especially her accent—people thought maybe she was French Canadian, which pointed an arrow up here. By the time the second woman had shown up, patients were dying, a few were already dead."

They possessed a good overview.

"I'm aware of your situation," Cinq-Mars revealed.

"You're aware?" Recchi asked. "We could've used a heads-up. A consult."

"As far as I know, every patient was contacted, told to cease their medication and seek treatment."

"That's another reason why we're here. We heard about that. What does that do for us, Sergeant-Detective? It sorts out the medical side of things, maybe, but I don't think it helps us out crime-wise, with the illegalities." Recchi liked to gesture with one hand as he talked.

Cinq-Mars imagined that a few perpetrators had been swatted by that hand over the years. He tried to redirect the conversation. "I understand, sir, that we're talking about two young, idealistic women, who thought they were helping. For years they *were* helping, before something went wrong. They never had any intent to do harm."

"Sir," McGibbon interrupted, "do you have any idea how many people ended up dead from their desire to do no harm?"

"Forty-two," Cinq-Mars replied, which startled both visitors. Both their heads shifted back as if from a blow. "You didn't know it was that many because we're not only talking about New York."

"We know about Jersey."

"Add on Philadelphia."

"Jesus," Recchi said.

"Baltimore," Cinq-Mars mentioned, "escaped by the skin of its teeth."

"Forty-two dead by your count," McGibbon summarized. "I think we have a crime here. I don't think it matters how idealistic they were."

"We have a crime," Cinq-Mars concurred. "But—behind the crime are men, and syndicates, who knew exactly what they were doing. People who deliberately killed others to advance science. The mob's involved. Around here, if something's big, the mob's always involved. They insist. Usually, all we have to do is figure out which gang. What I'm trying to say is, the women were pawns. If I've been protecting them, it might be because they're the only hope I have left to nail the real criminals."

This time, McGibbon and Recchi shared a covert communication. "We'd like to talk to them," Recchi said.

"No can do."

"Why not?"

"They're in hiding." Cinq-Mars saw no need to discriminate between Lucy and Camille. These men had no particular right to his knowledge.

"From who?"

"Not from me."

McGibbon turned his head to one side and nodded while looking down at the desk. He finally understood that the meeting was adversarial. "Are they police informants?"

"Would I tell you if they were?"

"I don't know why not."

"Would you?"

"That would depend." Under the stern gaze of Émile Cinq-Mars, McGibbon made a decision and spoke honestly. "Probably not."

"I won't tell you if they're informants or not."

"We're on the job, like you."

"Yes, you are. With respect, sir, I don't know you."

Recchi brushed a hand through his hair and breathed out with apparent impatience. "Tiddlywinks. We've got—how many, you said?—forty-two dead. You want to screw us around here?"

"We've got an officer assigned to this investigation beaten to death," Cinq-Mars told him. "We've got key witnesses blown up in their automobiles. I've had an assault upon my home and family. My partner's family's in hiding. I don't know you, sir." Cinq-Mars put both elbows on his desk and pointed a telling finger at the visitor. "I don't know you."

The four men were quiet awhile, each mulling avenues of possible reciprocity.

Recchi broke the silence. "Look, we're on your turf. What you say goes. We can't do anything here. We'd be lost. How can we make this work? How can we make this happen, Sergeant-Detective?"

Cinq-Mars leaned back in his swivel chair and issued a lengthy yawn. "All right," he declared when he snapped forward again. "We're driving out to a crime scene. If you want to tag along …?"

"What's the crime?"

"A cop was beaten and shot to death in his home. I want to revisit the scene. We can start there. See how it goes."

McGibbon checked with Recchi, who shrugged. "All right. Let's go."

Cinq-Mars jumped to his feet and grabbed his coat. "You guys armed?"

Reaching down, McGibbon retrieved the computer mouse that dangled just above his feet and put the object on the desk where he thought it belonged. The wee, plastic creature had obviously been irritating him. When he stood, he tapped his hip holster, and Recchi nodded.

"Good. I wouldn't want you reading tourist

brochures. I wouldn't want you thinking you've crossed into a safe country. It's not safe if you're law enforcement. This time of year, especially. The gangs are bomb-happy. This time of year, they might blow a man up just for using a word like 'tiddlywinks.' That wouldn't surprise me one bit. Show them your gold shields and tell them you're from New York, they might not be impressed."

"I got that message," Recchi said.

"What's so special about this time of year?" McGibbon asked.

"Boredom, maybe. Long winter nights."

"The mob here kills cops?" Recchi asked Mathers, as they followed Cinq-Mars out of the cubicle.

"Somebody does," Cinq-Mars told him over his shoulder.

"Cops. They kill cops?" Recchi, hurrying in pursuit, pressed the junior officer in a hushed tone, as if he wasn't sure whether he could believe the older guy or not.

Bringing up the rear, bobbing as he picked up his rubber boots on the fly, then reaching out to grab his overcoat off a hook, Mathers confided, "Lately."

Lucy Gabriel was standing by the highway, keeping an eye out for Camille's car. She had stepped out when she saw her friend coming, but was taken aback by the smashed window. Camille had covered it with a plastic sheet and so had to open the door to talk to her.

"What happened?" Lucy asked.

"Long story. Are you getting in?"

"Nope. Keep going down the road until you see a monk. He'll direct you."

Lucy disappeared into the trees on foot.

Camille drove on, and eventually a monk stood on the highway pointing to the parking lot of the monastery. She drove down and waited for the man to join her. He didn't say anything, but helped her unpack the car and guided the woman and her daughter to the ninth floor of the empty western wing.

Lucy came along quite awhile later, as though she'd been keeping watch, to confirm that Camille hadn't been followed, and the two women hugged. They wept for Charlie and Andy.

"Cinq-Mars is coming this afternoon."

"He is?"

"We'll have to tell him everything."

"We will," Camille agreed. "Oh God, Lucy! You lost Andy. I've lost Charlie!"

"Baby." They held one another again, and only the monk's return helped them pull themselves together.

"Does he talk?" Camille asked about Brother Tom.

"Not a peep. We communicate though, in our own way. Come on, Camille, pick a room. You might as well make yourself at home."

Camille put her things away in the simple room identical to Lucy's across the hall. Carole insisted on her own room and chose one two doors down. The little girl was permitted to unpack her own bag, and Lucy and Camille left her alone. Camille filled the little drawers in her room with her underthings and stacked her pants and blouses on the desk. She hung one dress on a small rack intended for a monk's robes. With Lucy's help she made the bed with the sheets and blankets brought in by Brother Tom, then Camille flopped down for a bed test.

"It ain't much, but it's home." Lucy tried to smile, but tears quickly sprang to her eyes instead. This time, Camille comforted her. "I guess if Cinq-Mars can't help us," Lucy said, dabbing her eyes, "he can always toss us in jail."

"Cheery thought."

"It keeps me going." She stuffed a Kleenex into the tight front pocket of her jeans.

"What do you do for fun around here?" Camille

called back over her shoulder as Lucy tagged along. They were off to check on Carole.

"Arm-wrestle Brother Tom. Yesterday I raced him down the hall after giving him a thirty-yard head start. I try to get him to talk, unsuccessfully so far. And I thought up a new game, where I give him a pat on the ass when he least expects it."

"You don't. Lucy! Poor Brother Tom!"

Camille was dragged away by Carole, who had taken it into her head that she wanted a bath. "I'm a guppy," she called back to Lucy.

Her mother turned on the bathtub taps. The seven-year-old seemed amazed that the bathtub was in a room all by itself, with no toilet and no sink. While they waited for the slowly pouring water, Lucy showed them the washroom.

"No urinals," Camille noted.

"Monks in robes, they'd rather sit, I guess," Lucy explained, and the women's laughter echoed off the tile walls and marble floor.

"Anyway, right now, only the fourth stall has paper, so that's the one we use."

"Gotcha." Camille tested the water in the bath while Carole got out of her clothes.

"Brother Tom will bring you banana bread and chocolate milk after your bath, Carole!" Lucy said. She wanted to protect the child from the sorrow she was feeling. It was all so horrible. Charlie, dead. Harry, dead. What was going on? How could they escape? She desperately needed to talk to Cinq-Mars. She desperately needed to trust him.

"I'm going to have a bath of my own," Camille decided. "There's more than one tub, right?"

"Dozens," Lucy confirmed. "Four on each floor."

Lucy returned to her room and stood looking out over the lake. She had done the right thing, she believed, bringing Camille here. She didn't want to lose another friend.

Mathers drove the police issue, their guests in the rear seat. They'd headed out to the ice-bridge with Cinq-Mars urging him to use a heavy foot. On the ice, though, he demanded that Mathers stop.

The officer braked the car slowly.

In the back, Detective McGibbon, seated directly behind Cinq-Mars, asked, "What're we stopping here for?"

Mathers was looked intently at his partner, as though he had the same question on his mind, only he knew better than to ask.

"I've made this," Cinq-Mars declared.

"What do you mean?" Recchi asked.

"I just have to figure it out." He was hardly noticing the men with him. In his own world, Cinq-Mars stepped out of the car and walked a hundred feet across the ice and snow.

"What the fuck is going on?" Recchi demanded to know.

Mathers said, "You guys stay here, all right?" He climbed out from behind the driver's seat.

"Is he nuts?" Recchi pestered him.

"Yeah," Mathers said, before he closed the door. "He's crazy." He watched his partner stop and crouch down, then place his head in his hands. Mathers waited a minute, observing him, before he walked up behind him. When he got close, he moved to one side, and saw that Cinq-Mars was trying to wipe away a tear. "Émile?" he asked quietly.

The man was embarrassed and tried to turn his head away. When he felt that he had done all he could to dry his eyes, he stood. "My dad's dying," he explained. "It's any day now. Maybe any hour."

"I know, Émile. I'm sorry about that. You want to take some time?"

Cinq-Mars shook his head. "God! What—is—it?"

After that outburst, Mathers was afraid to speak again.

Then Cinq-Mars said, "It wasn't Painchaud's house, Bill, it was Camille's!"

With his hands in his pockets, Mathers shrugged. "What was?"

"The clue I saw but missed." Mathers seemed confused, and Cinq-Mars shook his hands at him. "Her driveway. I'm sure, I'm positive, was full of cop cars. But there's no garage and her car was nowhere around."

"So?"

Cinq-Mars was taking large breaths, as though he was winded by an acceleration to his thinking. "So, where was her car?"

Mathers continued to stare at him, without comprehension.

"But I need it all, Bill. I need it all and it's coming. I tell you. I've prepared myself for this. I'm sorry if I don't know how to handle it."

"Émile—"

"Stettler wrote *lips lips lips.* He was concerned about lips, something about lips. Then Charlie has his lips sewn shut. You know I don't believe in coincidence. Coincidence is the biggest fraud going. Everything in life is interwoven, everything's connected. So Stettler knew about a problem with lips, something that confused him, upset him probably, so much so that a very secretive man wrote the words down and underlined them three times. As if he was trying to get his brain to figure it out. I know what that's like."

Cinq-Mars bent over at the waist, as if the adrenaline pumping through his system contorted him. "Stettler had some concern that he probably didn't understand about lips." He returned to an upright stance again. "And he bobs to the surface in Camille Choquette's fishing hut. Charlie is killed and he has his lips sewn shut, and his telephone is an open line to Camille's house. That's no coincidence. Two bodies, both connected to some place where Camille sleeps. Fishing *line*, telephone *line*—it all connects."

"All right," Mathers said, "I see where you're going. But we also have to deal with the small matter of proof."

"Yes, yes," Cinq-Mars agreed, impatiently. He had one hand in a pocket and the other he shook in midair, waist-high. "Let's just say you've killed someone and you run outside and you find out you've locked your keys in the car. What do you do? Call a locksmith? An automobile club? Do you go looking for a coathanger to jimmy the lock? No! Bill! We've already seen the shards of glass. You smash the damn window and get the hell out of there. But after *that*—"

Mathers had it now. "After that you don't park your car in the driveway, with the window out. It's Camille. We haven't even interviewed her yet, but we know now it's Camille. For some reason she wanted her boyfriend dead."

"Same reason that she wanted Andy dead," Cinq-Mars said. "They carried information. In her business, that's a deadly disease."

"Do we pick her up?"

Cinq-Mars nodded. "Let's go to her house. See if she can produce that car."

Camille undressed in private and donned her ankle-length bathrobe for the trek back down the hall. She organized her bathing items, her soaps and shampoo, cleansers and hairbrushes, and put them all in a pink toilet kit. Then she took Charlie Painchaud's pistol out of her bag and put that in the kit as well.

She checked her bath. The hot was too hot, and she added a little cold to the mix, stirring the water with one hand until she got the temperature right. Then she stood and locked the door.

Camille Choquette examined the pistol. She examined it as a woman in a particular mood might explore a dildo. She had one more tangle to unravel, and this would be the best way. The only way. Cinq-Mars was coming. Lucy was going to talk to him. She didn't know what Charlie had told him, but whatever it was, he was no longer alive to say it again. Lucy was a problem. Lucy connected her to the dead patients in the States. The dead patients in the States included two, one in New York and one in Paramus, New Jersey, whose lives she had taken and whose lips she had sewn. She had smothered Wendell in New York. She had slit the throat of the motel clerk in Paramus, then sewn the wound shut while he bled and died.

All night long, Camille had tossed and turned, knowing that she had made a mistake, that she should never have sewn Charlie's lips. She just couldn't help it at the time. She had wanted to do it so much. And now she had to kill the one person who could connect her to New York and New Jersey. One more death. She felt the weight of the gun in her hand and felt the urgency grow inside her. She wanted to do this. She wanted Lucy dead more than she had ever realized.

Camille turned off the taps, opened the door, and left the room. She moved down the hall with her right hand tucked inside her bathrobe, hearing her child splashing happily. That would be her next problem. Carole. She didn't want to think about that. She carried the gun under her left breast. She did not bother to knock but walked straight into Lucy's room, surprising her.

"Hey, girlfriend," Camille said.

"That was quick."

"The water's too hot. I'm letting it cool."

Lucy smiled slightly. "I was thinking about Harry Hillier." She came away from the window and sat on her bed, curling her legs under her. "I don't understand it." She pulled a blanket over her lap to protect against the chill and damp.

Camille seated herself on a chair that had been pulled close to the window. She kept her arms crossed.

"I talked to him," Lucy admitted.

Camille was surprised. "Harry? How come?"

"I found out that he was working for us after all, even though he didn't know we existed."

"What do you mean?"

"Well, I went to his office—"

"You, what?" Camille suddenly realized that if she kept Lucy talking she could learn a lot.

"Yeah, I went to his office to find out what he was doing, if anything, on our project. The data had to go through him, right? He's the only great scientist we have. Was he with the bad guys, or was he being duped, like the rest of us? Get this. Harry was suspicious. He didn't say anything, but he was beginning to figure out that the data had had to come from humans, not rodents, as he'd been told. I could tell from the file that he was working it out."

They heard a sound in the corridor, which startled Camille.

"Relax, it's only Brother Tom."

The two women waited while the monk ponderously made his way to the room. He greeted them with a smile and put down a tray with the offerings that Lucy had predicted, including a fourth cup, one for himself. He poured the hot chocolate from a white enamel pitcher, served them each a cup, and seated himself in the small chair at the edge of the desk. "This is like summer camp," Camille chuckled.

Lucy filled Brother Tom in. "I was just telling

Camille about our foray over to Hillier-Largent.
Anyway, I shook Harry up a little. I told him that I
knew what he'd done, and that I knew whose side he
was on. He probably didn't know what I was talking
about, he probably didn't know there *were* sides. But I
mentioned the file by its code name, *Darkling Star*. I
remember you told me that name. But I figured if
Harry was worried that he might be implicated in *Darkling Star*, he might cause a fuss around Hillier-Largent,
or over at BioLogika. Maybe he did. Maybe that's why
somebody blew him up."

"I didn't hear about any fuss," Camille mentioned.

"Would you have? I doubt if Harry and Randall
Largent would've had a public shouting match over
this one. I think they'd keep it pretty quiet, wouldn't
you?"

Camille nodded. She had made a mistake. If she had
heard of a fuss it would have been through Honigwachs, but she wasn't going to tell Lucy that. *It doesn't
matter any more, does it?* "It's a mystery to me. I don't
know why Harry's dead."

"Or poor Charlie," Lucy added.

"No, I know why Charlie's dead. He's dead because
I shot him. I was aiming for his fucking eye but I
missed, I think. I shot him in the head." Camille smiled
then, and held the icy grin frozen on her lips. She
thought that the shock on Lucy's face was a hoot.
Slowly, she withdrew the pistol from under the shelter
of her robe. "With this," she told them both. "I shot
him with this, his own gun."

Brother Tom was rising from his chair.

"Stay where you are monk-face," Camille told him.
She aimed the pistol in his direction. "I'll let you know
when you can budge."

Lucy and her guardian looked at one another, both
stunned.

"Sit down, monk-face."

Slowly, as though his weight was being lowered with the aid of a crane, as though he had lost the full use of his muscles, Brother Tom resumed his seat.

"That's better."

"Camille—" Lucy started to say.

"Ah, poor baby doesn't understand? She gets lost in the ways of the world? Ah, poor little Indian girl."

"What are you doing?" Lucy whispered, finding a portion of her voice. "This is insane."

"Ah," mused Camille, "no. Not a good word to use. I really object to that word. I mean, you're the bitch who killed forty-two people. Well, forty, actually, because I took care of a couple of those myself, put them out of their misery, anyway. You killed forty people and you have the nerve to tell me that *I'm* insane? Nope, it won't wash. Not with me, sister."

Lucy's eyes jumped around. The way her fear coiled and moved inside her, she was afraid she might retch. Her skin felt as if it would strip itself from her body and bolt. She had to fight to stay lucid, she was in a daze. She had faced military bayonets and boys in army boots who had looked as scared as she had been, boys who had been likely to do something rash at any moment and you just had to pray that they'd been well-trained. In that famous picture where she stood on an upturned police cruiser and taunted at the army with an automatic rifle in one hand, she had been feeling the fear of her men, the fear of the Warriors themselves, who had been willing to die and knew they might, but she had also understood that they were capable of humiliating themselves. As a woman, she could climb onto that car and screech at the army and no soldier would shoot her, she believed, because she was a woman. If one of the Warriors had done that, some giddy, schoolboy army sniper might have cut him down. And so, she had made a spectacle of herself. In a moment of panic and fright she had followed an instinct. She had focused attention on herself, and in doing so had released the pressure on everyone else. Her ploy had worked. She'd made the news, but more importantly, there had been no battle that day, where there might have been. This was different, but she had operated under fire before, and a voice inside her was screaming at her to function again.

"Camille, tell me. What's going on? What are you going to do?" She opted for a calming tone, but she heard the fear in her voice as well.

With her gun held up, Camille smiled more widely. Then suddenly she frowned. She spoke in a voice not much louder than Lucy's. "I'm going to shoot you, bitch. Do you know what a bitch you've been? I'm going to shoot you."

"Why? You won't get away with it." Lucy looked over at Brother Tom, whose wide-eyed gaze was fixed on Camille, his mouth open, drooling slightly. He seemed to be in shock.

"Sure I will, Luce. I'll say that I was in the bath when a killer attacked. I heard what I thought were gunshots and just stayed quiet, with the door locked. That's where I'll be when the cops arrive. In the bath. I'll be hysterical for them. My little girl will be weeping in my arms. She'll be my witness. I was taking a bath. The gun I'll drop here, it'll be identified as Charlie's, the same gun I used to shoot him. Clean the prints off, which any killer would do. If little bits of you land on me, I'll wash them off in the bath, then run fresh water. It's perfect. I'll get away with it, Lucy. I know that rots your socks, but I'll get away with it pretty easily. It won't even be hard."

"Camille, you can't do this."

"Sure I can."

"Why? Oh, God, *Camille!* What's the matter with you? What's happening?"

"Getting scared, are we? The bad news is sinking in.

Hang on a second, Luce. I need to have a word with monk-face first. Brother Tom," she told him in a hectoring voice, "you move that arm again, you shift that leg again, you wiggle around on your ass again, and it will be the last second of your life, understand me? Now I'm going to explain a few things to Indian-girl here, and I expect your full attention. Got me?"

The monk solemnly nodded.

Camille sneered at him. "Hey, maybe before the day is out I'll get Brother Tom to say a few words. What do you think? Would you like to live to hear that Lucy? Do you think he'll sit up and beg for us, if we give him the right encouragement?"

The squad car was speeding by the monastery when Cinq-Mars said, "Stop."

"What?" Mathers asked.

"*Stoooopppp!*" the senior detective shouted, and Mathers jammed on the brakes, fighting hard with the steering wheel to stay out of a spin. Each man was jostled and bruised by the car's swift halt.

"What, Émile, what?" Mathers demanded, recovering.

"It's a car. The monastery parking lot. I don't know. But it could be Camille's!"

"What the fuck's going on?" Recchi blustered in the back seat, but his words were no sooner spoken then Mathers was accelerating and turning the car on a dime, tires squealing, heading back the way they'd come. He bounded down the drive to the monastery, and every officer's head banged against the roof. He skidded to a stop next to the Mazda. Cinq-Mars and Mathers both stared at the window, which had been punched out and replaced with a sheet of plastic. Then Cinq-Mars and Mathers jumped from the car and drew their weapons.

At the sight of the guns, the New York cops suddenly sprang into action themselves.

"Big place," Cinq-Mars said. "We need to cover some ground. Everybody goes inside. Trust no one. Especially don't trust any women you meet who are armed."

They ran down to the nearest door. Mathers opened it, and the four cops burst inside.

"So, Brother Tom, you may want to shut your eyes, or maybe you prefer to die happy. Whatever. That's up to you." Camille stood. "I'm taking my robe off, in case I get any messy bits on myself."

She was careful, removing her robe, to move the pistol from one hand to the other so that it was trained continuously on Lucy Gabriel. The monk did not avert his eyes, nor did he seem either offended or interested by her nudity.

"This way, I can wash off easily," she said. Between the slight slump to her breasts and her sharply poking hip-bones, her ribs were obvious, and winter's pale progress showed on white skin, with only her face and hands weathered by the wind and sun.

Carole called from down the hall. "Mommy! I want to get out now!"

Camille returned to the door, keeping her eyes and the aim of the pistol on her captives. She shouted, "Stay there! Don't you dare move until Mommy comes back!"

"I want to get out *noooowwwww!*"

"Stay—the fuck—there!"

Her voice echoed down the hall.

"What?" she asked Lucy, noting her appalled expression and lifting her head to demean her with her look. "You don't like how I talk to my kid?"

"You need help, Camille."

"Nope! Wrong! Wrong thing to say! I don't like that, Luce, not one bit. And I don't take that shit from nobody. Now you take it back or I'll be mean to you.

I'll sew up your lips. Monk-face, you must have a needle and thread."

Lucy's face was quivering now, her lips trembling. Her hands also shook and her breathing caught in her throat.

"No, Camille, please, what's wrong with you— don't," Lucy implored her, and inched her way back on the bed, against the wall. "Please."

"Aw, Lucy, getting scared? I like that. Especially from you. Little Indian *warrior!* Brave little red-hearted girl with the rifle stuck above her head." She walked back and forth in front of her now, taunting her with her words and the pistol. "I always thought that was bogus. Who'd you kill, Lucy? Who'd you kill with that thing? You wouldn't have the guts."

"Mommy!" her daughter called from down the hall.

"Stay there, Carole!"

"Who'd you kill, Camille?" Lucy asked, turning the question on her. "Did you kill Andy?" Her mind raced. She had to buy time. She hadn't seen anyone except Brother Tom since her arrival. This wing of the monastery had truly been abandoned, and from what she understood there were hardly any monks in the main building either. Men just didn't become monks any more. Apparently, Camille wanted to talk about murder and Lucy held onto a single thread of hope. Cinq-Mars was supposed to visit her this afternoon. At no specific time. He was her only hope, and she had to keep Camille talking in the meantime.

"Andy was Wiener's big day," Camille revealed. "He botched it. Typical." She paraded in front of them, an arrogant swing to her hips accompanied her slow steps, her gun slightly upraised. "I don't know what's the big deal about killing somebody else. I was only doing humanity a favor. After Wiener shot him, Andy had to be drowned like a rat, and I had to tell Wiener to do it. He stepped on his head until the life went out of him. Sorry about that, Lucy, I know you liked the guy. After that I helped put him under the ice and stuff."

"Who's Wiener?" Brother Tom asked.

Neither woman turned her head, but both shifted their eyes to look at him.

"Monk-face is talking!" Camille sneered. "Your big chance to get into Heaven as a perfect, dutiful monk, Tommy. You blew it. Now I'll have to sew your lips to keep your mouth shut in Hell. Why not? I sewed Charlie up. It'll show we got the same killer here, which we do. I'll sew you up nice and tight, Brother Tom. You won't be babbling away throughout eternity. You too, Lucy. I'll sew up your lips. I'm sick to death of what comes out of your prying mouth. I'd love to do that."

"Mommy! Mommy!" Carole was screeching from her cooling bath.

"Oh, *God!*" Camille complained. "I'm going to have to snuff that child, too. Put her out of her misery."

Lucy pushed herself back against the wall, despairing now, convinced now that Camille was cracked, that she wasn't remotely sane. She was panting, afraid of dying here, but if she was going to die she wanted to be brave, at least.

"Who's Wiener?" Brother Tom asked again. He had a guttural voice, and he never looked directly at the woman with the gun.

Her pistol aimed at her old friend, Camille looked sideways at the monk. "Wiener is Werner Honigwachs, Tommy. Sorry, *Brother* Tommy. He killed Andy Stettler, an old friend of mine. I just helped him out a little. When the going got tough, the tough had to stand up and get the job done, you know? Yeah," she said, and she held her pistol with two hands and shifted her aim from Lucy's chest to her face, sighting down the lonely barrel and declaring with finality, "Now it's your turn, little Indian girl."

"No, Camille! Noooo!"

"Oh, yes," Camille taunted, her face crooked in a manic grin.

"Camille!"

"Mommy! I'm *cooold!*"

"For you, Lucy, right between the eyes."

"Oh God," Lucy whispered, and she turned her face away.

"Show me the whites of your eyes, Lucy. Come on. Come on. Don't be a baby. Turn to face me. That's it, honey. Turn. A little more. Come on."

Slowly, in increments, weeping, breathing in rapid gulps, Lucy Gabriel turned to face her.

"Open your eyes now. That's a brave little Indian girl."

She opened her eyes.

The blast of the gunshot exploded in the monk's cell, echoed down the corridor and through the wing of the monastery. A sound that was slow to decay, moving along the old stones and marble floors, resonant and shocking. As it struck the four detectives climbing the stairs, moving hurriedly with their weapons drawn, they stopped for an instant, then rushed on up.

Her body, contorting, convulsed, then collapsed onto the floor, the sound a mere thump, muffled, a life rapidly expiring.

Brother Tom stood up.

The bullet had passed through the fabric of his robe into the heart of Camille Choquette. He looked across at Lucy Gabriel, who had crumpled with shock and fright against the wall. He crossed the room quickly, stepping over the body, and pulled a file folder off the windowsill. Then he snatched up Lucy's car keys.

Lucy couldn't take her eyes off Camille's broken corpse, silent on the floor. The shock was welling through her. She felt dizzy, then frantic, then calm, then she she'd go through the spectrum once more. She couldn't believe it. *I'm alive! Alive!*

Brother Tom put his gun down on the desk and peeled his robe off over his head. She looked at him with a sudden overwhelming confusion and curiosity. He was wearing a mauve shirt and blue jeans, with a gun-belt around his waist.

"Sorry," he said. "I didn't understand you about that other guy."

She was breathing heavily again, but more regularly. "What guy?"

"Hillier. That Harry Hillier guy."

For a big man, he seemed light on his feet as he fled the room. He was carrying the file folder. Lucy heard him running down the hall. She tried to get up, but fell back. Her legs were wobbly and loose. She looked down at herself. She had peed. She saw Camille's open, dead eyes then, and uttered a sharp cry.

She heard other sounds, noises. Feet.

She forced herself up abruptly, wanting out of there. Lucy staggered against a chair and used it to steady herself, then stumbled on her way out to the corridor, where she slumped against the wall. Slowly at first, her body slid to the floor. Lucy sat there, her head in her hands, weeping, awaiting rescue. She was alive, she knew that, but for moments at a time the thought seemed to be more than she could bear.

She was surprised to hear footsteps again. So soon. She didn't know how much time had passed. Had monks come running? She'd thought they might. Looking up, she saw four men charge through the doors at the far end to her right.

The cops divided into pairs and each ran down a side of the corridor, checking the rooms as they made their way toward the weeping woman. They all heard a child's voice and moved as quickly as possible toward it, with all due caution. Cinq-Mars came upon a little girl, who had managed to crawl out of the hefty, cast-iron enamel tub and wrap herself in a towel, and when she saw the man with a gun she whimpered, "I'm cold. I'm cold. I'm *cooold!*" Mathers moved past his partner, tucked his gun away and wrapped the girl in his arms, but she would not stop reciting, "I'm cold. I'm cold. I'm cold. I'm cold." Her teeth were chattering.

McGibbon and Recchi made it all the way to Lucy Gabriel and knelt beside her. She was sobbing now and uttering plaintive cries, overcome with rage and sorrow and the miracle of her release. The two New York cops glanced inside the room and issued a precaution to Cinq-Mars. The detective crossed the doorway and saw the body on the floor in there. He pressed himself against the wall and crept toward the doorframe. Then he ducked his head inside and pulled it back out again. He took a second to process what he'd seen, then indicated to the other two that he was going in.

Cinq-Mars jumped into the room, finding it empty, save for the body of Camille Choquette.

He came back out to the corridor and knelt beside Lucy Gabriel. He held her upper arms in his hands. "You're Lucy? You must be Lucy." He pushed her hair back from her face. She was squirming around and moaning, and he caressed the side of her head gently.

Lucy nodded.

"Who did that, Lucy?" Cinq-Mars inquired. "In there. Did you do that?"

"Brother Tom," she managed to whisper.

"A monk?"

Lucy shook her head slowly. "That was no monk. He was no monk. Oh God. *Oh God!*"

"It's okay, Lucy," Cinq-Mars soothed her. "It's okay now."

"No," Lucy moaned. "You don't understand. He took it. He took it."

"What?" Cinq-Mars asked her quietly. "Who? He took what?"

"Brother Tom. He took *Darkling Star*. Oh God," she wailed, and Lucy clutched the detective's lapels. "Don't you understand? It'll happen again! He was no monk! He's a criminal! A killer. He took *Darkling Star!*"

BLOODWORK

17

KNOWLEDGE
IN A PARTICULAR TIME

The same day, late Wednesday afternoon, February 16, 1999

Émile Cinq-Mars decided to pay Werner Honigwachs
a visit in his office at the BioLogika Corporation to
educate him on recent developments. Offered a seat by
the company president, he declined, and instead took
up a more defiant position near the windows with a
view across the ice lake.

"How's your investigation coming along, Detective?
Any progress?" The man's confidence struck him as
boundless.

"It's been interesting." Clearly, his quarry had not
been worried by the death of Charles Painchaud.
Perhaps he did not know the implications, as Camille
might not have told him that she was ultimately
responsible. Cinq-Mars turned to face him. Knocking
Honigwachs off his high horse was shaping up to be a
pleasure. "The case has been solved. I only dropped by
to bring you up to speed."

"Solved! That's good news." Taking his chair,
Honigwachs swivelled around and calmly adjusted his
trousers. "You know who killed Andy?"

"I do." Cinq-Mars faced him. "You did. You took
Andrew Stettler's life, sir."

The accused managed a slight laugh, which degenerated into a faint cough. "Sergeant-Detective, you amuse me," he admitted. "I'll grant you that much."

"Glad to be of use, sir." Stepping away from the window, Cinq-Mars stalked Honigwachs in front of his impressive desk. From time to time he passed close to the cosmic clock, where the planets in their traces slavishly continued to orbit the sun. "Mr. Honigwachs—regarding your grey colt, Darkling Star. When I first said its name to you, you appeared startled. Now I know why."

Honigwachs put a foot up to rest across his opposite knee, as though relaxing into the discussion, hoping to convey the impression that Cinq-Mars did not make him nervous, or intimidate him or worry him in the least. The smile curling at the edge of his lips continued that smug declaration. "I don't follow. Why would I be startled by the name of my own horse?"

"Indeed you were. And no wonder, given that *Darkling Star* is also the code name that you gave your awful foray into the United States, sir, where you were personally responsible for the deaths of forty-two men—sorry, allow me to correct myself. I should say forty men, as Camille Choquette apparently took it upon herself to kill two of them with her bare hands—"

"Excuse me?" For the first time, the smirk was gone from his face. Pale, Honigwachs put his feet down on the floor, as if he suddenly felt the need for balance, for something solid underfoot.

"You didn't know that? I'm not surprised—why would she tell you? Most killers prefer keeping their lives as homicidal lunatics secret."

Strain showed across the man's jawline. "You're insane. Once again, you're rapidly depleting my patience."

"I've seen the pictures. Cops in New York and Jersey didn't think the whole thing was connected. Some lunatic killed two AIDS patients and sewed their lips shut."

"Sewed their lips—" Honigwachs repeated.

"That's right. Sewed their lips shut. They were more interested in who was sending AIDS patients into sudden death. The lip-sewer was just a sideline to their investigation. But everything is all woven together, isn't it, Mr. Honigwachs? Or crushed together. Not unlike knowledge flowing into a black hole. The weight of that gravity turns everything that is known into one hard ball of matter."

"What are you talking about?" His forehead was furrowed in concentration, as though he was frustrated by something that he could not understand or even begin to grasp.

"You don't know. That's regrettable," Cinq-Mars sympathized. "I'm also sorry to inform you, sir, that your girlfriend is dead."

"My girlfriend?" Werner Hongiwachs was not wearing his jacket, and the sleeves of his pinstriped shirt were rolled almost to his elbows. Cinq-Mars noticed the sweat stains expanding under his arms.

"Camille Choquette is dead, sir. She was executed by the mob."

Honigwachs did not reply this time, but stared at his adversary across the moat of the desktop. Cinq-Mars finally sat down in a visitor's chair, choosing one toward the end of the desk, near the cosmic clock.

"Before her death, sir, Camille happened to mention to Lucy Gabriel that you were the one who pulled the trigger on Andrew Stettler, that she only assisted with the cleanup. Would you care to confirm her report?"

"You're bluffing," Honigwachs taunted him. He tossed his head to dismiss the accusation as mere folly. "You're a scoundrel, Cinq-Mars."

This time, the detective smiled. "If I'm bluffing, sir, I'm doing a hell of a job. Before stepping into this room

I took a call from my partner. He's been interrogating Randall Largent. Apparently, Mr. Largent was somewhat upset to have had his business associate dropped into a blender." Cinq-Mars put up a hand. "Sorry, sir—police jargon for a carbomb. Insensitive, I know. Once we proved to him that Lucy had been in possession of Harry Hillier's copy of *Darkling Star*, well, sir, he got this faraway, worried look in his eyes, and after that he was willing to respond to our approach. Mr. Largent decided to talk the whole thing through, see if an agreement was possible on what his future might hold. He's anxious to make amends. With good behaviour, not to mention full disclosure, he might be out in time to see his year-old grandchild graduate from university, if he lives that long. It'll be touch and go."

Honigwachs scoffed. "You're bluffing. Randall Largent has no reason to be making up stories about me."

"Randall Largent, sir," the policeman explained, and he sighed with casual impatience but kept his look fastened on his prey, letting him know that he would give him no quarter, "understands the consequences of his actions. He's an intelligent, if somewhat misguided, human being. He'd rather not end up like poor old Harry. Lucy Gabriel conducted a telephone conversation with poor Mr. Hillier that was misunderstood, that's all that she did wrong in this particular matter. She's upset about it. She was fond of Harry, thought of him as an ally. Unfortunately, due to that misunderstanding, the mob went ahead and dropped poor old Harry into a blender. If that's what happens from a misunderstanding, imagine the results when she talks knowingly and specifically to the mob. Which she has done."

"What do you mean, 'which she has done'?"

Cinq-Mars smiled broadly again. He wanted Honigwachs to appreciate that he was enjoying this. He wet his lips with his tongue. "The mob took Lucy into custody, they tried to shake her down. They wanted to know who killed Andy, their boy. I'm sure they had a word with you, as well. Now, the Indians allowed that interrogation to take place, but they were also on hand to protect one of their own, and they initiated a plan to put her into hiding, in case somebody like you, or like me, wanted to harm her."

Honigwachs shifted his weight around in his chair, although he made a conscious effort not to seem to be squirming. He tried to appear both relaxed and bored, holding a knee in his hands for a moment, then letting it go again. Nothing worked satisfactorily for him.

"That was the significant variable in all of this," Cinq-Mars continued, drawing things out to increase the man's discomfort. "Blood. The blood connection between Lucy and the Mohawk Warriors, whatever their differences of opinion, was too strong for them not to look after her in a time of crisis. Lucy, after all, had fought alongside them and risked her life when the Warriors were under attack. What Lucy didn't know was that the Indians had allowed a mob gunman to go into hiding with her, in case she talked, in case she had something to say. The Mohawks were happy, because it gave her protection. The mob was happy, because it gave them a possible source of knowledge. That's all the players wanted in any of this, Mr. Honigwachs, even you— protection and knowledge. In your case, I'd add loot."

He paused to look at the intricacy of the clock, the moon and planets in strategic hold, a fearful symmetry, a precise gravitational dance in perfect balance. He gathered himself and carried on. "Today, sir, before her death, Camille Choquette confessed to killing Sergeant Charles Painchaud, and to helping you do away with Andrew Stettler."

"All right, Sergeant-Detective," Honigwachs intruded, "I've heard enough. I'm calling my lawyer. He'll take care of this. You're bluffing. Even if Camille spouted some nonsense, which I doubt because it's so ludicrous, a dead person can't be cross-examined. Any folly she might have uttered under duress can easily be dismissed in court. You know that. I know it too. If you think you can hoodwink me with some cockamamie scheme, you're twice as dumb as I thought you were, which is saying something."

Cinq-Mars burst out laughing. "Sir! My intelligence quotient is of no relevance! Whether I'm smarter than you or you are smarter than me won't help you! You're done! It's finished! It's over! Why play games? By all means, call your lawyer. Explain to him the following. Lucy Gabriel is in my hands now, and she's willing to talk at length. Lucy's been granted full immunity in exchange for her testimony, so she won't have to worry about incriminating herself. We have Luc Séguin, sir, her driver, who's not dead after all, as everybody thought. His demise was a story that Lucy made up, at Luc's insistence, to hide the fact that he was still breathing. He can corroborate a few details. We also have Randall Largent's testimony, and he will provide us with the paperwork, stating that you are the principal owner of Hillier-Largent Global, and that you were conspiring to cheat BioLogika of its knowledge. How am I doing? Not bad, wouldn't you say? Also, tell your lawyer this, in case he doesn't see the whole picture for himself. None of what I've just told you will be coming into play."

Cinq-Mars was not going to continue without his adversary asking him to do so. He wanted that final satisfaction.

"Why's that? No, don't bother telling me—it's all a bluff."

"I won't need any of that evidence, sir, because you are going to write a full confession of your crimes. You will provide me with a detailed, written account of the murder of Andrew Stettler, and you will reveal your entire part in the conspiracy to advance your science while callously disregarding human life."

Honigwachs was shaken, but he was willing to keep his head in the game. He relaxed and tensed his shoulder muscles, as if weighing various options. "Okay, I'm interested. Why am I doing this?"

"You will confess, sir, or I will refuse to arrest you."

Honigwachs chortled. "This is some sort of Cinq-Mars word game. I suppose I have to ask you what you mean by that now." He returned the Cinq-Mars glare, choosing to take him on and not back down.

"It's simple. The mob knows you killed their man," explained Cinq-Mars. "Camille Choquette inadvertently informed them. Trust me, they believed her. Even if it's not true—although we know better, right, sir?—but even if it's not true, it's what the mob believes. Now, they beat the living crap out of Sergeant Painchaud before they decided that he didn't do it. Poor fellow, he was having a bad run of luck. He called his girlfriend for help and she came along and shot him instead."

Honigwachs scrunched his eyes tighter, as if he was trying to either narrow or intensify his gaze. Cinq-Mars maintained that eye contact, burrowing into his head.

"You see," he added in a confidential tone, "I'll tell you this for free, as an example of my insider knowledge. Not only will you confess to the crime, sir, but you will plead guilty to murder in a court of law. After that, after we've locked you up for the Stettler murder, the Americans—two of whom are outside the door as we speak—the Yanks will do their best to tackle the more complicated charges against you. They'll have your confession, of course, which will make things easier. They'll have Lucy's testimony, and Luc's. So, you'll be trying to avoid the death penalty in a couple of states, sir, but at least you'll be alive for that fight.

Serving time, but alive. That's the best I'm offering. We can't predict how that will go. All we know for sure is how things will go if I *don't* arrest you."

"Nice speech, Cinq-Mars." Honigwachs had to clear his throat. He finally dropped his staring contest with the detective, and when he spoke his voice was weaker, and parched. He started to blink rapidly. "I still say you're bluffing."

"That's fine. You can say whatever you want. But I'm not finished with you yet, sir. You will also take what assets you have left in BioLogika and your satellite company, Hillier-Largent Global, and you will use them to compensate the families of your victims. You're on the event horizon, sir. You know what that means." Cinq-Mars pointed his right index finger and coldheartedly stabbed three orbiting planets in succession. Suddenly, the cosmic clock was in disarray. Mars had lost ground to Jupiter, Saturn had vaulted forward several eons. "What comes next is the long, traumatic, terrifying dip into the black hole, sir, and down you go. The choice, of course, is yours." Cinq-Mars stood. "I'll go now. Please, remember, full confession to murdering forty men in the United States, a guilty plea in Stettler's murder, and compensation to victims' families—or no arrest. Ask your lawyer if he's ever heard of a bluff like that before."

Cinq-Mars walked to the door, opened it, and turned around for a final word.

"Just fuck off," Honigwachs told him. His jawline had hardened. The veins on his neck had bulged and darkened.

"A word of caution, sir," Cinq-Mars added. "I imagine that the mob has received word of your misdemeanours by now. The first thing that I expect them to do, even before their nasty job on you, is to sell off their shares in BioLogika. Doesn't that sound likely? Check, sir. If there's a selling frenzy underway, if the price per

share plummets, if it appears that your largest shareholders can't dump stock fast enough—hickory dickory—consider what that means. Then ask yourself and
ask your lawyer how I bluffed that one. Good day, sir.
Oh, and don't trouble yourself too much about all of
this. We've all been living in a time warp. We're just
catching up to you now."

He walked out then and, joined by McGibbon and
Recchi, left the building.

"Where to?" McGibbon asked him outside. He was
thinking that he'd had an interesting day.

Dusk was falling. "Back to HQ. Wait for a phone
call."

The call came within three hours.

Cinq-Mars talked to the lawyer and made certain
that his demands were being met to the letter. Honigwachs was obliged to plead for his arrest, and Cinq-
Mars reiterated to the lawyer that he would not do the
paperwork on his client or take him into custody unless,
beyond a reasonable doubt, he fully proved his guilt.

"Counsellor?"

"Yes, sir?" the attorney asked.

"Do you have any children?"

"What does that have to do with our discussion?"

"Indulge me. Do you?"

"Two. One of each."

"Don't drive in with Honigwachs. See that he comes
in alone. Our body count is high enough. If he gets
whacked, don't be in the vicinity."

"A little dramatic, don't you think, Sergeant-
Detective?"

"Maybe. But think of your kids, counsellor, that's all
I'm suggesting."

Cinq-Mars put the phone down and nodded to
Mathers, McGibbon, Recchi, and Lieutenant Tremblay, all gathered in his cubicle. "Late this afternoon,
between three and four, according to Honigwachs's

lawyer, BioLogika shares were savaged by a steep decline," he announced. "The company has experienced a sell-off on heavy volume. Honigwachs is coming in. Dead or alive—that remains to be seen."

Eleven days later, Sunday afternoon, February 27, 1999

Émile Cinq-Mars was alone in his house—his wife had gone into the local village with their weekend house-guest—when he received the phone call he'd dreaded the most. Snow was heavy in the fields as he gazed out the second-floor window and listened. The day was unseasonably warm, and the horses shuffled around in the outdoor paddocks closest to the barn, relishing the breezy air that, weathermen were saying, had originated in Texas. He caught sight of a squad car turning onto the lengthy drive up to the farmhouse and stables, and after he had hung up he went downstairs and stepped outside to greet the unknown visitor, not bothering with a coat. Only when the vehicle turned sideways to him and stopped did he see that it belonged to the local police department. He identified the officer behind the wheel as the Chief of Police.

The man had to work a little to get himself out of the car and upright. Expecting trouble, Cinq-Mars was surprised when the chief, wearing sunglasses to protect his eyes from the bright glare off the snow, approached him with a smile. "Jean-Guy Brasseur," the visitor announced. He had adopted a different voice from the cranky tone he'd employed during their first meeting on the ice lake. Apparently, whatever chip had been on his shoulder then had eroded away.

Cinq-Mars met him at the bottom of the stairs and shook his hand. "I remember. How are you, Chief?"

"Good enough. Sick of winter. Detective, I have some news." He shuffled his feet around. He raised his head when a horse snorted, and Cinq-Mars looked across at the animal. The horse was gazing at him, probably wondering if he was coming over with a sugar lump or an apple.

Cinq-Mars shrugged. "What's that?"

"We've made arrests that might interest you."

"What's the crime?"

"Car theft."

He looked around his yard. He was thinking that he would remember this day. That the sadness in his heart and lungs and belly, the pain behind his eyes, would never completely vanish. He was thinking that after this cop left he'd go over to the horse who was still watching him and hug his neck. Then, he'd weep. "Okay. I'll bite. Why does that interest me?"

The chief grinned. He bobbed his chin continuously as if the information he was hoarding might pop a valve. "Same MO as before, Sergeant-Detective. You'll remember we had a snow squall Friday night. Lasted an hour or two. During the blow a Jeep Cherokee was heisted off a farm about twenty clicks down the road. One set of tire tracks left the farm, one set only, the Jeep's. Snowmobile tracks crossed nearby. Same thing could've happened to you, bud. A perp figured these farmhouses run so far off the roads nobody bothers locking doors. Let's face it, farmers run ten different types of machines, leave the keys in the ignition every time. Until now, they had no cause for concern. But somebody's out there stealing. No bomb that night. There wasn't any dynamite. No bikers. Just a couple of rough boys out to score a four-wheeler."

"Ah," Cinq-Mars cottoned on. "You're telling me that the attack on my house was random."

"It no longer looks isolated, that's all I'm saying."

"Thanks for driving out with this."

"Just filling you in, bud. I'll see you, Cinq-Mars.

You take it easy now." The chief got into his car and rolled down the window. "You know what it means?" he asked.

Cinq-Mars nodded slightly. The chief had done his best to mask his pride, and a measure of his disdain, although he had not been wholly successful. He was taking pleasure in the news, as the information was meant to belittle the city cop, knock him down from his high station. The chief was telling him that he was not such a vaunted legend of law enforcement that gunmen vied to be his assassin. He was not the target of the worst criminals in the land. Gangs were not willing to risk everything merely to take him out. He had been the random victim of an auto theft, like thousands of others, and the fact that he hadn't figured that out suggested that maybe he wasn't such a hotshot detective after all.

Cinq-Mars had been willing to let Chief Brasseur have that satisfaction, but then he changed his mind. He walked across to his car. "Do *you* understand it, Chief? Do you know what just happened here?"

The chief smirked. "Sure I do. You're not on anybody's hit list."

"No," Cinq-Mars told him. "I just got taken off."

"What do you mean?"

"They came at me, the mob did. Andrew Stettler, before he was killed, talked them into that. Not out of revenge, they're not that stupid, but because I was about to interfere with a major part of their business. Then Stettler got bumped off. As it happens, I solved that murder for them. Now, I have no way to interfere with their business any more, I have no way to disrupt their cash flow. Plus, I did them a favour. So they arranged that little heist Friday night, and somehow they put a bug in your ear to come out here and tell me about it. Am I right?"

The chief's eyes shifted to one side, then back again,

as though he didn't know where to hide.

"So I'm right about that. Do you know what it means now? The mob sent me a message. I'm off their hit list. I was on, and now I'm off. They want peace between me and them. You, sir, you were their messenger. Nothing more than that."

The chief stared up at him, his teeth clenched, and then stepped lightly on the gas and turned the car away. Cinq-Mars watched him go down the drive, amazed once again by the pettiness of human relations.

As he was watching, the squad car passed his Pathfinder returning. Cinq-Mars waited outside for the return of the two women. He felt the eyes of his father upon him. When he looked over, the horse continued to observe him. Cinq-Mars looked down again, and his eyes filled.

The vehicle parked in its usual spot and Sandra jumped down from the driver's seat holding up a little white bag. "I filled your prescription!" she called. "Celebrex, Émile! No more achy hands!"

"Yeah, well," Cinq-Mars grumbled. He'd been deliberately procrastinating on that one. Lucy Gabriel was stepping out of the vehicle also, and she let Sally the dog free from the back seat to bark at the departing car.

"What did he want?" Sandra nodded toward the driveway.

"To break my balls. Typical police behaviour. Lucy! Tell me, how many lab rats had to get sick for that little bottle of pills?"

"Human or rodent?" She smiled, for the first time in ages.

Sandra spun the cap off. "Come on," she coaxed, "open up! Wouldn't you rather shoot straight? Do you still want to be a cop or not, Émile?"

The question was a good one—did he still want to be a cop?—and Émile Cinq-Mars gave it more serious attention than perhaps his wife had intended. Apparently, he was already losing his partner, although he hadn't given up on that front, and that was more than he could stomach. At least Mathers was continuing in the force, for his photograph had been published holding little Carole Choquette in his arms, and his wife, affected by that, agreed that it was important that some people take risks to protect others. That he himself had encouraged the newspaper to publish the photo was knowledge Cinq-Mars was keeping to himself.

In the end, to answer his wife's question, he opened his mouth wide, and she popped in the pill. He gagged on the tablet, and made a face, and hugged his chest as he choked on it, but he managed to swallow it down, and the women laughed at his pantomime.

Muddied, Sally was circling the yard, wanting to play. Lucy found a stick, a branch that had come down during the last storm, gave it a good long toss, and the dog took off. They watched Sally run, then scamper back with the stick, and Cinq-Mars put his arm around his wife's shoulders. The dog begged Lucy to throw it again, and she teased the animal, feinting in various directions before lofting her precious stick high and far. Émile Cinq-Mars and Sandra watched as the young woman entertained the dog, and Sandra frequently shot a glance at her husband, noticing his red eyes.

Cinq-Mars smiled a couple of times when Lucy laughed. She was recovering from her trauma, but she had also educated them all concerning the gravity of the ongoing situation. She told them that *Darkling Star* could teach other firms the technique to accelerate an illness in order to track, isolate, and comprehend its progress. A pharmaceutical firm had already reported that they'd been approached. So the mob was out there, getting into a new business, offering death for sale, and the possibility was very real that soon someone might buy for the sake of the knowledge they'd gain.

Death had been put up on the auction block.

Cinq-Mars was sufficiently knowledgeable about humankind to know there would be bidders.

He whispered to Sandra, "Dad's gone."

And he wept then. His body shook. She put an arm around him. While the dog and the young woman played, while the horses lifted their heads and snorted, while the breeze prevailed, warm and brisk, Sandra and Émile Cinq-Mars turned and held one another in their arms, in the peace of their barnyard, silently, and they remained clasped, long after Lucy had taken the dog inside to leave them to their private sorrow.